LEFT FOR DEAD

BOOKS BY JOY KLUVER

Detective Bernadette Noel series

Last Seen

Broken Girls

LEFT FOR DEAD

JOY KLUVER

bookouture

Published by Bookouture in 2022

An imprint of Storyfire Ltd.
Carmelite House
50 Victoria Embankment
London EC4Y 0DZ

www.bookouture.com

Copyright © Joy Kluver, 2022

Joy Kluver has asserted her right to be identified as the author of this work.

All rights reserved. No part of this publication may be reproduced, stored in any retrieval system, or transmitted, in any form or by any means, electronic, mechanical, photocopying, recording or otherwise, without the prior written permission of the publishers.

ISBN: 978-1-80019-999-6
eBook ISBN: 978-1-80019-998-9

This book is a work of fiction. Names, characters, businesses, organizations, places and events other than those clearly in the public domain, are either the product of the author's imagination or are used fictitiously. Any resemblance to actual persons, living or dead, events or locales is entirely coincidental.

In memory of Ray

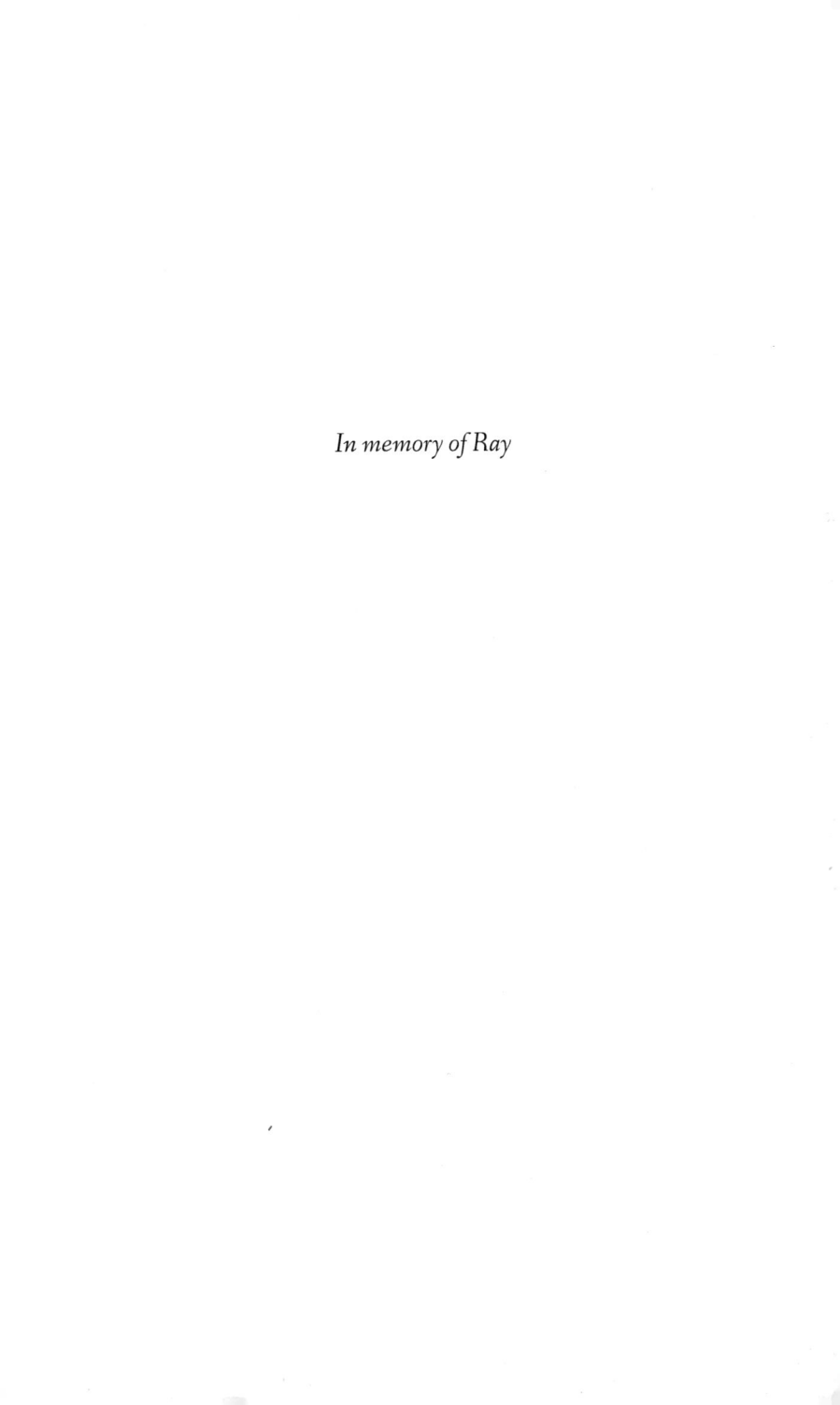

1

MONDAY

Bernie hit the snooze button. 6.30 a.m. *What day is it?* She tried to focus for a few seconds. *Monday.* She moaned. She really wanted a few more minutes' sleep but the pressure on her bladder was all-consuming. She was about to get up when her phone began to ring.

She snatched it up. 'DI Noel,' she said as she got up and walked to the bathroom.

'Sorry to ring so early, Bernie. I hope I didn't wake you up.'

Bernie recognised DS Kerry Allen's voice. She sat down on the toilet and willed her wee to be quiet.

'No, you didn't wake me. What's up?'

'We've got a woman attacked in Swindon. Looks similar to the sexual attacks that have been happening over the past few months.'

Bernie sighed, more with relief at emptying her bladder than at the attacks. 'Thought that was being handled in Swindon.'

'Yes but— What's that noise? Are you on the loo?'

Bernie laughed a little. 'Yes, sorry. I was desperate. It's not much fun having a baby pushing on your bladder. But it's no different from when we go to the loo at work for our little chats. Carry on.'

'Gee, thanks. I'll try to not let it put me off. OK, the woman was found this morning in Town Gardens. As I said, it looks like the same MO but this time he's upped his game. Not just sexual assault – as if that's not bad enough, he hit her on the head and left her for dead.'

'Left for dead? She's alive?' asked Bernie. She stood up, flushed the toilet and washed her hands, cradling her phone between her ear and neck.

'Barely. She's in a bad way. She had her bag with her still and there were family contact details in her purse. A car is on its way now to them. Hopefully they'll give us permission to take forensic evidence.'

Bernie looked in the mirror above the sink. The shadows under her eyes were darkening with disturbed sleep but her light brown skin glowed with the effects of pregnancy hormones pumping round her body.

'Strange that her bag was left. Presumably, we have a name?' she said.

'Yes, Keira Howard. Maybe he left the bag because he was disturbed by someone else having a late night – or early morning – jaunt. We don't have timescales yet. It was the park ranger who found her. He was taking his dog for a walk before opening the gates and said no one else was around and the paramedics said she was very cold.'

Bernie thought that when people looked at the pros and cons of having a dog, they should also factor in the possibility of it finding a body.

'OK. Where are you going to first?' she asked.

'Scene and then the hospital. We won't be able to see her until after the doctors have assessed her.'

Bernie glanced at the time on her phone: six forty-five a.m.

'Text me the details and I'll meet you at the scene. I'll try to be there before eight. See you soon.'

Bernie wandered back into the bedroom, hoping Dougie hadn't been woken up. Instead, he was also on his phone, his normally slicked back dark hair tousled from sleep.

'I haven't forgotten about the data, sir. Tom's sorting it out for us this morning. We'll have time to go through it all before the raid... Yes, I'll see you later, sir.' He hung up and rubbed his face before looking at Bernie.

'What've you got?' he asked.

'Sexual assault and attempted murder in Swindon. You?'

'A reminder that I have a briefing at eight. Like I'm going to forget. The DCI's panicking because someone's coming from the Met.' He shook his head. 'This county lines drugs case is huge now. And there's still so much to get through before the raid. I'll probably be late tonight.'

Dougie Anderson got out of bed and hugged Bernie. 'Did you sleep OK?' He smoothed her hair away from her face and kissed her.

'I had to get up twice for the loo. The midwife said it should get a bit easier in the second trimester. Hasn't so far.'

Dougie winced. 'Not fun. Hey, it's second scan this week, isn't it?'

Bernie knew what was coming. 'We've been through this. If you come, I have to ask Alex too.'

'But he's with Ali now. If you just took the test—'

'I'm not risking the baby for your precious ego. Same for Alex.'

'No, you don't have to risk the baby. I've been looking into it. There's a blood test you can do now to test paternity. It costs quite a lot but I'm willing to pay.'

Bernie sighed. She knew how desperate Dougie was to find out if he was the father or not. Wrongly, or rightly, Bernie had walked straight into Dougie's arms after she'd discovered her previous boyfriend, Alex, had cheated on her. 'I'll think about it, OK? I know you've got this briefing but can I jump in the shower first please?'

Dougie gave a broad grin, his dark eyes suddenly mischievous. 'Yes... or we could share one...'

Bernie gave him a playful shove. 'We haven't got time for that now.'

'Oh,' said Dougie. 'Spoilsport.'

2

Bernie drove slowly along Quarry Road, taking in the surroundings. There was open land to her left – some tennis courts and a playground – but the area quickly became residential. There would have to be house-to-house enquiries. The Town Gardens were to her right; a green oasis in the centre of town. She turned right and saw all the response vehicles parked on the double yellow lines. Forensics were already there, along with three police cars and Kerry's car. An officer stood guard by the wrought iron gates. A small cottage was next to them, just inside the grounds. Did the park ranger live there?

Bernie pulled her phone out and rang Kerry.

'Hi. I've just arrived. Where are you?'

'I'm at the bandstand. It's where the woman was found. I'll walk up to the gate to meet you. There are some forensic suits with the officer at the gate.'

'Right. Quick question – why isn't the whole park sealed off? I noticed another gate as I drove past.'

'Ah.'

Bernie could hear Kerry taking a deep breath. It wasn't going to be good news.

'About that,' said Kerry. 'The first response officers spoke to the park ranger, Malcolm Keats. He lives in the little cottage and was woken up by a noise late last night but thought it was a fox. He looked out but didn't see anything. The assumption was made that the victim and assailant went through the front gate rather than any of the others. The investigator working the other sexual assaults agreed, as it seemed to fit the MO for her cases – women being abducted and attacked after getting off a bus. There's a stop right outside the park gate.'

Bernie got out of the car and looked down the road. The stop was just a single post, not particularly obvious.

'Maybe it does all fit together but we can't assume anything, you know that,' said Bernie.

'I know. Look, wait for me to get to you.'

'You can't speak freely at the moment?'

'No. Give me five minutes.'

Bernie was suited and booted by the time Kerry arrived. The forensic suit fitted snugly over her bump – she wondered if they had maternity ones. She'd locked her bag in the boot of her car and slipped her keys and phone into her jacket pocket before pulling on a pair of blue gloves.

Bernie looked up and gave her DS a quick smile. The petite officer looked tired – her blue eyes were jaded and her short, blonde hair was in disarray. She'd obviously jumped out of bed and gone straight to headquarters.

'Please tell me that we have an inner and outer cordon,' said Bernie.

'We do. The crime scene manager is at the inner.'

Bernie made sure they were out of earshot from the officer on the gate before she asked her next question.

'What the bloody hell is going on? If this turns into a murder investigation then we'll be stuffed if we don't deal with this properly from the beginning.'

Kerry put her hand on Bernie's arm and gently pulled her to the side of the path.

'Look, this local crime investigator, Leigh Roberts, wasn't too impressed to see me either. There have been four other attacks over the last six months that she's been investigating, and as I said on the phone, this attack has a similar MO. So as far as Leigh's concerned, this is her case.'

Bernie shook her head. Having different teams for different crimes was all well and good until the lines became blurred. And why was an LCI – a civilian position rather than an actual police officer – investigating?

'Why have we been called in then? Surely Leigh Roberts has started to build on the information given by the other victims,' said Bernie.

'I've not managed to get much out of Leigh yet. We're here because this victim was hit on the head, the others weren't. They escaped serious injury and... well, let's just say that the next twenty-four hours are crucial for this woman. And even if she does wake up, there are no guarantees she'll make a full recovery. She probably has swelling on her brain. She's due to have a scan this morning. Thank God the temperatures were above freezing last night, otherwise...'

'Game over,' said Bernie. She looked around the park. Spring was slowly making an appearance. Daffodil shoots were coming up and crocuses were scattered through the lawns. March – the month that's meant to come in like a lion and go out like a lamb – was finally beginning to turn warmer after the cold, wet and windy days of winter. There were even pockets of blue, breaking through the metallic, grey clouds. Birds in an aviary were chirping furiously, fighting over some seed.

Bernie sighed. She didn't need the hassle of another officer being possessive over a case. But she understood it all too well. She hadn't been happy when she'd been kicked off a murder case the year before.

'OK. I'll tread carefully. If this is connected with the other attacks then we'll need Leigh Roberts,' said Bernie. 'I'll try to keep my hormones in check.'

Kerry gave a wry smile. 'Hormones? I didn't say anything about your hormones.'

They started to walk down the path towards the crime scene.

'Although, you have been a bit grumpy in the mornings,' said Kerry.

'What do you mean "grumpy"? I'm positively delightful in the mornings.'

'Hmm,' said Kerry. 'Maybe by eleven o'clock.'

3

Even dressed head to toe in a forensic suit, Bernie recognised Lucy Thomas, the forensic officer. There was something about the way she moved, a grace that was evident, despite the rustle of the white suit.

'Lucy,' said Bernie, as she approached the bandstand.

'Morning, Bernie. How's bubs?'

Bernie smiled. Before being pregnant, she'd never considered all the different names people gave to babies – bubs, sprog, nipper, bean and her favourite, bun.

'Seems to be OK. Almost halfway now. Got another scan soon. What've you got for me?'

Lucy shook her head. 'Not a lot, I'm afraid. No obvious weapon anywhere. There's vaginal secretions and blood – I'm guessing that both are from the victim. No semen that I've found so far, so maybe he wore a condom. I'll need to check the victim's clothes and ideally swab her and take samples from under her fingernails. Take photos too. She was whisked away before I got here. Obviously, I won't do any of that without permission. But the sooner we can do it, the better.' Lucy nodded towards a woman talking on her phone. 'That's Leigh

Roberts, the local crime investigator. She's just ringing the hospital now.'

Bernie looked at the woman on her phone. She'd pulled down her hood on the protective suit to make the call, her dark brown shoulder-length hair tucked behind her ears. The hand holding the phone had an array of silver rings, almost mimicking a knuckleduster. Bernie had a vague recollection of seeing Leigh at a talk she had done the year before when she was off active duties due to a broken wrist. If she remembered correctly, Leigh had asked some difficult questions at the end. She was clearly an ambitious officer. She wouldn't give up this case easily.

Leigh looked over and gave Bernie a brief nod but no smile. She finished on the phone and walked over to them, pulling the hood back over her hair.

'So sorry that you've been dragged out of bed, ma'am,' said Leigh. Her accent was local. 'It really wasn't necessary. I have everything under control.'

Bernie did her best to give an easy smile. 'Given the severity of the injuries, it makes more sense for MCIT to take over now, rather than later. DCS Wilson has given me the go ahead to be SIO. So, we need to close the gardens to the public today and seal it off completely. The perpetrator and the victim may have come in one gate but he may have left by another. I'll arrange for more officers to come and do a thorough search. If this is your man, then he's upped his MO and we need to find him quickly before he strikes again.'

Leigh lowered her eyes. 'Of course. I understand you need to take over. I'd like to come to the hospital, though, ma'am, to see the victim.'

Bernie turned to Kerry.

'I'm happy to stay and run the search,' said Kerry.

'Well, it's what you do best,' said Bernie. She turned back to

Leigh. 'Searches are a special strength of DS Allen's. She tends to spot things that others don't.'

Bernie hadn't meant it as a barbed comment but Leigh's face dropped. 'I was only doing what I felt was best given the resources I have.'

'I completely understand that. We just need to step it up now. What did the hospital say?'

Leigh tucked a loose strand of hair back into the hood. 'Yes, they said we could go now and do the forensic checks. The family are there and are desperate for this man to be caught. She's had a brain scan and is currently stable but we need to go asap.'

Bernie nodded. 'Did you hear that, Lucy?'

The forensic officer stood up, a sample stick in her hand. 'Yes, no problem. Give me ten minutes.'

Bernie gazed around the gardens. 'What can you tell me about this place, Leigh?'

The local crime investigator swung her eyes down again as she spoke. 'It gets quite busy. There's a café, a bowls club and in the summer they have live music on the bandstand here. It's a really popular park.'

'So we need to move fast if we're going to close it for a bit,' said Bernie. 'Kerry, speak to Malcolm Keats – get a statement from him too – and then get on to the Parks department at the local council and explain to them what we need to do. See how many extra officers we can rope in. Get Matt over here to help as well. Leigh, let's head back to my car and you can fill me in on these other attacks.'

They stripped off their suits and placed them in the dedicated rubbish bag by the gate. A lot more people were around now, their eyes drifting towards the police presence as they walked past on the other side of the road. Little children pointed excitedly on their way to school – 'Look, Mummy, police cars!'

'We'll need to do house-to-house fairly quickly. I'll get Matt to sort that out.' Bernie turned to face Leigh, her belly prominent now without the forensic suit.

'Oh,' said Leigh. 'Congratulations.'

Instinctively, Bernie stroked her bump. 'Thank you.'

They started to walk towards Bernie's car.

'I hope you don't mind me saying this, ma'am, but I've been looking for this guy for the last six months. I'm surprised you've been put on this. I mean, it won't be that long before you'll be on maternity leave.'

Bernie stopped and stared at the other officer. 'I'm not due until July. I think we stand a pretty good chance of finding him before then.'

'Oh, I see.' Leigh smiled without a hint of embarrassment. 'Must be a big baby then.'

Bernie's eyes narrowed. Despite her promise to Kerry, she could feel her hormones rising up and readying themselves to take aim. She reached into her jacket and pulled out her car keys. She pushed a button and the car doors clicked open.

'Get in the car, Leigh.'

4

Bernie was still smarting slightly from Leigh's comment about the size of her bump but was doing her best to stay professional. She had to find out about the other victims while they waited for Lucy.

'So, fill me in on these other attacks.'

Leigh took a deep breath. 'Well, ma'am, the first attack took place last year at the end of September. In that instance, the victim was grabbed after she got off the bus and dragged into an alleyway. He attempted to grope her but she managed to get away. The second victim was attacked on Hallowe'en. She'd been to a fancy dress party at a nightclub in the town centre. She was very drunk. She remembered waiting for a bus. The next thing she knew, she was on the ground behind some large bushes, with a man on top of her, his hand in her knickers. It was dark and he was dressed in black. She managed to push him off and run away.

'The third victim was on her way home from a work Christmas party. She was only metres away from her house when she got off the bus. She was forced behind some garages and sexually assaulted. Not a full rape but violated with his hands. She'd drunk a bit of wine but was with it enough to take in a few more details. She thought the perpetrator was possibly black, wearing black clothing. He was wearing a hoodie which was drawn tight over his face.'

Bernie nodded. 'That fits with what the second victim said then. Did the third victim say anything else?'

Leigh shook her head. 'No, she was very shocked. She, and the others, did the wrong thing but a very natural thing afterwards.'

'They showered,' said Bernie.

'Yes, and washed their clothes. So no DNA at all.'

Bernie sighed. She could see why Leigh Roberts hadn't been able to make headway.

'What about the fourth victim?'

'Finally, we have a victim who wasn't drunk at all. She'd been working at a supermarket and was on her way home when she was grabbed after getting off the bus. She was pulled into an empty car park and assaulted in the same way as victim three. Afterwards, she was wandering around in a state of shock when a passing patrol car spotted her and took her to the sexual assault referral centre. She said he had latex gloves on. She could remember the smell. He also spoke to her when she tried to scream. He told her to shut up or he'd slit her throat. He had a London accent. She kept her eyes tightly shut, though, so wasn't able to add to the physical description.'

Bernie noticed that Leigh hadn't pulled out her notebook once to tell her all that information, and despite herself she was impressed.

'When was the last attack?' she asked.

'In February.' Leigh paused. 'I think he's planning the attacks carefully each time. Watching the women and then following them. He knows where to take them.'

'And,' said Bernie, 'they were either at a bus stop or had just got off the bus. Whereabouts in Swindon? Any CCTV footage from the buses?'

'The second one was in the town centre but she was grabbed before getting on the bus. The other three were north of the railway line, all of them heading home. There is some CCTV footage but you can't see his face. Head down, hood up. But for the last attack when he got off the bus, there's a glimpse of white gloves against the black cuff of the sleeve.'

Bernie felt a twinge in her side. Her scar was starting to stretch with her bump. She gently rubbed it. 'And now we have a possible fifth victim. South of the town centre and this appears to be rape and attempted murder. Far more physical this time. He's stepped up.'

'I don't think there's much doubt about it. She has vaginal bleeding,' said Leigh.

Bernie turned towards the local crime investigator. She spotted Lucy, over Leigh's shoulder, heading towards them.

'We don't assume anything. Not until we have forensic results and we've looked at the CCTV on the bus. Here's Lucy now.'

Bernie pressed the button to wind down the passenger door window.

'Lucy, is it easier for you to come with us?' Bernie asked.

'Thanks but I'm going to take my van. Then I can go straight to the lab afterwards. I'm guessing you want Therese to start processing everything as quickly as possible.'

'Yes please. Leigh was just filling me in on the other cases. There doesn't seem much to go on forensically.'

Lucy shook her head. 'No, not really. We managed to get a few trace fibres from the fourth victim's clothes – some strands of black material. Might be useful in matching with a suspect's clothes but that's about it. Maybe this latest victim will have more.'

Leigh's mouth pulled slightly into a smile. Bernie could

guess what she was thinking – why look elsewhere when there was a prime suspect already? Even Lucy thought it was the same perpetrator.

'OK, we'll see you at the hospital. We'll meet at the main entrance.'

Bernie started the car and then pulled away. Leigh was wisely keeping quiet but the faint smile hinted at smugness.

5

The traffic was heavy as Bernie headed back towards the M4 and the hospital.

'Leigh, can you ring the hospital please and let them know we're stuck in traffic? As important as forensics are, if any treatment is needed then that should take precedence. Do we know anything else about Keira Howard, other than her name?'

'No, that's all the info we have at the moment so it's crucial we talk to the family as well.'

'I agree. Hopefully they'll have some idea of her movements last night. After we've spoken to them and Lucy has taken her samples, we'll head over to the bus depot and see if we can find out if Keira was on a bus. And see if your mystery suspect was there too.'

Leigh pursed her lips. 'He's not a "mystery suspect" – he's real and I'm sure it's him this time as well.'

Bernie glanced across at Leigh. 'That's not what I meant. I said "mystery" because we don't know who he is, rather than I think you're making him up. Leigh, I'm here to work with you, not against you. Now, make the phone call to the hospital and tell them our ETA is fifteen minutes.'

. . .

Bernie pressed the buzzer by the ICU door. There was a crackle, followed by a voice.

'ICU.'

'Yes, this is Detective Inspector Bernie Noel. We're here to see Keira Howard. You should be expecting us.'

'Yes, of course. Come in.'

The magnetic catch clicked open. A nurse in blue scrubs was waiting for them.

'Hello, I'm Rachel Bell. I'm looking after Keira. If you'd like to come with me please.'

Bernie, Leigh and Lucy followed the nurse to a side room. A couple sat on either side of the bed.

'Mr and Mrs Howard, this is Detective Inspector Noel,' said Rachel.

The couple both turned. Their faces were etched with tear tracks. Bernie held out her hand to each of them in turn.

'Mr and Mrs Howard, I'm so sorry that we have to meet in these circumstances.'

Bernie looked at the young woman lying on the bed. She almost looked peaceful. Her face was like porcelain. Despite the trauma, she was still beautiful. She had a white bandage over her forehead and an IV drip in her arm. A CPAP mask was over her nose and mouth. Her heart rate, oxygen saturation levels and blood pressure were all stable, according to the little lines moving up and down on the monitor. Bernie suddenly felt a memory start to surface, but she pushed it away. She steadied herself before speaking further.

'In a moment, I would like to talk to you about your daughter's whereabouts last night but I think you've been made aware that there are... certain things that my forensic officer needs to do.'

A slight tremor from Mrs Howard's head indicated a yes.

'I know that you don't want to leave her but it might be better if you step out of the room for a few minutes. Do we have your permission to do this?'

Mr Howard coughed. 'Yes. Anything that you need to do to catch the bastard who did this to Keira.' He reached over to his wife and squeezed her hand. 'Come on, Julie. She'll be in safe hands.'

Slowly, Julie Howard rose from her chair. She was struggling to stand. Leigh reached out her hand.

'Let me help you, Mrs Howard.' Leigh looked across to the nurse. 'Is there a room Mr and Mrs Howard could wait in please?'

'Yes, we have a family room. If you'd like to follow me.'

Bernie waited until they'd all left before shutting the door quietly. She snapped on a pair of gloves.

'What can I do to help, Lucy?'

The forensic officer opened her large bag. 'If you could label and seal please. We'll both need to initial. The officer who went in the ambulance with her bagged up her clothes in A&E so I'll fetch those afterwards. She was wearing a short, plum-coloured puffer jacket and a black jersey dress. Trainers on her feet, with high heels in her bag.'

'Sensible girl.' Bernie glanced at the young woman. 'If it wasn't for the bandage on her head, you'd think she was just asleep.'

Lucy looked at Keira's notes. 'She's sedated. They'll keep her like this until the results of the brain scan.' She gently peeled back the sheet and blanket over Keira. 'If this is the same attacker, then I'm expecting bruising in the same places. Assuming the bruises have come out. Yes, here we go.'

Lucy grabbed a camera and a ruler. 'Look at this bruising on her wrists. It's a bit hard to tell with the IV in her right arm but it's clearer on the left. He holds them so tight that you can see individual fingermarks.'

Bernie leaned in closer to see the marks. 'The others had this too?'

'Yes, all of them. I've seen the photos. They were taken at the sexual assault referral centre. So, not by us.' Lucy clicked away with her camera. 'There may be some on her inner thighs as well. The third victim had bruising on one leg.'

She pulled the bedding lower and very carefully raised Keira's hospital gown. There were marks on her left inner thigh.

Bernie briefly closed her eyes. An image flashed into her head. 'So, he probably held her wrists with his right hand and used his left to force her legs apart before assaulting her. He went much further with Keira than the others,' she said. Her stomach lurched. It didn't matter how many victims she saw, dead or alive, the thought of such violence always got to her.

The camera clicked again as Lucy took more photos. 'Yep. It's a big escalation. He's getting bolder. I'll do the worst bit next,' she said.

'I'd rather you leave that until later. It always feels like we're violating the victim all over again,' said Bernie. She sat down in the chair next to the bed. She didn't want to admit to it but being in ICU was starting to get to her.

'OK. I'll do fingernails instead. Maybe you should swap with Leigh. I know you don't find these things easy at the best of times but given your current condition, things might be a bit more... heightened.'

If anyone else had said that, Bernie would have considered it patronising but she knew Lucy meant well.

'You're probably right. I've barely eaten. I grabbed a slice of toast as I left and swigged down some decaf coffee.'

'Decaf? I'm impressed.'

Bernie smiled. 'Got to keep the blood pressure down somehow so the doctors are happy. On the other hand, I'm bloody knackered without my daily caffeine hit. Right, I need to get Leigh here but I don't have her number to call her.'

Lucy put down her camera and pulled off her gloves. 'Don't worry, I do.'

A few minutes later, Leigh popped her head round the door. 'You want to swap, ma'am?'

'Yes please,' said Bernie. 'I'm not feeling so great. The downside of dashing out without eating a proper breakfast. Apparently, growing babies need food. I'll talk to the parents and you can help Lucy. Have you got very far with them?'

Leigh shook her head. 'No. Julie Howard is too upset to talk at the moment and the father, Geoff Howard, was out all evening so doesn't know what Keira was doing.'

'OK, I'll see what I can get out of them.' Bernie's head started to spin as she got up. She grabbed the chair to steady herself. 'Oh, got up a bit quick there.' She waited until the room stilled before walking. There was concern on Leigh's face.

'There's a water cooler just outside the family room, ma'am. Maybe you should have a drink before talking to the Howards. It's at the end of the corridor, on the left, just before the entrance door to ICU.'

'That's a good idea. Thanks, Leigh.' Bernie took off her gloves and deposited them in the bin. She grabbed her bag and left the room. As the door closed behind her, Bernie heard Leigh speaking to Lucy.

'See? How can she lead this investigation? She's not up to it.'

6

The water trickled into the plastic cup. The cooler was nearly empty. Bernie downed the drink in seconds, the cold hitting the back of her throat. She could hear all the beeps from the machines on the main ICU, beating rhythmically until a discordant alarm affected the tempo. Looking across, she watched as a nurse immediately jumped up and twiddled dials until the alarm stopped. That was the noise that Bernie remembered most from her time in an ICU bed, after the stabbing. Far from being peaceful, it was full of constant sound – not just the machines but staff talking to each other, to patients and to family members. It had been months before Pops, her late grandfather, had spoken to her about it – what it was like to sit there and watch someone you love so ill. Not just the endless tubes and machinery but also quiet desperation and hopelessness invading every thought; of holding it together at the bedside but falling apart in the family room; finally hearing the words, 'She's turned a corner', only to see another family leave in tears.

'I prayed for everyone on that ward, not just you,' Pops had said. 'It was all I could do.'

Bernie pulled herself back to the present and was about to go in search of Keira's parents when she heard a voice behind her.

'Hello, stranger.'

Bernie turned to see Debs, Kerry's partner and also an ICU nurse. 'Debs, hi.' Bernie hugged her. 'Haven't seen you in ages. How are you?'

Debs pulled a face. 'Not so good. Had a death this morning, just before the changeover. I've been dealing with the family and the paperwork. Anyway, I'm now on my way home to bed. I take it Kerry isn't with you?'

'No. I'm here for Keira Howard. Kerry's working at the scene.'

'I thought she might be,' said Debs. 'Tell her I said hi. You see more of her than I do. Bloody shifts. We never seem to get them coordinated.'

'Hmm. Let me know your shifts for the next few weeks and I'll see what I can sort out. Can't promise anything, though, especially with this new case.'

'That's OK. I do understand.' Debs leant forward and kissed Bernie on the cheek. 'Thank you for thinking of us. I'd better go. You take care of little one. See you soon.'

Bernie watched Debs leave. The polar opposite of Kerry, she was tall and willowy, with long brown hair scooped up into a bun. Bernie understood the hassle of both partners doing shift work. With Anderson now working in a different team, their time together was often brief.

She knocked on the door of the family room before entering. Rachel was still with the Howards. Bernie sat down opposite Keira's parents. Geoff had his arm around his wife's shoulders.

'Sorry about us swapping over. Rachel, if you need to leave and check on Keira then please feel free,' said Bernie.

Rachel took the hint and left the room.

'OK. There are a few questions that I would like to ask you and also I'd like to explain what we're doing,' said Bernie, pulling out her notebook and pen from her pocket. 'I'm the senior investigating officer so I'm in charge of your daughter's case. I intend to do everything in my power to find the man responsible. I know a lot of TV dramas show things happening very quickly but this isn't always the case in real life. So please bear with me as we try to track this man down. It would be really helpful if I could trace Keira's last movements. Are you up for a few questions?'

Julie Howard looked up. 'I'll try. It's all a bit too much,' she said.

Bernie remembered what Pops had told her – the quiet desperation and hopelessness. 'I understand. We'll go slowly. Let's start with how old Keira is.'

'I'll answer,' said Geoff. 'She's nineteen.'

'And is she working or at college?'

'Both. She works at a solicitor's office in town. She wants to be a lawyer but she didn't get high enough grades in her A-levels. She's retaking them, though, this summer. She's been working very hard.'

Bernie jotted down a few notes.

'And where was she last night? Or supposed to be?'

'I'm not sure. Julie?'

Julie Howard wiped her nose with a tissue that she then tucked up her sleeve. 'She'd been out celebrating a friend's birthday. They'd been to a club, I don't know which one. A whole group of them. I don't really know them. We live in the opposite direction from her friends. But I'm sure two of them are called Caz and Mia. Anyway, she said she'd stay over with one of them.'

'Did she say who?'

'No.' Julie wiped a stray tear. 'She's done it before. And Monday is a college day but she doesn't have to be in until eleven a.m. So plenty of time to come home in the morning and get changed, and then go back out again. I wasn't worried. I should have been, though, shouldn't I?' She closed her eyes and breathed deeply.

'It's not your fault, Mrs Howard. Your daughter's an adult.'

'Is she? She's still my little girl, always will be.' Julie nodded towards Bernie's stomach. 'You'll find that out soon enough.'

Bernie squirmed a little in her seat. She was still getting used to her pregnancy being public property.

'You said that this has happened before – staying over at a friend's house. Can you remember when this was?'

Julie thought for a moment. 'I can't remember exactly but it's happened a couple of times this year. February half-term, I think, and New Year's Eve.'

'And had she been clubbing both of those times?'

'Yes, she had.'

'And does Keira have a boyfriend?'

'No,' said Geoff.

Bernie looked up. She thought he'd answered that a little too quickly. 'Has there ever been one?'

Geoff Howard looked decidedly uncomfortable.

'Mr Howard?'

Geoff rubbed his face before speaking. 'There was a boy she knew from college. They went out a few times. He was quite serious about it all but Keira wasn't. It got a bit... messy.'

Bernie put down her pen. 'Define "messy".'

Geoff looked at his wife who nodded back at him. 'Well, there were abusive text messages and phone calls. He found out our landline number and we would get silent phone calls in the middle of the night. He vandalised her locker at college and he... put photos of Keira on social media. Quite explicit ones.'

Bernie picked up her pen again and wrote down what she'd just heard. 'Did you go to the police?'

'No,' said Julie Howard. 'We went to the college. They were

very annoyed about her locker. They told him to either leave college of his own free will or face the police. He left and as far as we're aware, Keira hasn't heard anything from him since. He took the photos down as well.'

'Which college is this? And when did it all happen?'

'It's Western College and it happened last autumn. He left just before Christmas and didn't return in January,' said Geoff.

'And his name?' asked Bernie.

Julie gasped. 'You don't think he did this, do you?'

'I need to consider everything. His name, please, and a description.'

Julie bit her lip. 'Isaac Campbell. He's eighteen. Not very tall. Slim. Black. He seemed nice enough to begin with but then things changed. As Geoff said, Isaac thought the relationship was quite serious whereas Keira didn't.'

Bernie nodded as she wrote in her notebook.

'Mr and Mrs Howard, I will do my best to find out whoever has done this. I'm going to check and see how the examination is going and then I'll come back to you.' Bernie stood up. She thought about Leigh's suspect – and how one of the victims thought he was black. Was it Isaac Campbell? 'You've been very helpful. Thank you.'

Bernie was about to walk back into Keira's room when the door flew open and Rachel came rushing out.

'Is everything OK?' asked Bernie.

'No,' said the nurse as she buzzed past.

Bernie walked into the room. 'What's going on?'

Lucy was standing by Keira and looked up. 'Slight problem. I've just done the vaginal swab. I was expecting there to be some blood but not this much.' She indicated the pool of blood on the sheet.

'Shit. Period or miscarriage or internal bleeding?'

'That's what Rachel needs to find out. She's calling for a doctor and a sonographer.'

'I think I might know the answer,' said Leigh.

Bernie turned behind her to find Leigh pulling something out of a bag.

'This is Keira's bag. It was put in the ambulance with her. And this' – she held up an object – 'is a positive pregnancy test.'

7

All hell seemed to break loose as Bernie and the others were shoved unceremoniously from Keira's hospital room.

Bernie looked at Lucy. 'I hate to ask this but did you get everything you need?'

'I think so. I could have done with getting a few more swabs but it will have to do for now. She might need surgery. Poor girl,' said Lucy. 'I had high hopes for her clothes but they've been handled by quite a few people so getting any trace evidence will be tricky. Maybe Therese can find something. I just need to take DNA samples for elimination purposes from anyone that's dealt with Keira and then I'll take everything to the lab.'

Leigh stood behind them, holding Keira's handbag wrapped in an evidence bag. 'We need to examine this back at the station first, ma'am, before sending it on to Forensics.'

'I agree,' said Bernie. 'We particularly need to look at her mobile.' She glanced at the door of Keira's room. A sonographer had turned up a few minutes before with a portable ultrasound and a doctor had rushed in too. She thought of Keira's parents. They had no idea what was happening. Was it her place to tell them? She thought not. That was for the doctors to do. Her questions could wait for now.

'I'm just going to give my details to Keira's parents,' she said to Leigh. 'I'll be back in a minute.'

The pain on the Howards' faces was still evident.

'Is she OK? Have you finished now? Can we go back in?' asked Geoff.

Bernie tried to keep her voice calm. 'The doctor is with her at the moment, doing some tests. I'm sure Rachel will be back in a few minutes with an update. In the meantime' – she reached into her bag and pulled out a card – 'here's my number. I will need to speak to you again, and fairly soon. But there are some things that we're going to look into first, including Isaac Campbell.'

Geoff's fingers trembled slightly as he took the card. 'Thank you.'

'I don't suppose you know the pin code for Keira's phone, do you?' asked Bernie. 'We'll need to have a look at it.'

Geoff gave a brief smile. 'It's two, five, one, two. I know, Christmas. Not very original and possibly not very safe. But Keira's rubbish at remembering numbers.'

Bernie didn't bother to jot it down. Even with baby brain, she thought she'd remember it. 'Thank you. Take care of yourselves. We'll be in touch.'

Bernie opened up the boot of her car and grabbed a banana from a carrier bag.

'Do you want anything, Leigh?'

Leigh rummaged in the bag. 'Do you have anything healthier? It just seems to be crisps and cereal bars mainly.'

'Oh, sorry,' said Bernie, with a mouthful of banana. 'This was the last of the fruit. I found I needed lots of dry food when I had morning sickness.'

Leigh wrinkled her nose in disgust. 'So have some of these been in your car for weeks?'

Bernie sighed. It wasn't going to be easy working with Leigh. 'No. I just kept buying the things I knew I could eat that would stop me from chucking up every five minutes. You don't have to have anything.'

'I might pass for now, thanks.'

'Fine.' Bernie shut the boot. 'Let's head over to the bus station. See if Keira got a bus to the gardens. And on the way there, I want you to start looking into a few things for me.'

'Such as?'

'Isaac Campbell, a former boyfriend of Keira's.'

Leigh opened the passenger door. 'Oh, do you think he's the father?'

'Unlikely, split up last year. He hassled her for a while.'

'Shouldn't we be looking for the father of Keira's baby?'

'Isaac Campbell is black.'

Leigh's eyes widened. 'Well, in that case, maybe we should find him first—'

'Or maybe we shouldn't assume,' said Bernie. 'We need to check the bus CCTV.'

The man at the bus depot scratched his head.

'You two don't use buses in Swindon, do you?' he said.

Bernie shook her head. Living in a small village outside Devizes, she drove everywhere.

'I don't live here, so, no, I don't,' said Bernie. She turned to Leigh. 'What about you?'

'I tend to drive,' Leigh replied. 'Don't really like public transport.'

The man shook his head. A few flakes of dandruff fluttered down onto his suit jacket.

'There aren't any buses at that time of night; well, not on the routes you're asking about.'

Bernie paused. *How did Keira get there then? Cab? Walk?*

'We did have some night buses on Fridays and Saturdays but people didn't use them enough. It's not like we're London here.'

Something triggered for Bernie. She hadn't been on a bus since leaving London for Wiltshire. The memory of trailing someone and then meeting them 'by chance' on the bus flooded into her mind. Her scar began to itch again. She rubbed it, easing the memory as much as the physical symptom.

'OK, you've been very helpful. Thank you,' she said.

The two women walked out of the office back to Bernie's car.

'Of course, it doesn't mean that it's not the serial attacker,' said Leigh. 'He could have followed her from the town centre—'

'Leigh, we don't actually know where Keira was,' said Bernie. 'What she told her mother and what she actually did could be two different things. I'm not saying it's not the same guy but we need to look at other possibilities. Starting with Keira's phone. That will give us some idea of where she was last night. Rather than trying to find evidence to link her attack with the others, we need to work with what we have. And so far, that's precious little.'

A sulky expression crossed Leigh's face and her eyes darkened. Bernie didn't need a petulant officer.

'I suggest a little trip to headquarters,' she said.

'But all my notes are in Swindon, at Gable Cross station. Photos, the victims' statements—'

'Leigh. My digital media investigator is at headquarters and we need him to look at Keira's phone. We might set up an incident room at Gable Cross in the future but for now, I'm going to Devizes. Are you coming with me or not?'

Leigh bit her lip. She slowly nodded. 'I'll come.'

8

As Bernie walked through the door of police headquarters, she felt herself relax. She was back on home ground. At the same time, Leigh visibly stiffened.

'We'll need to sign you in at reception. Get you a pass,' said Bernie.

Leigh followed her to the main desk. Bernie smiled at the older woman there.

'Morning, Sally. This is Leigh Roberts. She's an LCI in Swindon. She's going to be working with us today.'

Bernie glanced towards the stairs as she heard a familiar voice. 'I'll be back in a minute.'

She met Anderson as he reached the bottom step. He was on his phone.

'Yes, I understand that, sir, but...' He mouthed 'hello' to Bernie. She could hear a stern voice coming through the mobile.

'OK, sir. I'll be back in thirty to forty-five minutes.' He hung up and then smiled at Bernie.

'I'm so glad to see you,' he said, kissing her on the cheek.

'Bad morning?'

'The worst. The Met officer arrived late and now he's

trying to take over my op. I've offered to go and buy sandwiches just to get out of the room. Of course, the DCI knew exactly what I was doing. The phone call was a little reminder that I need to behave myself. Fancy a walk to the bakery?'

'I'd love to, but' – Bernie glanced over her shoulder towards Leigh – 'I have a newbie with me.'

'Oh. Any good?'

'About as frustrating as your Met officer.'

Anderson smiled. 'That good, then. Have you got lunch? Shall I get you some? A bun for the "bun"?' He stroked her belly.

Bernie grinned. 'This child is going to look like a pastry when he or she comes out. I haven't got any proper lunch. Plenty of crisps in my desk drawer though.'

'You know that's not good enough. I'll buy you something. What about Miss Knuckleduster over there? That's a serious amount of rings she's wearing. She could do some real damage with them.'

'Hmm. She tends to wound with her words rather than her fists.'

Anderson pushed Bernie's hair back from her face. 'What did she say?'

Bernie sighed. 'That I must have a big baby. She thought I was further along.'

Anderson did his best to conceal a smile.

'It's not funny,' said Bernie.

'No, it's not. And you're beautiful. Sure you don't want to go for a walk? There's a lovely little bench by a pond. Great for a quick kiss.' He winked.

Bernie touched his arm. 'Very, very tempting but there's a victim in ICU and we need to find her attacker. But maybe this evening.' She tilted her head to one side.

'This evening, you'll be asleep before the news. I'd better go.

If your newbie wants anything, text me.' He brushed her lips with a kiss. 'I'll drop the food to you in MCIT.'

Anderson walked away as Leigh came up to Bernie.

'Just a bit of paperwork to fill out. Honestly, you wouldn't think that I already work for Wiltshire Police,' said Leigh. 'Who was that man?'

Bernie allowed herself a glimmer of a smile. 'Detective Inspector Anderson. He's with Serious Organised Crime. He's my partner.'

'I bet he's excited about the baby.'

Bernie's heart lurched. Despite everything, not knowing whether he or Alex Murray, Bernie's ex, was the father, Anderson did seem excited. At least he hadn't mentioned the paternity test again.

'He is,' said Bernie. 'He's gone to get some lunch. Do you want anything from the bakery? I can text him.'

'No, it's fine. I have a pasta salad with me. I made it last night. I like to have everything organised. You never know when you're going to be able to eat.'

'True. Come on up and meet the rest of the Major Crime Investigation Team.'

DCs Alice Hart and Mick Parris were sitting at their desks when Bernie entered MCIT.

'Morning, ma'am,' said Mick. 'Or rather afternoon.' He grinned.

'Cheeky. Some of us have been at work since eight a.m.,' said Bernie.

'I know,' said Mick. 'DS Allen has called in. She's making headway with the search. Nothing interesting been found yet.'

'OK. Mick, Alice, this is Leigh Roberts. Leigh's a local crime investigator with Swindon. Leigh, this is DC Alice Hart and DC Mick Parris. You've already met DS Kerry Allen. DC Matt

Taylor makes up the rest of our little team and he's helping Kerry. We're under the supervision of Detective Chief Superintendent Wilson. But the person I need right now is Tom and his tech magic. Alice, could you give him a call please and ask him to pop up?'

'Yes, ma'am. Oh, Jane Clackett was looking for you earlier. She's already had some journalists sniffing around the "woman in the park" case.'

'Oh God, that's all we need.' Bernie looked across to Leigh. 'Jane runs the press office for us. She terrifies journalists, which is a good thing.'

'Oh,' said Leigh. 'Should I be worried?'

'No,' said Mick, 'you're a woman. It's only men she eats for breakfast.'

'Mick!' Bernie laughed. 'And for that, you can be the one to get back to Jane and say we have nothing to share with the media at present.'

'Can I email her rather than see her in person?'

'Wimp. OK, but only because I have another job for you, DC Parris. Look up an Isaac Campbell, probably living in Swindon. See if we have anything on him.'

'Can't I do that?' asked Leigh. 'I mean, can I help with that please? I did start looking him up when we were driving over but I didn't get very far.'

Bernie looked between Mick and Leigh.

'Fine by me,' said Parris.

'Go ahead then,' said Bernie.

She went over to her own desk and pulled Keira's phone out of her bag. It was tempting to check out the mobile before Tom arrived but she remembered a conversation she'd had with the super when she told him she was pregnant.

'Great news, Bernie. And now you can start acting like a proper detective inspector. Delegate. Stop trying to do everything yourself.'

Bernie's fingers were itching to tap in the pin code but the super was right. What was the point in having the experts if you didn't use them? She picked up a pen and began to write a list of things she needed Tom to look for. Now she'd seen Keira, there was no time to waste. They had to find this man before he struck again.

9

Tom appeared a few minutes later.

'You got here quick, Tom,' said Bernie.

The young digital media investigator laughed, his blond wavy hair shaking. 'I always come running when you ask for me, ma'am.'

'Well, I have a list of things I want from this phone please.'

'Let me guess. You want to know exactly where this phone has been in the last twenty-four hours. Plus text messages, phone calls, social media, et cetera.'

'Spot on, as usual. In particular, look for any messages from a Caz and a Mia. Those were two names her parents mentioned. Her mother wasn't sure what clubs Keira was going to visit last night so we definitely need the geographical position. In particular, the last position should be in the Town Gardens area. I want to know how long the phone was there for. That should help to narrow down the time of the attack.' Bernie rubbed her bump as she felt the fluttering movements once more. She resisted the urge to smile and say hello to her bump. She'd only been having these movements for a couple of days.

'OK. Sounds like all the normal stuff. I'll have to wait for the network provider to come back to me but I can start on the other stuff straight away. Do you have a passcode?' asked Tom.

'Two, five, one, two, according to her father but I wouldn't put it past Keira to have changed it. You might expect parents to know that kind of info for maybe a thirteen-year-old, but nineteen? Although Keira was being hassled by an ex-boyfriend so maybe her father wanted access to her phone. Have you found out anything on Isaac Campbell yet, Mick?'

Mick Parris looked up from his computer screen. 'Not much yet. He does have a couple of cautions for being drunk and disorderly, though, so I have an address for him.'

'Excellent. Send it to me along with his caution details. I want to see when those happened. See if they tie in with when he was hassling Keira.'

Bernie walked over to a whiteboard and picked up a pen. She wrote 'Keira Howard' in black capitals at the top of the board and then underlined it.

'Leigh, I know you're desperate to link this with your other cases but for the moment, we're going to work it separately. When there's evidence to prove it's the same man, then we'll bring in everything you have. I don't want to go down one road, only to find it's the wrong one. OK?'

Leigh twisted the rings on her fingers. Her face hardened. *Is she really going to argue with me in front of everyone?*

'I understand that, ma'am,' said Leigh. 'I guess you won't be needing me then.'

'I didn't say that,' said Bernie. 'You're the one with local knowledge. Except for bus routes.' She half-smiled. 'Not that I know any better.'

Leigh flushed. 'Sorry. I never use the bus. I really don't like public transport at all. I drive everywhere. In fact, my car is back at the Town Gardens.'

Bernie took the hint. 'Don't worry. We're going to head back later after lunch. We need to visit Keira's college anyway and see if we can track down Caz and Mia, whoever they are. I'm sure Tom will have some more detail for us by then, won't you, Tom?'

'I'll do my best, ma'am.'

'Great. By the end of today, I want some details on this board,' said Bernie.

As Tom headed to the office door, Anderson arrived with lunch.

'Oh, DI Anderson, glad I've caught you,' said Tom. 'I've left the data you needed for your county lines case in Swindon on your desk. I've printed it out in triplicate as you requested.'

Anderson glared at Tom but his Scottish voice was as smooth as silk. 'Thank you. I'll go and collect it.'

Tom left, seemingly unaware of Anderson's anger but Bernie had noticed it. She remembered the phone call he'd had that morning from his DCI about the case.

'Hey, good timing,' she said, laying her hand on his arm as he came over to her. 'I definitely need lunch now. Baby too.'

He gave a brief smile. 'Can we have a quick chat outside please?'

'Yes, sure.'

The corridor was empty.

'What's up?' said Bernie.

'I can't believe Tom just said that. We're trying to keep this case quiet.'

'That's not why you're cross though.'

'No.' Anderson rubbed his forehead. 'They've brought the raid forward. Which is ridiculous because there are still things we need to go through. That data, for example. It's from a mobile phone we've been tracking and there's one number in particular that's been ringing in. I think it's important; the DCI and the Met officer disagree with me. Anyway, it's going to be tomorrow at four a.m. I might not make it home tonight.' He sighed. 'I'm sorry.'

Bernie took his hands and placed them on her bump. 'Don't be sorry. I didn't want to say before as I wasn't sure but I think I'm starting to feel the baby move now. You probably won't be able to feel it yet. It's more like a fluttering than a kick.'

Anderson smiled. 'That's fantastic.' He moved his hands up to cup Bernie's face and kissed her. 'I can't wait to feel it kick.' He leaned his forehead against hers. 'I'm sorry about this morning. It's up to you to decide when you want to do a paternity test, OK? I love you, DI Noel.'

'And I love you, DI Anderson. Thank you for understanding.'

'Now, go and eat your lunch and don't go too mad with this case of yours. OK?'

'Yes, sir.'

Bernie opened up the bag from the bakery to find a chicken panini and a Belgian bun. There was a decaf latte to go with it. Leigh was already eating her pasta salad.

'Oh, Alice, could you ring the hospital and ask how Keira is doing? And then after that, I'd like you to process Keira's handbag,' said Bernie.

'Sure, no problem.'

Bernie pulled a bag of crisps out of her desk drawer to add to her lunch and saw Leigh roll her eyes. Bernie chose to ignore the LCI's indignation at her eating habits. Maybe she was reading too much into Leigh's behaviour but there was something about Leigh that still bothered her. Something she couldn't quite put her finger on. 'You know in your knower,' Pops had used to say when she was younger and unsure about things. And he'd been right. If something was slightly off, there was normally a reason for it. Bernie's hands hovered over her keyboard. Should she look up Leigh's record? It really wasn't the done thing. But she needed to find out more about Leigh Roberts if they were going to work this case together. She tapped Leigh's name into the staff database.

10

Western College was a 1970s educational establishment in desperate need of renovation. A building works sign next to the main entrance suggested that improvements were slowly happening.

Bernie parked her car in the staff car park. Apart from a couple of upmarket models, the other cars suggested that the college lecturers didn't make much money. Leigh had phoned ahead to make an appointment with the principal, Stephanie Lawson, and Bernie suspected that one of the more expensive cars belonged to her.

They didn't have to wait long in reception for Stephanie Lawson to arrive. In her forties and dressed in a smart navy suit with matching shoes, she looked more like a director of a company than a head teacher. Bernie mused that education was rapidly turning into a business.

'Ms Lawson, I'm Detective Inspector Bernie Noel and this is my colleague, Leigh Roberts.' Bernie held out her hand. Stephanie Lawson's grip was strong.

'You want to know about Keira Howard,' said Stephanie.

'We had noticed that she hadn't arrived today. Come through to my office.'

Despite the bleak exterior of the building, the principal's office was reasonably modern – clutter free and painted white. Apart from a small amount of open paperwork, the desk was completely empty. *I bet she hasn't got packets of crisps stuffed in her desk drawers.*

Bernie's look hadn't gone unnoticed.

'We operate a clear desk policy here as staff have to share. I don't make an exception for myself.' Stephanie gestured to two chairs in front of her desk. 'Please, take a seat. Do you want any refreshments?'

'No, thank you,' said Bernie. 'We really need to get on with our investigation. Leigh told you the basic details.'

Stephanie sighed. 'Yes. It's terrible to hear Keira's been hurt and is in hospital. Are you allowed to tell me any more?'

Bernie paused. 'I can only tell you for now that it was a very serious assault. We're trying to piece together her movements last night. Her mother told us that she went out with some friends, Caz and Mia. Are they students here?'

'Yes, they are – Caroline Prince and Mia Turney. The three of them study the same subjects – Law, History and Politics. Keira is very serious about doing law at university. She works part-time at a local firm of solicitors called Markhams and has a conditional place at Bristol. She's studying very hard and is determined to get good grades this time.'

'And the other two?' asked Bernie.

'Well... the other two aren't quite as conscientious as Keira. They're not the best influence.'

'So that might explain why they all went out clubbing on a Sunday night,' said Bernie.

Stephanie nodded. 'Yes, I saw them both at lunchtime, looking a bit green about the gills.'

Bernie caught Leigh looking confused.

'They had hangovers, then,' said Bernie. The confusion on Leigh's face cleared.

'Absolutely. Those two know how to party. I'm guessing you need to speak to them.'

'Yes please, but I'd like to do it separately,' said Bernie. She quickly glanced at the clock on the wall. It was already three thirty p.m. and they needed to find Isaac Campbell too. 'Do you have another room we could use as well please? Leigh could interview one of the girls while I see the other.'

'Yes, I can arrange that. Shall I pull them out of class? They finish at three forty-five.'

'In a few minutes,' said Bernie. 'I'd like to talk about Isaac Campbell first.'

Stephanie Lawson's face darkened. 'Ah. I'm guessing Keira's parents told you about him. He's a bright lad but he was obsessed with Keira. They hadn't been together very long when she broke it off with him. And then he started harassing her. Put up explicit photos of her on social media. She came to see me about it and I spoke to him. He did remove the photos but overall, things didn't improve. When he vandalised her locker, it was the last straw for me. I wanted Keira to come to you but she begged me not to call the police in. Her parents were insistent that something had to be done so I excluded him permanently.' Stephanie's fingers were rubbing the corners of the paperwork on her desk. 'It wasn't pleasant.'

'What kind of vandalism are we talking about?' asked Leigh.

'He'd written some very abusive terms on her locker using a permanent marker. We couldn't remove it.'

Bernie looked across at Leigh. Something was clearly bothering her. She caught Leigh's eye and gave her a nod – permission to continue.

'But don't you get graffiti like that all the time in a place like this? What else was there?' asked Leigh.

Stephanie flushed. 'You're right. There is more. I really shouldn't have listened to Keira. She begged me not to contact the police or tell her parents. And as she's over eighteen, it was her decision to make. It wasn't the graffiti that was the problem as such. It's what was in her locker. There were' – Stephanie's eyes focused on the paperwork in front of her – 'condoms, wrapped up in a tissue. Used condoms. And a note... threatening to kill himself if she left him. I'm so sorry. I should have told you. I shouldn't have listened to Keira.' Stephanie's composed mask had slipped. 'You said a serious assault. And there's a good chance that Isaac's responsible. I've failed Keira. Expelling him wasn't enough.'

'Do you still have the condoms and the note? Or take photos at the time?' asked Leigh.

Stephanie's eyes flicked up. 'Good God, no. Especially the condoms. Everything was thrown away.' She shook her head. 'I've been so stupid.'

'We don't know that Isaac is responsible,' said Bernie, 'but we will need to speak to him. Thank you for being honest with us. Perhaps you could arrange for us to see Caz and Mia now.'

'Yes, of course. I'll just ask reception to sort it out. I'll be back in a minute.'

Stephanie Lawson left the room with considerably less self-assurance than she'd had when they first met.

Bernie turned to Leigh. 'We need to ask the girls the same questions. Do you want to write these down?'

'No, I'll remember.'

'OK. We want to know where they went last night. What time did they meet and where? What time did they leave? How were they all planning to get home? Were they hassled by anyone? Does Keira have a boyfriend? Got that? Who do you want, Caz or Mia?'

'I don't mind,' said Leigh.

'OK, toss you for it.' Bernie pulled out her emergency parking one pound coin from her pocket. 'Caz is heads, Mia is tails.' She flicked the coin into the air, caught it, and opened her hand. It was heads. 'Looks like you've got Caz.'

11

Mia twiddled a strand of her long hair with her fingers. When Bernie had explained what had happened to Keira, she thought Mia was going to throw up.

'Oh God, no. I knew we shouldn't have let her go off by herself.'

Bernie reached for her notepad and pen. 'What time was this?'

Mia rubbed her face with her hands. 'About eleven, I think.'

'And where were you?'

'The Plaza.'

'From what time?'

'About ten.'

'And there were no problems with anyone? No men hitting on you?'

Mia shrugged her shoulders. 'There were a few who tried it on but we weren't interested. Too busy having a drink and a laugh. It was Caz's birthday.'

Bernie tapped her pen against her notepad. 'How much did you all drink?'

'I'm not sure. Enough for a hangover but not so much that I can't remember things.'

'OK. So what do you remember?'

Mia released her hair, leaving a curl behind. 'Keira left first, about eleven, as I said. Caz and me went about eleven thirty. I promised my parents I wouldn't stay out late because it's "a school night".'

'And how did you get home?'

'Cab. Although I didn't actually go home. I stopped over at Caz's. My parents knew. Keira was going to do the same but then she changed her mind,' said Mia.

'So she went home instead?' asked Bernie.

There was a slight hesitation before Mia replied, 'Yes.'

Bernie uncrossed her legs and stretched out her back. She gave Mia a hard stare. 'Are you sure about that, Mia?'

Mia's eyes darted round the room. She swallowed. 'Um... I think she was going home.'

'Mia, did Keira have a boyfriend? Was she still seeing Isaac Campbell?'

'That piece of shit – no way! Sorry, I shouldn't swear but what he did to Keira was awful. No, her new guy...' Mia stopped and put her hand to her mouth.

'I think you need to tell me everything you know, Mia. Keira is in intensive care. We have to find the man responsible.'

The young woman started to cry. 'Is she going to die?'

'I hope not,' said Bernie. 'But if she does, then this all becomes a lot more serious.'

Mia wiped away her tears with her hand. 'OK. I don't know much. She's being seeing someone since December. I don't know who. No one from college. I think he's older.'

'Married?' asked Bernie.

'Possibly. I don't know.'

'And it was a sexual relationship?'

Mia squirmed in her seat. 'Yes.'

'We found Keira in the Town Gardens area. Does this man live there?'

'Maybe. I don't know. She just left last night after she got a text and said she had to go.'

Bernie's eyes lit up. 'She got a text?' She made a mental note to check in with Tom.

'Yes. Oh shit. She... she got a text, smiled and said she had to leave. She's done that a few times before. But I'm telling you the truth when I say I don't know who he is. Caz doesn't know either. Keira is a year older than us. We all have a great laugh together but sometimes... it feels like she's a grown-up and we're not. Like it's OK for her to have a secret lover because she's more mature than us. She can be a bit patronising at times.'

Bernie nodded. She already knew Keira was keeping secrets. 'So, was Keira going to catch a bus?'

'No. There aren't any that time on a Sunday night. We always get cabs. Unless we've run out of cash. Then we have to walk. That's not much fun.'

'I bet.' Bernie put her notebook away. 'Thank you, Mia. I know you must think that you've betrayed Keira but you really haven't. It's essential we find the man responsible so he can't do it again. In the meantime, I suggest staying home for a bit. Watch a movie, eat popcorn. And definitely don't walk alone after dark.'

Bernie and Leigh sat in the car, comparing notes and watching the students spill out of the college doors. Bernie spotted Mia, head down, shoulders hunched. Another young woman, with black hair and dip-dyed pink ends, was hurrying after her.

'Is that Caz?' asked Bernie, pointing.

'Yes. She wasn't giving much away. Like Mia, she said Keira had left early. But she didn't mention the text or the secret boyfriend. I don't understand it. Why not tell the truth like Mia?'

Bernie watched as Caz caught up with Mia. 'I don't think Mia planned to tell me. It slipped out. It's stupid really. They think they're protecting Keira, protecting her reputation. I don't care about her reputation. I care about getting a violent man off the streets.'

Caz was standing in front of Mia, holding her shoulders. She didn't appear to be shouting but it didn't look like a friendly chat either.

'I think Caz might know who Keira's lover is. Do we go over?' asked Leigh. 'Perhaps you'd get more out of her.'

'I doubt it. She's prepared now. The element of surprise has gone. We'll keep an eye on them though. In the meantime, I think we need to check out Isaac Campbell.'

Bernie pulled out her phone and checked the email from Mick Parris. 'The two cautions for Isaac Campbell are for last year. One in October and one in December. That might fit with the break-up with Keira and then being excluded from college. His address is Shrivenham Road. Do you know where it is?'

'Ah. Yes. I do. It's by the football ground,' said Leigh. She grinned.

Bernie was puzzled by Leigh's response. 'Is there a problem, Leigh?'

'No. As long as you're good with roundabouts.'

12

'Holy shit,' said Bernie. 'Where the hell do I go?'

Bernie looked at the large road sign. It looked more like a mathematical diagram than road directions.

'Welcome to the magic roundabout,' said Leigh. 'It's not that difficult really. Take each roundabout as it comes. Don't try and think about all of it. Believe it or not, we don't often have accidents here. I think it's because drivers are a bit more cautious. So at this first one, turn right.'

Bernie hesitated. 'Aren't I going the wrong way round the roundabout?' She hadn't even driven abroad so to go right went against her natural instinct.

'Yes, but it's fine. Go now.'

Bernie pulled out cautiously. Even though she'd lived in Wiltshire for over a year, this was her first encounter with the magic roundabout.

'OK,' said Leigh. 'At this one, we're going to go left but then you'll need to get into the right-hand lane for the next one.'

Bernie waited for a break in the stream of cars to her right. She was more aware than ever of the precious cargo she was carrying. She turned left but then pulled right. She still couldn't quite take in what she was seeing. It was like watching a ballet with cars, as the streams of vehicles wove in and out of each other.

'Go right now,' said Leigh, 'and this is our road. It'll be down near the end.'

Bernie drove past the football stadium on her left. She spotted a CCTV camera that was probably very helpful on match days. The road was a mixture of terraced houses on one side and semi-detached and bungalows on the other. She slowed down to check on the house numbers.

'Don't worry, ma'am. I'm keeping an eye on the numbers. It'll be near the end on the left,' said Leigh.

'Do you know this road well then?'

'I grew up in this part of Swindon. I had a friend who used to live on this road. Here we are, it's the house with the white door.'

The curtains were pulled and no one answered when Bernie rang the bell. She thumped on the door and called out, 'Police. Open the door please.' She knew that often got a response, as neighbours would glance out of their windows, so people would open up just to avoid a scene. It worked. The door opened.

A woman in her forties stood there, an air of weariness about her.

'What do you want?' she asked.

'Mrs Campbell? We're looking for Isaac,' said Bernie.

'It's Ms and he's not here.'

'Really? Do you mind if we come in and have a chat anyway?' asked Bernie.

'I do mind.' The woman tried to shut the door but the sound of a metal dustbin crashing to the ground rang out from the back of the house.

Bernie sighed. Leigh pushed past the woman and ran into the house, and then into the garden. She then dashed back.

'He's gone over the fence. Wait here, ma'am.'

Leigh flew up the road and then disappeared down an alleyway.

Bernie turned her attention back to Isaac's mother. 'Ms Campbell, it really is in your son's interest for him to talk to us. We've just been speaking to Stephanie Lawson.'

The woman laughed. 'And you're going to listen to him, are you? Like that bitch of a principal did? I don't think so. Unless you have enough to arrest him for a crime, don't come back here without a warrant.' The door was slammed in Bernie's face.

She waited by the car for Leigh to return. She came back five minutes later, red-faced and out of breath.

'Sorry, ma'am. Lost him. There's a park behind here. He'll be hiding somewhere. Did you get anything from his mother?'

'Only a door in my face. And not to return without a warrant.'

'Sounds guilty to me, ma'am.'

'Hmm. Or maybe he was tipped off.'

The colour in Leigh's face was starting to return to normal. 'I can certainly think of two people who might have done it.'

'Really? Who?'

'Caz and Mia.'

'Definitely not Mia. Not with the way she was talking about Isaac.'

Leigh grimaced. 'I've learnt the hard way that what people say isn't always what they mean. Life would be so much easier if it was.'

Bernie thought back to the two teenage girls they'd seen at the college. Had one of them contacted Isaac? Even if they had, there was no chance they'd admit to it. She flexed her left wrist. A previous encounter with a suspect armed with a hammer had left it weak. Coupled with hormones flooding her body and relaxing her joints, and lots of driving in one day, it was really starting to ache. She looked back down the road. She wasn't sure if she could cope with the magic roundabout again.

'Do you fancy driving, Leigh?'

'Sure. Where are we going?'

'Back to Town Gardens. I need to check in with Kerry and you need to collect your car.'

A smile crept onto Leigh's lips. 'You don't want to drive round the magic roundabout again, do you?'

'You got me.'

The rush hour traffic was heavy as they cut across town, but Leigh knew some cut-throughs which helped shave a few minutes off the time. It was almost six p.m. when they arrived at Town Gardens, and dusk was starting to set in. They found Kerry at the gate, debriefing the search team.

'Ah, ma'am. We're just finishing up for today. No weapon found, I'm afraid,' she said, grimacing.

'Did you find anything useful?' Bernie asked.

There was a ripple of laughter through the group.

'We found *plenty* of things that weren't useful, but just before we finished, PC Harman over there made a fantastic discovery,' said Kerry.

Bernie looked to where Kerry was pointing and smiled at the male officer.

'Well done, PC Harman. What did you find?'

'A carrier bag in a bin. It had a used condom and some tissues in it. It was pushed down quite deep.'

'And where was this bin?'

Harman gave a brief smile. 'The other side of the gardens, ma'am, by another gate.'

Bernie nodded. 'That's good news. Let's get that to forensics asap. If it has Keira's DNA on it then we'll have our man's DNA too. Thank you, all of you, for your work today. We may need to continue the search tomorrow. I'll decide in the morning. You're free to go back to your stations.'

13

Bernie pulled into the car park at headquarters. She really wanted to go home and soak in the bath but that would have to wait. News of Keira's mystery boyfriend meant she needed to check in with Tom. Were there any texts on Keira's phone that could lead them to him?

She trudged up the stairs, praying she wouldn't bump into Anderson. If he saw her this tired he would send her home. She'd been working for almost twelve hours without any proper breaks.

MCIT was quiet when she walked through the door. Mick and Alice had already messaged to ask if they could go home. Both had young children. Would she be doing that in a year's time? Leaving bang on time to collect her baby? She slumped down at her desk, trying not to think about the future. But she couldn't help herself. Without any family around, how would she and Dougie cope? Unless it wasn't his baby but Alex's. Then it would be even worse. It was becoming increasingly obvious that Alex didn't want to jeopardise his relationship with Ali. And would Dougie stay? He hadn't said anything to suggest it but there was a niggle at the back of Bernie's brain. That was partly why she didn't want to do a paternity test yet. If he wasn't the father, he might just walk away. She didn't want her child to grow up without a father around, like she had. And there was the nub of the problem – her own insecurity and abandonment issues. Not that it was her father's fault. Both her parents had only been fifteen and her father, Gary, had been pushed very firmly away by her maternal grandparents. He was doing his best to make up for lost time now though.

She felt a flip in her stomach. She smiled and rubbed her belly.

She jumped as she heard a whoosh from the office door.

'Ah, ma'am. You're back. I was about to leave a note on your desk.'

Bernie smiled as Tom came over to her. 'Please tell me you have some good news.'

'Well, I have some. The phone company hasn't come back with the data yet for location but we should get that tomorrow. However, I have been through Keira's text messages. It seems as though she might have a boyfriend.'

Bernie raised an eyebrow.

'But of course, being the ace detective you are, you already knew that,' said Tom.

'I know there is one but no name.'

'Unfortunately, I can't give you a name either. What I do have is a pay-as-you-go mobile number. The last text she received came from that number, asking her to meet up. To be precise, the text read "Are you free? Meet usual place?" and she replied, "Yes. There in twenty mins."'

'That confirms what I was told earlier by one of her friends. Are there other texts from this number?'

'Oh, yes. Daily. And some of them are... how shall I put it? X-rated?' Tom blushed a little. 'I mean, that case I worked with you last year – the teenage girls being groomed online – that was bad but... I suppose this is different, two consenting adults, but it's still hard to read. Anyway, there was one interesting message that I think he sent to her by mistake.'

Bernie arched her back in her chair. 'Tell me more.'

'It was "Got some nose whisky. You in?" She replied with question marks.'

'Hmm. Nose whisky is slang for cocaine. Wonder if he was selling or had bought it to share with someone. Why don't you send the transcripts over to me and I'll take a look at them.' She rubbed her eyes. It was going to be a long night.

14

'What's so important that you're still here at nine p.m.?'

Bernie turned round in her chair to see Anderson in the doorway of MCIT.

'This.' She held out the transcript of Keira's texts.

Anderson sat down next to her. 'Whoa. This reads like a really bad porn script.'

'It's definitely not a good one.'

'Bernadette Noel! I don't think I want to know how you know a good porn script.' Anderson winked at her. 'This is the woman you found in the park?'

'Yep.'

'So this guy has to be in the frame now as a possible suspect.'

Bernie nodded slowly. 'If we can find him. Pay-as-you-go phone. It's not going to be easy.'

'No. But you're not going to find him tonight. You need to go home, have something to eat and then go to bed.' Anderson pulled Bernie up to standing and wrapped her in his arms.

'I wish you were coming home with me,' she said.

'I know. I'd much rather be coming home instead of pulling

an all-nighter here. But this case has become so big now. What looked like a simple cuckooing case initially has blown out of all proportion. Our drug-dealing cuckoo is just the tip of the iceberg. It's a full-on county lines case and we need to nip it in the bud before it spills out into all the major towns in Wiltshire. And it all connects with this gang in London. Hence the Met guy being here.'

Bernie pulled away from Anderson. 'I ought to let you get back to it if you've got this raid booked for tomorrow early morning.'

Anderson kissed the top of her head. 'On one condition – that I walk you to your car now and you go home. There's leftover lasagne in the fridge from Saturday. Blast it in the microwave for about four minutes.'

Bernie looked at the paperwork on her desk and the empty whiteboard. 'I really ought to write some of this up on the board.'

'Or you can do it in the morning before the briefing. Come on. Pack this stuff away.'

'Is that an order, *Detective Inspector* Anderson?'

'Yes, it is, *Detective Inspector* Noel.'

Bernie allowed her legs to float up in the bath. The lavender candle was making her feel drowsy. But she couldn't switch off completely. A vision of Keira in the hospital kept dancing about in her head. Was it Isaac Campbell who had hurt her? Or this new mystery man? A sex game gone too far? Leigh's suspect from her other cases? Or someone else entirely? The smell of the lavender was overpowering and she was aware of her eyelids becoming heavy.

When she woke up, the water was cold and the candle was barely flickering. Any good that the hot water had done for her had disappeared with the temperature. She shivered as she got out, her back and legs feeling stiff. She dried herself quickly before hurrying across to her bedroom. It wasn't any warmer in there and she looked at her cold, uninviting bed. Dougie always warmed her up. She wouldn't sleep easily without him there. Pulling on her PJs and dressing gown, she headed downstairs. The paperwork was at the office but she could look at Tom's email.

Sitting on the sofa with a blanket around her, Bernie opened her laptop and signed in to her work email. There were lots of attachments on Tom's message. Bernie didn't fancy any more porn texts so she looked at other SMS threads instead, in particular the ones to Caz and Mia. She examined the more recent ones first, starting with the last text she'd sent to Caz.

Hi Birthday Girl! Looking forward to partying with you tonight. Not 100% sure I'm staying over though. I'll confirm later.

Bernie glanced over some older texts about homework and nights out until one caught her eye.

Sorry for bailing this evening. But you know I can't resist him when he calls.

Bernie checked the date. It was from two weeks previously. She scrolled through the messages. They continued to be mostly routine but then one stood out, from New Year's Eve.

OMG Caz! I have to go. Can't believe he was in the club tonight. I'll call you tomorrow.

Bernie pulled the blanket tighter around her. Who was in the club? Isaac? Was Keira scared? Or was it the secret man and she was excited? It was so hard to tell from a text message. Her eyes were stinging from tiredness and looking at the screen. She was reluctant to put the laptop away, not least because it was keeping her warm. She'd get one of the others to go through all the messages, emails and social media accounts tomorrow. Do a proper analysis. Matt Taylor was good at that.

Her legs were like lead as she went up the stairs. Keeping the blanket around her shoulders helped to dampen the shock of the cold bed. She balled up initially to stay warm but slowly stretched her legs out. Relief flooded through her body as her legs were finally allowed to rest. Sleep swooped in.

Bernie flicked at her face as the buzzing grew louder. It took her a moment to realise that it wasn't a fly but her phone vibrating on the bedside cabinet. She tried to turn but immediately became tangled in the sofa blanket. By the time she freed herself to reach for the phone, the buzzing had stopped. She sighed. She grabbed the phone anyway and swiped to unlock it. The time was 4.23. There was a voicemail. She jabbed at the phone to make it play.

'Oh God, Bernie.'

It was Anderson. Something was wrong. He wouldn't normally call her in the middle of the night.

'Sorry, I probably shouldn't have rung. I didn't know who else to ring.'

Even though she was still sleepy, she recognised the panic in his voice.

'Oh God. It's all gone tits up here. We arrested our suspect. As he was being brought down the stairs he tripped up one of the officers holding him and managed to break free. I couldn't stop him. He ran out into the road, with handcuffs on. There was a bloody supermarket lorry. The driver couldn't help it. There wasn't enough time to brake. Oh God, Bernie. I think the suspect is dead.'

15

TUESDAY

Anderson's phone went straight to voicemail as Bernie called him back. He was either on the phone to someone else or had turned it off. Bernie sent him a text instead.

Do you need me to come?

She sank back into the bed, her heart racing. She knew all too well what lay ahead for her partner. There would have to be an internal investigation and he would probably be suspended while that took place. All the hard work would collapse and the drugs gang would know that they'd been rumbled. They would disappear before they could be arrested. She thumped the bed with her left fist and immediately regretted it. Her wrist throbbed.

Wide awake now, Bernie couldn't resist her nagging bladder. She felt a rush of acid rise from her stomach as she sat up. Heartburn. The joys of pregnancy. She took her phone with her in case Anderson replied, switching the sound back on so she would easily hear a call or a text.

After finishing in the bathroom, Bernie wondered what to do. She willed the phone to ring but it stayed stubbornly silent. She contemplated calling headquarters but she wasn't really supposed to know about the county lines case, plus she wanted to keep the line free. Knowing she wouldn't sleep, she went downstairs to make a herbal tea. She hated the stuff normally but had found a lemon and ginger one that helped with morning sickness. The woman in the health food shop had listed all the benefits and had already told her she would need raspberry leaf tea if she was overdue.

'It helps to induce labour. Along with lots of walking, ripe pineapple, a hot curry, a hot bath and' – the woman had lowered her voice a little – 'plenty of hot sex.'

At that point, Dougie, who had been looking at something on a shelf, had come over and wrapped his arms around Bernie's waist.

With a wink, he had said, 'I'm sure we can manage the last one.'

The woman had blushed deeply. Dougie had that effect on women.

Bernie smiled at the memory as she poured boiling water into the mug. She watched the tea bag bob around, infusing in the water. The aroma of lemon and ginger filled her nostrils. Sometimes the smell alone was enough to calm her.

She took the mug across to her little kitchen table and sat down. Sipping the hot drink, she pulled her phone out from her pocket. Still no call or text from Dougie. She opened up her personal emails. There was one reminding her of her scan at the end of the week. She placed her hand on her bump.

'Maybe we'll find out who you are, little bun.' Bernie smiled as she felt a small movement underneath her hand. But her smile disappeared as she thought about the blood oozing from Keira. Had the doctors managed to save the baby? If not, maybe they could get a DNA sample to find the father. Bernie made a mental note to contact the hospital in the morning.

She walked into the lounge to look at her laptop. She was about to open up the email from Tom when her phone rang from the kitchen.

Damn. Left it on the kitchen table. She ran quickly and answered just before it switched over to voicemail.

'Dougie?'

'Yes. Oh God, Bernie. This is a major shitstorm. The paramedics have managed to resuscitate him and he's on his way to hospital now. There'll have to be an investigation. Maybe even the IPCC. Shit.'

'What are you doing now? Are you coming home?'

Anderson sighed deeply. 'I wish. I'd much rather be with you. I have to go to headquarters and give a statement. I might still be there when you come into MCIT. I'll come and see you.'

'Oh, my love, I'm so sorry. Is there anything I can do?'

'Not really. Unless you want to calm the Met guy down. He's gone apeshit at me. Reckons the whole operation is blown. They've gone ahead with their raids in London anyway but it's all compromised now. He's looking for someone to blame and he's aiming for me. God, I could lose my job over this.'

'You? Why?'

'Can't go into it now. I have to go. I'll see you later. Love you.'

'Love you too.'

Bernie walked back into the lounge and flopped onto the sofa. She was worried about Dougie. A Met officer gunning for him didn't sound good and if the Independent Police Complaints Commission became involved then it all became a lot more public. She glanced at her phone. It was five a.m. She couldn't decide whether to go back to bed or not. Her alarm upstairs was due to go off at six thirty. She'd probably feel wretched if she did grab some more sleep but she might get through the day better if she did.

The bed was cold on Anderson's side but there was a very faint imprint of warmth on Bernie's. She settled into it, turning onto her left side. Despite everything, sleep came remarkably quickly.

16

The newsreader's voice slowly penetrated Bernie's brain.

'Reports are coming in of an incident in Swindon earlier this morning. A man arrested by police broke free and was hit by a lorry. He's now in hospital in a critical condition. Wiltshire Police are due to make a statement later today.

'In Trowbridge, an accident has—'

Bernie reached over and switched off the radio alarm. She rubbed her eyes before looking at her phone. There were no texts or calls from Anderson. She'd have to go into work to find out what was happening. They'd obviously not been able to put a blackout on the media. Her brain slowly whirred into life. The news report had mentioned there would be a statement later. Bernie could think of one person who would be dealing with that – Jane Clackett. And maybe, just maybe, she'd be willing to talk.

Jane closed a drawer on her desk. She looked tired but her efficiency wasn't diminished.

'You know I can't tell you everything, Bernie. As much as I may want to.' Jane sighed.

'Do the family know?'

'They're being notified.'

'Name?' Bernie knew she was pushing her luck.

'Absolutely not. More than likely he'll be named in the statement issued later this morning. What I will say is, this is serious. The chief constable has already been on the phone to one of the Met's assistant commissioners. It was a big operation at the Met's end. Don't worry about Anderson. He's a big boy. He can take care of himself. In a weird way, this helps you.'

'Helps me?' Bernie stretched uncomfortably in the chair. Her trousers were getting a bit tight.

'Yes. This has taken the press away from your case. I was starting to get phone calls from a couple of journalists yesterday, asking if there's a serial rapist in Swindon that we're keeping quiet about. You've not exactly been forthcoming on that one so I had to fudge it a bit.'

'Yeah, sorry. I'm not sure. If it is all the same guy, he's been sexually assaulting but not raping – until now. I'll let you have some details as soon as I can.'

'Don't worry too much. The journos are focused on this now. The best thing you can do is get on with your case and find the perpetrator pretty darn quick. Wiltshire Police needs some good publicity at the moment.'

'Yes, of course.'

Bernie stood up to go. She had a briefing to get ready for.

'Try not to worry. It won't be good for the baby. Besides, Anderson's like a bloody cat – always lands on his feet.' Jane smiled. It was a rare occurrence and her face lit up.

'Thanks, Jane.'

. . .

MCIT was starting to get busy. Everyone in the normal team was there. Only Leigh Roberts was missing, which Bernie thought a little odd. Leigh had seemed so determined to find the attacker yesterday. Bernie stood by the whiteboard. Her chat with Jane had delayed her preparation. The board was blank except for Keira's name.

'Good morning, everyone,' said Bernie. 'I don't need to tell you that... something happened this morning. There's bound to be a media presence here today as well as Swindon. Obviously, we're not allowed to talk to the press.

'We need to remain focused on Keira Howard. We were all a bit spread out yesterday looking at different aspects of this case so I thought it would be good to bring everything together this morning before divvying up jobs.'

Bernie picked up a whiteboard pen and began to write. 'As far as I see it at the moment, there are four possible suspects here. Firstly, let's start with the one person we can name – Isaac Campbell. He was harassing Keira at college and ended up being permanently excluded for his behaviour. Leigh and I went to see him yesterday but he did a bunk. Mick, I think you were looking at him as well.'

Mick coughed. 'Yes, ma'am. He has a couple of cautions for being drunk and disorderly and disturbing the peace. These were at the end of last year. I need to check dates again but this might be a reaction to being kicked out of college. Otherwise, nothing else.'

Bernie nodded. 'Thanks, Mick. Tom did some sterling work yesterday with Keira's phone. One of her friends mentioned to me that Keira had a secret boyfriend and since it looks as though Keira might have suffered a miscarriage yesterday morning, we can assume it was a sexual relationship. Texts found on Keira's phone confirm this. When she left the Plaza on Sunday night, she was on her way to meet him.'

'God, the Plaza's a dive,' Matt said.

'Really? Have you been there?'

'Once. My sister went a few times and then swore blind she wouldn't go back. I don't know what happened – she wouldn't tell me.'

'Thanks for the intel. I'll bear that in mind. Getting back to this guy though.' Bernie wrote on the board – 'Secret Lover'. 'Maybe their meeting went wrong. Maybe she told him about the baby. Who knows? We need to find out who this man is.'

Bernie then wrote 'Swindon serial attacker' on the board. 'Unfortunately, Leigh isn't here yet, but she's been looking into a series of sexual assaults over the past few months in Swindon. He's mainly attacked women after they've got off buses or when they've been waiting to catch one. But there were no buses at that time on Sunday evening. However, I don't think we should rule him out and he needs to be caught, regardless of whether he attacked Keira or not.

'And then for the fourth option, well, person unknown.' Bernie drew a question mark on the board. 'Keira's attacker could be anyone else. Which obviously narrows things down a bit.' She half-smiled. 'But for now, we need to concentrate on these other three men. Isaac Campbell will hopefully be the easiest one to find. He'll go home eventually. We need to find out what we can about Keira's secret man. His phone records might help with that so we'll see what Tom can dig up. If we're really lucky we might get a location. And when Leigh gets in, she can look again at her Swindon attacker.'

Bernie noticed Kerry pull a face. 'What's up, Kerry?'

'It just seems we're spreading ourselves a bit thin. Wouldn't it be better to wait for the forensic results on the condom we found?'

'Perhaps. I was also wondering if Keira did miscarry, did the hospital keep the foetus? We might be able to find out who the father is.'

'Ma'am?'

Bernie turned to Matt.

'Yes?'

'Sorry, I forgot to say. Therese called from Forensics. She's had to put our stuff on hold as she's been ordered to process everything from DI Anderson's case first. The order's come from the top so we're going to have to wait a bit longer.'

Bernie rubbed her forehead. The day had barely started and was already going wrong.

'OK. Kerry, could you get on to the hospital please and find out if they kept the foetus? Matt, I'd like you to start going through Keira's emails, texts and social media. Alice, I'd like you to help Matt with it. Mick, I'd like you to look at Isaac Campbell a bit more and put an alert out to Swindon police to be on the lookout for him.'

'What about the search in the gardens?' asked Kerry. 'Do you want that to continue? We still haven't found the weapon, presuming the attacker didn't take it with them.'

Oh God, I really am dropping the ball here.

'I think it's going to be hard to get hold of other officers to help today,' said Bernie. 'Most of them are being used for the incident in Swindon this morning.' She thought about what Jane had said to her earlier. Wiltshire Police needed good news. 'But we need that weapon and we can't afford to miss evidence. See how many officers you can get. It'll be reduced from yesterday.'

'That's OK. There isn't much more that needs searching.'

Bernie glanced at her watch. It was eight twenty. They needed to crack on. But where the hell was Leigh?

17

Bernie had just picked up her phone to call Leigh when she tumbled through the door of MCIT.

'Finally,' said Bernie. 'I was about to call you. It's nearly nine o'clock. We start at eight.'

'Yes, I know. I'm very sorry. The traffic was bad. I'll allow more time tomorrow. I need to change my routine to accommodate that so I'll go to bed earlier tonight. So I'll need to eat earlier too—'

'Whoa. Stop. You just need to leave a bit earlier so you don't get caught in the rush hour,' said Bernie.

Leigh shook her head. She looked agitated. 'No, you don't understand. I have a set morning routine but it's linked to how much sleep I get. I need nine hours' sleep to function properly so if I have to get up earlier then I need to go to bed earlier. And I normally allow three hours between my meal and going to bed so my food starts to digest properly. Otherwise I get indigestion and then that affects my sleep—'

'OK, OK, I get the picture. I just don't need to know about it all.'

'Sorry, ma'am. My hours are a bit more set in Swindon.'

'If this is going to be a problem for you then I can send you back to your duties as LCI.'

Leigh looked up sharply. 'No. I want to do this. I just need to work out a new routine.'

Bernie thought again about what she'd read on Leigh's record. Leigh was autistic – routines would be important to her. She nodded. 'That's fine. We need to get on now. Come and look at what we have so far.'

They walked over to the board and a small smile appeared on Leigh's face.

'You've put up my guy,' she said.

'As a possible suspect, yes. There are some things that fit but there are plenty of things that don't.' Bernie pointed to 'Secret Lover'. 'Finding this man is my top priority at the moment. Matt and Alice are going through Keira's social media, see if that gives us anything.'

'So you think we might be looking at an abusive partner rather than my suspect?'

'I guess that depends on who he is and if he knows about the baby. Maybe she'd just told him and he got angry and attacked her.'

'Hmm, I'm just not convinced, ma'am. You'd normally expect a man to punch a woman in the stomach if he knows she's pregnant. But Keira didn't have any bruising on her abdomen.'

'But the rape was brutal enough to cause a miscarriage.'

'Except it didn't,' said a voice behind them.

Bernie and Leigh turned round to look at Kerry.

'I used my personal contact at the hospital to find out about Keira. I thought it best.'

Bernie nodded. Debs would be discreet.

'It seems they managed to stem the bleeding enough for the

baby to be saved. Keira is still pregnant. So no chance of DNA for the time being. Hopefully it will stay that way if that's what Keira wants.'

Bernie rubbed her head. 'I'm pleased for Keira but obviously that doesn't help us.' Bernie caught sight of Leigh staring at her. 'Sorry, I didn't mean it in a bad way. I'm very glad Keira is still pregnant. Kerry, what else did Debs say?'

'She's stable but still critical. Well enough to be moved onto the main ICU ward though. The swelling on her brain is slowly going down. And now they know she's pregnant, they can tailor her treatment. Her parents have been there all night. Apart from when she was rushed into theatre, they haven't left her side.'

Bernie sighed. 'OK. I'll try and see them later if I get the time. I think it's unlikely but maybe they'll have some idea about this secret boyfriend. Matt, anything for me yet?'

'No, ma'am. Still working on it.'

Bernie turned back to the board. Her eyes glanced over Isaac Campbell's name.

'Mick, have you asked Swindon police to look out for Isaac?'

'Yes, ma'am. And those dates when he turned up in custody do seem to fit with when he was dumped by Keira and then permanently excluded from college. He hasn't been in trouble since then. Or rather, he's not been caught.'

'Hmm, that's possible. He certainly wasn't keen to see me yesterday. I assumed it was about Keira but it could easily be about something else. And until I have enough for a warrant, there's no point in going back to see his mother.'

Bernie tapped her foot. She was restless. The best thing to do would be to head over to Swindon and check out the club where Keira had last been seen. But Anderson was on her mind. She wanted to see him before heading off to Swindon.

'I was just thinking, ma'am, that it might be best if we visit the club,' said Leigh. 'They might have some CCTV footage and then we can see which way Keira went and if anyone followed her. We could check any other cameras to see if they picked her up at all.'

'You must be able to read my mind, Leigh. I was just thinking about that. We could pop into the hospital as well. There won't be anyone at the club for a while. But there's something else I need to do first. Would you help Matt and Alice for a moment? I'll be back soon.'

As Bernie headed to the door, Kerry followed with her coat and bag.

'I've been promised three officers so I'm heading over to the Town Gardens. I guess I'll be there all day. Better go to the loo first.'

Bernie took the hint. Kerry wanted to chat.

They made sure the toilets were empty before they spoke.

'OK, what do you want to tell me, Kerry?'

Kerry leaned against the sinks. 'I don't know if Anderson is going to get out of this mess. A friend who was there told me that Anderson was ordered to wait by the front door and then personally walk the suspect to the van. I don't know why – that was the order and it came over the radio so everyone heard it. But he didn't do that. Instead he opened the front door and walked out to the van to get it ready. So with no one guarding the front door, the suspect took his chance to escape. It makes it look as though Dougie was in on it. They're going to haul him over the coals for this. They may bring in Anti-Corruption.'

Bernie ran her fingers through her hair. 'Do we know who the order came from?'

'My friend seemed to think it was whoever was in charge.'

'So it might have been this Met guy. Oh, that's typical of Dougie. He's so stubborn. He doesn't like this officer so obviously decided he wasn't going to be ordered about.' Bernie shook her head. 'I was hoping to see him before I went out.'

'It's unlikely. He's being questioned now.'

'But he's not slept in twenty-four hours.'

'The Met are baying for blood. He won't be let go until they're satisfied with his answers. Don't expect him home anytime soon.'

18

Bernie leaned back in the car passenger seat. After her disturbed night, she didn't feel safe to drive. Besides, Leigh knew Swindon better.

'So, hospital first then, ma'am.'

'Yes please, Leigh. I very much doubt that there'll be anyone in the club before eleven.'

Bernie looked out of the window as they drove past the standing stones at Avebury. No one was really sure about their true significance but they were impressive to look at. She had brought Anderson here to tell him about the baby.

'You want to go where?' he had said.

'The standing stones at Avebury. It's National Trust.'

He had kissed her on the forehead. 'National Trust? We're like an old married couple.'

It had been a rare, dry winter's day in Wiltshire. The sun was bright but the wind was raw. Bernie pulled her scarf tighter around her neck and stuffed her gloved hands into her coat pockets. She was still feeling a bit queasy but now that she had made her decision, she had to tell Dougie. And then she would have to tell Alex.

She'd shivered as they walked round the stones.

'This is ridiculous, Bernie, you're freezing. Let's go and find a coffee shop and get out of the cold.'

'Wait.' Bernie turned to face him. 'There's something I have to tell you.' The wind was at her back now, whipping her coat. She tried to look at him but struggled to make eye contact. She closed her eyes and blurted out the words. 'I'm pregnant. But—'

'What? You're pregnant?' There was a lightness to his voice.

Bernie opened her eyes. 'Yes. But—'

'But that's amazing. That's incredible.' Anderson had a broad smile on his face. 'I know this is something that we hadn't really talked about yet but—'

Bernie placed her hand on his lips. 'But.' She sighed. 'It might not be yours. Judging by my dates, I probably conceived that weekend we went to that pub and saw Alex with another woman.'

Dougie looked confused. 'So, how can it not be mine?'

Bernie looked over his shoulder at the standing stone behind him. 'Because I had sex with Alex that Saturday morning. You know, when Alex and I were still together.' She bit her lip. She had deliberately chosen to tell Dougie in a public place so that he wouldn't cause a scene.

'OK. When will you know who the father is?'

She dared to look at him briefly. He looked crushed, his earlier happiness dissipated.

'We can do a test after the baby is born.'

'Can't one be done before? What's it called? Amniocentesis or something like that?'

Bernie looked down at the ground. Her boots were splattered with mud.

'Maybe. I'm not sure how safe the test is for the baby. And I'm not going to risk losing it. So the question is, can you cope with this? With a baby that might not be yours?'

Bernie looked at Anderson, searching his face for an

answer. He had just gone through a whole gamut of emotions. He cupped her face with his gloved hands. The fleece material was soft on her cheeks.

'You don't have to cope on your own.'

'But if it's Alex's?'

'Do we have to tell him?'

Bernie sighed. She could see Anderson was desperate for the baby to be his. 'Yes, we do. I spent all of my life not knowing anything about my father until last year. I'm not letting my child go through that.'

Anderson released his hands from Bernie's face and drew her into him.

'Then, assuming Alex wants to be involved, this baby will be spoilt with having two daddies.'

It only seemed like moments later that she and Leigh were at the motorway roundabout.

'You OK there, ma'am? You've been very quiet. We're almost at the hospital.'

'I'm just tired. I didn't sleep very well.'

'I guess you must be a bit worried. I heard what happened.'

Bernie sighed. There probably wasn't a police officer in Wiltshire who hadn't heard by now. 'Yes. I've not been able to see him.'

'I'm sure it will all get sorted out, ma'am.'

'Let's hope so.'

They had reached the hospital and Leigh pulled up outside the main entrance.

'Why don't you go on up and I'll find a parking space?'

'OK. I'll see you up there.'

. . .

Bernie leaned against the back of the lift as it steadily moved up past the floors. She checked her phone but there was nothing from Anderson. She'd wanted to go down to custody to try and find him but knew it wasn't wise. She wouldn't be allowed to see him anyway. The Police Federation rep would be with him when questioned so he wouldn't be alone. She just had to trust that he'd be OK.

The lift doors opened opposite ICU. Bernie pressed the buzzer and announced herself. The catch on the door opened and she went in. She was rubbing antibacterial gel on her hands when she noticed the armed police officer. His face was familiar. He nodded at her. 'Ma'am.'

'I'm sorry, I've forgotten your name. Baby brain and all that.' She smiled.

'PC Joiner.' He jerked his head behind him and lowered his voice. 'The suspect from this morning. The one hit by the lorry.'

'Oh.' Bernie looked into the long ward. The curtains were partially drawn around most of the patients but the closest one to the entrance on the right had the curtains completely closed.

'Are you here to see him?' asked Joiner.

Bernie shook her head. She looked down to the end of the ward on the left and spotted Rachel, the nurse she'd seen the day before. 'No. I'm here to see someone else. Keep up the good work.'

As she walked down the ward, her shoes clicking quietly, she wondered about the suspect lying in the bed. Who was he and why did he need an armed guard? Was he that dangerous or did he need protecting?

19

'Rachel, isn't it?'

The nurse turned as she closed the curtains around Keira's bed. 'Ah, DI Noel.'

'How's she doing?'

'She's stable. I sent her parents off for a tea break not that long ago if you wanted to see them. Really, they need to go home to bed. They're done in.'

Bernie took the hint. 'I don't need to ask them any questions at the moment. I just wanted to see for myself how Keira's doing. I heard about the baby.'

Rachel tilted her head to one side. 'What exactly have you heard?'

'That the baby's been saved.'

'Yes, for now. But we have to be careful with Keira's treatment. Our duty, foremost, is to save her.'

Bernie looked past Rachel to the blue curtains around Keira's bed.

'I'd prefer it if you didn't see her right now. Not without her parents here.' Rachel's face was resolute.

'I understand. Will you let her parents know that I came by? And you're right – they must need some sleep.'

'Her older brother is on his way. He's a medical student at Bristol. They've said they'll go when he arrives. Now, if you don't mind, I have a few more checks to do on Keira.'

Bernie tapped her foot. She hated wasting time. She could go and track down Keira's parents but they clearly weren't going to be in the best state for questioning.

'OK, I'll leave you to it. Either I or one of my team will ring later for an update. Please let us know if anything major happens.'

'Yes, of course.'

Bernie walked slowly back along the ward, her eyes fixed on the other bed with its curtains pulled all the way around. She stopped when she reached it, her fingers almost brushing the blue material. She desperately wanted to pull them back and see the man lying in the bed; the man responsible for Anderson's problems. Just who was he?

'Ma'am.'

Bernie pulled her hand away quickly, her eyes darting towards the voice. It was Leigh.

'Sorry, I took a while to find a space.'

'Unfortunately, it's been a waste of time. We can't see Keira and her parents are too exhausted to speak to us. We might as well head over to the club.'

Bernie started to walk away but glanced back. She thought she saw the curtains move slightly. As she reached the entrance to the ward, she spoke quietly to the armed guard.

'Is there someone in with the suspect?'

'Yes, ma'am. A detective from London. I don't know his name.'

Bernie nodded. She thought it was probably the Met officer running the operation. He was just as intriguing as the suspect.

. . .

Bernie wiped her hand after knocking on the door of the club. It was sticky. The smell of vomit and urine lingered from the alleyway to the side of the building. No one was answering the door.

'Such a delightful place,' she said. She glanced at her watch. It was almost eleven a.m. 'We'll come back in about fifteen minutes, Leigh. It might be worth our while looking for any private CCTV along the shops here. I'll take this side of the road, you can take the other. Meet you back here in fifteen.'

Leigh stiffened but then nodded her head.

'Everything OK, Leigh?'

'Yes, ma'am. Everything's... fine.'

Leigh walked towards a newsagent, her shoulders slumped a little. She paused on the threshold before pushing open the door. Bernie wondered if she'd done the right thing in sending Leigh off on her own but she couldn't stay cocooned in the police station for ever. She had to be prepared to meet the public. The words on Leigh's work record danced around in Bernie's head: *She has the makings of a fine officer in so many ways but her lack of social skills prevents her from moving forward in her training at present. Recommend that she looks at a station-based civilian role.*

Load of crap, thought Bernie. Leigh just needs the right support and encouragement. And I'm going to give it to her.

She turned on her heel and walked into Poundland.

Twenty minutes later, Bernie returned to the club.

'You're late,' said Leigh. 'You said fifteen minutes.'

'I know. But I saw some interesting footage. There's a camera on the bank and on the ATM. They're getting the tapes ready for me to take back to HQ. We'll need to pop back there after we've been to the club. How about you?'

Leigh was twisting her rings. Bernie pretended not to notice.

'A couple of shops have CCTV but they reuse the tape every twenty-four hours unless something happens to their place. The guy at the newsagent lives in the flat above. He said he didn't hear or see anything out of the ordinary on Sunday night. What was the interesting footage from the bank?'

'Ah. Keira used her card. She didn't get any money out though. Either she was checking something or she was overdrawn. Her account is with a different bank so we need to look into that. But the main thing is that someone walked behind her and then came back a minute later. We need a closer look. Anyway, there should be someone in here by now. Even if it's just a cleaner.'

Bernie banged loudly on the door. It was still tacky. She wiped her fist again. The door opened. A young woman with a pale face and straw-coloured hair opened the door a fraction. Bernie held up her badge.

'I'm Detective Inspector Noel. I'd like to see the manager please.'

The young woman's eyes darted down.

'He's not here.' She had an Eastern European accent. Bernie thought she might be Polish.

'Is anyone else in?'

'Barman.'

'Well, I'd like to see him then please.' Bernie pushed the door. 'If you don't mind?'

The woman relented and opened the door fully. 'Come in. Be careful. I'm cleaning floor.'

Bernie and Leigh stepped around a mop and bucket. The water inside was already brown. The floor was damp and slippery. Bernie trod carefully. The artificial lights barely lit the large, darkened room, and there was little daylight from the tinted front windows. At the end was a small stage with sound equipment. To the right was a long bar. A black man, dressed in jeans and T-shirt, was drying glasses. As they approached, he turned. He had a tattoo of a swallow on his neck. Bernie knew that a swallow sometimes signified that a person had done time. Had he been in prison and if so, what for?

She held up her badge. 'Detective Inspector Noel.'

'Oh bloody hell. What is it this time?'

'A young woman was here on Sunday evening. We think she's a regular – Keira Howard. She was attacked after leaving here. And your name is?'

The man continued to dry up. 'Carl Smith. Well, if it was after she left, it's not my problem.'

'What time did you close on Sunday?'

'About one a.m., I think. It was quiet and almost empty.'

Bernie leaned on the bar and immediately regretted it. It was as sticky as the front door. Numerous circles and spillages had dried on the counter, having not been cleared up properly.

'This place isn't particularly clean, is it?'

The man put the glass down. 'We've come in early to sort it out. Got very messy last night. Had a big birthday group in and they got a bit sloppy with their drinks. If you think this is bad, you should see the state of the toilets. Let's just say they had a few too many cocktails. Magdalena's got that to look forward to.' He nodded towards the cleaner as she mopped the floor. 'Think she's putting it off. Don't blame her.'

'Anyway, Keira Howard.' Bernie held up a photo.

The barman leaned forward. 'Oh yes. I know who you mean. She was in with her friends. Think they had a birthday celebration as well. I don't know when she left.'

'Maybe your CCTV could help us out with that,' said Leigh.

'Probably. But I don't deal with that. You'll need the manager and he won't be in until after lunch. Last night's birthday girl got an extra present, if you know what I mean.'

Bernie's stomach heaved. 'I didn't think people behaved like that any more – staff getting off with the punters.'

The guy laughed. 'Most don't. But Jules is old school. Still thinks it's the nineties.'

'What time will your manager be in then?'

'Not sure exactly.'

Bernie drew a card out of her jacket pocket. 'Perhaps you can give me a text when he arrives.' She tapped the card on the counter. 'We're looking at attempted murder for Keira. It'll be much better publicity for the club if you cooperate.' Bernie pointed to his neck. 'Nice tattoo.'

Carl Smith covered his neck with his hand. 'I'm straight now.'

'Good to hear.'

'I mean it. I'm straight. So don't even think about pinning this one on me.'

20

'What do we do now, ma'am?' asked Leigh.

'We wait. I'm not so sure that Boy Wonder in there will text me when the manager turns up. Or if he does, he might wait until after they've checked the tapes. There's a café over there. Come on. I'll treat you to lunch.'

A wave of anxiety washed over Leigh's face. 'But I have lunch back at HQ. It's in the fridge.'

'Let me guess. Pasta salad.' Bernie glanced up at the sky. Grey rain clouds were starting to push in, taking the warmth of the March sun away. 'You need something warm today. Like a jacket potato. Look, there's a board here on the wall.'

Bernie pulled Leigh over to see the menu on the chalkboard. 'I was right. Lots of fillings to choose from. What would you like? I'm going to have baked beans and cheese. God knows, I need the fibre. Pregnancy plays havoc with your digestion. Sorry. That's probably too much info.'

'Ma'am, please.'

Bernie looked at Leigh. Her face was pale. She was twisting her rings again.

'Bottle of water?'

'Yes. That would be great, thanks. I can wait until we get back to HQ.'

Bernie nodded. 'OK.' Leigh was going to need more support and encouragement than she'd first thought.

Bernie tucked into her jacket potato. Leigh drank straight from her water bottle, declining a glass.

'So, Leigh, how long have you been an LCI?' Bernie knew full well how long Leigh had been in the job.

'About eighteen months.'

'And you're enjoying it?'

'Yes. I like piecing the evidence together and then confronting the suspect.'

Bernie smiled. 'I like that part too. Am I right in thinking that you're a civilian LCI? Have you thought about joining the police?'

Leigh grimaced. 'I did try. The training... was more than I expected.' She looked at the table. 'When I was told about the Local Crime Investigator role, it seemed ideal. I've always wanted to be in the police. Some little girls play hospitals and schools with their toys but I never did. I used to arrest my teddies, interrogate them and then charge them with various crimes.'

Bernie put down her knife and fork. 'Which one was the naughtiest?'

'Big Brown Bear. He was always beating up the other bears and kicking them off my bed. He got sent to prison a lot.' Leigh started twisting her rings. Her eyes were still fixed on the table. 'You've read my file, haven't you?'

Bernie picked up her glass of water and drank a large mouthful before answering. There was no point in lying. 'Yes. I have. It's important for me to know who I'm working with.'

'So? What? Are you testing me? Seeing if I'm going to fail? If I'm up to the job?'

Bernie held up her hand. 'Whoa. I'm not testing you. Leigh, you show a lot of potential. I want to help you. Encourage you to be an even better officer. You went into those shops today and spoke to members of the public. That's great. I know you don't find that easy.'

'I only went into two shops. I couldn't do any more. I can cope at the station when I interview people but...' Leigh twisted the rings harder and faster.

'That's fine. You tried. It can't be easy with your disability...'

'It's autism. And OCD. I don't think of it as a disability. I'm just... different. My brain works in a different way to yours. That's all it is.'

Bernie looked at Leigh's hands. She was worried that Leigh would give herself friction burns with the ring twisting. She laid her hands on Leigh's.

'Stop. I understand that looking at me might be tricky for you at the moment. So just listen. I'm not trying to catch you out or make you fail. If I didn't want you on this investigation then you wouldn't be here now. You will see things that others miss. That I miss. You're very much needed.'

Bernie pulled her hands away but caught one of Leigh's rings. It slid down, revealing criss-cross lines on the finger. Leigh pushed it back quickly.

'Leigh, do you have those marks on all your fingers?'

Leigh was silent. But her fingers were busy twisting the rings.

Bernie leaned back in her seat and looked out of the café window to the club across the road. No one had been in since they'd sat down.

'My mum called me "fidget fingers" when I was a kid. I couldn't keep my hands still. And I would drop things. And they'd break. And Mum would shout at me. My fingers would get me into trouble.'

Bernie turned her gaze back to Leigh. Her fingers were working overtime with the rings.

'So, like your teddy bears, your fingers had to be punished?'

'Something like that. It was my early teens. I wasn't diagnosed until I was eighteen.'

'And, am I right in thinking that your rings have two purposes? One, to hide the scars and the other is the equivalent of an elastic band on your wrist. You twist the rings when feelings of self-doubt or anxiety arise?'

'Yes. It helps to calm me down. I focus on the rings rather than the problem. Does that make sense?'

Bernie looked at the eight rings on Leigh's hands. 'Yes, it does. They're pretty rings. But none on your thumbs.'

'No. Mum said I was "all fingers and no thumbs". Funny how things stick in your head. My thumbs were good.'

'I think you're good, full stop.'

Something caught Bernie's eye. A man in a shiny suit with spiky hair was at the front door of the club.

'I think the elusive "Jules" has just turned up.' She looked down at her plate. The jacket potato was half-eaten. 'Oh well. At least I got some food in me to keep baby happy. We'd better go.'

The two women stood up to leave.

'Leigh, I genuinely want to help you. If you think I'm pushing you too hard, then say so. But you're more capable than you realise.'

Leigh's long hair had swung in front of her face like a curtain. She didn't push it back.

'Sometimes it's better just to leave things as they are,' she said.

21

Magdalena sighed as she opened the door.

'Floor is still wet. He's in bar.'

Bernie smiled as she stepped gingerly around the wet patches. As they approached, Jules was turned away from them but Carl Smith spotted them.

'Detective Inspector, I was about to call you. I was just filling the boss in on your visit.'

Despite the good-natured tone of his voice, Bernie didn't believe Carl for a second.

Jules turned round and extended his hand. His face was perfectly composed. 'Jules Verne, at your service.'

Bernie raised an eyebrow. 'Seriously?'

'Ha! You caught me there, Detective Inspector. I was originally Julian Farmer but it's not exactly a hip name for this industry. So I changed it by deed poll. Most of the kids these days haven't even heard of the original Jules Verne. They just think it's me – DJ Jules Verne. I was very big in Ibiza in the nineties. Maybe you saw me there.'

Bernie's hands automatically started to clench with annoyance. 'I was a child in the nineties.'

'Oh right. Sorry.' Jules' face flushed a little under the fake spray tan. 'Um, I hadn't expected a detective inspector to be so young.' He rubbed his hands together. 'Anyway, what can I do for you? Can I get you both a drink?'

Bernie didn't even have to look at Leigh to know her reaction. 'Thanks, but no. We have something to discuss with you and we'd like to see your CCTV footage please.'

'Yes, of course. Come up to my office.'

As she and Leigh followed him up the stairs, she wondered if he'd taken any young women there, and shuddered at the thought. Her fears were confirmed when she saw an oversized couch in the corner.

Jules noticed her staring at the sofa. 'It's a sofa bed. I sometimes sleep over if it's been a late night.' He gestured with his hand to sit down.

Bernie spied a couple of chairs at the desk. 'Think it might be better if we sit here for now.' Forensics would have a field day with the sofa, given what Carl Smith had said about his boss. And then she remembered what Matt had said about his sister. Had Verne tried it on with her? What about Keira?

'So, what can I do for you? Carl mentioned something about a young woman at the club on Sunday night.'

'Yes, her name is Keira Howard.' Bernie reached into her pocket for her phone to find a photo of Keira. 'She was here on Sunday evening with two friends, celebrating one of the other girls' birthday. I guess you must get a lot of birthday party groups in here. Carl said you had one last night.' Bernie stared at Jules, looking closely for any response.

Jules shuffled in his chair. 'Er, yes. Lots of parties come in here.'

Bernie passed her phone over to Jules. 'Do you remember seeing Keira on Sunday?'

Jules looked at the photo on the phone. 'Yes. She's a regular. Her friends too.'

'Well, that's interesting. Because one of the girls turned eighteen at the weekend.' Bernie gave a brief smile.

Jules held his hands up. 'What can I say? They all look older these days and most of them carry fake IDs anyway. Good ones at that.'

'I'm not here to close you down for underage serving. I'm interested in seeing your CCTV and finding out when Keira left. And, more importantly, if anyone followed her.'

'So what's happened to her?'

'She was attacked. She's in a bad way.'

'Oh no, that's awful. I'll get the tapes ready for you to look at. Back in a minute.'

As Jules left the room, Leigh turned to Bernie. 'Do you think we can trust him?'

'Not sure.' Bernie stood up and scanned the room. It wasn't particularly big. Faded music posters, featuring bands Bernie remembered from her childhood, were pinned up on the walls. There were photographs of local celebrities at the club on a large cork board. The ceiling was stained yellow with cigarette smoke, even though there was a 'No Smoking' sign above the door.

Verne returned a few minutes later with a tape. 'Here you go. We have four cameras in total. One at the front door, one at the rear, one above the bar and the last one overlooking the dance floor. It doesn't cover everywhere but does most of it. That's for Sunday night so Keira should be on there.'

'Thanks. Do you remember seeing Keira leave?'

Verne shook his head. 'No. Impossible to see anyone clearly when I'm on stage. Hopefully, you'll spot something on there that will help. Is there anything else I can do for you? If not, I need to get ready for tonight.'

'That's all for now, thank you.' Bernie stood up to leave. She pulled a card out of her jacket pocket. 'These are my contact details if you or your staff remember anything.'

She walked carefully down the stairs. They were just as sticky as the rest of the place. Clearly, Magdalena hadn't cleaned them yet.

Verne showed them out of the front door, a slightly forced smile on his face. Did he have anything to hide?

'Ma'am, would you like me to get the CCTV footage from the bank?'

Bernie looked at Leigh. 'Yes please. If you're all right to do that?'

Leigh gave a slight nod. 'It's my local branch so I can cope with going in there. I'll be back in a few minutes.'

Bernie glanced back down at the tape in her hand and remembered what Verne had said – it covered almost everywhere. But what about the blind spots? Had Keira been in any of those areas? Had something happened that no one else had seen?

22

Bernie pushed open the door to MCIT, carrying the two tapes. She smiled at Matt, Alice and Mick, as they worked at their desks. 'Afternoon,' she said. 'Hope you've all been working hard.'

'Of course,' said DC Matt Taylor. 'What've you got there, ma'am?'

'CCTV footage from an ATM and the club where Keira was on Sunday night. Four cameras for the latter, so I'm guessing it's a split screen.'

'Oh God, I hate those. Impossible to have your eyes everywhere.'

'Well, Alice and Mick can help you.'

'OK. Where's Leigh?'

'She's gone to eat her lunch. Have you heard anything from Kerry?'

Matt looked at the clock. 'She called about an hour ago. They haven't found anything else.' He picked up the tapes. 'We'll start on these. I'm guessing you want them detailed as evidence.'

Bernie sunk into her desk chair. 'Yes please.' She rubbed her eyes. The energy from her half-eaten lunch was wearing off.

'Maybe you should close your eyes for a few moments, ma'am. You look done in,' said Matt.

Alice got up from her desk to join them. 'I agree. Pregnancy's hard enough at the best of times. Get your head down. We'll let you know if we find anything.'

Bernie gave a weary smile. 'Thank you. You are the best team. But don't let me have any longer than forty-five minutes, OK?'

There was just the ticking of the clock on the wall as Bernie rested her head on her arms on her desk. It lulled her off to sleep.

'Bernie, time to wake up.'

The voice was male and deep and Bernie struggled to place it. She knew it couldn't be Pops because he had been dead almost a year. Her neck clicked as she raised her head. Her eyes flickered open. Her eyes were blurry so she blinked a few times to see properly. Detective Chief Superintendent Wilson came into focus.

'Oh sir, I'm so sorry. I don't normally fall asleep on the job. I just needed a few minutes' rest.'

'It's fine. I know you had a disturbed sleep last night. Plus you're growing a human being. I remember how tired my wife was. Matt said you'd asked for forty-five minutes but I doubled that time.'

'What? I've had an hour and a half? I don't have time for that.'

Wilson laid his hand on Bernie's arm. His frog-like eyes were soft. 'Everything is under control. Your team is doing a great job. Matt Taylor has taken charge. But I haven't woken you to tell you about that. I want to talk to you about DI Anderson.' There was a seriousness to Wilson's voice.

Bernie sat upright and stretched out her back. It wasn't going to be good news.

'I'm afraid I have to tell you that Anderson has been suspended pending further enquiries.' He squeezed her hand gently.

'Are the IPCC going to get involved?'

Wilson swallowed slowly.

'Not just Police Complaints. Anti-Corruption are sniffing round as well.'

'What?' Bernie stood up quickly, too quickly. She placed her hand on her desk to steady herself. 'Dougie is not corrupt! He might be a pain in the arse and incredibly stubborn but he's honest.'

'I know, I know. Bernie, please sit down.' Wilson paused as she took her seat. 'Things are moving quickly and... stuff is coming out about the suspect. Plus, the Met is leaning quite heavily on the chief constable. I can't tell you any more about it for now. An officer has taken Anderson home for him to get some sleep. If you would like to go home too then I'm happy for you to do so. He's going to need you.'

Bernie glanced at the clock. It was close to four p.m. She'd hit the school run traffic if she left now. 'I'll wait a bit longer. I ought to check in with my team first. And if Dougie's asleep, I don't want to wake him.'

Wilson looked at her quizzically. Did he know she was making excuses? Did he realise this was bringing back memories of her own suspension and investigation when she was in the Met? She wasn't sure.

'OK. Well, the offer is there for you to go early if you want. I'm sure you could both do with some decent home-cooked food tonight and a good night's sleep.'

Bernie grimaced. Home-cooked food was not her speciality.

Anderson was the chef in their house. But the pub across the road from them had recently started doing take-out. Sue's pie and mash combo sounded like a good idea.

Bernie stuck her head round the door of the viewing room. Leigh and Alice were sitting in front of one screen and Mick and Matt in front of another. Bernie glanced at the screens. It was obvious what each pair was looking at. Mick and Matt had drawn the short straws and were trying to look at two cameras at once from the club, whereas Leigh and Alice were focusing on the bank camera.

Matt turned round. 'You're awake. Did the super speak to you?'

Bernie came into the room and stood by Matt. 'Yes, he did. I'm going home soon. Found anything?'

'Yep,' said Matt. 'We have her arriving at the club, at the bar a few times, on the dance floor for quite a while and then leaving about eleven p.m., which fits what her friends said.'

'Can we see which direction she went when she left? Is there anything on the CCTV footage from the bank?'

'Yes,' said Leigh. 'She turned right out of the club and walked to the bank to try and get out some money. I've spoken to the manager at her bank and Keira's overdrawn. So I'm assuming she was going to get money for a cab but didn't have enough. That's why she walked. But the CCTV from the club and from the bank shows that person you'd spotted. Can you find it, Matt?'

Bernie wanted to smile. Leigh was taking charge. Would Matt cope with that?

Matt rewound the footage and then pressed play. 'Yes, here we go. This is Keira leaving the club. We know that she goes to the bank which is just a bit further down. Now, look here at this guy.' Matt paused the tape. On screen was a shadowy figure in dark clothes, standing in a shop doorway opposite the club. He pressed play. The figure moved about twenty seconds after Keira left, shuffling down the road, dressed in a dark hoodie with the hood up, and jeans, his hands stuffed in the hoodie's pockets.

'He's on the bank footage as well. Same sort of thing. Hanging back from Keira while she's at the cashpoint but then follows her as she leaves,' said Alice.

Bernie looked at Leigh and then back at the screen. With his hands in his pockets it was hard to tell if he was wearing gloves. But he looked very familiar, especially from the back. It appeared to be the same man from the bus CCTV – Leigh's sexual assault suspect. She caught Leigh's eye, expecting smugness but instead saw only sadness. The journalists that had contacted Jane were right. They had a serial sexual assailant on their hands who was becoming more dangerous with each attack. They had to find him, and fast.

23

Adrenalin was buzzing through Bernie's body. Going home early was no longer an option. It was better to let Anderson sleep anyway. Jane Clackett wasn't in her office. Bernie looked for the super but couldn't find him either. *Where are they?*

Bernie popped down to reception to see if they had left already.

'No,' said Sally, 'they're in the press conference.'

'Oh. I thought they did that this morning.'

'No, it was postponed. They're all in the press room. It's about to start.'

Bernie made her way quickly to the relevant room. She hovered by the door, desperate to go in but knowing that it wasn't wise. Some of the local journalists knew her well. She pressed her ear to the gap between the double doors. She could hear the chief constable speaking.

'I apologise for the delay of this press conference. It was important to ascertain the facts as much as possible. This is an ongoing investigation so I'm not at liberty to tell you everything. What I can say is that a suspect, who was arrested early this morning in a dawn raid, broke free from officers and was hit by a lorry. He is in a critical condition. His family have been notified but I am unable to confirm his identity at present. An investigation has begun into what happened and all the officers involved in the raid have been questioned. That's all I can say at present. Are there any questions?'

The chief constable sounded serious.

'Chief Constable, can you confirm this raid was part of a joint operation with the Met?'

Bernie wanted to look through the square glass panel to see who had asked the question but she didn't dare raise her head.

'Yes, it was part of a joint operation. Their raids were not affected by this incident.'

Bernie didn't believe that last bit.

'Will this case be looked at by the Independent Police Complaints Commission?'

'That's not been decided yet.'

'Chief Constable, Clive Bishop of the *Salisbury Journal*.'

'I know who you are, Clive.'

'Well, it's polite to introduce yourself. I think some of my colleagues here have forgotten their manners. Can you tell me if there's any truth that an officer has been suspended and that Anti-Corruption will be getting involved in the investigation?'

Bernie stepped back from the door as though her ear had just been burnt. *How does he know that? Who's been talking?*

'As I said earlier, Clive, this is an ongoing investigation. We will work with whoever is deemed most appropriate to handle the case. Now if you will please excuse me, we have a lot of work to do.'

There was a bustling sound as people got up. Bernie darted down the hallway and into an empty meeting room, shutting the door behind her. There were footsteps outside and then lowered but angry voices in the corridor.

'How the hell does Bishop know that?'

Bernie recognised the chief constable.

'Sir, I don't know.' It was Wilson.

'If we have a leak then we have to find out who, and fast. We're up to our earholes in shit as it is. And what about DI Noel? How much did you tell her?'

Bernie's heart thumped as she heard her name mentioned.

'Only what we agreed. That DI Anderson has been suspended and that Anti-Corruption may have to come in.'

'Could she be Bishop's source?'

'No. I think that's highly unlikely. Bernie's a good officer.'

'And you didn't say anything to her about the suspect?'

'Absolutely not. I'm very aware she mustn't be told.'

'But will Anderson tell her?'

'Anderson doesn't know the suspect's real name. Only one of his aliases. His identity is safe for now.'

'Good. We need to keep it that way. Now, I need to go and make a phone call to Scotland Yard. Hopefully our press conference will have appeased them a bit.'

Bernie could hear another set of footsteps approaching the two men outside the door. She recognised the tap-tapping of kitten heels – Jane Clackett.

'Jane,' said the chief constable, 'thank you for setting that up. I think it went well, don't you?'

'To a certain extent. Clive Bishop managed to agitate things a bit. We'll have to liaise carefully with the Met as to how much information should be released.'

'Yes, indeed. I'm going to call someone at the Met now. I should be able to tell you more later.'

'I'd better go and check on Bernie's team,' said Wilson. 'They're sifting through CCTV, looking for Keira Howard and her attacker.'

'Some good news about Keira Howard would be most welcome.'

There were more footsteps as the people outside walked

away. Bernie waited until she heard the swing doors at the end of the corridor close.

'You can come out now,' said Jane from outside the door.

Bernie froze.

'Bernie, I know you're in there.'

She cracked the door open a little. Jane stood there with her hands on her hips.

'How did you know?'

'Your perfume. It's very distinctive.'

Bernie pulled the door open.

'But I'm not wearing any perfume.'

Jane laughed. 'I was standing by the door in the press conference. I glimpsed you through the glass. I made sure you were in this room before I opened the door for the chief constable and the super. Come to my office. We'll chat there. I might even have some chocolate if you're really lucky.'

Bernie sat back in the chair and allowed the chocolate to melt in her mouth.

'Did you have lunch?' asked Jane.

Bernie wrinkled her nose. 'Sort of. Half a jacket potato.'

'Why only a half?'

'Needed to have a little chat with the owner of a nightclub so had to leave my lunch.'

'Could he be the secret boyfriend Tom mentioned to me?'

Bernie smiled. Tom was like a rabbit caught in headlights with Jane – most men were. Jane was the master of finding out information. She should have been a detective, herself. 'Unlikely. Keira left the club to see this man. She wouldn't need to if it was Verne. But that doesn't mean he didn't try it on with her at some point. His barman suggested he went home with a punter last night. Leigh and Alice have spotted something interesting on the CCTV camera, though, from outside the club.

There's a man who appears to follow Keira and he looks suspiciously like the Swindon bus attacker.'

'Have you got some stills from the footage? Do you want me to put it out to the press tonight?'

'We can get stills—'

A knock at the door interrupted Bernie.

'Come in.'

The super appeared. Bernie wanted to laugh. Even he was scared enough of Jane to wait for her to answer. But then she remembered the conversation she overheard and her humour evaporated.

'Oh, Bernie. I thought you'd gone home.'

Bernie turned in her chair but didn't trust herself to fully look Wilson in the eye. 'I was going to, sir, but the team found some interesting CCTV footage. I came to talk to Jane about it.'

'Yes, they've just told me. It might be best to release the footage tomorrow. You'll need to speak to her parents first anyway. Go home and come back fresh in the morning. You look worn out.'

Bernie was tempted to argue with Wilson but she was tired and his earlier words kept ringing in her ears. She wasn't comfortable with him any more. She eased herself out of the chair before breaking off another row of chocolate from the large bar on Jane's desk.

'Oi.'

Bernie winked. 'One for the road.'

24

Bernie found Anderson asleep on the sofa. She gently pulled the throw over him. It was tempting to let him sleep but Bernie knew from experience she would need to wake him soon, feed him and then send him to bed properly. Otherwise he would wake in the night absolutely starving. She'd get the food first though.

The Marchant Arms wasn't too busy, and as she waited for her order her stomach rumbled loudly in the quiet bar.

There was a loud laugh. 'Someone's hungry.'

Bernie turned to see Paul Bentley, the local vicar. She smiled. It was always nice to see a friendly face.

'Yes, this baby is very demanding when it comes to food. I haven't the energy to cook tonight and Dougie's asleep on the sofa.'

'You've both had busy days then. I saw the news earlier about what happened in Swindon. You're not tied up in that, are you?'

Bernie looked at Paul's concerned face. If anyone else had asked that question she would have thought him or her nosy. But not Paul.

'I'm not...' She paused.

Paul gave an understanding nod. 'Ah. But Dougie is. I'm sure there's nothing that I can do to help but Anna and I are here if you need us.'

'Thank you. That means more than you know.'

Sue, the landlady, called out, 'Steak pie and mash, times two?'

'That's me,' said Bernie. She carefully hopped off her bar stool and glanced back to wave at Paul. She trusted him but would Dougie?

Bernie put the kettle on to make some instant gravy to go with dinner. As it boiled, she heard a noise in the lounge. She popped her head round the door.

'Hi, sleepyhead.'

Anderson groaned.

'I'm just getting some dinner ready. I got pie and mash from the pub.'

Anderson rubbed his face with his hands. 'I feel like shit.'

Bernie came into the lounge and crouched down next to him. She kissed him on the forehead. 'I know you do. You'll feel better after some food. Then later on, have a shower and go to bed early.'

Dougie smirked. 'Now, you're talking.'

'Honestly, you've been suspended and feel shit but you still want sex.'

He sighed. 'I just want to be close to you. To know that someone's on my side.'

'I'm always on your side. Let's talk over dinner.'

Bernie cut into her puff pastry pie, little flakes breaking off and soaking into the gravy. She speared a tender piece of steak which melted in her mouth as she chewed.

'Mmm, Sue makes the best pies.'

'Can't argue with that one. Although my mother's recipe for lasagne is better than the pub's.'

'Well, yes, that's true if your version is anything to go by. Have you spoken to your mother recently? Any chance I might meet her soon?'

Anderson lowered his head. 'I spoke to her last week. It's not convenient to see her at the moment.'

Bernie put down her knife and fork. 'Have you even told her about me?'

'Yes... but not the baby. I mean... how am I supposed to tell my mother, a staunch Catholic, that my girlfriend is pregnant but it might not be my baby? She would think badly of you and I don't want that.'

She stiffened. The niggle that Dougie might leave if he wasn't the father was back. 'Right. Your mother would think I'm a tart, maybe even a whore and definitely not worthy enough for her son. Or maybe you don't have to tell her anything because it's none of her business.'

'That's not what I meant.'

'Then what did you mean?'

'Oh God, Bernie, can we not do this now please?'

She picked up her cutlery and started to attack the pie. In her mind, she understood what Dougie was saying. But her heart still felt the shame. Even her own mother and father had been shocked when she had told them.

'You're pregnant but you don't know who the father is?' Denise had said.

'Says the mother who had me at fifteen!'

'Bernie,' said Gary, 'we're not judging you.'

'Could have fooled me.' She sounded like a petulant child.

Gary gave a broad grin. 'I missed out on your whole childhood but it sounds as though we're about to get a rerun of your teenage years.' He reached out and took her hand. 'We are pleased but we know it won't be easy for you. We'll support you however we can, won't we, Denise?'

Denise sniffed. 'Yes, of course. But you're going to make me a grandma before I'm fifty. Mind you, I did that to my mum. Oh God, don't tell Granny you don't know who the father is.'

Bernie nodded. Her grandmother would not be so understanding.

Now, as she ate her pie, she remembered that Anderson's mother was closer in age to her grandmother than her mother. Maybe waiting would be better.

'I'm sorry,' she said.

'I'm sorry too.' Anderson squeezed her hand.

'Do you want to talk about what happened this morning on the raid?'

He shook his head. 'Not yet. Maybe later.'

Bernie lay next to Dougie, his hand resting on her naked bump. The baby kicked against it.

'Oh, did you feel that?'

Anderson's eyes flickered open. 'Feel what?'

'The baby just kicked your hand.'

'Really? I didn't feel it.'

'You will soon. Do you want to talk?'

'No. Too tired. We'll talk in the morning.' He turned over, facing away from her.

She sighed and turned onto her back. Within a few minutes the baby started kicking. 'OK, OK,' she muttered and moved back onto her side. She snuggled into a sleeping Anderson, spooning him. She was exhausted but her brain started to race as soon as she shut her eyes. The conversation between the chief constable and the super kept playing in her head. If Anderson hadn't been told the suspect's real name, who was he? And more importantly, why wasn't she allowed to know?

25

WEDNESDAY

Bernie could hear a familiar voice and it took her a few seconds to realise that it was the newsreader on the radio. After her previous disturbed night, she had slept soundly with Anderson next to her. He was still snoring gently. Bernie turned the radio off and padded out to the bathroom, wrapping her bathrobe round her naked body.

In the bathroom, she pulled back her robe and turned sideways to the mirror. Her rounded belly was more obvious this way. And so were her breasts. They were filling out and ached a little. Her bra was definitely too small – Alice had mentioned something about special maternity ones. Bernie had looked at some online but they were so ugly. Maybe she'd ask Alice where to get some nice bras. She was going to need maternity clothes as well, especially work trousers. Bernie sighed. She didn't know when she was going to get time to do any shopping.

She turned the shower on and waited a couple of minutes before stepping in.

. . .

When she came out of the bathroom, Bernie could smell toast. She got dressed quickly and headed downstairs. There was a plate full of buttered toast on the table along with jam, chocolate spread, marmalade and Marmite. Anderson glanced her way as he poured hot water into a cafetière.

'Breakfast is served, madame.'

'Thank you.'

'Least I could do since you looked after me so well last night.' He winked. 'Very well, in fact.'

Bernie shook her head and laughed. 'Honestly.'

Dougie brought the coffee over to the little kitchen table. 'I wasn't sure what you would like on your toast this morning. I know it's normally jam but you've had some strange food requests recently.'

'Hmm. I actually want Marmite this morning.'

'But you don't like it.'

'I know! What's wrong with me?'

'You probably need vitamin B or whatever it is that's in it. The baby's telling you what it needs.'

'Yes, that must be it.' Bernie smiled at Anderson. Eating breakfast together was a rarity as they were normally dashing off to work. But Bernie couldn't fully enjoy it knowing that they still had to talk. She spread the Marmite thickly on her toast.

'God, Bernie, it's not chocolate spread, you know.'

She bit into the toast and grimaced. 'OK. Maybe a bit too much.' She scraped some off. 'So, I guess we need to talk about the elephant in the room.'

'An elephant? Where?' Anderson glanced over his shoulder. 'Looks more like a hippo to me.'

'Dougie.'

'OK, OK. I'm not sure where to start.'

'Begin with the raid.'

'OK. Everything had gone smoothly. We were in position at the right time. We had the battering ram to gain entry. The team went in and we had the suspect cuffed within a matter of minutes. There were a couple of other people in the property but they weren't of interest. We already knew that this guy had wormed his way into their home and they weren't involved in the drugs at all. Anyway, the suspect was kicking off a bit, you know – shouting and swearing – as he came downstairs. So I went outside to make sure the van was ready so he could be put in straight away. Which was obviously the wrong thing to do. I shouldn't have left the front door until he was completely downstairs. But there were two officers with him, and he was handcuffed. I had no reason to believe that he would try to escape. By the time I heard the others shouting, the suspect was running into the road and the lorry was right there.' Anderson put his head in his hands and breathed deeply.

'Did you see the impact?'

Anderson nodded and then raised his head. 'I'm not going to get that image out of my head anytime soon.'

Bernie remembered what Kerry had told her. 'Were you told to wait by the front door?'

'Yes. And I did. But when I could see how difficult he was beginning to be, I thought I'd better get the van ready.'

'Wasn't there anyone else who could have done that? Sorry, I'm not questioning your decision. I'm just trying to work out where everyone else was.'

Anderson pushed the plunger down on the cafetière. The brown liquid swirled. He poured it out into their mugs. 'I've been going through this over and over again. There should have been someone by the van but I didn't see anyone when I looked out. I think he must have come in to help deal with the other two. They were getting worked up about it all.'

'So' – Bernie moved a few things round on the table – 'let's say the chocolate spread is the van. How close is the front door to the van?'

'About five metres. It's a small front garden but the van was parked outside next door.'

Bernie placed the jam a short distance away from the chocolate spread. She picked up two teaspoons. 'You're one and the suspect is the other. Show me where you were and what the suspect did.'

Anderson took the spoons. He placed one by the chocolate spread. 'That's me. At the back of the van, opening up both the outer and inner doors. I hear shouts and I look up. The suspect is sprinting down the path. He's fast.' Anderson moved the other spoon. 'I step to my left to run after him but realise that I can't catch him. So I step to my right, to intercept him in the road but then the lorry is there and it's too late.'

Bernie placed the Marmite. 'The lorry. Was there anything to suggest that it being there was out of the ordinary?'

'No. It was making its usual delivery at its usual time.'

The word 'usual' stuck in Bernie's head. Like Leigh's routines. Always on time. Was it just a tragic accident or did someone know that the lorry would be coming at that precise hour?

'Any concerns about the driver?'

'None as far as I'm aware. He was slightly over the speed limit but not much. His tachometer has been examined. He was in a right state afterwards.'

'And what questions were they asking you?'

'Pretty much the same as yours. Why did I leave the front door? Why didn't I stop him?' Anderson paused. He reached out and took her hand. 'I'm going to be honest with you – I'm worried. Something isn't right here but it's not me. Yet, it's all on my head.'

The super's words were almost shouting in Bernie's mind. She had to ask Anderson.

'Can you tell me the suspect's name?'

Anderson squeezed her hand. 'I wish I could, but I don't think it's wise. I've probably told you too much as it is.'

Bernie stuffed the last of the toast into her mouth. It might not be wise but she had to find out the name of the suspect. It wasn't just about Dougie any more.

26

She'd left later, so the traffic was starting to build up. Anderson had been staring out of the kitchen window, absent-mindedly doing the washing-up when she'd kissed him goodbye.

Tapping her fingers on the steering wheel as she waited for the traffic lights to change, Bernie glanced at the clock on the dashboard. It was after eight. She wondered if Leigh would be in before her. That would be ironic.

Her team were all at their desks when Bernie came into MCIT. Leigh was sitting with Alice.

'Guys, I'm so sorry. It's amazing how leaving ten minutes late can affect everything. Right, where did you all get up to last night? I hope you didn't stay late.'

Kerry looked up from her computer. 'No. The super sent us all home by six thirty. Told us to get a good night's sleep. You certainly look better than you did yesterday.'

Bernie smiled. 'Yes. Slept much better with Dougie home.' She walked over to the whiteboard. 'Let's get this updated then.'

The others got up from their desks and faced the board.

'Alice and Leigh – did you find out anything else about the man following Keira?'

Leigh coughed nervously. Bernie thought she wasn't used to speaking up in team meetings. 'Well, I compared the footage with the CCTV we have of the bus attacker. There's nothing definite to say it's the same man but they are very similar. Same build and height and same dark, unbranded clothing. But without seeing the faces, we can't be sure. We've got some stills done, ready to go out to the press.'

'Excellent. We need to check for any more cameras in the area to see if we can spot that elusive face. Matt and Mick – anything else suspicious from the club?'

Matt shook his head. 'Not that we could see. Caz and Mia left before midnight. They were pretty drunk. No one followed them. The club shut at one a.m.'

'Tell you what, though, ma'am,' said Mick, 'Keira didn't seem drunk. She was walking normally. She'd have had her wits about her.'

'What are you thinking, Mick?'

'Well, it's all a bit odd, isn't it? She was found in the gardens but the gates were all locked. How did he get her over the gate? I know this Swindon attacker has dragged his other victims into out-of-the-way places but this doesn't seem to fit – the other locations were all easy to access.'

'She was hit over the head,' said Kerry, 'so she might have been easier to manoeuvre. But thinking about it, those gates are quite high.'

'But the fences aren't,' said Leigh. 'He could have dragged her over.'

'Except they have sharp points on them and Keira doesn't have any injuries consistent with that,' Kerry replied.

'Yeah, and, there's no nice way of putting this,' Mick continued, 'but so far this guy's been using his hand to assault – not full rape. To me, that sounds like he can't get it up. So how has he managed to inflict such terrible internal injuries on Keira? It just doesn't add up, for me.'

Bernie looked at Leigh. Her face was flushed. It was difficult to have your hard work rubbished by a team you've only just met.

'But we have the condom,' Leigh said quietly.

'Yes, we do,' Bernie replied, 'so let's keep an open mind about the suspect for now. And when Keira wakes up, hopefully she'll have some answers for us. In the meantime, we need to gain more information on her. Keira's college principal mentioned that she works for a law firm called Markhams. Do you know anything about them, Leigh?'

Leigh still looked a bit disheartened after Mick's comments. 'Yes. Probably the biggest firm in Swindon. Takes most of the defence cases at Gable Cross. Anthony Markham is the main partner and he's pretty cunning, arrogant even. It's normally a "no comment" interview with him. Keira's done well to get work experience there.'

'Sounds a good place to start then. Kerry, can you contact them please and see if you can set up a meeting today? They might not know about Keira yet, so tread carefully. Leigh, I know you're not going to like this but I think it would be a good idea for Alice and Mick to review your sexual assault cases. Fresh eyes and all that. In particular, it might be worth visiting the sexual assault referral centre in Swindon. Lucy said the forensic evidence for the other victims was collected there. See what you can pick up from them.'

Alice and Mick nodded but Leigh looked away.

'It's all right, Leigh. I have something else for you. I want you with me when we see Anthony Markham. You're the only one who seems to know him.'

Bernie turned to Matt. 'Have you seen all the CCTV now? What about Swindon Council cameras?'

'Not quite. Got up to the point where the club has shut but

the outside cameras are still recording. Don't think we'll get anything else but I'll keep watching. I contacted Swindon Council CCTV and the last sighting they have of Keira is on Commercial Road. She probably turned right onto Eastcott Hill as that's the most direct way to the gardens from there. But no council cameras from that point onwards.'

'Good. OK. While you all get on with that, I'm going to see Jane Clackett. It seems that the media have got their teeth into the Swindon attacker story and we need to give them something to keep them happy.' Although, Bernie thought, if Mick's right, then we have two attackers on the loose. And that's more danger to local women. The press will have a field day with that.

Bernie spent the morning with Jane, sorting out a press release. They used the stills of the possible attacker from the bus as well as pictures of Keira outside the club. They were also putting out a request for any private CCTV or video doorbell footage. They needed more confirmed sightings of Keira. Trying to phrase the press release, though, was proving difficult. And Bernie wasn't ready to mention the possibility of a second attacker until she was sure.

'We need to mention there's been a series of attacks,' said Bernie.

'Yes, I understand that,' said Jane, 'but it needs to be done in a way that doesn't raise alarm.'

'Jane, we're looking at a possible serial sexual attacker in Swindon. We need women to take care.'

Bernie picked up her pen and began scribbling. 'How about this? "There have been a number of attacks on women in the last few months in Swindon. Police now have strong reason to believe the attacks are connected and are the work of one man. We urge women to take care if they're travelling home alone, especially late at night." Is that OK?'

'In what way is that not alarmist?'

'There's only one man. "Strong reason to believe" means that we, the police are doing our job.'

'Yes but "urging women to take care"?'

'Yes, I know how it sounds – as though it's the woman's fault when it isn't. We definitely need a new approach in policing this area, one where we target the men. But until we catch him, we do need them to take care, Jane. Keira was probably only hours away from death when she was found. Protecting the public is more important than the force's reputation.'

Jane took the notepad from Bernie. 'Talking of reputations, did you talk to Dougie?'

'Yes. He told me what happened. I don't know why the focus is on him leaving the front door and going out to the van, when the officer who was supposed to be outside had come inside.'

'Everyone is being questioned.'

'To the same extent as Dougie?'

'I should hope so.'

'Hmm. I'm not convinced.'

'Well, as long as the suspect survives, the outcome shouldn't be too bad.'

'And if he doesn't?'

'Let's not go there yet.'

There was a knock at the door.

'Come in,' said Jane.

Matt opened the door. 'Ah, here you are, ma'am. Thought you might like to know that Kerry's made an appointment for us to go to Markhams law firm this afternoon. Kerry wants to go with you, and I wouldn't mind going as well. Sick to death of watching CCTV. And Alice and Mick are going to the sexual assault referral centre.'

'Bloody hell, Matt, it sounds like we're going on a team outing to Swindon. The ice creams are on you.'

27

Bernie noticed a twitch at the blinds as they all got out of the car outside Markham's office. Four officers was definitely a show of force – perhaps even overkill. But at least Markham and his staff would have to take them seriously.

'OK. We've been clocked already,' said Bernie. 'What was their reaction like when you called, Kerry?'

'Very helpful. I spoke to Anthony Markham himself and he was very shocked. There are two other partners as well and there are three secretaries. So a reasonable sized practice for Swindon.'

'They take most of the defence work,' said Leigh. 'So among the criminal fraternity, they have a good reputation.'

'Hmm. We'll need to keep our wits about us then. Kerry, I'd like you to pair up with Matt, and Leigh, you're with me. As well as finding out how Keira got on here, ask about any cases she was helping with. We've got three interviews each. Leigh and I will take the partners and Kerry and Matt, if you can take the secretaries—'

'Actually, ma'am,' said Leigh but then she stopped. 'Sorry, I shouldn't question your decisions.'

Bernie looked at Leigh. She obviously had something on her mind. 'No, say it. We aim to work as a team here.'

'Well, I was just thinking that maybe it would be a good idea to question the partners and then their corresponding secretaries.'

'That works for two of the partners but not the third. So either us, or Kerry and Matt, would be doing two extra interviews.'

'Oh yes. I didn't really think that through, did I?' Leigh looked away. Bernie sensed her reluctance to make eye contact.

'But it's not a bad idea. It would keep the questioning consistent. I'm conscious that we need to fit in a hospital visit as well. So, Kerry and Matt, you're probably going to hate me for this, I think you should do four interviews and Leigh and I will pop over to see Keira after we've spoken to Markham and his secretary.'

Kerry nodded her agreement but her mouth was pulled tight. She wasn't happy about Leigh's idea.

'Sounds fine to me, ma'am,' said Matt. 'But then anything is better than watching CCTV all day.'

'Right then. Let's go and meet Keira's work colleagues.'

Anthony Markham was dressed impeccably in a smart black suit, dark hair slicked back with a little silver showing at the sides. Bernie thought he was probably in his forties. He sat in a dark brown leather chair behind a large, solid oak desk. The décor of his office and the rest of the building was tastefully decorated in pale grey with fixtures and fittings that screamed money. No expense had been spared and Bernie wondered how a provincial solicitor could afford this. He appeared relaxed, which surprised her. She expected him to be more agitated by the vicious attack on his intern. Perhaps he'd already processed his feelings. Or maybe it was his normal poker face when dealing with the police. He jumped up as they approached. Bernie introduced herself and Leigh.

'Please sit, DI Noel and LCI Roberts.' He nodded at Leigh. 'We've met before, haven't we? But I've not had the pleasure, DI Noel, although your reputation goes before you. I hear you're quite formidable in the interview room. I wasn't sure if I was supposed to say anything or not to the others but I thought it best not to. I know how you officers like to use the element of surprise; I've seen it done often enough in an interview.'

Bernie and Leigh sat down opposite him at his desk. 'We only do that with suspects, Mr Markham, not witnesses. Although, lawyers are definitely the trickiest people to question,' said Bernie. 'But we're not trying to catch you out. We're simply building up a picture of Keira.'

Markham nodded. 'Of course. I'm forgetting my manners. Would you like anything to drink?'

'Just a glass of water please,' said Bernie. She already knew Leigh's answer.

'Nothing for me,' said Leigh.

Markham buzzed an intercom on his phone. 'Joel, could you bring in a glass of water please?'

He looked up. 'Now, where do you want to begin?'

Bernie pulled out her notebook and pen. Leigh did the same.

'Let's start with how Keira came to be here in the first place.'

'Now that's easy. I go fishing with her father. It's a nice way to while away the time. We were chatting last summer about Keira's exam results and I offered for her to come and do work experience here. Thought it would help with spurring her on. And as far as I can tell, it has. She's been a real asset and her grades at college have been going up.'

'Are there any particular cases that she's been working on?'

'She's been helping out with quite a few. I deal with criminal law, as does Richard Dunne. Penny Coleman, my other partner, handles family law cases so that includes divorce and child custody, maintenance – that sort of thing. We've shared her around, so to speak. Given her experience of very different cases.'

'With the criminal cases, has she come into direct contact with your clients?'

There was a knock at the door. A young man came in with a glass of water. Bernie thought he was in his mid-twenties. Slim but not tall; good-looking in a boyish way. Could Joel be Keira's secret lover?

'Thank you, Joel,' said Markham.

He waited for Joel to leave before answering Bernie's question.

'She didn't have direct contact as such. She came with me to court on occasion; Penny also. She sometimes sat in on meetings if notes needed to be taken, although another secretary was always present. We didn't wholly rely on Keira's notes. But she was never left alone with a client, if that's what you mean.'

Bernie jotted down some notes of her own.

'The clients that you do have, Mr Markham, are any of them sex offenders?'

Anthony Markham leaned back in his chair. 'As I'm sure you are well aware, DI Noel, Swindon is infamous for the amount of sex cases it has, especially flashing. Whether I want to represent these people is neither here nor there. I can only conclude that Keira's attack was sexually motivated and you're wondering if a past or even present client of mine is responsible.'

'And this is why lawyers are tricky to question.' Bernie smiled.

'We know the dance too well, Detective Inspector. I think it's unlikely that one of my clients is involved but I'm willing to cooperate with you.'

'That's good to hear. How about this man?' Bernie took out a photo from her bag. It was a still from the CCTV footage of a man dressed in black. She passed it to Markham.

'It would be difficult to recognise anyone from this photo,' he said. 'But, looks like a black man to me.'

'Possibly. Although we have no guarantees he's our man. But he's certainly a person of interest. Maybe we could have a list of who you've seen since Keira started here.'

Markham waggled his finger. 'Small matter of client confidentiality there, DI Noel. However, Keira is a valuable member of our team, so, in this instance, I'll get Joel to draw one up for you. I've had a few clients that might fit the bill. Some are local lads, others are from London who appear to have relocated here, bringing their "businesses", so to speak, with them.'

Bernie looked up sharply. Had Markham been approached to represent Anderson's injured suspect? She had to be careful with what she said next.

'Yes, there does seem to be an increase in that – branching out of London.' She caught Leigh's eye but she didn't appear to pick up on Bernie's subliminal message. Kerry would have done in an instant.

'If there isn't anything else you want to ask me, I guess you would like to speak to Joel next.'

Bernie closed her notebook. 'Yes. We'd very much like to talk to him.'

28

Joel looked nervous, a vein pulsing in his neck. He eyed his employer's chair.

'I don't think Mr Markham would mind in this instance if you sat in his seat.' Bernie gave a reassuring smile.

Joel sat on the edge of the chair, leaning slightly forward.

'So, Joel, I'm Detective Inspector Bernie Noel and this is my colleague, Local Crime Investigator Leigh Roberts. We're here to ask you about Keira Howard. I'm sorry to have to tell you this but Keira was attacked Sunday night.'

There was a sharp intake of breath. 'Oh God. Is she...'

'She's alive but she's in intensive care. We're trying to find out more about Keira's life. It helps us if we can build up a picture of the victim.'

Joel nodded. 'I understand. I'm not sure if I can tell you much. Keira's been here about six months. She's very keen to learn. We work well together.' He rubbed his face.

'Do you ever talk about your personal lives? What you might be doing at the weekend, for example?'

'Sometimes. She mentioned that it was a friend's birthday and they were going clubbing on Sunday night.' He stopped.

'Have you remembered something?' asked Bernie.

'No. It's just… it's a bit odd to go clubbing on a Sunday, isn't it? I normally go either Friday or Saturday night so I have time to recover before Monday.'

'Have you ever been clubbing with Keira?'

'No. We've sometimes been to the pub on a Friday evening after work. We're the only two single people here. And young. Everyone else is rushing home to their families.'

'I see. So Keira didn't mention any boyfriends to you?'

'Hmm, there was one guy but he wasn't her boyfriend as such. He was hassling her at college but then he left. That was last year. She hasn't mentioned anyone since. Well, not to me. I suppose she may have spoken to the other secretaries but I doubt it. They're both in their fifties.'

Bernie stretched in her chair as the baby kicked her.

'So, you're the two young single people in the office then. Did you ever think about being more than work colleagues?'

Joel flushed. 'Er, not really.'

Bernie waited.

'Well, not unless a drunk, awkward, Christmas kiss counts.'

'Just a kiss?'

'God, yes!'

Bernie wrote something down. 'I'm sorry, Joel, but I have to ask this – where were you on Sunday night? All night?'

'I was at home. I still live with my parents. They can give me an alibi.'

'How old are you?'

'Twenty-six. I'm saving for a deposit so I can get my own flat.'

'OK. We may have to speak to your parents to confirm that. Otherwise, I don't have any more questions. Leigh, do you have any?'

Leigh looked up from her notepad where she'd been scribbling down notes. 'No, ma'am.'

'Thank you, Joel.' Bernie reached into her jacket pocket and pulled out a card. 'If you think of anything that might help, then please call me.'

Joel reached across the desk and took the card. 'Is she going to be all right?'

'We're not sure yet. But the doctors are doing everything they can.' Bernie stood up and held out her hand. 'Thank you for your help.' Joel's hand was clammy in hers. She resisted the urge to wipe her hand on her trousers until after he had left the room.

'So, Leigh, what do you think about Joel?'

'Well, he's definitely saving up his money. His collar and cuffs are frayed. And he fancies Keira.'

Bernie smiled. 'I agree. And Anthony Markham?'

Leigh gave a brief glance. 'Oh, he knows how to spend. Designer suit and shirt. Leather shoes. And this isn't cheap office furniture either.'

'I think I might end up being Watson to your Holmes, Leigh. Let's see how the others are getting on.'

Kerry and Matt were just coming out of another office as Bernie and Leigh stepped into the main reception area.

'How are you doing?' asked Bernie.

'We've spoken to Richard Dunne and his secretary, Sandra. About to see Penny Coleman and Tracey,' said Kerry. Her mouth was still tight.

What's going on? thought Bernie. You asked to come here.

'OK. Anthony Markham is going to give a list of his clients. We'll pop over to the hospital now to see Keira and her parents and then we'll come back to collect you. If you finish before we get back, maybe you could start looking at Markham's client list. The same with the other two partners. See if anyone stands out.'

Kerry nodded slowly.

Bernie pulled her aside. 'Spit it out.'

'Is it wise for you to be visiting ICU?'

'I've already established a relationship with Keira's parents.'

'You know exactly what I mean. Anderson's suspect is there. Maybe it would be better if Matt and I went. You could finish the interviews here.'

Bernie stared at Kerry. 'Are you suggesting that I would be so unprofessional as to—'

'I'm not suggesting anything, *ma'am*. But you can't afford to do anything that might jeopardise Dougie. And you can't tell me you wouldn't be tempted to have a sneaky little look around those hospital curtains.'

Bernie's cheeks burned. She remembered how close her fingers had indeed been to pulling the curtains back, to finding out who the suspect was. And the Met officer too. Kerry was too insightful for her own good, sometimes. But she did want to see Keira's parents and her brother.

'How about this? I leave Leigh here with Matt and you come with me, to make sure I behave myself. Deal?'

'Deal. But I will go into ICU and ask Keira's family to join us in the canteen.' Kerry's eyes were hard. This was the best Bernie was going to get.

'Fine. You win.'

They walked back to Matt and Leigh.

'Slight change of plan,' said Bernie. 'Kerry's going to come to the hospital with me. Matt, I'd like you to conduct the last two interviews with Leigh.'

If Matt was puzzled by the change of plan, he didn't show it. 'All right with me, ma'am.'

'That OK with you, Leigh?'

She started to twist her rings. She gave a nod though.

'I'm leaving you in capable hands. Matt's a very good officer. Keep doing what you did in the other interviews. You obviously pick up on things that we might miss.'

Seemingly reassured, Leigh stopped twisting her rings.

29

'So, have you been told to babysit me?' Bernie kept her eyes on the road as they drove towards the hospital.

'I don't know what you're talking about,' answered Kerry.

'Really? The super didn't have a word with you last night to keep an eye on me?'

'Don't be so daft. I'm watching out for you and Dougie.'

'Hmm.'

'For God's sake, Bernie! Dougie is up to his neck in shit. The raid didn't go well at all. Apart from the obvious, a little birdy has told me that no drugs were found. Cash, weapons – including a gun – were discovered, but only a small amount of drugs were recovered. Nothing like what was expected. Dougie set up the raid, so his reputation is on the line here. And I know you. You'll want to sort it out for him.'

Bernie mulled over the conversation she'd overheard the night before. Could she trust Kerry with the information? She shook her head, cross with herself for doubting her sergeant.

'What's wrong? You're shaking your head,' said Kerry.

Bernie stuck her right-hand indicator on and pulled out

onto one of the many roundabouts in Swindon. She couldn't think of another place that had so many.

'I heard a conversation last night,' said Bernie. 'One I wasn't meant to hear. There's something else about the suspect. I don't know what it is but I'm definitely not allowed to know anything about him.'

'Who was talking?'

'The chief constable and the super.'

Kerry ran her hand through her short blonde hair. 'God, Bernie. All the more reason I should be the one to go up to ICU. If the highest ranking officer in Wiltshire is saying you need to be kept out of this, then you need to keep your nose out.'

'There was something else. Dougie doesn't know the suspect's true identity. But the chief and super do. I've been wondering. It's a county lines case with connections to a London gang. What if it's a gang I dealt with when I was in the Met? That would explain why I'm not allowed to know who the suspect is.'

'Did you get any threats at the time?'

'I can think of a few.'

Bernie pictured possible culprits; one in particular. She wanted to voice her fear to Kerry but couldn't bring herself to do so. She needed to check first if he was still in prison. She was supposed to be notified if he was released early but he hadn't even served half of his sentence. Common sense told her it wasn't possible. Yet, the scar on her left side from the stab wound was starting to itch like crazy.

The car park was, unsurprisingly, full. They circled three times before finding someone pulling out.

'Right, I'll go to ICU and see who's there with Keira,' said Kerry. 'I'll meet you in the hospital café. Mine's a medium latte and a large piece of cake.' She winked.

'Honestly, the amount of respect I get.'

Kerry took Bernie's hand and squeezed it. 'I'm just trying to take care of you.'

'I know. Skinny latte?'

'Yes please. Got to balance out that cake somehow.'

Kerry hopped out of the car and headed off to ICU while Bernie walked towards the café. She placed her hand on her side to quell the itching and her rising anxiety. She would do a check when they got back to headquarters.

The café was busy but she was able to find a fairly secluded table. She had Kerry's latte and a hot chocolate for herself. There were two pieces of chocolate cake. The baby definitely loved chocolate, or at least, that was Bernie's excuse. The thick warm liquid revived her as she waited for Kerry and Keira's family. She'd half-eaten the piece of cake by the time Kerry appeared, a young man with her. Judging by his similarity to Keira, he was her older brother. She stood up and held out her hand as they approached.

'Hello. I'm Detective Inspector Bernie Noel. You must be Keira's brother. Can I get you something to drink and eat?'

'I can get it.'

'No, I insist.' Bernie pulled out her purse and handed a ten pound note to Kerry. 'Seriously, what would you like?'

'Just a small latte please. And maybe a sandwich if that's OK. Any filling will do. I haven't eaten since I arrived here just before midday. Thank you.'

'No problem. Please sit down. Sorry, I don't know your name.'

'Adam.' He nodded towards her cake. 'I know it's tempting but try to not have too many of those while you're pregnant. You don't want to get gestational diabetes.'

Bernie raised her eyebrows.

'God, I'm sorry. I'm a fourth-year medical student. I'm

doing obstetrics at the moment. I'm actually writing an essay on gestational diabetes. Sorry. None of my business.'

'Oh, I don't know. You have a point. My diet is pretty poor at the best of times. The hazard of being a police officer. You have to grab food when you can and it's not always healthy. But, talking of babies—'

'Did I know that my sister was pregnant before today? Not for sure but I suspected it. She came to visit me, not this weekend just gone when she was... attacked, but the weekend before. She was definitely off-colour. She vomited. I went through the usual checks of what she'd eaten, asked if there was a stomach bug going round college – it all seemed OK. Then I asked her outright if she was pregnant. She denied it.'

Kerry returned with the coffee and a toasted cheese and ham sandwich.

'Hope that's OK.'

'That's amazing. Thank you.' Adam bit into the sandwich, while Bernie relayed to Kerry what he had just said.

'Had she mentioned any boyfriends to you?' asked Kerry.

Adam shook his head. He swallowed his mouthful. 'No. I knew about the harassment from last year. She hasn't mentioned anyone since.' He took a gulp of coffee. 'But when she said she wasn't pregnant, there was something about her. She looked shocked. Not because I had the audacity to ask her but more that it was at that point she realised maybe she was pregnant. Like it had just dawned on her. Maybe I'm reading too much into it.' He took another bite.

'On the contrary, I think you read the situation correctly,' said Bernie. 'We found a pregnancy kit in her handbag with a positive test. I'm guessing she took a test because of what you'd said.'

Adam rubbed his face. 'I wish she had trusted me. I could have organised a test for her the weekend she was with me. Do you think... Could it have been the father who did this to her and not some random guy?'

Bernie drank some of her hot chocolate. 'We have a number of lines of enquiry. The father is one of them. We're waiting for some forensic evidence to see if that helps us at all. But until Keira wakes up and tells us what happened, then we don't know for sure.'

'Hmm.' Adam looked thoughtful. 'It might not have anything to do with it but she went to a party on New Year's Eve. She was a bit agitated when she came home. I wondered if she'd taken something but her pupils were normal. Maybe something happened that night.'

30

'So Keira's parents didn't want to come down then,' said Bernie.

'I think it was more the case Adam didn't want his parents to hear what he had to say,' said Kerry. 'He offered to come down pretty quickly. He played the "concerned" son – "Let me handle it, Mum and Dad". Hmm. Not surprising, considering what he told us.'

Bernie finished eating her cake. 'But in some sense, he didn't tell us very much. Only that he thought she was pregnant and something happened on New Year's Eve. He has no idea about the father. I think Keira's friends, Caz and Mia, probably know far more than they're letting on.'

'Or Keira really did keep it quiet.' Kerry drank the rest of her latte.

'Then she must have had a very good reason for doing so.'

'A married lover then?' asked Kerry.

'I'm beginning to think so. What was Richard Dunne like?'

Kerry put her mug down. 'Hmm. Early fifties, bald and not exactly in the best shape. Anthony Markham seemed a bit more suave.'

'True. Leigh noticed he wore very expensive clothes. He's obviously doing well for himself.'

Kerry pulled a face.

'What's that look for?'

'Leigh.'

'What's wrong with her?'

'Well, apart from the fact that you couldn't stand her to begin with, she's a bit... weird. And now appears to be your best buddy.'

Bernie laughed. 'Oh, Kerry, are you jealous? You'll always be my right-hand woman. Leigh is...' Bernie paused. She'd already breached protocol by reading Leigh's record in the first place. To tell Kerry would make it worse. 'Let's just say Leigh is quirky and has her own way of doing things. She's used to working mostly alone so it's not easy for her to adapt. And yes, I did find her annoying at the beginning. But she has a lot going for her and, with support, she could be an excellent officer.'

'I'm assuming she'll be going back to Swindon after this case. She's brought her own mug with her, as though she's got her feet under the table already.'

Bernie smiled. She knew exactly why Leigh had brought her own mug and it had nothing to do with staying in the team. 'I just think she prefers her own mug. And we don't know how long this case will take. So I think it's important to make her feel welcome. Anyway, we've gone off track. Anthony Markham goes fishing with Keira's father. Would she sleep with one of her dad's friends? Who knows?'

'Stranger things have happened. Who was the other guy, the young one?'

'Joel, Anthony's assistant. He admitted he and Keira had a drunk Christmas kiss. Claims he was home with his parents on Sunday night. We ought to check his alibi.'

'Even if his alibi checks out, it doesn't mean he's not the father. It would just mean that someone else attacked Keira.'

'True.' Bernie checked her watch. It was just after four thirty. 'We ought to head back to Markham's office and collect the others. We've been here longer than I planned so they must be done by now. I'm just wondering if they'd like a drink and something to eat. I'll text Matt.' She quickly typed a message. She rubbed her eyes while she waited for a reply.

'Tired?'

'Yes. I'm sure the cake and drink will kick in soon.' Her phone buzzed. 'Ah, here we go. Large latte for Matt, bottle of water for Leigh. I'll just get those and then we can go.' Bernie pushed herself up from her seat, her legs a little stiff from sitting.

'I have to say that you've behaved yourself this afternoon, *ma'am*.'

'What do you mean?'

'You haven't asked me once about Anderson's suspect.' Kerry winked.

As they exited the car park, Bernie noticed a car entering.

'I'm sure that was Anthony Markham,' she said.

'Where?'

'In the Mercedes.'

'He's probably coming to see Keira.'

'Hmm. Maybe. But there was something he said earlier. About some of his clients. He mentioned he's represented men who have come from London and brought their "businesses" with them.'

'What did he mean by that?'

'I'm assuming drugs and other gang-related crimes. Exactly the sort of stuff Dougie was looking into. Maybe he's not just seeing Keira.'

Kerry sighed. 'Is this your way of getting me to speak about the suspect? The curtains were still around his bed. The only bed to have all the curtains pulled. So I don't know if he's awake and asking for a lawyer. Or maybe the family have contacted him. Or maybe, Markham has just come to see his employee.'

'But it's something to bear in mind,' said Bernie. 'I wouldn't put it past Markham to combine business with a hospital visit. I think he grabs as many clients as he can. He must do to be able to afford designer suits like that.'

Matt and Leigh were waiting outside the office when they arrived.

Bernie pulled up and opened her door. 'Did they kick you out?'

Matt rubbed his jaw. 'Not exactly. The last secretary we spoke to was wearing a rather overpowering perfume. It was too much for Leigh. We left as soon as we could.'

Bernie looked at Leigh. 'You OK?'

'Yes. I was coughing a bit. Feel better since we've been out here. It's quite fresh today. Think it might rain soon. I can smell it on the wind.'

Bernie looked up. White clouds were skipping across the sky but there was a hint of darkness in the distance. 'Well, we'd better get back then. Happy to drive, Matt?'

'Sure, no problem.'

Kerry got out from the front passenger seat. 'You sit in the front, ma'am. You've got longer legs than me.'

'Are you sure?'

'Yes, of course. Besides, it will give me a chance to talk to Leigh. I've barely said more than hello.'

Bernie glanced at Leigh. Her hands were already twisting her rings.

'Or maybe Leigh can tell us about those last interviews,' said Bernie. 'I'm interested to know what you picked up. And I'm sure Matt will give us his thoughts too. Kerry, can you do me a favour and find out where Mick and Alice are? I'd like to do an update before we all head home tonight.'

Bernie knew she had just undermined Kerry. But she had to protect Leigh. Although Bernie had found Leigh difficult to begin with, by spending time with her, she was finding attributes that she really liked about her. Leigh definitely saw the world in a different way; something that would only help with the investigation.

31

Black clouds had ripped up the previous blue sky and rain was drumming on the car roof. The wipers were on double speed. Bernie didn't want to distract Matt as he drove but she did want some feedback.

'So it sounds as though you didn't get much from the other two partners and their secretaries,' she said.

'No, not really,' answered Matt. 'Just that Keira was very conscientious. The client list may prove more helpful. Leigh and I thought it would be better to check the names on our database. Anthony Markham has certainly had a lot of clients in the last six months.'

'I wonder what his hit rate is like in terms of getting people off.'

'He tends to go for plea bargains,' said Leigh. 'Especially if he knows he's not going to win. But he doesn't make it easy at interview. He'd rather do deals with the CPS than the police.'

'Hmm. Any news on Mick and Alice, Kerry?' Bernie turned in her seat to look behind her.

'Yes. They've just got back. Alice wants to know if you want the briefing room set up.'

'Yes please.' Although, Bernie was concerned they still knew so little. Maybe Mick and Alice would have found out something.

Matt dropped them by the entrance to save them getting too wet. Alice had been true to her word and the room was set up ready.

'Thanks, Alice. I don't know if it's just the rain but it feels colder out there now,' said Bernie. 'I thought spring was on its way.'

'Good job we're not up north,' replied Alice. 'They're getting snow tonight.'

'Thank God it's not here. I bloody hate snow.'

'Really? I can't wait to build a snowman with my little boy. He's walking now.'

'Well, it's great for kids but not for me. I've got too much Caribbean in my blood. Give me heat and sunshine any day.'

'Yeah, me too,' said a male voice.

Bernie turned round to see Matt, dripping from head to toe. 'Oh, Matt, I'm so sorry. I meant to say there's an umbrella in the side pocket of the driver's door.'

'Not to worry. I always keep clean clothes in my locker. I'll be back soon.'

Fifteen minutes later, the team were all sat down, even Bernie. She held up a whiteboard marker.

'Alice, would you mind scribing for me please? My legs have officially given up. Right, let's see where we're up to.' She eyed the board. 'Hmm. Let's focus on Keira for the moment.'

Alice drew a circle around Keira's name.

'So, she's worked at Markham's office for about six months,' said Bernie. 'She's helped all the partners but has spent more time with Markham and his secretary Joel. Oh God, did we ask Joel's surname?'

'It's Davies,' said Leigh. 'I got it and a number for his parents after you left. So we can call them after this.'

'Well done, Leigh. Glad you're on the ball. Pregnancy brain strikes again.'

Bernie looked at the board. Alice had written Markham's and Joel Davies' names down.

'Something we need to consider, is whether either of these two men are Keira's secret lover. Davies confessed to a drunken kiss. Markham is a friend of her father's. Just put their initials for now under the "Secret Lover" heading.'

'Ma'am, do you really think Markham could be Keira's secret lover, given that he's a friend of her father's?' Matt asked.

'He wouldn't be the first man to try it on with a woman young enough to be his daughter so we'll leave his name there for now. Moving on, Kerry and I met Keira's brother, Adam, this afternoon. He's a student doctor and he diagnosed her symptoms when he saw her a week and a half ago. She denied she was pregnant but I'm wondering if his question is what led Keira to do the pregnancy test found in her bag. If she was on her way to see this secret boyfriend to tell him, maybe this was her proof.'

Alice wrote up 'Adam, brother, diagnosed pregnancy'.

'Have we had any response to the press release?' asked Kerry.

'Good question. Mick or Alice, did you hear anything when you came back?'

They both shook their heads.

'OK, I'll check in with Jane after this. Mick and Alice, as an aside, how did it go in Swindon at SARC?'

'They were a bit cagey to begin with,' said Mick, 'until I explained that we're investigating another possible victim. Then they opened up a bit more. Although to be honest, they didn't tell us anything we didn't already know through Leigh's notes. Except for one thing that one of the counsellors told Alice.'

'Yes,' said Alice, standing by the board. 'The third victim, attacked after a Christmas party, has really been struggling. So much so that she ended up in ICU last month after taking an overdose.'

'What?' said Leigh. 'I knew nothing about that.' She looked alarmed.

'Don't worry, Leigh. She's only just started going back to counselling so they only found out recently. Sounds as though she was worried about us finding out. She has some mental health issues and didn't want to be considered an unreliable witness. Poor woman. Anyway, she's doing better but it'll take time. I left my card with them just in case anyone remembers anything else.'

Bernie shifted in her seat. She looked again at the board and the four possibilities for suspects. 'OK. Thanks for going there. Any news on Isaac Campbell?'

'No,' said Mick. 'We popped into Gable Cross to ask. He's keeping his head down at the moment. But he's not at his mum's house. They're keeping an eye out for him though.'

'Good. Thanks for doing that. Right. We've two possible secret lovers and, of course, there's always the completely random guy we know nothing about. I'm still also concerned that we don't have a weapon. Maybe the attacker took it with him. But I'd like to go to the gardens again tomorrow. I know you've done a thorough search, Kerry, but I need to get a feel for the place. Mick was right earlier: we need to find out how Keira got into those gardens. Kerry and Leigh, I'd like you to come too. In fact, Leigh, you can meet us there. Save you coming here first.'

Leigh nodded but Kerry didn't look impressed.

Bernie let out a long sigh. Detective Chief Superintendent Wilson was bound to ask for a progress report by the end of the day. She would have to tell him the truth – despite chasing up a few leads, they still had no idea who attacked Keira. Maybe the forensic results would finally come in and they'd get some valuable information from the press release.

32

'Give me some good news, Jane.'

Jane put down her pen. 'It went out this afternoon on the website and social media but no helpful response yet. Just the normal "shoot the bastard" comments on Twitter. It's about to go live on the local evening news bulletins and will be on the late-night session as well. We might get something from the TV appeal. We normally do.'

Bernie's stomach rumbled.

'Someone's hungry. Please tell me you ate lunch today.'

Bernie looked to the side. 'I had a piece of cake this afternoon. And a packet of crisps at lunch. I would have had more but we had to go to Swindon.'

'Honestly, Bernie.' Jane shook her head. 'Now, if we get some phone calls later, how do you want to handle it?'

'Which telephone number was given?'

'Switchboard.'

'In that case, take details of all calls, unless we know they're crank, and then send through to us in MCIT any that seem credible. Especially if the same name keeps cropping up.'

'Great. I'll pass that on. In the meantime, go and get some food.'

'I'm going to order pizza for everyone.'

'No, you are not. The little grocery shop down the road has started stocking those frozen gourmet meals.' Jane pulled a leaflet out from a desk drawer. 'Here's the range. Then everyone can have what they want and it might actually work out cheaper. And you'll give that baby of yours something decent to eat.'

Bernie took the leaflet. She stood up slowly, her back aching. 'You know, it's hard to believe that less than a year ago, I hated your guts.'

'I know. And now I'm your mother. Go. Eat. Get ready to take phone calls.'

Bernie speared a piece of chicken on her fork. 'This is really good stuff.'

Matt swallowed a mouthful of food. 'I agree. This curry is knockout. It was an excellent idea of Jane's. We should do this again sometime.'

The phone on Kerry's desk started to ring.

'OK. Here we go,' said Bernie.

Kerry picked up the phone. 'Hello, this is DS Allen, how can I help you?' She picked up a pen and started writing notes.

Bernie wandered over to Leigh who was just finishing her meal.

'Was that OK for you?'

Leigh nodded. 'Yes, thanks. I can cope with frozen meals like this because, in a way, I'm still cooking them. Even if it is in the microwave.'

'You don't have to stay if you don't want to. I'm not sure how late we're going to be. And I know you still have a long way to get home and you need your sleep.'

'Well, I've been thinking about that. We're assuming that these calls will relate to people in Swindon. As I'm already there in the morning, I can start looking things up for you and maybe cross-reference with Markham's clients. Then I might have something for you when we meet at the gardens. So staying later tonight isn't a problem.'

Bernie nodded. 'Sounds good to me.'

Bernie went and sat at her desk. She was impressed by Leigh's willingness to work and fit in. Her desk phone started to ring. She picked it up.

'DI Noel. How can I help you?'

A couple of hours later, the phone calls had trickled off.

Bernie stood up. 'OK, so what do we have? Any one name that stands out?'

'Yes,' said Alice. 'I've had the name "Frank Green" three times.'

'Yep,' said Mick, 'I've had him too.'

'He might be worth looking at then,' said Bernie.

Leigh laughed. 'I don't think so, ma'am.'

Bernie turned to Leigh. 'Why's that then?'

'The joys of working at a local level means you really get to know your community. Frank is well known. He's probably one of our most prolific flashers.'

'Maybe he's moved on to the next level,' said Kerry, glaring at Leigh.

Leigh twisted in her seat to look at DS Allen. She seemed oblivious to Kerry's displeasure. 'I very much doubt it. Apart from anything else, Frank Green is white and in his seventies. His name comes up for everything sexually related because his neighbours hate him and want him out. Unless the description from the victim is of an old man in a flat cap and a long coat, we know it's not Frank. And if we do suspect him, we just go straight round to his house. It doesn't go on the TV news.'

'Let me guess,' said Mick, 'he raises his flat cap to his victims as well as—'

'Yes, thank you, Mick. Right, we ignore the Frank Green calls,' said Bernie. 'Anything else of significance?'

'Yes, ma'am,' said Matt. 'I had a call from a woman who lives near Town Gardens. She said that over the last few months, she's noticed a man who seems new to the area. She's seen him dealing drugs in the service road behind her house. She has reported him but he always disappears before the police turn up. He's normally dressed in black with a hood up. She's not had a clear look at his face but says he's definitely black.'

Bernie leaned against her desk. 'Could be a possibility. But then how many black men are there in dark clothes with a hood? Worth checking, though, especially as it's near the gardens. Leigh, that's one for you to look into tomorrow morning – there might be a link with the Swindon attacker. See if you can find the original report.'

Matt passed a slip of paper over to Leigh.

'Anyone else got anything?'

'I got three different names,' said Kerry. 'Martin Barry, Neil Rogers and Dean Foster.'

'Any of those sound familiar, Leigh?'

'Yes. Martin Barry is another flasher. Neil Rogers is regularly done for kerb crawling. But Dean Foster is new.'

'I've already looked into him,' said Kerry. 'He doesn't have a record.'

'Were you given an address?'

'No. But the caller mentioned he lives in the Broadgreen area.'

'Hmm. Worth checking up on. He might even be our mystery drug dealer, working a new area. Did the person ringing give you their details?'

'No. Just gave the name and area and then got off the phone as quick as possible.'

'Then that's definitely one to look into. Pass the name to Leigh. So tomorrow, Kerry, Leigh and I will go to Town Gardens. Mick, I want you to keep checking on Isaac Campbell. Matt, touch base with Tom about Keira's phone. Alice, I want you to chase up Forensics. I know Therese said they've been ordered to deal with Anderson's case first but this is ridiculous. We've got a serial attacker on our hands and we need to know if that condom found in the Town Gardens has any bearing on this case.'

33

THURSDAY

Bernie stirred in her sleep and turned over. She blinked as she opened her eyes. One of the bedroom curtains was pulled back and Anderson was silhouetted by the window.

'Dougie?'

'Oh sorry. I didn't mean to wake you. Come and see.'

Bernie eased herself out of the bed. 'What?'

Anderson put her in front of the window. He slid his arms around her waist and kissed her neck. 'See?'

'Oh God, it's Narnia.'

The one street lamp in the village, by the pub, illuminated the perfect snow. Marchant was normally quiet anyway but even the silence seemed muffled, as though cotton wool was stuffed in their ears. The branches of the bare trees were iced white. A few green daffodil stalks stood valiantly with just their tips showing.

'I thought we weren't supposed to be getting this,' she said.

'We weren't but the late forecast on the news was different. It changed direction slightly. We haven't got too much though. And you're right, it does look like Narnia. I'm half expecting Mr Tumnus to appear.'

Bernie nestled into Anderson. 'I loved those books as a child. Pops used to read them to me at bedtime.' The thought of Pops made her eyes smart. Her grandfather would have adored her baby.

'Who was your favourite character?' asked Anderson.

'Lucy.'

'Why?'

'Because she was the first one to believe and she never doubted. She wasn't afraid to get stuck in and despite being the youngest, she showed more leadership than her siblings.'

'Let me guess, Pops said you were like Lucy.'

'He did. Oh God, I miss him. It'll be a year soon. He'd have loved this little one.' She rested her hand on her bump. Anderson added his on top. A thought popped into Bernie's head. 'Oh no. I'm supposed to be going back to the crime scene today. And I've got my scan on Friday. How long is this weather supposed to last for?'

'It'll probably be dirty grey slush by the morning so should be fine. That reminds me. Alex popped by yesterday.'

Bernie twisted in Dougie's arms to face him. 'I hope you were nice.'

'I was politeness personified. He wanted to talk to you in person but we agreed it was probably better if I passed the message along.'

'What message?'

'He said thanks for the invite to the scan but he can't make it. In fact, he won't be coming to any appointments. It'll be awkward for him.'

'Well, we both know that—'

'No, there's more to it. He'll be going for other appointments with Ali. He can't risk the midwives seeing him with a different woman.'

'Ali's pregnant too? God, when's she due? Not the same time as me?'

'No. September sometime. So, it really is just you and me in this now, even if Alex is the father.'

Even in the semi-darkness, Bernie could see the pain in Anderson's face. Maybe she should take the blood test. She shivered.

'Sorry, you're getting cold. One last look at Narnia and then back to bed. I need to warm you up.'

The small back garden was a patchwork of green and white as the snow melted. Bernie imagined disappointed children across the county, hoping for a snow day. She could do with a snow day herself.

'Doesn't look like Narnia so much this morning,' said Bernie as she spread Marmite on her toast. 'I think the magic lies in the first sight of snow.'

'And lamp light,' added Anderson.

'Hmm.' Bernie bit into her hot toast. 'This is so good. I could eat this all day.'

'Better for you than cake.'

'Oh yes, who've you been talking to?'

'Jane. She called yesterday evening to see how I was doing.'

'And how are you doing? I'm sorry. I was only fit for bed when I got in.'

'Apart from being bored out of my head, I'm OK. If you want I can drive you in today.'

'Is that wise? Should you be at headquarters?'

'Is it wise that I let my pregnant girlfriend drive herself to work along narrow, twisting, slippery country lanes?'

'Is it that bad?' Bernie had another bite of toast followed by a swig of decaf coffee.

'It's a bit icy. I'd rather you played it safe.'

Bernie pulled out her phone and started looking at the weather apps. 'I'm sure it'll be fine. I'm going to Swindon again today anyway. Back to the scene. There are a few things that don't quite add up still and I want to see it again for myself. I didn't stay very long on Monday morning.'

'Make sure you wear boots and a coat then. The snow might be melting but it's still cold out there.'

'Yes, Dad.' Bernie finished her toast and gulped down her coffee. She kissed Dougie on the cheek. 'See you later.'

Bernie sat in her car in the car park at headquarters. There was a phone call she had to make but she didn't want the rest of her team to know. Ever since seeing the curtains drawn round Dougie's suspect's hospital bed, a thought had been twisting in her brain. She knew it wasn't possible but she had to check. She scrolled through the contacts on her phone and dialled a London number.

'Probation Service, Annalisse Vickers speaking.'

'Hi, Annalisse, it's Bernie Noel.'

'Oh hi, DS Noel. I haven't spoken to you for a while.'

'I know. I'm a DI now but I prefer Bernie anyway. You're probably wondering why I'm calling.'

'Well, yes.'

Bernie placed her hand on her side. 'I need to know if... he's out.' She couldn't bring herself to say his name.

There was a pause. 'Not as far as I'm aware. You should have been notified if that was the case. But as we all know—'

'Yes,' said Bernie. 'Mistakes are made.'

'Look, I'll check for you. Your number came up on my screen. Is that the best one to use for you?'

'Yes. You can text if that's easier. In fact, it might be better as I'm out on enquiries today. I understand this is a delicate thing to ask.'

'It's no problem. Hopefully I can put your mind at rest. I'll make some calls now and get back to you.'

'Thanks, Annalisse. Bye.'

Bernie slipped the phone into her pocket, making sure it was on vibrate. She didn't want to miss Annalisse's message.

34

Matt raised his head as Bernie walked into MCIT. He was the only one in.

'Morning, ma'am. Got some good news for you.'

'Oh, yes?'

'Someone called in this morning to say she thinks she might have Keira on her video doorbell footage. She caught the news earlier and looked it up. Best thing is, she's in Quarry Road which suggests our possible route for Keira from the club to the gardens is right, assuming it is her.'

'Excellent. Ring her back and see if we can visit her this morning please.'

Bernie sat at her desk and switched on her computer. She brought up maps and searched for Town Gardens. As well as the main map, she also found a hand-drawn map for the gardens.

'Matt, the woman who rang last night about a drug dealer in a service road near the gardens – I know you passed it on to Leigh but do you know exactly where?'

Matt checked his notepad. 'Yes, I have the details here.' He came and sat next to Bernie. 'It's on the west side of the gardens. Here, Goddard Avenue.'

Bernie switched to street view. 'Ooh, these are nice terraced houses. Look Edwardian to me. It's a good area. No wonder this woman isn't happy.' She clicked and moved along the street. 'Ah, here we are. A little lane that I guess leads to the service road at the back.' Bernie clicked on it but the view stayed put. 'Looks like they didn't record down there. That's a shame.' She continued and saw that each time there was a break in the terrace, there was a little side lane. 'Lots of ways in and out.'

'It's the same on the other side of the road as well,' Matt said.

Bernie clicked again and put the map back to normal. Using the mouse, she pointed out a pathway. 'This seems to connect the service road with the park.' She switched tabs to the hand-drawn map. 'And this map is showing a gate in that corner.'

'So the assailant may have left that way,' said Matt. 'In which case, he might also be the drug dealer. Using the routes he knows.'

'Exactly. I'm kicking myself for not going back to the scene earlier.'

'But if he was following Keira, he probably didn't go in that way, assuming it is Keira in Quarry Road.'

Bernie nodded. 'I think you're right, Matt. Contact the woman in Goddard Avenue as well. It would be good to chat to her too.' She glanced at her watch. Nearly eight a.m. Kerry was normally in by now. 'Any sign of Kerry?'

'No, ma'am.'

Bernie's phone vibrated in her pocket and she grabbed it quickly, hoping Annalisse had got back to her. Instead, it was a text from Leigh.

What time do you want to meet at the gardens?

Bernie thought for a moment. With Kerry not in yet, it was pointless going for an early time. The gardens were still sealed off anyway so they didn't have to worry about others being around. Bernie texted back.

Let's meet around 10am in Quarry Road by the gardens. Someone there we need to talk to first.

Leigh's reply was swift.

OK. See you then.

As Bernie put her phone away, Kerry walked in, looking dishevelled.

'What's happened to you?' Bernie asked.

'Oh, don't. The flat upstairs from us is unoccupied and it had a burst pipe last night. Right above our bedroom. Been up half the night. I've had to leave Debs to sort it out.' Kerry rubbed her eyes. 'Think you might have to drive today. Sorry.'

'No worries. We're not meeting Leigh until ten a.m. so we don't have to go just yet. Time for a cuppa first. I'll make you one for a change. Tea?'

Kerry nodded.

'Matt, what about you?'

'Coffee please.'

The kitchen was just down from the super's office and Bernie heard voices as she walked past. She caught Anderson's name. She leaned towards the door.

'How soon can we get DI Anderson out of this mess? It's not helpful being a senior officer down.' It was the super.

'I appreciate that but our hands are tied at the moment.' Bernie recognised the chief constable's voice.

'Tied by whom? The IPCC or the Met? Just because it's London, doesn't mean they're better than us.'

'I know. But we have to wait for the family too. His mother's arriving this weekend sometime.'

Bernie stepped back as her phone buzzed. She pulled it out and saw a text had arrived from Annalisse. She went to the kitchen before opening it.

Done a check. He's still in and not going anywhere for quite some time. You're safe.

Bernie gave a huge sigh of relief as she texted back her thanks. The man who stabbed her was still in prison. Not in a bed in ICU. It wasn't his mother who'd be in Swindon this weekend. But if it wasn't him, why were the chief constable and super still keeping the suspect's identity secret from her?

35

Quarry Road was quite narrow and not easy to park on. Leigh was already there. Bernie found a space further down and then she and Kerry walked back, Bernie pulling her coat around her as they went. Dougie was right. It was cold. The snow had melted away to a grey slush but a stiff breeze kept the temperature low. Kerry still looked tired but the cold seemed to be waking her up a bit.

'Morning, Leigh,' said Bernie. 'We just need to pop into a house up here first. The owner rang in earlier to say she thinks she has footage of Keira. This top bit's very narrow, isn't it? No pavement at all.'

Leigh nodded. 'Bit dangerous walking down here in the dark, really.'

Bernie checked the address on her phone and then pointed to a modern house. 'This one here. Mrs Devlin.'

She led the way up the drive and rang the doorbell, the camera presumably capturing them. Bernie got her warrant card ready. A dog started to yap.

'Ssh, Trixie,' came a voice from inside. The door opened a crack, the chain on.

'Mrs Devlin, I'm DI Noel. One of my colleagues rang earlier to say we'd be coming. You have some video footage to show us.'

'Yes, that's right. Just wait a minute.'

The door closed and the yapping dog sound became muffled. A minute later, the door opened again.

'Sorry about that. Trixie gets a bit excited about visitors. She's in the kitchen now,' said an older woman with short white hair. 'Come in. Would you like some drinks?'

'No, thank you, Mrs Devlin. This is DS Allen and LCI Roberts.'

'Come and sit down and I'll get my iPad.' She showed them into the lounge, immaculate apart from the white dog hair that covered all the chairs.

'Think I might stand,' muttered Leigh.

Bernie didn't blame her. She perched on the sofa, not wanting to get white hair on her black coat. Kerry sank into an armchair, clearly too tired to care.

Mrs Devlin joined them a minute later and sat next to Bernie. She opened the doorbell camera app on her iPad. 'Here we go. I didn't even think about checking until I heard the request on the news. I heard what had happened. I normally walk Trixie in the gardens but obviously not this week. A friend of mine lives opposite the main gate and she told me. Said she saw a young woman taken away in an ambulance. I do hope she's all right—'

'She's doing OK,' Bernie said. She pointed to the iPad. 'The footage?'

'Oh, yes. I've got it set up for you. Eleven twenty p.m. – movement outside your house. Here she is.' Mrs Devlin pressed play.

Even in dim light, Bernie could see Keira walking past, on the side closest to the house. She didn't appear scared or concerned about her surroundings. She was facing forward, not looking around her. Her dress wasn't much longer than her jacket, high heels ditched in favour of trainers, a bag over her shoulder. She seemed a million miles away from the young woman in ICU.

Bernie nodded. 'That's her. Did anyone else walk past?'

Mrs Devlin shook her head. 'No one else shows up until the morning.'

'Can I see?'

Mrs Devlin scrolled the footage on. No other motion was detected. Bernie sat puzzled for a moment. If the man seen near the club had followed Keira, why wasn't he picked up on the camera too? Could being dressed all in black fool it into not sensing motion? Or maybe there was a cut-off point for the range covered?

'Thank you, Mrs Devlin. It would be useful to have that footage please.'

'Of course.' She frowned. 'How do I do that? My son set it up.'

Bernie smiled. 'We give the iPad to DS Allen and she does it for you.' She passed the tablet over. 'Did you hear anything that night? Anything at all?'

'No, I didn't.'

'What about Mr Devlin?'

The older woman shook her head sadly. 'He died last year. Just Trixie and me now. The children and grandchildren visit quite a lot which is why I keep such a big house. I have to say, I'm a bit nervous with this attack. It's normally fine round here.'

'I'm based in Swindon, Mrs Devlin,' said Leigh. 'How about I ask some of the police community support officers to check on you every so often? I know they walk through the gardens as part of their beat so it won't be a problem for them.'

Mrs Devlin smiled. 'Really? That would be very reassuring.'

Bernie gently touched her arm. 'We're going to find this

man. And you've helped us enormously. Kerry, have you sent it to headquarters?'

'Yes, gone to my email.' Kerry put the iPad on a coffee table.

'Right, we won't keep you any longer, Mrs Devlin. I'm sure Trixie will want to be let out. Thank you for your help.'

Bernie stood. Mrs Devlin showed them out. She waved to them before closing the door.

'That was a nice thing to offer, Leigh. Do you think the PCSOs will mind?' said Bernie.

'No, I know the two on the beat round here. They're always up for a chat. Besides, she seems lonely.'

Bernie looked at Leigh and wondered if she was lonely too.

A man with dark, curly hair, wearing a green fleece with Swindon Council stitched on it, was waiting for them by the gate just round the corner from Mrs Devlin.

'DI Noel? I'm Malcolm Keats, park ranger. LCI Roberts thought it was better to open up for you here, rather than making you walk all the way down to the main gate, especially as the pavements are a little bit slippery.'

Bernie smiled. 'Thank you. That's very helpful. Particularly as we now think this is where Keira got in.' She looked at the metal gate behind him. It looked rather old and dilapidated and a lot taller than the metal railing fence. If Keira had come in this way, it was more likely she climbed over that than the gate.

Malcolm Keats caught her eye. 'We're hoping to get this gate restored back to its former glory. You think your girl came in this way? The spikes on the fence could do some damage but put a coat over them, you could then probably climb over.'

'Do you have a problem with people coming in at night?' Bernie asked.

'Not as far as I'm aware. I live in the cottage at the front and I've got a dog. He barks at anyone who comes in that way, even at night. But there are other gates too. Do you want me to show you?'

'Yes please. I particularly want to see the one that has a pathway leading to a service road behind Goddard Avenue.'

'That's just down here.'

They followed Malcolm past trees that were springing back into life after winter, not bothered by the sprinkling of snow that was fast melting away. A few crystals edged green shrubs. It didn't take long to reach the old, ornate green gate.

'Here we are.' Malcolm reached into his pocket and pulled out a bunch of keys. He unlocked the gate and it swung open, revealing a pathway beyond it.

They'd only gone a few minutes when they reached a brick wall covered in graffiti to their left.

'This is interesting,' Bernie said. She was thinking about the man spotted in the service road. Had he tagged this wall at some point?

'Yeah, it gets graffitied quite a lot. They all paint over each other's tags.'

Bernie looked back at the path that now started to wind uphill.

As if reading her mind, Kerry said, 'Why don't Leigh and I check out the rest of this pathway? Save your swollen ankles.'

Bernie smiled. She hadn't wanted to admit it but her ankles were beginning to ache inside her boots. 'Sounds like a plan.' She turned back to Malcolm. 'Do you know any of the people painting the graffiti?'

Malcolm shook his head. 'No. They normally do it late at night and I'm at the other end of the park. I do check round here every few days, though, just in case they leave any empty aerosols around.'

'And when did you last do that?'

'Yesterday. I was given the all-clear to walk round the gardens, doing jobs.'

'Don't suppose you still have them?'

'Well, they're in the bin, but I could fish them out for you.

I'll go now. When your colleagues come back, just pull up the gate and close the padlock. Keep right on the path and it will bring you down to the gardener's yard. I'll be there.'

'OK. If they're in a bag, don't take them out. I might want to send them to Forensics.'

Bernie studied the brick wall as Malcolm walked away. Some of the graffiti was large, brightly painted words. Others just looked like squiggles but meant something to the person who sprayed it. She spotted one tag in the bottom right-hand corner that caught her breath. It looked familiar, like one she'd seen in London a few years before. She bent down and looked closer, steadying herself with her hand on the ground. She reached into her pocket for her phone and took a photo of the tag, all the while trying to match it with an image from her memory. It was very similar but she knew it couldn't be the same person. Annalisse had assured her he was still in prison. Even so, her heart was thumping hard.

36

Bernie's heart rate was almost back to normal when the other two returned.

'Where's Malcolm?' Kerry asked.

'He's gone to the gardener's yard. He picked up some spray paint cans yesterday. I thought it might be worth sending them to Forensics.'

Kerry stared at her. 'We searched here on Monday. There were no cans. They must have been dropped since then.'

'Doesn't mean the graffiti guys weren't out here on Sunday evening. They might have tidied up for a change. Just think it's worth checking. Besides, it might tie in with the drug dealer reported to us last night.'

Kerry shrugged. 'Fine.' She was definitely out of sorts and Bernie wondered if she and Leigh had just had a bust-up. But Leigh seemed fine.

'So, Leigh, does the path lead to the service road?'

'Yes, it does. I can see why the residents are getting annoyed.'

'Well, we'll be visiting one of them after this. I told Malcom we'll meet him at the gardener's yard. Come on.'

They walked back to the gardens, locked the gate and then followed the path past more shrubbery and trees to the gardener's yard. Malcolm was waiting, with a black bin bag in hand.

'Here you are. I haven't touched them again. And I kept them separate from the other rubbish so they could be recycled safely.'

Bernie smiled. Here was a man good at his job. 'I'm assuming you've already given us a statement, Malcolm.'

'Yes, to this officer.' He nodded towards Kerry. 'My missus too. I heard a fox around midnight – at least I thought it was a fox – but nothing else. I'm now wondering if it was actually the victim. Feel really bad about that. Wish I'd found her sooner.'

'Do you mind just running through what you saw again please?' Bernie thought it unlikely that Keats was involved in Keira's attack, but she wanted to make sure. It was always worth eliminating people from an enquiry.

'Of course. I took the dog out for a toilet break and a walk a bit before six thirty – I like to see the sunrise. The birds were already chirping away in the aviary. As I walked past the bandstand, the dog started barking and I saw what I thought was a bundle of clothes but then I realised it was a person – a young woman. There was blood on her head and also from, you know, down below. It was along her legs. I felt for a pulse and was so relieved to find she was alive. I dialled nine nine nine and you got here really fast. I'd only just put a blanket over her and unlocked the gate when the police car came and then the ambulance. How's she doing? Is there any news?'

Bernie shook her head. 'Nothing's changed so far. But the doctors are hopeful.' She held out her hand for the bin bag. 'Thanks, Malcolm.' As she took the bag, she noticed something further back behind him. 'What are all those rocks by the tree there?'

Malcolm turned. 'Oh, those. Just rocks that we might use around the gardens to make a feature or repair a wall.'

Bernie looked at Kerry. 'This was all checked out by the CSIs, right?'

Kerry hung her head and muttered, 'Shit. No.' She looked up. 'The doctor's report on Keira's head wound didn't mention any dirt or gravel so we discounted these. Plus the bruising is rounded.'

Bernie was about to have a go at Kerry when she realised she was just as bad. This was her first trip back to the scene since Monday and she hadn't stayed long then. She spoke gently. 'Ring Lucy and ask her to come back with a team. One of these rocks might be the weapon. They all need to be checked for blood.'

As Kerry rang Lucy, Bernie's phone began to buzz. Debs' name was flashing on the screen.

'Hi, Debs. Are you trying to get hold of Kerry?'

'No, you. I've just heard from one of my ICU colleagues that Keira's awake. Thought you'd like to know.'

'That's wonderful news. Do you think she's up to visitors?'

'Not sure but you can go along and see.'

'Thanks. Bye, Debs.'

'Bye, Bernie.'

She pocketed her phone. 'Great news. Keira's awake. I think we should get over there as fast as we can.'

Kerry ended her call. 'Lucy'll be here in about forty minutes. Can you wait that long?'

'Not sure. By the time we've spoken to Lucy, it'll be well over an hour before we get there.'

'I have an idea,' said Leigh. 'Why don't I wait for Lucy and tell her what needs doing? And after that, I can go and see the woman in Goddard Avenue. Then you'll have plenty of time with Keira.'

Bernie looked at her very sullen DS and thought Leigh's idea was a good one. As it would just be the two of them, maybe then she could find out what was going on with Kerry.

'That sounds like a plan.' Bernie turned to Malcolm. 'Thanks for your help. Could you let us out at the Quarry Road gate please?'

37

Kerry was silent on the journey to the hospital. It was so unlike her and Bernie wondered if she and Debs had had a row that morning. That would explain why Debs called her rather than Kerry. The hospital car park was fairly empty for a change and they had their pick of spaces. She hoped it would be the same the next day when she came with Dougie for her scan. Bernie was just about to get out of the car when Kerry stopped her.

'Bernie, do you think it would be better if it was just me who went up?'

Bernie paused before answering. She thought Kerry had volunteered her services a bit too quickly. Was the super behind it all? Using Kerry to keep tabs on her?

'Why? Is there a problem with me going up there?'

Kerry sighed. 'No. I guess not.'

'Good. Let's go.'

Bernie pressed the buzzer to be let into ICU, and they followed the usual routine of rubbing hand gel into their hands. Rachel, Keira's nurse, was waiting for them.

'She's very confused so I'm only giving you five minutes,' she said.

Again they walked past the bed with all the curtains pulled closed. Bernie deliberately kept her eyes facing forward, not wanting to attract Kerry's attention. But she had noticed that the armed guard wasn't there. Was he or she on a break or had the officer been stood down?

Bernie smiled as she approached Keira's bed. Her parents and brother were there. They were exhausted but there was relief on their faces.

'Good morning, Mr and Mrs Howard; Adam. I've heard there's been some good news.'

Julie Howard gave a brief smile. 'Yes. She woke up a couple of hours ago. Spoke a few words. Had a few sips of water. She's sleeping again now. I suppose you came because you want to speak to her.'

'Yes. But we can wait if she's sleeping.'

Keira moaned and turned her head slightly.

'She's stirring,' said Adam. He reached out and touched her cheek. 'Keira, the police are here.'

Keira slowly opened her eyes. Adam and Julie moved away from the bed, allowing Bernie to get near.

'Hi, Keira. My name's Bernie Noel and I'm the detective leading your case. Do you think you could manage to answer a few questions?'

'Hmm.' Her eyes were slightly glazed.

'Couldn't this wait?' asked Geoff Howard. 'The poor girl's been through so much.'

'I understand that, Mr Howard. And if Keira isn't up to it, we'll stop.' Aware that there were some questions Keira might not want to answer in front of her parents, Bernie added, 'Maybe you'd like to go and get some food? You must all be hungry.'

'I'm not leaving her,' said Geoff.

'Come on, Dad,' said Adam. 'We're leaving her in safe hands. Let the police do their job.'

The family shuffled out and Kerry stepped closer.

'So, Keira, as I said, I'm Bernie and this is my colleague, Kerry.' Now wasn't the time to baffle Keira with rank. 'I'm sorry but I do need to ask you a few questions. What do you remember?'

'Not a lot.' Keira's voice was quiet.

'Do you remember being at the club with Caz and Mia?'

'Mmm. Caz's birthday.'

'Do you remember leaving?'

Keira blinked her eyes. 'Yes. I needed to go...' She stopped.

Bernie wondered if Keira was trying to think up a lie. 'Keira, we know you got a text message from a man. Telling us the truth really is the best option.'

Keira bit her lip.

'Who texted you? Who were you going to see? Did he do this to you?'

Keira turned her head and winced. 'Head's banging still. He didn't do this. I can't tell you who he is.'

'But he's the father of your baby?'

Keira's eyes widened slightly. 'I'm still pregnant? Do my parents know?'

'Yes and yes. But let's focus on you leaving the club. What can you remember?'

Keira sighed. 'Went to the cashpoint to get some money for a cab but didn't have enough. So I walked. Think I put my earphones in to listen to some music. Going to meet a friend. Nearly there but then... nothing. I don't remember any more than that.'

'Were you aware of anyone else around you?'

'No, not really.'

'You were found in the Town Gardens. Were you going to meet your friend there?'

Keira gave a slight nod. 'Yes. I climbed over the fence by the Quarry Road gate. We've met there before.'

'I know you don't want to tell us but we really do need to know so we can rule him out and also let him know you're here. He must be worried about you. We won't tell your parents.'

Keira opened her mouth and shut it again. She looked at Bernie. 'Do you promise not to tell my parents?'

'Yes.'

'Right, that's your five minutes up.'

Bernie looked up and saw Rachel standing behind Kerry.

'We haven't finished here yet.'

'Yes you have. I said five minutes and you've actually had more than that. Keira's only just woken up. She needs to rest. You can come back another time.'

Bernie shook her head. She looked back at Keira but her resolve to speak had weakened. She closed her eyes, shutting them out. Bernie gently squeezed her hand.

'Well done, Keira. We'll come back another time.'

Bernie glared at Rachel but the nurse wasn't backing down.

'We'll find Keira's family and let them know that we're leaving. For now.'

Bernie pushed past the nurse. With Kerry behind her, she allowed her eyes to dart across to the screened bed. She was relieved to know the man responsible for her scar wasn't lying there. But who was he?

Bernie pulled out her phone as they left the lift and headed out to the car. There were some new emails and a missed call from Therese at Forensics.

'Therese rang. At last! Oh wait, she's sent an email too. Maybe we'll finally have some news on that condom.' Bernie stopped still as she read it. 'Nothing on Keira's clothes... I don't believe it.' She turned back.

'Where are you going?' asked Kerry.

'ICU.'

'What? You heard what the nurse said. Keira needs to rest.'

Bernie pushed the button for the lift. 'It's not Keira we need to speak to.'

38

'Bernie, are you going to tell me what's going on?'

Kerry looked nervous.

Bernie hammered the buzzer to be let back into ICU.

'Bernie, you're worrying me. What did Therese say in her email?'

'She apologised for the delay but she had to get someone else to retest the semen from the condom. She was concerned about cross-contamination from another case – Dougie's raid. The results are back. There's no cross-contamination.'

Bernie turned away from Kerry. She headed into ICU.

'Bernie, wait. You can't go in there. The super said—'

'So I was right. You have been babysitting me. Is that why you've not been yourself today?'

'Please, Bernie, you have to trust me. It's for your own good.' Kerry tried to grab her arm but she pulled it away.

'I understand this could compromise Dougie but we have DNA proof. We have Keira's attacker.'

Bernie walked quickly towards the screened bed.

'No, Bernie. This has nothing to do with Dougie. This is to do with you.'

Bernie ignored Kerry and pulled back the curtains. A young black man lay on the bed, tubes everywhere. She gripped the bar at the end of the bed as her brain registered who she was seeing.

No, it's not possible. I spoke to Annalisse. He's still in prison.

And then a movie played in her head, one that she had tried so hard to block out. Her left hand went to her side as the stabbing pain started, warm blood pumping out while the rest of her turned cold. There was laughter. 'That's it, stab the fucking pig!' said a male voice. More laughter but then sirens. Lots of sirens until she heard a familiar voice.

'It's all right, Bernie. I've got you. It's OK.'

Her old boss, DI Jack Thornton.

That's not right. That's not what he said. It was 'We've got them'.

She turned her head slowly towards the man standing next to her, her eyesight clouded by tiny coloured dots, the ringing in her ears increasing. Older now, but the broken nose still recognisable.

'Sir?' she whispered.

'I've got you.'

Her legs gave way as blackness swooped in.

The smell of fresh laundered linen filled her nose. Her natural instinct was to turn over but something was stopping her.

'Ah, here we go. Welcome back to the land of the living.'

Bernie forced her eyes open. Rachel was standing next to her. Slowly the sounds of beeping machines returned.

'What happened?'

'You fainted. Fortunately for you we had a bed free. We put you in the recovery position. There's a wedge behind you.'

'I want to move.'

'Not for the moment. Let's make sure you're completely back with us first. Your blood pressure is all over the place.'

'It's normally high.'

'I know. We looked up your notes. But the pressure dropped dramatically. I was about to hit the crash button when it came back up. I'm just waiting for a doctor to come and check you over.'

'I don't need a doctor.'

'Don't argue with me. But while we wait, you can speak to your colleagues.'

'Colleagues? But there's only Kerry.' And then she remembered the face she had seen before the blackout. Why was he here?

'Oh thank God! Dougie would have killed me if anything had happened to you.' Kerry took her hand and squeezed it. 'I'm sorry. I should have been honest with you. I hated keeping info from you but the super made me promise. Said it was for your own good. Maybe he was right.'

'I don't understand.'

'Bernie, you fainted—'

'No, not that. The man in the bed. He's supposed to be in prison. I checked.'

'He still is,' said Jack Thornton. The other colleague. But not for a long time.

'I thought I'd imagined you,' said Bernie.

'No. I've been here for a few days.'

'Been avoiding me then.'

'Something like that.'

DI Jack Thornton smiled. His face wrinkled. Definitely older but the flattened nose was unmistakable.

'So, if it's not Danny Ambrose lying there, who is it?'

'Think about it, Bernie. You'll work it out.'

Laughter. 'Stab the fucking pig.' Boys turning into men.

'Zac Ambrose. He was seventeen when I last saw him.'

'Well, he's almost twenty-one now. The same age Danny was when he stabbed you. Understandable that you thought it was him.'

'So Zac Ambrose is Dougie's suspect?'

'Yes. You know DI Anderson then?'

'Intimately.' Bernie raised her eyebrows.

'Ah. That makes things a bit awkward. What made you pull the curtain back today? I know you've been past a couple of times.'

The memory of Therese's email came back to her. Bernie looked at Kerry.

'How far away is Keira's bed?'

'At the other end of the ward.'

Bernie lowered her voice anyway. 'The DNA on the condom has come back. Definitely has Keira's on it, and... Zac Ambrose's. I don't know what you have on Zac but we need to add rape and attempted murder of Keira plus possible other sexual offences.'

'Shit,' said Kerry.

Bernie closed her eyes as the ramifications of all this hit her. Not only was Dougie's suspect now her suspect for Keira's attack, she should have been told that he was in Swindon. The super and chief constable had deliberately kept that information from her. How could she trust them again? She opened her eyes to see two concerned faces.

'Sorry, have you two introduced yourselves? Jack, this is DS Kerry Allen and Kerry, this is Jack Thornton, my old DI. I don't know what your rank is now.'

'DCI.'

'Must be a very big case for you to leave London.'

'It is. And if this new evidence is correct, it really complicates things.'

'What do you mean, "if"? Therese had a second test done by someone not involved in either case. There's no "if" about it.'

Rachel appeared with a sonographer. Bernie recognised her from her first scan.

'Right, visitors out for the moment please. We need to check Mum and baby.'

Thornton nodded as he left. 'I need to get back to my post anyway.'

'This conversation isn't over,' said Bernie.

'It is for now.'

Kerry squeezed her hand again. 'I'll just be outside.'

Rachel pulled the curtains round the bed.

Bernie smiled at the sonographer. 'Hello. You did my twelve-week scan. I'm actually due the next one tomorrow.'

'Oh, yes. Police officer. I remember you. Well, in that case, let's get you over to Maternity and do your full scan now. Save you coming back tomorrow.'

'Oh, but my partner—'

'Can he get here in the next fifteen minutes?'

'Not really.'

The sonographer frowned. 'I'm sorry but I really need to check baby out quickly. You took quite a fall, apparently.'

Bernie pictured Dougie's face. He'd be so disappointed.

A head popped back round. 'Can I come with you?'

Bernie smiled. She understood why her DS had been so sullen today. She'd been put under pressure by the super to stay quiet and Kerry hated that kind of thing.

'Of course.'

'Great,' said the sonographer. 'I'll just get a porter and a wheelchair.'

Despite her protests that she was capable of walking, Bernie reluctantly sat down. As she was wheeled away, she looked back, first at Zac's bed, and then Keira's. Having the suspect and victim on the same ward was difficult enough but with Zac being Danny Ambrose's brother, Bernie had a good idea as to what the super was going to say.

39

Maternity Outpatients was half-full. Last time Bernie had been there for her first scan, there had barely been an empty seat. A forty-five-minute wait had taken its toll on her bladder and she'd had to run to the toilet after the scan. The pictures had been great but it was the second one she was really looking forward to. She wanted to know if the baby was a boy or girl.

'Don't you want to be surprised?' her mother had asked.

'No. I want to know who this baby is. Decide a name.'

'But you won't know exactly who this baby is, will you? And when you do find out the father, shouldn't he have a say in the name?'

'What? Like my father did?'

'That's not fair. I wanted Gary to be a part of it all but Pops wouldn't have it. I should have fought harder for Gary but I was only fifteen. You're a grown woman. Don't make the same mistakes I did.'

The gel was cold on Bernie's abdomen. She shivered slightly.

'I'm sorry,' said the sonographer, 'I wish there was a way we could warm it up. By the way, the obstetrician wants to see you afterwards too. Make sure you're OK.' She turned the screen towards Bernie and Kerry. 'Here we go. Here's your baby, looking very good so far.'

Bernie stared at the screen. Last time had been amazing but now the image was so much clearer. She saw an arm up and moving around as though waving.

'I think the baby's saying hello,' she said.

'Yes. Which is helpful because that gives me a clear view of the chest and abdomen so I can check baby's organs.'

Kerry touched Bernie on the arm. 'Thanks for letting me come in and see. This is incredible.' She beamed.

'Now,' said the sonographer, 'I have lots of things I need to check and measure so don't mind me for a moment. You just enjoy watching your baby.'

Bernie was enthralled as the baby moved around on the screen.

'Will Dougie be cross?' asked Kerry.

'Probably. But it would have taken him an hour to get here.'

'It's my fault anyway,' said the sonographer. 'So, I'm going to take lots of photos for you to make up for it. We normally only do a couple but I think I can do a few more for you today. This little one has the cutest nose. And looking at the measurements, I think this one is going to be tall like you. Everything else is looking good for baby. No harm done in the fall, at all. Now, your placenta. Did they say anything to you about it at your last scan?'

Bernie thought. 'I think they said it was a bit low.'

'Yes, it still is. So I'm going to recommend that you have another scan around... hmm, let's say twenty-eight weeks. Hopefully your partner will be able to make that one. Do you have any questions? Maybe one in particular?'

'How did you know?'

'I have a sixth sense about this. I can normally tell. I currently have a very good view.'

Bernie smiled. 'Yes, I'd like to know.'

'Or you can wait for the next scan with your partner?'

Bernie looked at little Bun waving at her on the screen. First and foremost, this was her baby. 'No, I'd like to know now please.'

40

'Dougie is going to go apeshit when you tell him all of this,' said Kerry.

'Tell him what?'

They were driving back to headquarters. Bernie had wanted to go back to Town Gardens but Kerry had persuaded her to go back to MCIT.

'Where should I start? You had the scan without him. Thank God little bubs is OK. Dougie's suspect is our main suspect for Keira's attack and the other sex offences. The suspect is also the brother of the man who stabbed you and was there when it happened. And the big cheese from the Met is your old boss.'

Bernie rubbed her face. 'Yep, it's been one hell of a day so far. I'm looking forward to some late lunch when we get back. Perhaps we can pop into the baker's. I fancy a bacon roll. Must be craving the salt.'

'Bernie, this is serious.'

'You think I don't know that? I need to talk to the super before Dougie. And I need to eat before that. The doctor told me I have to have more regular mealtimes.'

'We've been telling you that for weeks. OK. Baker's first and then headquarters. And after you've seen the super, I think you should go home. We have our man and he's not going anywhere.'

Detective Chief Superintendent Wilson wiped his forehead with his hand.

'Bernie, I want you to know that I had your best interest at heart.'

'Really? How long have you known?'

'Only a couple of weeks. I tried to pull Anderson off the case but he wasn't having any of it.'

'But you didn't tell DCI Thornton about Dougie's connection with me. He looked surprised when I mentioned it.'

Wilson wiped his head again. 'No. There were enough complications as it was.'

'Bit more complicated now with the DNA results.'

'Yes. You do realise you're going to have to give up the case?'

Bernie had already suspected that this would be the super's response but she was willing to fight. 'No. No way. I owe it to Keira. I won't question him. I'll pass that to Kerry and Matt.'

'Bernie, once the Ambrose family know you're in charge... well, all hell's going to break loose. You don't want to be accused of setting him up.'

Bernie thought back to the last time she had seen Jade Ambrose, Danny and Zac's mother, at court. She'd made her feelings about Bernie very clear.

'Where is she? I'm surprised she's not at the hospital.'

'She's visiting family in Jamaica. She knows about Zac and is trying to get a flight home. We expect her to arrive this weekend sometime. You might want to stay away from the hospital. In fact, as all the evidence for Keira's attack points to Zac Ambrose, you don't have to be here at all for the next few days. You have an excellent team and I'm sure Kerry can build the case.'

Bernie sighed. 'You're sending me home?'

'You fainted today. Kerry said that your blood pressure was all over the place. Your baby comes first. A few years ago, you experienced a horrific attack. You had counselling at the time but considering your reaction today, I'm wondering if you might need more. Post-Traumatic Stress Disorder doesn't disappear overnight. I'm going to arrange for you to see a counsellor. And I'd like you to see your GP and get yourself signed off for a week at least.'

'But I'm not ill.'

'That's an order.'

Bernie clenched her fists. Being removed from the case was bad enough but being told to go home just added to her frustration. And maybe she could cope with that but with Anderson at home as well, she wondered if they would survive the week.

'What about Dougie? He's in the dark about the independent investigation into his case. He's not saying it but I know it's getting to him.'

'I'm afraid he's going to have to wait a bit longer on that front. But what I will say, no matter what your feelings are about Zac Ambrose, you need to pray he pulls through. Because if he doesn't, Jade Ambrose will be baying for DI Anderson's blood.'

The GP surgery was busy but Dr Forbes fitted her in as soon as she heard that Bernie had fainted.

'Honestly, Bernie, what am I going to do with you?'

'According to my boss you're going to sign me off for a week.'

'But you don't want that.'

'No, of course not.'

Dr Forbes smiled kindly. She'd been the one who'd told Bernie she was pregnant. 'You know, you and I have been in this together since the beginning. I never judge my patients but I was so relieved when you decided to continue with this pregnancy. You've been honest with me about paternity and now I'm going to be honest with you. I've read the notes from the doctor at the hospital about what happened earlier. Regardless of what your boss wants, I'm telling you that you need to rest. So I am going to sign you off for a week.' She turned from Bernie and started typing on her computer. 'I also want to see you in two days' time to check your blood pressure again. If you feel faint before then, call the surgery and I'll see you.'

'But two days' time will be Saturday.'

'I will see you.' The printer sprang into life and the sick note was printed. 'In the meantime, get that lovely Scotsman of yours to look after you.'

Bernie sat in her car outside her cottage. She placed a hand on her abdomen and received a kick in response.

'Hello, little Bun. We've had a bit of a day, haven't we? But now I know who you are, I'll have to think of a name for you.' She smiled.

Her phone buzzed in her pocket. It was a WhatsApp from Dougie.

What are you doing?

Sitting in the car.

I can see that. Come inside. It must be cold out there.

It's not too bad. I've had a crap day.

I'm sorry you've had a crap day.

Bernie sniffed.

I've got lots to tell you but I think you're going to be cross with me.

The tears were flowing now. Bloody hormones. She didn't want an argument.

The passenger door opened and Anderson climbed in.

'Hey, it can't be that bad.' He wiped her tears.

'It is. I had the scan.'

'What? That's meant to be tomorrow. Why did you have it without me?'

'Because I fainted in ICU and they had to check the baby was all right. And when I said I was having a scan tomorrow, the sonographer decided to do a full scan today.'

'You fainted? Are you OK? Is everything all right with the baby?'

Bernie couldn't bring herself to look at Dougie but the tension was palpable.

'I'm fine and so is baby but I have a low-lying placenta so I need to have another scan in seven weeks' time. You can come then.'

'Hmm. All right. Did you get any pictures?'

'Yes.' Bernie reached behind for her bag and pulled out the envelope containing the scan photos. Anderson's face melted as he looked at them.

'Wow. That's such a cute nose.'

'I know. That's what the sonographer said.' She paused. 'I asked. Do you want to know?'

Anderson looked up from the photos. He nodded.

'Beautiful little... girl.'

Anderson nodded again, tears forming in his eyes. He put

the photos down and took her face in his hands. 'We're having a little girl.'

Bernie didn't have the heart to remind him that the baby might not be his. 'Yes.'

He kissed her deeply. 'That makes it a good day, not a crappy one.'

'Oh, Dougie, you don't know the half of it.'

41

Bernie was curled up on the sofa with a blanket over her legs and a mug of hot chocolate warming her hands. She could smell something delicious cooking in the kitchen.

'What have you made for dinner?' she asked.

'An Italian beef stew. A family recipe. It's got another hour to go.' Dougie appeared in the doorway between the kitchen and the lounge, with a tea towel over his shoulder. It reminded her of the first time they worked together, looking for a missing five-year-old girl. He'd been the family liaison officer, looking after the girl's family. He'd been both arrogant and attractive. She smiled. He still was.

'So' – he sat down next to her – 'I have time to hear all about your crappy day. You've told me about the scan, which wasn't crappy. What else happened?'

Bernie took a sip of her hot chocolate. Dougie had put cream and marshmallows in it. She wiped away the cream that had stuck to her top lip.

'We got the DNA results back on the condom. It definitely has Keira's DNA on it. And there's a match for the suspect.'

'But that's brilliant news, isn't it? You know who you're looking for.'

Bernie shook her head. 'It's not that simple. Therese had to get another team member to retest it to make sure there'd been no cross-contamination with another case. Your case.'

'What?' Anderson looked confused. 'My case? You mean my suspect in hospital is Keira's attacker? And they're both in ICU? Shit.'

'Exactly. Neither one is well enough to move just yet but Keira's awake so they might be able to swap her to a different ward soon.'

'She's awake? What does she remember?'

'Nothing much. She had earphones in and was listening to music as she walked. She remembers climbing over the fence into the gardens to meet her boyfriend and then everything went black. She nearly told us who the father of her baby is but the nurse interrupted us and told Kerry and me to leave.'

'Did you know the DNA results when you spoke to her?'

'No, we saw Keira first. It's why we went to the hospital in the first place. We were just leaving when the results came through.'

Anderson stroked her curled-up legs. 'I'm not sure if I dare ask the next question – did you go back to ICU to see the suspect?'

Bernie drank more of her hot chocolate. She nodded.

'Shit, Bernie. That might have compromised me with this investigation.'

'I know. I'm sorry. But there's more to it than just you. The other day I overheard the super talking with the chief constable. They were saying it was really important that I didn't find out the suspect's true identity and that, in fact, you don't know his true identity either.'

'What are you on about? Of course I know his name. It's...' Anderson stopped.

'You might as well tell me,' said Bernie. 'Because it's not his real name.'

Anderson sighed. 'Dean Collins. Although he sometimes uses Foster. But there's no record for a Dean Foster and only a handful of cautions for Dean Collins.'

'Dean Foster – that name came up in our enquiries. He was mentioned as a possible drug dealer. Leigh's been looking into him.'

Anderson laughed. 'More than possible. And not just drugs. He's a front for lots more and it all comes from London. Hence the Met involvement.'

Bernie nodded. She hadn't even got to that part yet. 'His real name is Zac Ambrose. If we were to look him up, we'd see some convictions and, more importantly, his connections. We're talking some pretty serious stuff here. I was part of a Met operation a few years ago. I went undercover to infiltrate the gang his brother ran. Or rather to befriend the girls in the gang.'

Bernie took another mouthful of hot chocolate. She noticed her hands were beginning to shake. She gripped the mug tighter. Images were trying to force their way into her mind. She couldn't stop the shaking now.

'Hey, it's OK. Let me take your mug.' Anderson drew her into him. 'You don't have to tell me if you don't want to. But I'm guessing this is where your scar comes from. Am I right?'

Bernie buried her head into Anderson's shoulder. 'Yes.' Cortisone was starting to flood her body as her stress levels increased. The baby began kicking like mad.

'Oh, I felt that,' said Anderson. 'Little Bun's going nuts. You don't have to tell me any more for now. Except: did he do this to you? Did Zac Ambrose stab you?'

Bernie lifted her head. 'No. It was his brother, Danny. He's in prison. But Zac was there, egging Danny on to stab me. If the rest of the team hadn't turned up at that point, Danny would have killed me. I have no doubts about that.'

. . .

The stew was delicious. Bernie marvelled at how Anderson managed to produce such thick, rich sauces.

'Dougie, this is so good. Just what the doctor ordered. Quite literally. The doctor I saw this morning...' She stopped.

'What doctor? You said you had a scan.'

She put her fork down. 'Now I'm calmer, I can tell you everything else that happened today. After I got the DNA results, I went back to ICU. Kerry tried to stop me. I wouldn't listen to her. Turns out the super had Kerry watching me, making sure I didn't go near Zac. But I did. I pulled back the curtains and there he was. Lying on the bed, tubes everywhere. And then suddenly I was back there.'

Anderson took her hand and kissed it. 'You're safe now.'

'Am I? How long has he been here? I should have been told he was on my patch. The whole reason I came to Wiltshire in the first place was to get away from it all. There were death threats. Jack Thornton suggested I should leave the Met and go elsewhere.'

'Wait, DCI Thornton. You know him?'

Bernie nodded. 'He was my boss at the time. He was running the operation.'

'Then he would have known you were here. You're right. You should have been told. Me as well. I would have come off the case and we could have gone away while someone else dealt with it all. And then I wouldn't be in the shit and you wouldn't have the past coming back to haunt you. Sorry, I interrupted you. What happened after you saw Zac?'

'I fainted. I guess it was the shock and the memory of it all. Jack Thornton was there and caught me. The nurse came and when I woke up I was on a bed. I had the scan to make sure the baby was OK. And she's fine. Then I saw the obstetrician who told me I need to eat better.'

'Well, as you know who your man is, you don't have to work over the weekend. He's not going anywhere, is he?'

'No, he's not. But he's not my man any more. Wilson has told me to take a week off work. Dr Forbes signed me off.'

'In other words, he's kicked you off the case.'

'Exactly. He's getting Kerry to take over. But whether Zac ever gets charged is another matter.'

'Does Keira and her family know?'

'Not yet. It wouldn't be wise to tell them that the attacker is only a few beds away.'

42

FRIDAY

Friday morning dawned with neither of them needing to get up. Dougie had brought her breakfast in bed.

'Are there any restrictions on you travelling, Dougie? Do you have to stay here in case you need to be questioned again?'

'I'm not sure. I'd probably have to let them know where I was going. What were you thinking? We can go to London to see your mum if you want.'

Bernie bit her lip. She knew her suggestion wasn't going to go down well. 'I was thinking we could go to Scotland.'

Dougie drank his tea. He didn't look at her as he replied. 'The snow's hit them bad up there. It wouldn't be wise to go.'

Bernie considered pushing the subject but knew it wasn't worth it. 'It was just a thought. And I have to see Dr Forbes tomorrow anyway to get my blood pressure checked.'

Her phone began to buzz on the bedside cabinet.

'So much for being signed off. It's Kerry.' She answered the phone. 'Hi, Kerry.'

'Hi. I thought you might like to know that Keira's well enough to be moved off ICU later today. The super's thinking I should tell her family, after she's settled on the new ward, that we know who's responsible for the attack and we'll be making an arrest very soon.'

'I guess the super's hoping they won't find out her attacker has only been a few beds away from her.'

'No. That would not look good. At least we can start putting the evidence together. What do you want me to do about Leigh? She was looking into this Dean Foster guy.'

'Ah.' Bernie wasn't sure if she should tell Kerry or not. But it was pointless having Leigh look into an alias. 'It looks as though Zac Ambrose was using two other names – Dean Collins and Dean Foster.'

'OK. I'm not going to ask how you know that. But it means Leigh can stop trying to find him.'

'Yes. We know where he is but it'll be worth her while looking for evidence to link him to the other attacks. Lucy should be able to help with that. Find out if there were any dark clothes taken when the police raided Ambrose. There might be some of Keira's DNA on them. And maybe some of the other victims too. I know Therese said there was nothing on Keira's clothes but ask her to check again for Zac's DNA. And what about the woman in Goddard Avenue? Did Leigh get anything useful from her?'

'Yeah, she did. Some CCTV footage showing a man dealing drugs in the access road last Sunday night. You can't tell if it's Zac Ambrose though. As for the rest of it, I might need to talk to the super first. I don't know how much access we're going to get to Ambrose's belongings. It's a Met operation really.'

Bernie sighed. She really wanted to be back in MCIT and directing this all herself. But it was important Kerry played by the rules.

'OK. Talk to the super and let me know how you go. Oh, the rocks. Anything found there?'

'No blood on any of them so weapon still out there somewhere. I'll ask if anything was picked up in the drugs raid.

Anyway, you enjoy a few days off. Come back to us fit and healthy. Bye.'

'Bye, Kerry. Say hi to everyone for me.'

Bernie put her phone down.

'You're going to struggle not working, aren't you?' said Anderson.

'And you're not?'

'Touché. You're right. We should do something to take our minds off of this.' He leaned across and kissed her. 'But not Scotland. At least not for now.'

A pub lunch seemed to be the best option for the day. It wasn't long before Paul Bentley and his wife, Anna, joined them.

'We don't often see you in here at this time of the day,' said Anna. 'A rare day off?'

Bernie didn't really want to explain. 'Something like that. Do you want to join us? Haven't spoken to you in ages.' Bernie looked at Dougie. 'You don't mind, do you, Dougie?'

'No. Be our guests.'

There were occasional moments when she'd wondered if she'd done the right thing at the beginning of the year, and it had been Anna she'd turned to before telling Dougie; Anna's arms she had sobbed in.

'I just don't know what to do,' Bernie had said.

They had been in Anna's car, parked outside the Well Woman Clinic.

'It's all such a mess. Dougie keeps asking me what's wrong. How do I tell him? Christmas was awful. I told him I had a stomach bug but I can't keep that up much longer. The logical part of me says that this is the only way. But.' She shook her head. 'What do I do, Anna?'

Anna had gently wiped the tears from Bernie's face. 'Only

you can decide that. Whatever you choose to do, I'll be here for you.'

And she had. Not once had she judged Bernie.

'How's baby? I think you're due for a scan soon,' said Anna.

Bernie blinked the memory away. 'Yes, I had it yesterday. Everything's fine.'

'That's good news.'

Anna smiled but there was sadness in her eyes. Bernie knew they had lost a baby daughter to cot death. She wanted to tell them she was having a girl but thought it wise not to. Besides, she hadn't even told her own parents yet.

Paul placed a couple of drinks down on the table. 'Sue will bring the food over when it's ready. Good to see you both together. I guess that doesn't happen very often.'

Bernie smiled. 'No, it doesn't. I was just telling Anna I had my scan yesterday. Everything's OK.'

'Fantastic. Now, I'm not sure how best to broach this so I'll just be upfront. I know you have different Christian backgrounds – Catholic and Baptist. So I don't know what your plans are for after the birth but if you want to christen the baby then just let me know. But equally, if you'd rather have a dedication type service, I'd be happy to do that. Or maybe you don't want to do anything.'

Bernie looked at Dougie. 'We haven't really thought about it, to be honest. I think it's something we'll discuss after the baby's born.'

Anna squeezed her hand. 'There's no rush.' Unlike her husband, she was aware of the full situation. If Alex turned out to be the father, would he want a say? And if he was, would Dougie really stay?

43

SATURDAY

Dr Forbes unstrapped the blood pressure band.

'Fantastic,' she said. 'Still a little high but that seems to be your norm anyway. Keep doing whatever you're doing.'

'What? Not working?'

Dr Forbes smiled. 'Try not to work too hard. Besides, I heard on the news this morning the man responsible for the attacks in Swindon has been found. I'm assuming that's what you've been working on.'

'Very perceptive of you,' said Bernie. 'Maybe you should become a detective.'

Dr Forbes laughed. 'I'm happy to stay a GP. But your team should have this all wrapped up by the time you go back. Hopefully it will be a while before you're having to investigate anything else.'

'I doubt it. People do stupid things all the time. Actual premeditated murders are rare but a stray punch or a push down the stairs in a moment of madness are far more common.' Bernie sighed. 'It would be nice to have a breather for a while but I think I'd go mad if I didn't have something to investigate.'

'Well, I'm happy for you to go back to work next week. Any

dizzy spells or bad headaches – just contact me. And think of these next few days as bonding time with your baby. She can hear you now, so talk to her. Get Dougie to do the same.'

That's a good idea – get Dougie to bond with the baby now.

'Thank you, Dr Forbes. I'll see you soon.'

Bernie walked back to her car. She'd heard the news report earlier that had mentioned the attacks. It had probably been Jane's idea to release the information the police had their man. It had been carefully worded. No mention of arrest or being questioned, just that he had been found. Definitely ambiguous. Bernie wondered how Keira's parents had taken the news and if they were still none the wiser that their daughter's attacker had only been a few metres away from them.

Her phone vibrated in her pocket. She pulled it out, saw Kerry's name on the screen and swiped to answer.

'Is this my daily check-in, making sure I'm behaving?' Bernie asked.

'Something like that. I just thought you might want a quick update. I guess you heard the news this morning.'

'Yes, I did. Let me guess – Jane's idea?'

'Totally. A bit of good news for Wiltshire Police. Of course, no one mentioned that the suspect is the same man hit by a lorry after a police raid. There won't be a press conference for it. But you know what Clive Bishop is like. He always finds out info somehow.'

Bernie smiled and thought about the older journalist from Salisbury. Other officers dismissed him as a washed-up hack but his years of experience of working in local newspapers made him a valuable asset. Bernie recognised his worth.

'He's a good guy really. Any other news?'

'Oh yes, I nearly forgot. Debs told me that Zac Ambrose's mother turned up at the hospital this morning. She's caused a bit of a stir apparently. She threw out your old boss – what's his name again?'

'Jack Thornton.'

'Yes. Told him to go away, with quite a few expletives added in. Debs had trouble settling her down. Anyway, she's by her son's bedside now and has said she doesn't want to see any police until after Zac wakes up.'

'If he wakes up.'

'Debs has said that he's doing better. It's still early days but they're more hopeful that he'll recover.'

'Good. I want to see him face trial for what he's done to Keira and the other victims.'

'You're not afraid to see his mother again? Debs said she's quite formidable.'

Bernie pictured the woman she had last seen a few years before. Jade Ambrose – hair in box braids, gold hoop earrings and a heavy gold chain around her neck (bought for her by her sons) and long nails painted in vibrant colours. She had dressed up to the nines for Danny's court case. Jade Ambrose could never be accused of being understated. But hiding in her shadow, with his head down and shy smile concealed, had been her youngest son, Joshua. Bernie wondered what had happened to him. A young teenager with Down's syndrome, his brothers had cruelly used him to carry drugs for them. Was he still living with his mother?

'I don't mind seeing her again,' said Bernie. 'But I'm more than happy for DCI Thornton to handle this one.'

There was a vague warmth to the sun as Bernie sat in her little back garden with Dougie but she still had her coat pulled in tight.

'So Mum said it was fine to come?' asked Bernie.

'Yes. Said something about it being good timing. Gary's over, apparently.'

'It'll be nice to see him.'

Although Bernie had only known her father for less than a year, he was starting to feel part of the family. And her parents rekindling their relationship was the icing on the cake.

'What time do you want to leave in the morning?'

'Not too early. Maybe about ten. Gary's going to cook a full-on Jamaican lunch.'

'Light breakfast then.'

'Yes. I'll need to go and get petrol before tomorrow. Best price is in the opposite direction of the M4.'

'Go now if you want.'

Anderson took her hand and kissed it lightly. 'I'd much rather just sit here with you for now. I'll go later this evening.'

Bernie zipped up her large overnight bag. Apart from a few toiletries, she had everything she needed packed for the next couple of days. Going to London normally made her apprehensive but knowing that Zac and Jade Ambrose were in Swindon made her feel easier. Plus Dougie would be with her and her father would be there. She felt the baby move. She remembered what Dr Forbes said so she started chatting to her unborn child.

'So, little Bun, we're going to see Grandma and Granddad tomorrow. They're going to be so excited when you're born. We all are. Although...' The thought of paternity tests made Bernie stop.

'Who were you talking to?'

Dougie was standing in the bedroom doorway.

'The baby. She can hear us now. Dr Forbes was encouraging me to talk to her. You too.'

'Was she now?' Dougie put his hand on Bernie's belly and

bent his head down. 'Hello, baby girl. I've been very silly and forgot to get petrol. I'll have to go now.'

Bernie looked at the clock. 'But it's almost ten. We can get it in the morning. It doesn't matter if it's a bit more expensive.'

'I'd rather go now and then we don't have to stop when we hit the M4.' He kissed her. 'I don't mind going. I won't be long. You go to bed. I'll make sure I'm quiet when I get back.'

44

SUNDAY

The car was packed, ready to go. Bernie knew, in a few months' time, it wouldn't be as easy as slinging two bags in the boot. There'd be a buggy, changing bag, car seat, travel cot, baby sling...

'Ready?' Anderson gave her a huge grin.

She had been fast asleep when he'd come back from getting the petrol. Not working had definitely improved her sleeping patterns.

'I might just go to the loo one more time. Especially if you don't want to stop.'

Anderson laughed. 'God, Bernie. If you're like this now, what are you going to be like when you're full-term?'

Bernie was just washing her hands when she felt her phone buzz in her trouser pocket. She dried her hands quickly and pulled it out. It was Kerry.

'Seriously, you don't have to check in with me every day. I promise I'm behaving myself. We're just about to go to London.'

'Unfortunately, I don't think you are. I'm really sorry, Bernie, but you and Dougie need to come to headquarters.'

'Why?'

'Because... Jade Ambrose is here, screaming blue murder.'

'That doesn't surprise me. That woman causes a commotion wherever she goes.'

'No, she's literally screaming murder. Zac Ambrose died last night. She's gunning for Anderson.'

They were silent as they made the short journey to Devizes. Bernie had rung her parents to say they would be late, if they got there at all. Gary had been disappointed. He'd started cooking at seven a.m.

'I'm really hoping we can still come, Gary, but I'm not sure. I'll give you a call later.'

'I hope so too. Got a lot of food here!'

'We'll try.'

Anderson pulled into headquarters and parked the car. He reached over and squeezed Bernie's hand. 'I'm sure it won't take too long, whatever it is. It's probably just the super letting me know the IPCC investigation will ratchet up now that Zac Ambrose has died.'

Bernie looked at him. He seemed calm but there was a hint of worry in his dark eyes. 'It doesn't make sense though. Debs told Kerry yesterday that they expected Zac Ambrose to recover. So why is he now dead?'

'We'll have to wait for Nick White to do the post-mortem.'

'Assuming he's allowed to do it. The Met might want to bring in one of their London pathologists since he was injured during their operation.'

'Well, we won't know if we stay out here. Are you worried about seeing his mother, given what you've been through because of Danny Ambrose?'

Bernie paused. She'd told Kerry yesterday she was fine to see Jade Ambrose but that was when Zac was still alive. But now he was dead – what did that mean for Dougie? Once Jade knew the connection between them, Dougie wouldn't have a hope. Her scar began to itch.

'Come on,' said Dougie, 'let's get this over and done with. Then we can drive on to London.'

Bernie heard Jade Ambrose before she saw her. Her south London accent boomed down the corridor from the super's office.

Jane Clackett was standing nearby. 'Oh, thank God you're here. Come into my office for a moment.'

Bernie and Anderson shuffled into the small but very neat space. Bernie sat on the spare chair.

'What's going on?' asked Anderson. 'She doesn't sound very happy.'

'She's not,' said Jane. 'Until the post-mortem is done, we're not very sure what's happened. Yesterday, Zac Ambrose was making progress. His mother said he briefly woke up and spoke to her. The doctors were confident he would recover. But overnight, he slipped away.'

'So how could that be murder?' asked Bernie.

'According to Jade, his vital signs were good. Apparently she used to be a nurse. She went off for a cigarette and to go to the toilet around eleven p.m. When she came back about thirty minutes later, his vital signs were dropping and the alarms on the machines were going off. The doctors and nurses did their best but couldn't save him. She thinks something happened while she was away.'

Bernie rubbed her forehead. There was a stab of pain in her temple. She could almost feel her blood pressure rising. Why are we here? she thought. We were nowhere near the hospital yesterday. And then she remembered. Dougie had gone out for petrol and she had no idea what time he'd come home. Surely he hadn't done anything stupid?

'What do we do? Knock on the super's door?' Bernie asked.

'No, I'll call him,' said Jane. She picked up her phone.

Bernie spoke quietly to Anderson. 'I don't understand why she wants to talk to me. Last time I saw her, she told me she'd see me in hell. Unless she's found out about Keira and knows I was leading the investigation. Or maybe she knows we're together and plans on taking us both down.'

Anderson put his arm around her. 'We know the truth and we just have to say it, no matter how painful it might be for Jade Ambrose to hear.'

'You sound like Pops.'

'I'll take that as a compliment.'

Pops had come with her to Danny Ambrose's trial when she'd had to give evidence.

'You don't have to come with me. I have given evidence before in court,' she'd said.

'Yes, I know. But you hadn't been stabbed and left for dead those times. More than that, I want to see him. I want to see the man who nearly stole you from us. And I want to see his mother. I've heard about her. She claims to be a God-fearing woman but she isn't. You just tell the truth and the good Lord will do the rest.' And Pops had held her, just as Anderson was doing now.

'Right,' said Jane. 'The super will see you both now.'

45

Jade Ambrose had her back to them when they entered Detective Chief Superintendent Wilson's office.

'Ah, DI Noel and DI Anderson. Thank you for coming in when you're supposed to be having some time off.'

Mrs Ambrose still didn't turn round but Bernie noticed her shoulders stiffen at the mention of her name.

'DI Anderson, I only have one spare chair. Perhaps you could go and grab another from somewhere.'

Bernie didn't want Dougie to leave her. Her throat was tightening and the throb in her head was increasing.

'Yes, sir.' He brushed his fingers on her thigh as he left the room.

The super smiled at her. 'Please sit down, DI Noel.' He was deliberately keeping it formal.

Keeping her eyes forward, she pulled back the chair and sat down. The office door opened and Anderson placed a chair in between her and Jade. Bernie was grateful for his consideration in protecting her.

Wilson laced his fingers together. 'Well, as I said, thank you for coming in. DI Noel, I know you have already met Mrs Ambrose. DI Anderson, this is Zac Ambrose's mother.'

Anderson turned his head and nodded. A handshake was not appropriate.

'Mrs Ambrose and I have been speaking at length this morning.' Wilson paused, seemingly lost for words. 'I have offered her our condolences for the death of her son, Zac. Mrs Ambrose is keen to know what happened to her son. I have explained to her that the IPCC will conduct a full investigation. However, Mrs Ambrose isn't fully satisfied with that and has an unusual request.'

Wilson looked directly at Bernie. 'It involves you, DI Noel. It might be better if Mrs Ambrose explains it herself.'

Bernie knew she had to look at Jade. It would be rude not to. She turned her head to the right and looked past Anderson. Jade was looking forward. She now had a natural afro but still had the gold hoop earrings and necklace. There were streaks of mascara on her cheek, and as Bernie watched, she raised her hand to wipe away a tear. Her nail polish was lime green but a couple of the nails were broken.

'Jade, I'm sorry for your loss,' said Bernie.

'No, you're not. You're worried about lover boy next to you.' Jade turned her head and stared directly at Bernie. 'He's the one who put Zac in hospital.' She nodded at Bernie's abdomen. 'I see he's also put a baby in your belly. Congratulations. I hope you're ready to be a mother. Then you'll know what it's like to have your heart ripped out. You're not just living for yourself any more.' Her hand came up to her cheek again.

'You still have Joshua, Jade. And he needs you very much. How is he?'

'Don't you mention Joshua!' Jade's nostrils flared. 'He's a good boy.'

Bernie's hands were clammy. She tried to keep her voice

even. 'I know he's a good boy. Although I guess he's a young man now. I'm assuming he's being looked after.'

'He's still in Jamaica with my aunt. I had to ring him this morning and tell him his brother is dead. He's the reason why I'm here. You made a real impression on him all those years ago.' Jade shook her head. 'He's such an innocent. He really liked you.'

Bernie thought of the sweet-natured boy who'd followed her round the youth club when she was undercover. 'I liked him.'

'Well, he doesn't understand that you were there to deceive us. That you're the one responsible for putting Danny away.'

Bernie's scar itched. She opened her mouth to retort but changed her mind. Jade had never believed her eldest son was capable of such violence; had always insisted that the police had stitched him up.

Jade looked away. 'When I told Joshua I thought someone had hurt Zac, he said, "Ask Bernie to help. She's a good police officer." And as much as I dislike you for what you did to Danny, Joshua's right. You were only following orders back then. You are a good officer.' Jade looked back at Bernie. 'Which is why I want you to investigate Zac's death.'

Bernie's mouth dropped open. 'What? I'm not sure that's going to be possible. There are so many reasons why I shouldn't. It's not standard practice, to begin with. It should be the IPCC. And that's even before the complication of DI Anderson being the one investigated over Zac's escape. Plus, it looks as though Zac was responsible for a string of sexual offences that I was looking into.' Bernie looked at Wilson. 'Sir, I can't. I won't.'

Wilson shrugged. 'Sorry, Bernie. Top brass have agreed you can investigate.'

Bernie looked away, shaking her head, angry at what she was being asked to do. She was supposed to be taking it easy, decreasing her stress, not escalating it.

'Oh, you'll do it,' said Jade. 'Apart from the fact you owe me for sending my eldest son to prison, I think you're very fond of this one here.' She pointed at Anderson. 'At the moment, he's the one who's going to be hung out to dry for Zac's death. Out of interest, where were you last night, DI Anderson?'

Dougie looked bemused. 'I'm not sure you have the right to ask me that.'

'Humour me.'

'I was at home with Bernie.'

'All night?'

'Yes... ah, I went out for petrol.'

'What time?'

'Just before ten p.m.'

'And what time did you get back?'

'I'm not sure. About ten thirty.'

'And she can confirm that?'

'No, she was already asleep but I have a receipt and there's CCTV at the garage... Sir, this is ludicrous.'

Jade Ambrose crossed her legs. 'It would be so easy to make a case against you. When Zac woke up yesterday, he told me a few things. He was worried someone wanted to kill him. So he passed crucial information on to me. I wrote it all down.'

'But it's hearsay, Jade, it won't stand up in court,' Bernie said.

'No, of course it won't. I'm not stupid. But you can use it to find out who killed Zac. Because, trust me, someone wanted him dead.'

'Then you need to hand it all over to the IPCC. Sir, this is ridiculous. I'm signed off sick. Dougie's suspended because of Zac's accident.'

'It was no accident,' insisted Jade.

Bernie stood up. 'No, I'm not doing this. It's a massive conflict of interest with DI Anderson being investigated. I don't understand why the chief constable has agreed to it. We were on our way to see my family and that's what we're going to do.

Come on, Dougie.' Bernie's hand was on the door handle when Jade spoke again.

'I understand. Thank you for at least listening. Of course, it's such a shame you won't find out the truth about what really happened to you when you were stabbed.'

Bernie stopped and turned back to Jade. 'What do you mean?'

'You've always thought it was your fault you blew your cover.' Jade shook her head. 'Find Zac's killer and I'll tell you who grassed you up.'

46

'What? We can't investigate this. That's just stupid!' Kerry dumped her tea bag in the food waste. 'She's having a laugh, right? It's not like we'll be any better than the IPCC.'

Bernie leaned back against the work surface in the small kitchen. 'Sadly, she's not. Jade Ambrose has me over a barrel. We might not be better than the IPCC but there's more of a chance that people will talk to me than a formal hearing, especially if they want to stay anonymous. Besides, if I don't do it, she'll drop Dougie in the shit. Claim that he's responsible somehow.'

'All because he went out for petrol last night? How did she even know that?'

'She didn't. But she figured on me being asleep. Difficult to truly alibi someone when you're sleeping.'

'Yeah, but the super heard her threaten you.'

It wasn't the threat that had persuaded Bernie. She knew Anderson would prove his innocence in the end. It was the question that had haunted her for the last few years – why had her undercover operation gone so wrong? If Jade Ambrose really knew the answer, then Bernie was willing to do anything to find out.

'I'm not sure it matters that the super heard. Jade Ambrose has a loud voice and she's not afraid to use it. She made a small fortune selling her story after Danny's trial. She did the whole "he's such a good boy" routine – claiming it was self-defence, which makes a mockery of those really good kids who get stabbed and killed, whether it's mistaken identity or simply wrong time, wrong place. And she used Joshua for those articles. "Look at me with my poor disabled son." She sensibly kept Zac out of the way though.'

Bernie rubbed her forehead. The throbbing was constant. She longed to take some ibuprofen but knew she was only allowed paracetamol. They barely touched the pain but it was better than nothing.

'Anyway,' Bernie continued, 'is everyone in? We need to start looking at this.'

'Yes,' answered Kerry. 'Even Leigh.'

Bernie looked at her team sitting around the large table in the meeting room – Matt, Alice, Mick and Leigh. She'd given the pen to Kerry to scribe on the whiteboard. Zac Ambrose's name was written in the middle, with DECEASED written underneath.

'Thank you for coming in on a Sunday, especially as you were all expecting a rest day today. OK, this is slightly unusual, but we've been asked to investigate Zac Ambrose's death.'

'Shouldn't we wait until the post-mortem?' asked Matt. 'We don't know that it's suspicious.'

'No, we don't. Which is why I said death rather than murder. At the moment we have no idea. I've been told that Nick White will do the post-mortem this afternoon. But in the meantime, we have to start thinking about possibilities. And quite honestly, I need your help here. So give me your ideas, no matter how mad they might sound.'

Bernie heard the clock ticking as the room went quiet, her team lost in thought for a few moments.

'I still think it's natural,' said Matt. 'Not many people get hit by a lorry and live to tell the tale.'

'True. Put that up, Kerry.'

Kerry drew a line out from Zac's name and wrote – 'NATURAL CAUSES. DIED FROM INJURIES SUSTAINED FROM THE ACCIDENT'.

Alice raised her hand. 'Ma'am, it could be natural causes from something not damaged in the accident, like a heart attack.'

Kerry drew another line.

'It could be human error,' said Mick. 'You know, wrong drugs given by accident.'

'In that case,' said Bernie, 'we're looking at negligence on the hospital's part. Although a coroner may judge it as misadventure.'

Bernie looked at Leigh. Her eyes were glazed over, her mind somewhere else.

'Leigh, any thoughts?'

Leigh's head shook slightly as though startled. 'Sorry, ma'am, I was just trying to work something out. It's a bit like a "locked room" mystery.'

'Sounds like an Agatha Christie book.'

'Well, in a way, yes. ICU has a buzzer on the door. You either have to be buzzed in or have a pass to gain access. So, if Zac was murdered...'

'How did the murderer get in?' said Bernie. 'Good idea, Leigh. Keep thinking along those lines.'

Bernie looked at the board. Kerry had just written up Leigh's idea.

'So we've covered natural causes, misadventure and murder,' said Bernie.

'Or it could be manslaughter,' said Kerry. 'Someone wanted to keep Zac quiet but not necessarily kill him.'

'Yes, add that as well.' Bernie looked at the clock. It was almost midday. They needed a list of actions.

'Do we know if the scene has been contained?' she asked.

Kerry shuffled slightly. 'I'm not sure. I didn't think to ask as I assumed we wouldn't be looking into it. I'm hoping it has been. Along with all the medical equipment.'

'Particularly his IV drip,' said Leigh. 'If Zac was poisoned via the drip, there may be remnants of the drug in the fluid. Might be easier to check than wait for toxicology results from the body.'

'Or it could have been administered straight into the blood stream with an injection,' said Bernie. 'There must be lots of needle marks on his body with his treatment. Another one could easily go unnoticed. Right, first port of call is the hospital. Do we know if the CSIs have been called?'

'Yes,' said Kerry. 'Lucy's going to meet us there.'

Bernie thought for a moment. Kerry wasn't going to like her next question. 'Is it wise that you come? Given that Debs works in ICU.'

'Is it wise that you lead this investigation, given that your partner is considered to be responsible for Zac Ambrose being in ICU in the first place?'

Bernie gave a wry smile. Only Kerry could get away with talking to her like that. 'Come on then. You as well, Leigh. Let's go and check out your "locked room". The rest of you, get me a full background check on Zac Ambrose. Find out who might want to harm him.'

47

Bernie leaned back in the passenger seat as Kerry drove to Swindon. She texted Dougie to see how he was. He'd had the job of telling her parents they wouldn't be coming.

Did they take it OK?

>*They were fine. I didn't tell them who you were dealing with though.*

No, don't tell them. Mum will go mad. And Gary doesn't even know about it all.

>*I don't even know it all! Maybe you could tell me sometime?*

Bernie scratched her head. How could she tell Dougie what had happened when she wasn't even sure herself?

I will one day. Just let me deal with this first. Don't know what time I'll be home. I'll text you later. X

Kerry found somewhere to park in the crowded car park. It was close to visiting time.

'You know,' said Kerry, 'I've been thinking about what you said and maybe I shouldn't interview any of the staff. I know quite a few of them through Debs. Do you want me to go and check out the CCTV footage instead?'

'I think that's probably a good idea. You do that, and Leigh, you come with me.'

They got out of the car and headed towards the hospital.

Leaving Kerry at main reception, Bernie and Leigh headed to ICU.

'Keep your eyes out for cameras, Leigh. Then we can give Kerry an idea of where to look.'

'DI Noel?'

Bernie turned to see Lucy a few paces behind them. She was carrying a large case with her and a camera. 'Hi, Lucy.'

'I saw you in the car park and I've been trying to catch up with you.'

'Oh, sorry. I was just saying to Leigh that the CCTV might be able to help us if someone else is involved. If I remember rightly, time of death was close to midnight last night. There couldn't have been that many people around at the time.'

'Oh, I don't know,' said Lucy. 'A&E is always busy through the night so there's often patients wandering around who need X-rays or whatever. It's never completely quiet here.'

They took the lift to ICU. It smelt strongly of disinfectant. Bernie had found that pregnancy had increased her sense of smell. The odour of the hospital would be multiplied by ten when they went to the post-mortem later.

When they reached ICU, Bernie looked for a camera. There was a small one above the door. She thought the staff probably used it to see who was waiting outside. But was it a recording camera? She pressed the buzzer and they were let in, squirting a blob of antiseptic gel onto their hands as they entered.

'Back again, DI Noel? Have you not got anything better to do? You can't seem to keep away.' It was Rachel, the nurse who had looked after Keira. There was a barbed tone to her voice. Bernie chose to ignore it.

'Well, you know. Hopefully there's nothing in this and Zac Ambrose died of natural causes. Plus, the sooner we can get a bed back in action, the better it's for you.'

Rachel nodded. 'I agree. We pulled the curtains round it and stuck a chair in front. That was the best we could do. And yes, we do need that bed back. We had to turn someone away earlier.'

Lucy put on a forensic suit before she headed over. 'I'm afraid I don't have any spares with me. I do have shoe covers though. So you can look, after I've processed everything.'

'OK. We'll chat with some of the staff as best we can,' said Bernie.

As well as Rachel, there were five more members of staff – four nurses and one doctor. They all looked quite busy. Bernie needed to know who had been on the night before. Who had dealt with Zac? She only knew Rachel so thought she'd stick with her.

'Sorry to bother you again, Rachel, but I need to know who was on duty last night.'

Rachel sighed deeply. 'Really you should deal with HR, because that's hospital policy, but I'll write down the names for you. It's all very sad but sometimes patients go downhill rapidly and die.'

'His mother disagrees. She said his vital signs were good. Even the doctors agreed.'

'Yes, but it's not uncommon for someone to rally just before they die. See it all the time. Maybe you should just wait for the post-mortem.'

'If we did that then the bed would be out of action for even longer.'

Bernie was aware of a flash behind her. Lucy had pulled back the curtains and was taking photos.

'Do you have to use flash?' asked Rachel. 'It's not helpful for some of our patients.'

'Sorry. I'll close the curtains again.'

'I'm going to need his medical records as well please,' said Bernie. She noticed Leigh was wandering around, muttering to herself.

'No can do, I'm afraid. They went with him to the morgue. You'll have to ask the pathologist for them.'

Leigh was now trying a couple of doors to see if they would open. 'What's in these rooms?' she asked.

'One's for storage, the other for cleaning materials.'

'Do you know the cleaners well?' Bernie asked.

'Used to. Until it got contracted out. Now it's rare to see the same cleaner twice in a week.'

'What time do they come?'

'Early morning and late evening,' said Rachel.

'And what about if you have an emergency spillage of bodily fluids? You know, blood or... other stuff everywhere. Is there someone available all the time?'

'Well, yes. In fact, I think someone said that happened last night. I'm not sure though. You'll have to check with the night shift. Here are their names. HR can give you more details.'

Bernie scanned the list. She was glad Debs' name wasn't on it. She turned to Leigh. 'Right then, Miss Marple, let's see if we can solve this locked room mystery.'

'I know I said it's a locked room mystery but there are ways around it. Obtaining a pass, for example. Or they're known to staff or have good reason to be there.'

'But to be there in the middle of the night?' asked Bernie.

Leigh paused for a moment. 'They might not have been there that late. If something was injected into Zac, it could be a delayed reaction. It might have been given earlier. And perhaps even unwittingly.'

Bernie stopped and looked at Leigh. 'So his meds could have been tampered with. Not just an accident like Mick suggested. Now, there's a thought.'

48

The woman in HR peered over her glasses at Bernie and Leigh. She looked stressed.

'I can't give you that information. Our systems went down overnight due to a failed data patch. I've had to come in especially to try and sort it all out. And even if they were working, that information is confidential,' she said.

'Well, how am I supposed to contact these members of staff then?'

'You're the detective.'

'Can you at least give me the details for your cleaning company then please? Maybe they'll be a bit more obliging. I don't think you understand how important this is.'

'I can give you that information but not our staff details. When you have proof of foul play then maybe I can help you further. I suggest you leave your number with the ICU staff to pass on to their colleagues. Then that way they can contact you directly. Sorry.' The look on the woman's face suggested she was anything but.

Bernie turned on her heel. 'Let's see if Kerry has got on any better with the CCTV.'

. . .

Kerry was deep in conversation with a security guard when they arrived.

'Hi, Bernie, do you want the good news or the bad news?' asked Kerry.

Bernie sighed. 'Let's get the bad news dealt with first.'

'There's no good news. The cameras went down for a while yesterday late evening. They managed to get the feed back but no recording.'

Bernie raised her eyes to the ceiling. 'Shit. What caused the problem?'

The security guard shrugged. 'Some kind of tech issue. The IT guys were running a data patch and it went wrong. Knocked everything out – all the hospital computer systems. Sorry.'

'Bloody hell, that's all we need. Let's head back to ICU and see how Lucy is doing.'

Lucy was just finishing up.

'Hi, DI Noel. All done. I've bagged up the evidence and taken photos. The ICU staff aren't going to like this but I'll need to take this heart monitor as well.'

There were brown paper bags and clear plastic ones lying on the bed.

'Do you have the IV fluid bag and tubes?' asked Bernie.

'Yes. That'll be the first thing the lab will test. They might have some results by the end of tomorrow but I can't guarantee. I'll need a copy of his notes to see what should be in there. That will help me narrow down any anomalies.'

'Good luck with that. The notes have gone with the body to Nick White.'

'No, it's OK. Rachel's printing out a spare set for me.'

'What?' Bernie's head began to throb. 'She told me I couldn't have the notes. I don't think she likes me.'

Kerry touched her arm. 'Leave it with me. She's probably just a bit defensive with everything going on. I know some of the other staff on today. I'll get a copy of the notes from one of them.'

Bernie rubbed her head. She wished she hadn't said yes now. And more importantly, she wished the IPCC had said no. She still didn't know how the chief constable had got them to agree. It was completely wrong. What she was most concerned about was how much power Jade Ambrose had in all of this. She was definitely Queen in this elaborate game of chess and Bernie was simply a pawn.

'DI Noel?'

Bernie pulled her hand away.

'Would you be able to carry down something for me to my van please?' asked Lucy.

'Yes. Although preferably something light.'

'Of course. The bedding isn't too bad. Leigh, could you take the IV stuff please? It's a bit more awkward to carry.'

Leigh picked up the bag and Lucy passed the bedding to Bernie.

'Why do you need the heart monitor again?' asked Bernie.

'Really just to make sure it was working properly. If it was faulty, it wouldn't have registered Zac's heartbeat properly. So in other words, he might have been going downhill for a while before anyone noticed. It's probably a bit far-fetched but worth exploring.'

'I'm not sure that anything's going to be too "far-fetched" with this case,' said Bernie. 'It's already pretty bonkers.'

Kerry appeared with an A4 envelope in her hand. 'Here you go. Full set of notes for Zac Ambrose plus the staff list for yesterday – day and night shifts. Thought it important that we look at all the staff.'

'When was Debs last on?'

'Previous night. She's on a break now for a couple of days.'

'OK. Well, I think it might be best to get Matt and Alice to look at the staff. It could be awkward for you if you know any of them.'

'I know. But looking at this list there might be one or two who might open up to me more, if you know what I mean.'

'What – gossip?'

Kerry gave a wry smile. 'If you think the office politics in the police force is bad, you ought to work in the NHS. God, Debs comes home in a right state sometimes.'

'Hmm, OK. But only the ones you think will talk to you. The credibility of this investigation is already wafer thin. Grab something for Lucy and then we'll get out of here for now.'

They left ICU and headed back to the car park.

'What are we doing next, ma'am?' asked Leigh.

'Ever been to a post-mortem?'

Leigh paled.

'I thought not,' said Bernie.

49

Bernie dozed as Kerry drove south across the county to the mortuary in Salisbury. The journey would take nearly an hour and a half, so she allowed her mind to wander. She played out the morning scenes, trying to make sense of it all. She still didn't understand why the super had given Jade such leeway. It was highly irregular. There had to be something else going on. But her befuddled brain held no answers.

There was a gentle tap on her arm. 'We're here, Bernie. Time to wake up,' said Kerry.

Bernie groaned. She hated post-mortems. She turned in her seat to look at Leigh. She was now the colour of chalk.

'If it makes you feel any better, Leigh, I hate these too. But it's part and parcel of the job.'

'Not for a local crime investigator.'

'Maybe, but you're part of MCIT at the moment.'

Leigh sighed. She was trembling. 'It's not just the actual body and all the medical stuff, it's the smell, the flickering of the strip lighting, the sound of the saw. I easily get overwhelmed with too much sensory stimulation.'

Kerry looked quizzically at Bernie.

As much as she knew she had to keep it confidential, Bernie thought she might have to explain a few things about Leigh to Kerry.

'It's OK, Leigh,' said Bernie. 'You can stay in the car. Maybe go through the paperwork from the hospital. See if anything stands out to you. Come on, Kerry.'

As they walked across the car park, Kerry looked back at the car.

'I don't understand why you let her off. Is there something you're not telling me?'

Bernie paused for a moment, weighing up what she should say. 'It's her first time and you know what I'm like. You don't want to deal with both of us fainting, do you?' She, too, glanced back at the car. She would need Leigh's permission before she could say anything.

Bernie was prepared for the smell that would hit with the whoosh of the doors opening but it was even worse than expected. It smelt like the entire contents of a fridge switched off for a month with the door shut. She staggered slightly. She didn't even want to contemplate what had caused it.

'Sorry,' said Dr Nick White. 'Had a particularly bad one this morning. I won't give you too much detail, DI Noel, I know what you're like. Don't want you in a heap on the floor. Hope you're made of stronger stuff, DS Allen.'

'Oh yes, Dr White, you don't have to worry about me. I'll keep an eye on Bernie.'

'Good. Right, let's get Mr Ambrose out here then.'

A technician wheeled Zac Ambrose's body into the room. Bernie gripped the rail on the viewing platform. It wasn't the sight of his dead body that shocked her, it was the serenity on his face that caught her breath. Zac Ambrose had always been full of anger. Now, he was at peace.

Nick White spoke aloud, his voice being recorded. 'We have the body of a young black male, aged twenty years. Name is Zac David Ambrose.' He paused and shook his head. 'Too young.'

Bernie bit her lip. *And now we'll never know why he brutally attacked Keira and those other women.* Keira. She mentally kicked herself for not visiting her when they were at the hospital in Swindon. She decided she'd wait until she could reveal that her attacker was dead. For obvious reasons, there was currently a news blackout.

Kerry took notes as the post-mortem continued. Nick White put up X-rays on the board and pointed out the injuries caused by the lorry accident – broken pelvis and left femur. Bernie knew other internal injuries would be found when White opened the body up. She could see the scar from the operation where he'd had his spleen removed. The pathologist closely examined Zac's body, pointing out each needle mark, scratch and bruise that he could see. It was important that White was thorough but it seemed to be taking much longer than normal.

Bernie struggled to concentrate. She glanced at her watch. It was close to five p.m. Her stomach rumbled. She hadn't eaten since breakfast. So much for her new good habits. She jumped when someone touched her arm and turned to see Anthony Markham behind her.

'What on earth are you doing here?' she asked.

He was as immaculately dressed as the first time Bernie had met him.

'Jade Ambrose has appointed me as her solicitor. She asked me to come to the post-mortem, make sure it was being done properly. I was hoping to be here for the start but got stuck in traffic.'

Bernie shook her head. 'I don't think that's a good idea.'

'It's OK, DI Noel, I have been to post-mortems before.'

'That's not what I meant. It's a conflict of interest for you.

We have evidence to suggest that Zac Ambrose was Keira's attacker.'

'What?' Anthony Markham took a step backwards, his eyes wide. 'Are you sure? How conclusive is the evidence?'

Bernie glanced at Kerry. 'I can't tell you what we have but enough to suggest that sexual intercourse occurred between them, and probably not consensual.'

'Shit.' Markham rubbed his face. 'You're right. I can't represent the Ambrose family now. And it's not like I can even pass it to another partner. I can recommend some other firms to Mrs Ambrose.' He looked across at the dead body on the slab. 'It's not how I like to see things done but I guess this is justice for Keira in one sense. She won't have to go through a trial.'

'No. Keira and her family don't know yet. I would be grateful if—'

'Of course. I won't say anything. It must be hard for you to have to investigate Zac's death now.'

Bernie sighed. Markham had no idea just how hard it was. 'It's not great but we have to be impartial in these things.'

'Yes. Like the doctors and nurses who treat them – victim and perpetrator. Incredible really. You're dealing with both Keira and Zac, just as my wife had to treat both of them.'

Bernie frowned. 'Your wife?'

'Yes. Rachel Bell. She refused to take my name when we got married. You might have seen her in ICU.'

Bernie thought about the obstructive ICU nurse and glanced at Kerry, who looked equally puzzled. 'Yes. We've met.' *But if Rachel knew who Keira was, why didn't she tell her husband?*

50

After another hour, the post-mortem still wasn't finished. Bernie was aware of Leigh sitting out in the car and guessed she would be starting to fret about getting home in time.

'How much longer, Nick?' she asked.

'Hmm. Not sure. This is a tricky one. I don't have an obvious cause of death at the moment. It's probably going to come down to toxicology and you know how long that can take.'

'Oh, great. Do you mind if we push off? We left a colleague in the car.'

'No, not at all. You've lasted much longer than you normally do, DI Noel. I'll try to send a provisional report to you tomorrow.'

'Thanks. Come on, Kerry. Let's hope Leigh's still all right.'

Leigh's head was buried in the paperwork. Bernie had had the foresight to text her before they came out so she wasn't startled by them. She looked up as they approached and smiled.

'God, you were ages. I was beginning to think you were trapped in there,' she said as they got into the car.

'You could have always come in and found us,' said Kerry. 'I left you the keys in case you wanted to get out.'

'No thanks. Think I'll stick to reading medical reports rather than actually seeing. Besides, this is fascinating stuff.'

'Really?' asked Bernie.

'Yes. Jade Ambrose was correct. Zac's vital signs were good. Then they suddenly dropped.'

'But Rachel said it wasn't uncommon for people to rally just before death,' said Bernie. 'Hey, guess what we've just found out about Nurse Bossy?'

'What?' asked Leigh.

'Guess who she's married to.'

'I don't know.'

'Have you had your head in the paperwork the whole time we were inside? Or did you notice anyone else around?'

Leigh shook her head. 'I've been focused on this.'

'So you didn't see Anthony Markham turn up then?'

'What? No. Why was he here?'

Bernie put her seat belt on as Kerry started the car. 'Jade Ambrose appointed him as solicitor. He'd come for the postmortem. Once I told him about Zac probably being Keira's attacker, he was out of there. Jade will not be happy. Quite like to be a fly on the wall for that one. She's going to go nuts.'

'And he's married to Rachel? The nurse who looked after Keira?'

'Yep. Right, Kerry, let's see if we can get back to headquarters by seven p.m. for a quick briefing and then everyone can go home. I'm definitely not pulling an all-nighter for the Ambrose family.'

Kerry dropped Bernie home just after seven forty-five p.m. She was exhausted. When she opened her front door she was met by a delicious – and familiar – smell.

'Dougie? Did Gary give you his recipe for jerk chicken?'

Anderson opened the lounge door and gave her a huge grin. 'Not exactly.'

'Is that my lovely daughter?' said a voice from the lounge.

'Gary?'

Dougie pulled back the door to reveal Gary Noel.

Bernie was overwhelmed with emotion and burst into tears. She fell into her father's arms.

'Couldn't let the chicken go to waste,' said Denise from behind her, tucking a strand of fair hair behind her ear. A good five inches shorter than her daughter she was standing in the doorway to the kitchen. She held out her arms to Bernie for a hug.

'Oh, Mum, Gary.' Bernie looked around at her family. 'This is exactly what I need. I've had such a shitty day.'

'Language, Bernadette!'

Bernie laughed. 'Oh, Mum. You sound like Granny!'

Anderson offered to dish up the food but Gary Noel made it clear that the kitchen was his temporary domain.

'Are you going back this evening?' Bernie asked her parents.

'No, we've booked a room at the pub for a week. Thought we'd have a little holiday,' said Denise and she squeezed her daughter's hand.

'I'm going to be working though.'

'That's OK,' said Gary. 'We're going to visit Bath and generally annoy Dougie.' He put plates of jerk chicken and rice in front of them all. 'Tuck in.'

Bernie's tongue tingled with the spices from the chicken. Her stomach was full. It was a squeeze with four of them around the small kitchen table.

Dougie took her hand and kissed it. He whispered into her ear, 'Do you want to tell them now about the baby?'

She smiled and nodded. 'So, we have something to tell you.' She waited until everyone was looking at her. 'Mum... Gary...'

He beamed at her.

'I had a scan last week and we're having a baby... girl.'

'Oh that's wonderful,' said Gary.

Denise started to cry. 'My baby girl is having a girl.' She leaned forward and kissed Bernie on the cheek.

'Do you think I should call Granny and tell her?' Bernie's grandmother had been lukewarm when she'd told her she was going to be a great-grandma.

Denise patted her hand. 'There's no rush. She's not exactly happy about me getting back with Gary.'

'OK.' She smiled at Denise. Her mother might have sounded like Granny earlier but Bernie knew she'd be a much better grandmother.

51

MONDAY

MCIT was already buzzing by the time Bernie arrived at work. She hated being late but her mother had insisted on cooking her pancakes for breakfast and she wasn't about to turn that down.

'Sorry, guys. My parents turned up last night so bit of a late one.'

Kerry smiled. 'Seeing that you're meant to be signed off sick, I think we can forgive you. This time.'

'Cheeky. Right, fabulous team. I'm going to grab a coffee and then we'll meet in the briefing room.'

Kerry took her position as scribe again.

'OK, we didn't make a huge amount of progress yesterday,' Bernie said, 'so we need a really big push today. We left Nick White still working on the post-mortem. I'm hoping Lucy and Therese might be able to come up with something. There was an IT failure at the hospital which meant the CCTV wasn't recording. So we're reliant on eyewitnesses. Have we got anywhere with the staff list and visitors to ICU?'

'Yes,' said Kerry. 'I got a phone call this morning from a

member of staff. Everyone is happy to talk to us and I also now have the names of others who came into ICU Saturday night.'

'Was there a name for the cleaner? Might be easier if we have a name to give the contractors,' Bernie asked.

'No. The person I spoke to said he was new and she didn't get a chance to ask his name.'

'Description?'

'Young, male and black.'

Bernie crossed her legs. 'Now that's interesting. Matt, your job today is to get on to the cleaning company and find out a name for our mystery cleaner. Did you get anything on Zac Ambrose yesterday?'

Matt shook his head. 'Not exactly. Access denied to his criminal record. Which is interesting in its own way.'

'It is.' Bernie thought for a moment. Who had done that and why? 'Anyone else, Kerry?'

'Well, it appears that Nurse Bell made a return visit after her shift had finished.'

'What? You mean Rachel Bell, aka Mrs Markham, Anthony Markham's wife?'

'Indeed I do.'

'Wait a minute,' Matt said. 'The lawyer who's Keira's boss? So does that mean she knows Keira and was treating her?'

'That's what I was wondering. I suppose Rachel might not have met her before. We'll have to ask her. Do we know if she's working today?' Bernie asked.

'She's not. Got a day off,' Kerry replied.

'Hmm. She's not a massive fan of mine. Mick and Alice, how about a little trip to Swindon? Chance to stretch your legs.'

Alice looked at Mick and nodded. 'Sure. Do you want us to call ahead first?'

Bernie pondered. 'No, I don't think so. A surprise visit would be better. OK, Kerry, who else popped into ICU Saturday evening?'

'Adam Howard, Keira's brother. Came in with some chocolates for the staff. And if I remember rightly, he's a student doctor.'

Bernie tapped her notebook with her pen after writing Adam's name down. 'We haven't told the Howard family about Zac Ambrose yet but is it possible that they, or maybe just Adam, found out somehow? I might need to have a chat with him.'

'Actually, Bernie, you might want to leave the Howard family to Leigh and me. There's someone else on the list that I think you need to talk to. And possibly with the super as well,' said Kerry.

Bernie was confused. 'Who?'

'DCI Jack Thornton.'

Bernie closed her eyes. 'Shit.'

DCI Jack Thornton pushed his sandy hair off his face. Bernie noticed it was a little thinner these days. A few more wrinkles around the blue eyes that had once dazzled her, convincing her everything would be OK. He leaned back in his chair. 'I'm a bit confused as to why I'm here.'

'We're just having a little chat, sir, about Zac Ambrose,' Bernie said.

'Oh come on. What's the "sir" nonsense about? And if we're just having a little chat, why is Detective Chief Superintendent Wilson here as well?'

Bernie leaned forward on the desk that separated her from her old boss. 'In case you don't like my questions and decide to pull the old "I'm not being questioned by a junior officer" crap.' She kept his gaze in an effort to steady her own nerves. Thornton broke away first.

'All right. Go on then.'

Bernie glanced down at her notebook. 'Apparently you

were at the hospital the night Zac died, despite the fact that Jade Ambrose had kicked you out. Why were you there?'

Thornton sighed. 'I wanted to find out how Zac was doing.'

'You could have rung. Why visit at' – Bernie looked at her notes – 'ten thirty at night?'

'I was hoping Jade wasn't going to be there. I thought she might have booked a hotel. Should have known she wouldn't leave his side. We argued and the nursing staff kicked me out.'

'And can anyone confirm that you left and didn't return?'

'Check the CCTV footage for the car park. It'll show me leaving.'

Bernie looked down.

'Oh, let me guess,' said Thornton, 'the CCTV wasn't working. You're screwed.'

'Or maybe you are. There's nothing to show you left the hospital area.'

'Except the CCTV at my hotel. Pretty sure that's working but I'll leave you to check it out. Besides, why would I want Zac dead? He's a crucial part of my case.' Thornton crossed his arms. 'Are we done?'

'Not quite. Why can't we get into Zac Ambrose's record?'

Thornton twitched slightly but covered it quickly. Not quickly enough for Bernie though.

'By "we", I'm assuming a lower-ranking officer has tried. Maybe a DC? Because of the nature of the county lines case, higher authority is needed. I can request you're given access. Wouldn't want you to think I'm hindering you in any way.' He gave her a brief smile. 'Are we done now?'

Bernie knew it would be pointless looking up Zac's record. Thornton might give her access but he could still redact vital information. She looked at Wilson.

He nodded.

'Yes, for now, sir.'

. . .

Bernie wanted to kick Thornton's empty seat. 'Smug bastard,' she muttered.

'Now, now, Bernie,' said Wilson.

'What? He is a smug bastard.' Bernie stood up and stretched her back. 'And you weren't much help, sir.'

'Come on, Bernie, you and I both know I was just here for decoration. With me present he had to answer your questions. And he was right about the cameras. I'll get someone to check the CCTV at his hotel. Is there any indication that the outage at the hospital was anything other than a failed data patch?'

'I can't see HR lying to me. And if there had been a cyber attack, I think they would have asked for our help.' Bernie shook her head. 'I still don't understand why I'm even doing this. You need to level with me.'

Beads of sweat appeared on Wilson's forehead. He was clearly uncomfortable. 'I'll be honest and say that I'm not happy about this either. But the order has come from the top.'

'The chief constable?'

Wilson wiped the sweat away with his hand. 'More than that – the Met Commissioner. The operation that Anderson was working on is more complicated than you think.'

Bernie sat at her desk in MCIT, trying to comprehend what Wilson had just told her. She was glad the room was empty. She'd come back to find a note from Matt saying he was going to the office for the cleaning company as no one was answering the phone. It would be a while before anyone else would be back. She had to talk to someone. She didn't want to call but there was no choice. Looking at the telephone number Wilson had given her, she dialled the number and waited. There was a click as the phone was answered.

'Hello?'

'Hi, it's Bernie Noel. I think we need to talk, Jade.'

52

The hotel was ideally placed. It was close to the hospital in Swindon and had easy access to the M4. Jade glanced nervously around the hotel lounge. It was virtually empty. They were sat in the corner on plush armchairs with a coffee table between them. Bernie was surprised Zac's mother was so on edge.

'Are you OK, Jade?'

'Hmm, yes. Just checking we're definitely alone.'

'If you're not happy we can drive somewhere in my car.'

'No, we can stay here. Plus I need coffee anyway.'

Jade caught the eye of a waiter and ordered.

'Thank you for meeting me,' Bernie said.

'Yeah, well, I'd have preferred it if my lawyer could have been here. But apparently I don't have one any more.'

Jade gave Bernie a hard stare. Her face was free from make-up for a change but there was still a flintiness to her look.

'I'm sorry about that, Jade, but given the circumstances, Anthony Markham couldn't represent you. Keira works for him and she's the original victim here. So are the other women we think Zac attacked.'

'He explained that but I don't believe it. Don't get me wrong here – I hate violence against women. I should know. I've had a couple of exes who hit me. But Zac isn't... wasn't like that.' She stopped as the waiter approached the table with her coffee. 'Thank you.'

The waiter turned to Bernie. 'Madam, would you like anything?'

'Oh, I think I'm OK, thanks.'

'Nonsense, woman! You've got a baby in there to feed,' said Jade. 'Let me guess, you're off caffeine.'

'Yes, how did you know?'

'Happened with all three of mine. How about a hot chocolate? And cake. Have you got any cake?'

'Yes, madam, we have Victoria sandwich.'

'OK, two pieces of cake and a hot chocolate.'

'Jade, I really don't need—'

'I insist.'

Bernie was still quite full from her mother's pancakes but maybe this could be an early lunch.

'All right then, but I'll pay.'

A glimmer of a smile appeared on Jade's lips. 'You think I'm paying for all this?' She pointed round the room. 'You think this fancy hotel is in my budget? Hell, no. Someone else is picking up the tab. And you don't need to know who.'

Bernie shook her head. Jade Ambrose hadn't changed. If she could get someone else to pay for things then she would happily accept. 'I won't ask, then. But what I do want to know is what Zac said to you when he was awake.'

Jade tapped her lime green nails on the table. 'I told that boss of yours. Hasn't he passed it on?'

'Some. I now understand why I'm investigating Zac's death. You think someone from the Met is responsible somehow.'

Jade tilted her head to one side. 'Not exactly. Zac said that he'd been working as an informant for the Met. When Danny went inside, Zac thought he'd take over the gang. But there were older members who had other ideas. He was still part of it all but was pushed away. He thought being Danny's brother meant something. It didn't.' Jade paused. The waiter was back with their order. He placed it quickly on the table and left.

Bernie picked up the long teaspoon and stirred her hot chocolate in the tall glass mug. She took a sip and waited for Jade to continue.

'So, it turns out Zac was a bit pissed off with the gang but he'd promised Danny he'd keep an eye on it for him. Except...' Jade lifted the cake and took a big bite. Crumbs dropped from her mouth as she spoke. 'The gang made a big mistake. They used Joshua to hide a gun. He got caught. And you know the penalties now. You can go to prison for hiding a gun for someone else. I was beside myself. Danny can cope inside but Joshua? You've seen him. How's a boy with Down's going to cope?'

Bernie took a mouthful of her drink. 'I don't think the CPS would have pressed charges. It would be pretty obvious that he'd been used.'

'That's not what the police were going to do. He was fourteen at the time. They threatened me with social services. They were going to take him away from me. Unless.'

'Unless what?' Bernie used a fork to cut a chunk of cake to eat.

'Unless Zac turned grass.'

Bernie put her fork down. 'Did you know at the time that Zac had agreed to that?'

'No. I'd always wondered why they'd changed their minds about social services. I thought the CPS hadn't agreed to the charges. It was all suddenly dropped. It was only the other night that Zac told me. Said what he'd been doing for the last few years. Doing it to keep Joshua safe.'

'Doing what, exactly?'

'Informing on the gang. It was clear they were getting bigger, getting into more serious stuff. Dealing in drugs and weapons. And then branching out of London.'

'County lines,' said Bernie.

'Yeah, that's it. The gang asked Zac to set something up in Swindon and his Met handler told him to do it. With Zac's information, the raid was set up. The plan was that he'd be arrested like everyone else. But his handler called him just before and told him he'd been exposed, that the gang knew. He suggested Zac should try to escape if possible. So he did.'

'Then he was hit by the lorry,' said Bernie. 'And you now think that someone ordered him to be killed.'

'Yeah. It's the only thing that makes sense to me. Either someone from the gang or even the Met.'

Bernie took another swig of hot chocolate before asking her next question, her heart racing at the thought that a police officer might have had a hand in Zac's death.

'And did Zac tell you the name of his handler?'

'Oh yes.'

Bernie nodded. She didn't need to ask who. It was obvious. It was the man who had led the raid, who hadn't left Zac's side in hospital until forced to and who she had spoken to only a couple of hours before. Most importantly, it was the man who had blamed Dougie for Zac Ambrose's accident. It was her old boss – DCI Jack Thornton.

53

As all the team were in the Swindon area, it made sense to meet up at Gable Cross Police Station. Bernie had rung ahead to ask if they had a spare meeting room. They met in the car park except for Matt who was still tied up at the cleaning company office. Bernie allowed Leigh to take the lead in showing them in. A young male officer with shorn blond hair and sparkling blue eyes beamed at Leigh as they entered reception.

'Hi, Leigh. Good to see you. Missed you. Where've you been?'

Leigh flushed a little. 'I've been at headquarters in Devizes with DI Noel here. We need to get them signed in.'

'Of course. I hope you're not going to keep Leigh for too long, ma'am. She's a great LCI. We've done a few cases together. We'd miss her if she left.'

Bernie bit her lip to stop herself from smiling. She wasn't sure how much Leigh was picking up but it was clear that the officer liked her. 'Oh, don't worry. Leigh's helping us with a case. I'm sure we can let her come back afterwards.'

Leigh glanced quickly at Bernie and then away again. She began twisting her rings.

Why's she stressed? She can't stay at MCIT unless she joins the HOLMES team. We need to have a chat.

'You're all free to go through. Just sign out when you leave. It's meeting room two. Leigh knows where that is.'

'Thanks...?'

'Oh, sorry, I'm PC Tim Hills, ma'am.'

'Thanks Tim. There's one more team member to come – DC Matt Taylor. If you could show him through please. He's about ten minutes away.'

'No problem. And feel free to grab some coffee and tea if you want.' Tim smiled and his eyes lingered on Leigh. Her brown hair hung down like a curtain, shielding her face, but there was a glimmer of a smile behind it.

'OK, Leigh, lead on,' Bernie said.

Bernie opened a window to get some air into the stuffy room. Although it still wasn't spring-like weather outside, the fresh air would help keep them all awake. Or maybe it was just she who was flagging. Growing a baby was exhausting.

Leigh came back into the room carrying a tray with a jug of water and glasses. 'Thought this might be quicker than making lots of tea and coffee. Plus the kitchen supplies are a bit low.'

'That's fine. I had a hot drink not that long ago,' Bernie said.

'Yeah,' said Kerry. 'We sort of dropped into the hospital café.'

'And we went to a drive-thru,' said Alice.

Bernie laughed. 'Honestly, the public will think that all we ever do is drink coffee and sit around. So we'd better get on with some work. Alice and Mick, how did you get on with Rachel Bell?'

Mick leant back in his chair. 'She wasn't in. A neighbour popped out to us and said that she was probably at Pilates or yoga.' Mick snorted. Alice elbowed him. 'What?'

'God, Mick. It's just an exercise class.'

'All sounds a bit poncey to me. Nothing wrong with just going for a run.'

'I prefer running,' said Leigh.

'See?' said Mick.

Kerry sighed. 'If you're not careful, Mick, I'm going to use you in my next WI self-defence class and you'll find yourself being thrown by little old ladies.'

'For God's sake, pack it in, all of you,' Bernie said. 'Alice, did you find out anything more about Rachel?'

'Well, the Markhams live in a very nice house in Lydiard Millicent. It's a small village just to the west of Swindon. They've been married for quite a long time but no kids. The neighbour's in her late seventies. I don't think she gets to chat to too many people so she was more than happy to oblige us. We waited for a while to see if Rachel would turn up but she didn't.'

'Could you see inside the house?' asked Kerry.

'No. They've got shutters and they were closed.'

'OK,' said Bernie. 'Strike one there. How about the Howard family, Kerry and Leigh?'

Kerry shuffled in her seat. 'Might be heading for strike two. Keira's parents were there but not her brother, Adam. As Keira's doing better, he's gone back to university in Bristol.'

'Well, this is good. Possible suspects doing a disappearing act,' said Mick.

'Except they might not be suspects,' said Alice. 'We still don't know this was murder.'

Bernie poured some water into a glass. 'True, we don't know for certain. But I had a very interesting chat with Jade Ambrose this morning. Not sure how much I'm allowed to reveal but... let's just say there are probably people who wanted Zac dead. I'm going to keep an open mind until the post-mortem results but it won't surprise me if murder is the outcome.'

There was a knock at the door.

'Come in,' said Bernie.

Smiley Tim popped his head round the door. 'Your DC has arrived. Is there anything I can get you, ma'am?'

Bernie smiled back. Tim's smiles were infectious. 'No, we're fine thanks.'

Tim pushed the door back and let Matt in. 'Well, if you do need anything, just let me know. Leigh knows where to find me.'

Matt pulled back a chair and sat down. 'Sorry for being late, ma'am.'

'No problem at all, Matt. We're hoping you have some information. We've not had the best morning.' Bernie wasn't ready yet to share the information on DCI Thornton. She needed to talk to Wilson first.

'At first I thought I wasn't going to get anything. I left you a note saying the cleaning company weren't answering their phone. Turns out there was a fault on the line. Anyway, once I got there, the office staff were really helpful.' Matt reached over and poured himself a glass of water. 'So, I got the name of the guy on shift that evening. He's new. Only joined last week. His name's Dean Foster.'

Bernie looked up sharply, Leigh too.

'What?' said Bernie.

'Dean Foster. Why? Do you know him?'

'Zac Ambrose used Dean Foster as an alias. Do you have anything else? Address? Other contact details?'

Matt smiled. 'Better than that. I have a copy of the photo taken for his hospital ID card.' He pulled out a piece of paper that had been folded into quarters and passed it down the table to Bernie. Despite the lines criss-crossing the photo, Bernie recognised him instantly. She turned the paper round for everyone to see.

'Look familiar?'

'Shit,' said Mick. 'That's Isaac Campbell.'

'Yes, it is. But what's he doing using an alias that Zac Ambrose used, and working on ICU? There's only one way to find out. And since we have a full team, we've got a much better chance of capturing him this time.'

54

Bernie and Leigh sat in Bernie's car. They were parked a little way down on the other side of the road from Isaac Campbell's house but they could see it clearly. The team were in place. Mick, Alice and PC Tim Hills were ready to knock at the front door. Kerry, Matt and two uniforms were behind the back garden.

'Go, go, go,' said Bernie into her radio.

Mick knocked firmly and said, 'Open up! Police!'

Bernie wondered how long to give Isaac's mother to answer. She didn't particularly want to break down the door. Not least because they'd then have the hassle of getting it fixed.

'Can you hear anything, Mick?' Bernie asked.

'I can hear some movement, ma'am. I'll knock again.'

Mick thumped hard. 'Police!'

Bernie spotted curtains twitching in one of the houses next door. 'She'll have to open up in a minute otherwise she's going to have an audience.' She spoke into the radio. 'Thirty seconds more, Mick. Then we'll get the battering ram out.' She watched the second hand on her watch tick round. 'Come on, Mrs Campbell. Open up.'

'Ms Campbell,' said Leigh.

'Oh yes, you're right. Damn. Time's up.'

Bernie changed channel to open comms. 'You're up, PC Hills. Break down the door please.'

There was a huge bang as Mick and PC Hills used the battering ram to break down the door. Leigh yelped and covered her ears, curling into herself.

There were shouts coming over the radio as rooms were searched but Bernie was concerned with Leigh. She was now rocking.

'Leigh? Is this a meltdown?'

There was a slight nod. Bernie didn't know what to do. Would distraction work?

'It's OK, Leigh. We'll be done here soon and then you can go home. What are you having for dinner tonight? My family are over so I think my father will probably be cooking.'

Leigh continued to rock.

There were more shouts from the radio and then the words Bernie was desperate to hear – 'Got him.' She recognised Kerry's voice. Alice came out from the front of the house and headed towards Bernie's car. As she drew close, she picked up speed. She opened the passenger front door.

'Meltdown?' Alice asked Bernie, seemingly unfazed by Leigh's behaviour.

'Yes, I don't know what to do. She won't stop rocking.'

'She's self-soothing. She's on the autistic spectrum, isn't she?'

Bernie nodded.

'I thought so. My brother's autistic. I recognised some traits in her. Changing teams and routines has probably taken its toll.' Alice gently placed her hand on Leigh's back. Leigh flinched. 'OK. Not gentle touch then. Would a big squeeze be better for you?'

Leigh raised her head a little. 'Hmm.'

Alice bent into the car and squeezed Leigh as tightly as she could.

'How does that help?' asked Bernie.

'Releases the tension. That's it, Leigh. You're going to be OK. Nearly there.' Alice looked at Bernie. 'We caught this one early. I guess you felt you couldn't tell us but it's better for us all to know. That way we can support Leigh and have strategies in place.'

There was a voice on the radio. 'Bringing him out.'

Bernie looked at Alice.

'You go, ma'am. I'll stay with Leigh.'

Bernie got out of the car and walked across the road to Isaac Campbell's house. She was slightly shaky. She'd thought she could help Leigh, encourage her and push her forward. She realised now that that approach was more about her than Leigh. Her being a great boss rather than Leigh's well-being.

Mick and Matt had Isaac between them, his hands cuffed.

Bernie shook her head. 'Seriously, Isaac, all we want to do is talk to you. Your mother's going to go spare when she sees her front door. Next time, just answer.' Bernie looked at Matt and Mick. 'Stick him in the van. We'll question him at Gable Cross.'

PC Tim Hills followed behind, the battering ram in his hands.

'Good work, PC Hills.'

'Thank you, ma'am.' His eyes drifted across to her car. 'Is Leigh OK?'

'Leigh? Um, yes.'

'Did she have a meltdown?'

'You know?'

'Yes. She told me. Said that's why we can't be together. It's not for want of trying. But I'm willing to wait for her.'

Bernie smiled. 'You're a good man, Tim. She'd be lucky to have you.'

Tim blushed. 'Right, I'd better get your man back to the station for you.'

There was a hand on Bernie's arm. She turned to see Kerry and Matt.

'Well, that was fun,' said Kerry. 'The look on his face when he leapt over the fence and saw us there – priceless. The daft boy tried to tackle me first.'

'Yeah, that was a mistake,' said Matt. 'Kerry tossed him over her shoulder before he had a chance to blink.'

Bernie laughed. 'It's very important to have a ninja on the team.'

'Alice is pretty good too,' said Kerry. 'Talking of Alice, what is she doing to Leigh?'

Bernie looked at her car. Alice still had Leigh in a tight grip. 'Ah. Leigh didn't feel too good. Alice is just helping her.'

'Hmm.' Kerry's smile had disappeared. 'I think it's about time that you level with us, Bernie.'

55

'Isaac, do you understand why you're here?' Matt asked.

The young man looked around the room but refused to acknowledge the two officers before him. Bernie thought he was going to be hard to crack but she trusted Kerry and Matt to find a way.

Matt pushed a piece of paper across the desk. 'This is a photocopy of your ID photo for the hospital. It's definitely you in the picture but it's not your name. Why are you using the alias Dean Foster?'

No response.

'See,' Kerry said, 'the interesting thing about the name "Dean Foster" is that it isn't the first time it's been used as a fake name. Another man has used it. Zac Ambrose. Do you know him?'

Bernie thought she saw Isaac flinch.

'Zac Ambrose died Saturday night. He was in ICU and you were on shift.' Kerry leaned forward in her chair. 'I'm interested in how you knew him. Was it as a drug dealer or did you hear what he allegedly did to Keira Howard, your ex-girlfriend?'

Isaac started to tap out a beat with his feet.

'Do you know what we think he did to Keira? A serious blow to her head, raped her and left her for dead. Thankfully she's OK now. But it was touch-and-go for a while. She could easily have died. I should think her family and friends would be very angry with the man responsible. Maybe want to exact their revenge.'

Isaac turned his head to the left and stared at the wall, his feet still tapping. Kerry looked at Matt to take over.

'Isaac, why are you using a false name for work?' Matt asked. 'Looks a bit sus.'

Isaac started tapping his hands on his legs, joining the two beats together like a drummer.

'You see, at the moment, you've been arrested for using a false name and false documents to obtain work. But as we dig deeper, we might be changing that charge to murder.'

The drumming stopped.

Bernie edged closer to the monitor screen. 'Come on, Isaac. You don't want to get sent down for murder.'

Isaac looked at Matt. 'Shit, man. You're not pinning that one on me.'

'Then explain to me why you've just got a new job cleaning on the hospital ward that Zac Ambrose was on, using an alias that he used to use.'

'I want a lawyer.'

Bernie was relieved to see it wasn't Anthony Markham that walked behind Isaac Campbell into the interview room. The lawyer was a woman in her late twenties. They sat down opposite Kerry and Matt.

'Thank you for giving me some time with my client.'

'It's his right,' said Kerry.

The lawyer gave a tight smile. 'We have a prepared statement to read. "I, Isaac Campbell, was approached at the end of last week by a guy in a club. I was offered money to take a cleaning job at the hospital. My role was to keep an eye on one of the patients in ICU – Zac Ambrose. I didn't get on to the ward straight away. Two days ago I had a late shift on ICU and I found Zac. I saw he was talking to his mother. I reported this back to the guy who hired me. He asked me to work a double shift and deliver a note to Zac for him. I managed to do that. I don't know what was in the note. It was sealed. I didn't touch Zac. I just gave him the note."'

Bernie wrote down a few questions for Kerry and Matt to ask. Isaac Campbell was clearly holding back information.

56

'Here are my questions.'

Bernie handed a piece of paper to Kerry. The DS scanned the sheet.

'OK. That's what I was thinking as well.'

Bernie pointed out one question in particular. 'We need the name of the club. I'm betting it's the Plaza. If so, we'll need to go back and get more CCTV tapes. See if we can spot Isaac and this man he's mentioned. Don't push for the man's name. Get the club.'

Kerry nodded. She went back into the interview room and Bernie sat down in front of the screen again. Isaac was looking twitchy. She saw Kerry appear.

'Interview resumed at sixteen forty hours,' said Matt.

'Thank you for your statement, Isaac,' Kerry said. 'Obviously we have some questions to ask you about it.'

'My client will be giving a "no comment" interview. We've provided you with an account.'

'Which is very helpful but we need to just clarify a few things. Isaac, do you know the name of the man who approached you at the club?'

'No comment.'
'What was the name of the club?'
'No comment.'
'Was it the Plaza?'
'No comment.'

Bernie rubbed her brow. She was starting to get a headache. She hadn't eaten since having the cake and hot chocolate with Jade before lunch. A thought occurred to her. *Where's the note Isaac delivered?* She sent a quick text to Lucy.

Hi. Quick question. Was there a letter in amongst Zac Ambrose's possessions? Thanks.

It seemed far-fetched but could there have been something in the envelope that could have caused his death? Ricin or something similar. She hoped not.

Isaac was continuing to evade Kerry's questions. He was starting to drum again with his feet. Where it had previously been because of arrogance, it now seemed more like nervousness, even fear. He had given enough information to clear himself but not so much that he dropped someone else in it.

Bernie picked up her pen and tapped her notepad. How could they get Isaac Campbell to crack?

Matt took over the questioning.

'Isaac, I need to ask you about Sunday evening a week ago. Where were you?'

The teenager stared at Matt but remained silent.

'What has this got to do with being arrested for using a false name?' asked the lawyer. 'What's the relevance?'

Matt turned to the female lawyer. 'Isaac was asked to use a false name to obtain employment at the hospital so he could spy on Zac Ambrose. We believe that Zac was responsible for the attack on Isaac's ex-girlfriend, Keira Howard. That attack took place on Sunday night. When officers tried to speak to Isaac about it, he did a bunk. We still need to rule him out.'

Matt looked at Isaac again. 'You liked Keira, didn't you? A lot. Which is understandable. She's a very pretty girl. I expect a lot of guys admire her.'

Isaac's nostrils flared.

'Have you been keeping tabs on her, Isaac? Did one of her friends, either Caz or Mia, tell you she was seeing someone else? We know you're in touch with at least one of them because you were tipped off last time we came to visit. Were you at the Plaza that night? Or maybe hanging around outside, waiting to see who she was with? Did you see her leave by herself? Maybe follow her?'

Isaac's breathing quickened. He clenched his fists.

'Perhaps we've got it wrong about Zac. Maybe she met him to have sex in the Town Gardens and you witnessed that. And that made you angry. Maybe it was you who raped her and hit her over the head and left her for dead.'

Isaac leapt to his feet. 'I would never do that. Never. I love Keira and I'd do anything for her.'

'Anything?'

'Yes.'

'Then answer our questions.'

Isaac looked around the room and spotted the camera. He looked directly at it. 'I want to talk to the person watching. And off the record. I'm not going to be sent down for this shit and more importantly, I'm not dying for it either.'

Bernie looked at the young man on the screen who was looking directly at her through the camera. She picked up her phone and texted Kerry.

OK. Give me five mins.

She was going to need some meds and food before she

tackled Isaac Campbell. Her phone buzzed once, then again. Two text messages. First, Kerry.

Sure. No problem.

The second was from Lucy.

No letter in his possessions. Maybe mother took it? Should have some results for you tomorrow.

Damn. She'd have to contact Jade Ambrose about the letter. And there were no guarantees she'd confess to having it. Not if she'd read it and it was of some use to her. Despite their earlier heart-to-heart, Bernie still didn't trust Zac's mother.

She rummaged in her bag for a cereal bar and some paracetamol.

The young man stared impassively at Bernie. She might have been wrong to give him time to calm down. Still, after watching Matt's questioning, she knew what buttons to press.

'OK, Isaac, the tape is off and we're not video recording you. It's just you, me and your lawyer. Let's get some details.' Bernie picked up her pen. 'Name of the club where you met this man please.'

Isaac sighed. 'The Plaza.'

'Thank you. Were you there the night Keira was attacked?'

'No.'

'Where were you? We need to be able to rule you out.'

'I was at home watching TV with my mum.'

'And she can corroborate that?'

'Yeah.'

'What were you watching?'

'What?'

There was something odd about Isaac's expression.

'The TV programme you saw. What was it?'

'Oh... it was a boxset.'

Bernie raised her eyebrows.

'It was... um, *Downton Abbey*.'

Bernie pressed her lips together to stop herself from smiling.

'It's my mum's favourite. She likes that shit. I was just keeping her company, you know.'

Bernie nodded. 'I understand. It was very sad when they killed off Matthew, though, especially as Lady Mary had just had the baby.'

'Yeah, and they showed that episode on Christmas Day. Fucking way to end the day.'

'Are you sure it's just your mum who likes it?'

Isaac looked away, clearly embarrassed. 'That tape's definitely off, right?'

'Yes.'

'Then yes, I do like it. We watched three episodes and then I went to bed. I was nowhere near the Plaza that night.'

'So why did you run when we came to see you the day after the attack?'

'I'd heard about it. And I didn't think you'd believe my alibi.'

Bernie drank some more water. 'Well, I think I believe you. Tell me about this guy in the Plaza.'

Isaac was quiet.

'You told us you'd do anything for Keira. Is that what you said to this man? Had he mentioned to you what Zac had done?'

Isaac shifted in his seat. 'Sort of.'

'What day was this?'

'Can't remember. End of last week some time.'

Bernie glanced at the lawyer. She glared back. She wasn't going to help.

'OK. What did he look like?'

'I didn't see him properly. It was kinda dark and shadowy. But he had a London accent. He didn't say his name. Just gave me some money and the paperwork to get the job.'

London? So maybe this is related to Zac's gang after all.

Bernie thought back to her visit to the club. There were plenty of hidden places. Maybe the man thought there weren't any cameras there. She was going to have to ask DJ Jules Verne for the tapes that came after Keira's attack. Then Carl Smith came to mind. The black barman with a swallow tattoo on his neck, indicating that he might have been in prison some time. She hadn't thought to check him out as he was still at the club when Keira was attacked. *Is he connected with the gang?*

'So, this man, it was dark and he was black, so you couldn't see his face?'

Isaac smirked. 'I never said he was black. He didn't talk like a black man. He was white.'

57

'Fuck, fuck, fuck.'

Bernie buried her head in her hands. She was trying not to jump to conclusions but a white man with a London accent who had the ability to get hold of false papers meant only one thing – DCI Jack Thornton. Especially since Isaac had used the same name that Zac Ambrose had had. That was careless.

She had asked Kerry to release Isaac without any charge, not even for using false papers. She didn't know how long she had before Thornton found out. She'd given Isaac her number in case he needed it but had a sneaking suspicion he'd probably do a bunk. She didn't blame him.

The interview room door opened and Kerry popped her head round.

'You OK?'

Bernie raised her head. 'Yeah. Just tired.' She couldn't tell Kerry about her fears.

'Did you get anything helpful?'

'He met this man at the Plaza at the end of last week. Didn't give me a day.'

'Well, while you were chatting to Isaac, I got on to our favourite DJ. Matt's gone to get the tapes.'

'How did you know?'

Kerry wrinkled her nose. 'I sort of listened at the door and as soon as I heard "Plaza", I went and contacted the club.'

Bernie was relieved. Hopefully it meant Kerry hadn't heard what else Isaac had said.

'Good work.' She tried to keep the strain out of her voice.

'Are you sure you're OK?'

'Yes. Just tired and hungry.' Bernie looked at her watch. It was after six p.m. 'Are Mick and Alice back yet?'

'I'll check,' Kerry said.

'Thanks. You can just text me.'

Bernie picked up her phone. She wasn't sure who to ring first – DCS Wilson or Jade Ambrose. Zac's mother hadn't mentioned a letter to her. Either she hadn't read it, or, more likely, she had and planned to use it in some way. It seemed more prudent to call the super first. She scrolled through her contacts.

Wilson picked up after the second ring.

'Bernie, do you have some news for me?'

She liked the fact he always cut to the chase.

'I think so, sir. We spoke to the elusive Isaac Campbell today. Turns out he was the cleaner on ICU and he claims he delivered a note to Zac. We don't have that note. Did Jade Ambrose mention anything to you about it?'

There was a pause. 'No. Not that I remember. Did someone give the note to Campbell then?'

'Yes. At the Plaza at the end of last week. Along with documentation allowing him to get the cleaning job under the name of... Dean Foster.'

Silence.

'Sir?'

'I'm here.'

'You understand the significance then.'

'Yes. Did Campbell describe the man?'

'He said it was too dark to see the man properly but he spoke with a London accent and he's white.'

'So, unlikely to be a gang member?'

'For Zac's gang, yes. We both know who this is. What do we do? Pull him in again?'

'Without the note, we have nothing. If Jade Ambrose has it, she may not be willing to give it up and is possibly using it for her own ends.'

'Blackmail?'

'Perhaps. Or maybe something else. I'll talk to the chief constable. We can look into it more in the morning.'

'But sir, don't you think we ought to act sooner? We've released Isaac Campbell. What if something happens to him?'

'Don't worry about that. We have eyes on DCI Thornton. He's not going anywhere without our knowledge. We'll chat tomorrow. Don't work too late tonight. Bye, Bernie.'

He hung up before she could reply. Bernie was confused. If there was surveillance on DCI Thornton, why did she need to be involved in the investigation at all? She took a swig of water from her bottle and grimaced. It was warm. Her phone pinged. A text from Kerry.

Mick and Alice are back. Matt too. We're in the meeting room.

Bernie felt slightly woozy as she went into the meeting room. The super was right. They shouldn't work too late. She pulled out a chair, relieved to sit down again, even though she hadn't walked far.

'So before we start, I guess I owe you all an explanation about Leigh. I spoke to her before she left earlier to make sure I could pass this all on to you. Leigh has autism and there are quite a few things she struggles with – change being one of them,' Bernie said. 'I don't fully understand all of this and I certainly haven't handled it very well. Alice has more knowledge so perhaps you could explain a bit more please.'

'Yes, of course,' Alice said. 'My brother has autism too, so I've grown up with this. We were fortunate today on two counts with Leigh. Firstly, we caught the meltdown quickly so it didn't get a chance to escalate. Secondly, Leigh was in the car so the meltdown was confined. She didn't have the opportunity to flee and thankfully her response isn't fight. She seems to freeze and curl in on herself. Shut the world out. The rocking is an attempt to self-sooth. Ma'am, I know you're concerned that maybe you pushed her over the edge but I'm guessing Leigh was already very stressed. Changing teams and routine haven't helped. She's tried really hard to fit in. It's just taken its toll today. A good sleep and she'll cope better tomorrow.'

'But what if this happens again?' Kerry asked. 'We can't have her flipping out whenever. And to be honest, she was a bit useless with me at the hospital this morning. She barely said a word.'

Bernie looked at Alice. The DC was biting her lip. 'Say it, Alice.'

'When I drove Leigh home, she said a few things. I'm sorry, Sarge, but she finds you quite intimidating.'

Kerry sighed. 'I suppose I have been a bit short with her. Now I know, I'll try harder to support her.'

'Good,' Bernie said. 'We need to find a way for us all to work together.'

'Do you mean she's staying with us beyond this case?'

'No, Kerry. But I think she should finish this investigation and I would prefer it to end well for her. So, Alice, if this is OK with you, I'm going to pair Leigh with you tomorrow. And then in the morning, we'll see what tasks need doing and pair up everyone else as necessary. In the meantime, what have you got for me?'

Alice smiled. 'Rachel Bell still wasn't at home but we spoke to another neighbour. They're clearly not the best of friends. Apparently the Markhams like to have big parties. The neighbour said they get up to all sorts.'

'Did this neighbour elaborate?'

'A bit. Definitely lots of alcohol and possibly drugs. Lots of people who stay over but perhaps don't stay in their own bedrooms – if you get what I mean.' Alice raised her eyebrows.

'No! The Markhams? Really?'

Alice nodded. 'Hard to believe but true, apparently.'

'I'm not sure I want to know how the neighbour knows this.'

'Noise, mainly, but saw some things out in the garden last summer when the weather was good.'

'Yuck.' Bernie hesitated as she thought of something. *Have Geoff and Julie Howard been to one of these parties? Has Keira?* 'At the hospital,' she said, 'did Rachel say that she knew Keira at all? Because I still don't understand why she didn't tell her husband that one of his employees was in ICU.' She looked at Kerry.

'I don't know. I can't remember. She was very protective of her though.'

'Hmm.'

'What are you thinking, Bernie?'

Bernie leaned back in her chair and stroked her belly. Baby had been a bit quiet today. 'From what the neighbour said to Alice, it sounds as though there's a lot of sex at these parties. I'm wondering if Keira went to one and met her mystery man there.'

'The mystery man she was going to meet in Town Gardens?' Matt asked.

'Yes.'

'Does it matter?' Kerry asked. 'We're fairly certain Zac

Ambrose was responsible for Keira's attack and he's now dead. The father of her baby is none of our business.'

'True. But when Matt suggested to Isaac that maybe Zac wasn't responsible, something nagged me. Jade Ambrose told me Zac wouldn't behave like that.'

'There are lots of things mothers don't know about their sons,' Mick said.

Bernie sighed. 'I'm still not sure. This all started with the attack on Keira. I'd like to have another chat with her tomorrow. And we still need to speak to her brother. In the meantime, I think we ought to head home.'

'What do you want me to do with the CCTV tapes from the club?' Matt asked.

Bernie remembered what Wilson had said about DCI Thornton. He wasn't going anywhere.

'It can wait until tomorrow.'

58

TUESDAY

Bernie stretched out in bed. Dougie was already up. She could hear the shower running. She was tempted to join him but a quick glance at the clock told her she didn't have time. She'd eat breakfast first. She padded down the stairs, wrapping her dressing gown around her. Although the worst of the cold was over, the temperature was still struggling to get into double figures during the day.

She filled the kettle and switched it on. Stuck two slices of bread in the toaster, then glazed over as she mentally ticked off the jobs for the day – chase the post-mortem report, speak to the super, visit Keira and her family and check on her brother, get statements from the hospital staff...

She was oblivious to the boiled kettle and the toast popping up. It wasn't until Dougie put his arms around her that she snapped to.

'Morning. Can I nab one of those slices please? And maybe I should make the coffee?'

'Sorry. Miles away. Yes to both.'

'Do you want to talk about it? You were very quiet last night.'

Bernie sat down and spread butter onto her toast. 'Oh, Dougie, it's such a mess. I don't know where to begin or if I'm even allowed to tell you.'

Dougie placed the cafetière on the table and stuck more bread in the toaster. 'Well, the reason I'm up early this morning is the super called me yesterday to ask me to come in. I think my suspension is going to be lifted. Rumour has it that the IPCC is no longer looking at me.'

'Oh that's brilliant. And by rumour, I guess you mean Jane. Why didn't you say last night?'

'Because you were totally gone.' He plunged the coffee and poured some into Bernie's mug. 'But still, only tell me what you think you can.'

Bernie's hand hovered over the Marmite before choosing strawberry jam. Dougie smiled.

'We finally caught up with Isaac Campbell yesterday. Found out a few helpful things.'

Dougie raised his eyebrows.

'Sorry. Can't tell you what. But one thing, though, we found out that Anthony Markham and his missus have sex parties.'

Dougie nearly spat his coffee out. 'Seriously?'

'According to the neighbours. Although it may just be malicious gossip. But I'm wondering if Keira went to one of these parties and met her mystery man there.'

'Possibly.' Dougie paused as he ate some toast. 'But are you sure? I've had Markham in interviews. He really doesn't strike me as the type.'

'God, I know. But if you find Markham unlikely you should meet his wife. She's the stern nurse on ICU who looked after Keira. But she never said to us that she knew her.'

'Doesn't stop her from treating her though.' Dougie got up and grabbed another couple of slices of toast. 'So what are you having on this one then?'

Bernie thought for a moment. 'Do you know what I really fancy?'

'No.'

'Fish paste.'

Dougie pushed the Marmite towards her. 'That, I can accept, but fish paste? Never.'

Bernie enjoyed being driven into work by Dougie. There were definite signs of spring now. The snow was completely gone and forgotten about. Trees were coming into bud and crocuses were scattered across the green near headquarters. A bank of daffodils greeted them as they turned into the car park. A weak sun had broken through the clouds. Bernie's mood lifted. She still didn't understand why she was carrying out the investigation into Zac's death but she was determined to find the answer.

Anderson went off in search of the super as Bernie headed into MCIT. Everyone was in, except Alice and Leigh.

'Morning.'

Matt raised his head. 'Morning, ma'am. I was about to head off to start watching the CCTV, unless you want a briefing.'

'I'll wait for Alice and Leigh. Where are they?'

Mick spun round on his chair. 'Leigh's car was left here yesterday so Alice has gone to pick her up.'

'Oh yes, I forgot about that. Something else I forgot – the post-mortem report. Has it come in?'

'Let me just check,' said Kerry. She tapped on the keyboard. 'No, not yet.'

'That's unusual. Nick White is normally quite prompt about these things. Can you chase it please, Kerry?'

'No problem. Anything else?'

'Yes. How were things left with Keira's brother?'

Kerry pulled out her notebook and flicked through. 'He's going to come in at some point this week.'

'Hmm. That's not good enough. Mick, get on to him and set an appointment time. And tell him that today would be better if at all possible. He's only in Bristol. We can see him this evening. Matt, yes please for the club CCTV.'

Bernie put her bag down on her desk. 'And Kerry, I'd like to see Keira today. Can you drive me please? Dougie drove in this morning. He's seeing the super now. We're hoping he's going to lift the suspension.'

'About time too,' said Kerry. 'No problem going to Swindon. In fact, there's a nurse who's quite keen to speak to us.'

'Really? Does she have info on Zac's death?'

'Yes. But she's also been to a party at Rachel Bell's house.' Kerry winked.

Bernie smiled. 'Check to see if she's free for a chat.'

Anderson was just leaving the super's office as Bernie walked down the corridor. He had a broad smile.

'Good news then?' she asked.

'Aye. Back on active duty as of now.' He kissed her cheek. 'Of course, I'm not working this particular case, just to be on the safe side.'

Bernie nodded towards the door. 'Does this mean he's in a good mood then?'

'He seems fine this morning. Good luck.'

She knocked on the door.

'Come in... ah, Bernie. Take a seat. Did you just see DI Anderson?'

Bernie sat down. 'I did. Thank you. It's a relief to get him back out of the house.'

'Quite. An unfortunate business all round. Talking of which...' Wilson sighed. 'I have to be honest and say that I'm not happy about it. Not happy at all.'

Bernie nodded. 'I'm being used, aren't I?'

The super made eye contact with her. 'Yes.'

She shifted in her seat. 'I'm cover for a covert operation. I'm guessing Anti-Corruption. Is it the Met?'

'Not exactly. They've asked Thames Valley to investigate DCI Thornton.'

Bernie nodded. 'Makes sense. The Met maintains integrity plus Thornton's less likely to recognise Thames Valley officers. So did Jade Ambrose actually ask for me?'

'Yes. Felt that you owed her. Thought it was some divine justice you should investigate. And given your past experience with DCI Thornton, it suited us too.'

'You thought he'd be looking in my direction and not spot other people watching him. Great. Is this why the post-mortem report isn't in yet?'

Wilson nodded slowly. 'We've asked Dr White to be incredibly thorough.'

Bernie narrowed her eyes. 'Is it possible Zac Ambrose died naturally and this whole thing is just a charade?'

Wilson stared impassively. 'Until we have the full report, we have no idea. Samples have been sent to toxicology and they could take weeks.'

Bernie's heart beat faster as anger started to rise up in her. She didn't like being played.

59

Bernie barked orders at her team when she came back from her meeting. Kerry didn't need to be told twice to bring her car round and she wisely waited until they were halfway to Swindon before asking any questions.

'So, I take it your meeting with the super didn't go so well?'

'No it bloody didn't.'

'Can you elaborate?'

Bernie bit her lip. There was a need for secrecy but at the same time she favoured integrity and transparency.

'We're being played. We're not the only team looking into this.'

'Didn't we already know that? The IPCC agreed for you to investigate. I doubt if they handed everything over.'

Bernie shook her head. 'Not them. And to be fair, this other team isn't exactly looking at Zac's death. But I'm pretty certain they have the note Isaac delivered.'

'OK. I'm confused. I haven't noticed anyone else sniffing around.'

'You wouldn't. One – they're very good. Two – we're a diversion tactic.'

Kerry slowed down at a junction and indicated left. 'You mean... a covert operation? They're watching DCI Thornton?'

'Looks that way.'

Kerry pulled out. 'Why you though? Why ask you to do this?'

Bernie looked at the fields rushing past her. It had taken a long time to settle in Wiltshire after being in London all her life. But she wouldn't swap it now. Not for anything. That case in London had almost destroyed her. If she hadn't been accepted on to the accelerated programme, she probably would have left. She was now convinced her old boss knew more about it than he had let on at the time. Had some idea as to who had blown her cover and put her life in danger. Throwing her into the mix was meant to unsettle him. Remind him of the past.

'Because he and I have history. I'm there to rattle him so he makes a mistake. And he has. Giving Isaac Campbell the same alias as Zac Ambrose was sloppy. But I'm guessing he didn't have time to get new paperwork in place. He needed to get a note to Zac urgently. A warning to keep his mouth shut.'

'Shut about what?'

Bernie looked at Kerry. 'I'm still working on that.' She didn't want to reveal what Jade Ambrose had told her about Thornton being Zac's handler, but she had her own thoughts and corruption was high on the list.

There was an overpowering smell of lilies on Keira's ward. Bernie wrinkled her nose. She wasn't keen on them at the best of times. There was a nurse walking towards them with the offending flowers.

'It's not visiting time yet,' she said.

Bernie pulled out her warrant card. 'I'm Detective Inspector Noel and this is Detective Sergeant Allen. We've come to see Keira Howard.'

'Ah, right. While you're here, perhaps you can have a quick word with the patient who keeps hiding lilies in her bedside cabinet. We haven't allowed flowers for years now.'

Bernie smiled. 'I don't think that's classified as Major Crime. Keira?'

'Far end, on the right.'

Bernie and Kerry walked down the ward. Kerry muttered, 'At least her parents won't be here this time. We might get some decent answers.'

Keira was sitting up in bed. She held her phone in her hand and had earphones in. Seeing the two detectives, she pulled one earphone out. 'Have you come to see me? Bernie, right?'

'Yes, and this is Kerry,' said Bernie. 'Thankfully there's no one else here for us to visit at the moment.' Not any more, she thought. She sat in the chair next to the bed. 'Kerry, can you pull the curtains round please?'

Keira was alarmed. 'What's happened? Is it my family?'

Bernie placed her hand on Keira's arm. 'No. Considering what you've been through it's better to have a little privacy as we talk. How are you feeling now?'

'Better. My head still aches but the doctor's impressed with my recovery.'

'And the baby?'

Keira put a protective hand on her stomach. Bernie recognised that sign.

'Good. Telling my parents was a bit difficult though. I'm glad Adam was here for that.'

'And did you tell them who the father is?'

Keira slowly shook her head. 'I can't. Not yet.'

'Do you know who it is?'

'God, yes. I'm not a slapper, you know.'

Bernie winced. She had to stop her own hand moving to her belly to protect her baby.

'It's just complicated. I'm not sure how my parents are going to respond.'

'Has he been in to see you?'

Keira shook her head again. 'No. It's too difficult with my family here all the time. But I know someone texted him to let him know. Anyway, I don't know what that's got to do with my attack. It's none of your business really.'

'Well, you were on the verge of telling us last time and we had to consider the possibility that the father was responsible for the attack.'

'It wasn't him.'

'OK. We could pick him up and bring him to see you outside of visiting hours, if you like, and then you wouldn't have to worry about your parents seeing him.'

Keira's eyes widened. 'No. I mean, thank you, but he'll come and see me when he can.'

Bernie's mind began to tick. 'Keira, does your boyfriend have a criminal record? Is that what you're worried about?'

Keira shook her head, unconvincingly.

'All right,' said Bernie. 'We've come today to see if you're OK. And... to give you some news. The man we believe was responsible for your attack has died. We weren't able to interview him prior to his death but we have forensic evidence that suggests he was your attacker.'

Keira reached out and grasped Bernie's hand. 'So it's all over? He won't hurt me again?'

'It's over. I'm sorry there won't be a trial...'

'God, I'm not. The thought of a trial... I'm glad I don't have to go through it. I'm just so relieved. Thank you for coming to tell me. Oh God.' Keira shook her head. 'I've had a couple of bad dreams. Hopefully, I'll sleep better now.'

'I'm sure you will but it'll be a good idea to get some counselling. I do have a couple of other questions to ask you, though, if that's OK. One of the nurses who looked after you in ICU, Rachel Bell, do you know her?'

Keira paused and thought. 'I can't really remember very much from ICU, to be honest. I was so drugged up. All the nurses looked the same in their scrubs.'

'OK. My other question is to do with your work placement with Anthony Markham. He's a family friend, I understand.'

'Well, he goes fishing with my dad.'

'Have you ever been to his house for a party?'

Keira hesitated. Her face and neck flushed. It was obvious to Bernie that the answer was yes. But why was Keira lying about not knowing Rachel Bell?

Kerry's phone beeped as they walked away from the ward. She pulled it out and read a text.

'That ICU nurse I mentioned – Olivia – can meet us in five minutes out the front. It might be best if we talk in the car.'

'Good idea. What's she like?'

'A really lovely and dedicated nurse. I'd be surprised if she'd killed Zac, if that's what you mean.'

'Well, yes, I suppose I did mean that. I trust your judgement. Do you want to wait for her and then bring her over?'

'Sure. Here are the keys.'

Bernie was glad to get a few minutes to herself. She called Anderson as she headed back to the car.

'Hey, beautiful. You OK?' Dougie said.

'Someone's happy to be back at work.'

'God, yes. It's a bit mundane at the moment but never mind. A weight's been lifted off my shoulders.'

'Yeah, I think it's been placed straight onto mine.' She told him what Wilson had said.

'Holy shit. You need to get out of this and fast.'

'I can't. If I pull out now Thornton will be suspicious.'

'Can't or won't?'

Bernie paused. She hated the idea of being manipulated but she was desperate to find out the truth about that fateful operation in London. 'Won't. I've come this far. I can't quit now.'

60

Olivia smelled of disinfectant and vomit.

'Sorry about the smell. Had to do a bit of a cleaning job this morning.'

Bernie wound down the window. 'Don't you have a cleaner to help with that?'

'He didn't turn up today.'

Bernie gave Kerry a knowing glance. 'Well, thank you for speaking to us. You were on duty the night Zac Ambrose died. Can you tell us what happened please?'

Olivia scratched her head. Her hair was pulled back in a tight bun. Bernie understood what Keira had meant about them all looking the same in their anonymous scrubs. Even so, surely she would have recognised Rachel? 'I was looking after him. Everything was OK. He was down to fifteen-minute checks and I gave him his scheduled painkiller injection at eleven fifteen.'

'What was in that?'

'Ten mg of morphine. It's the standard amount and he hadn't had any side effects to it. But just before eleven thirty, his heart monitor began to beep and his mother shouted for us. His heart rate was dropping rapidly and he crashed. Went into cardiac arrest. We did everything we could to save him but it was too late. He'd gone.'

'But he had been making good progress?'

'Yes, but sometimes that masks a problem we don't know about. He'd had surgery but there might have been an internal bleed that had been missed. The post-mortem should pick up anything like that. I know I did everything correctly. I followed his care plan exactly. I had a handover with Rachel...'

Bernie twisted round more in her seat in the car. 'Rachel Bell? She'd cared for Zac on the day shift?'

'Yes. She said you'd spoken to her already.'

'Hmm. In a manner of speaking. Who decided Zac would have fifteen-minute checks?'

'I guess the doctor did. Rachel told me. It was written on Zac's notes.'

'And you know Rachel well?'

'Quite well. We've worked in ICU together for about three years.'

'Well enough to be invited to her parties then.'

Olivia blushed. 'I've only been to one, which was quite enough.' She shook her head. 'Never again. I was so surprised. Rachel is quite prim at work, stern even. But God, she knows how to let her hair down.' She shook her head again. 'I mean, I expected alcohol and lots of drunk people. And maybe a few smoking cannabis, but they had a glass coffee table in their lounge that had lines and lines of cocaine. They weren't even hiding it. And then...' Olivia raised her hand to her mouth.

'Sex?' Bernie suggested.

Olivia nodded. 'Yes. I left at that point. Someone propositioned me and I was out of there. I'm engaged. I wasn't about to be unfaithful. It was all writhing bodies and... quite noisy.' She shuddered. 'I found Rachel at the door talking to a neighbour.

Well, I say talking... they were arguing. The neighbour was threatening to call the police. Rachel laughed and said the police were already there.'

'What? There were police officers at the party?' Bernie looked at Kerry. Her alarm was reflected in Kerry's eyes.

'That's what she said. Anyway, as I was leaving I saw a couple down the side alley and, well, they were... you know, having sex. There was a security light on so anyone walking past could see them. I couldn't quite believe it when she turned up in ICU and then him later.'

'What, you mean Keira and the cleaner?'

'The cleaner? No. Zac Ambrose.'

Bernie was confused. 'You definitely saw Keira Howard and Zac Ambrose having sex?'

'Yes.'

'When was the party?'

'New Year's Eve. My fiancé's a paramedic and was on duty.'

'Would that fit with Keira's pregnancy dates?'

'I'm not sure. I didn't look after her. I know Rachel had her for all her shifts until she moved to another ward.'

'And what about Adam Howard?' Kerry asked. 'Did you see him come in?'

Olivia turned her gaze to Kerry. 'Yes. He brought in chocolates for us all.'

'Did he go into the ward at all?'

Olivia hesitated. 'I don't think so. Someone else took the chocolates. We were discussing the plans for the night. He could have wandered in without us noticing. I honestly don't know.' She glanced at her watch. 'I really ought to get back. My break time is nearly finished.'

'You've been very helpful. Thank you,' Bernie said.

Olivia left but the smell lingered.

'What now?' Kerry asked.

'We go back to Keira and let her know that the father of her child is dead. Maybe then she'll tell us the truth. No wonder she didn't want to tell us.'

Keira was propped up on her pillows, her earphones back in again. She was flicking through a magazine. Bernie waved at her to gain her attention.

'Sorry to disturb you once more, Keira, but we've found out a few things and we need to talk to you about them.'

Keira pulled out her earphones slowly and then closed her magazine.

Kerry drew the curtains.

'One of those chats again, is it?' Keira said.

'We're thinking about you,' said Bernie. 'You might be upset by what we're going to say.' She and Kerry sat down. Bernie placed her hand on Keira's arm. 'I know you don't want to tell me about the baby's father but I have to ask you if the name Zac Ambrose means anything to you.'

Keira looked puzzled. 'No, I don't think so.'

Bernie paused. 'What about Dean Foster?'

Keira gasped. She didn't say anything. She didn't have to.

'You know how I said your attacker had died.'

Keira nodded.

'We thought Zac Ambrose, or as you knew him, Dean Foster, was your attacker.'

Keira clasped her hand to her mouth to stifle a sob. Her shoulders moved up and down.

Bernie stood and placed an arm around her. 'I'm so sorry, Keira. When you're ready, we need to ask you some more questions but I'm going to give you a few moments.'

Keira buried her head into Bernie as tears ran down her cheeks. Bernie looked at Kerry and mouthed, 'We got this all wrong.'

Kerry mouthed back, 'I know.'

Keira stilled and lifted her head. She grabbed a tissue from a box on the bedside cabinet and blew her nose. She wiped her tears with her hand. 'OK. I'm ready now.'

61

'I first saw Dean at the Plaza last autumn when I was with Isaac. Dean was dealing and Isaac wanted to score. I thought he was lush – a proper man, you know. And he was eyeing me up big time. Next time I saw him was at the Markhams' house for a party. I'd been to their house before with my family but this time I was invited alone. I didn't think much of it really until I turned up and saw what it was like. God, they were behaving like randy teenagers. It was gross – old people copping off with each other. Anthony came up to me and I'm sure he wanted to have sex with me but Dean got in there first, said I was already taken. He was really sweet to me.

'So we started dating. I dumped Isaac which really pissed him off. I couldn't tell my parents the real reason why Isaac was so angry and I definitely couldn't tell them that my new boyfriend was a drug dealer.'

'Did you go back to the Markhams' for another party on New Year's Eve?' Bernie asked.

'Yeah, I didn't want to. I was at the Plaza with the girls but Dean was working and I didn't want to snog a stranger at midnight. So I came along. He provided the gear for them.'

'Someone saw the two of you having sex in the alleyway.'

Keira blushed. 'Oh God. I hoped that no one had seen us. Dean didn't seem to care. Actually, I don't know why I'm embarrassed. We had far more clothes on than that lot inside. Urgh. So much wobbly flesh on display.'

Bernie smiled. She wanted to tell Keira that she'd have wobbly flesh one day but decided against it. She thought carefully about her next question. 'We've also heard that Rachel had an argument with a neighbour about the noise. The neighbour threatened to call the police but Rachel laughed. Said the police were already there. What did she mean by that?'

Keira shrugged. 'I don't know. I guess some of them may have been off-duty officers. It was mostly the same people from the autumn party. I think they do this fairly regularly. Actually, there was one guy who was at both parties who spoke to Dean. He was different from the rest. He didn't get involved – well, he didn't seem to.'

Bernie leaned forward. 'What did he look like?'

'Oh, I don't know. Old. Fair hair. Had what my dad would call a boxer's nose. London accent. They disappeared into another room for a while...' Keira blanched. 'Oh God, were they having sex?'

Bernie thought about DCI Jack Thornton and what she knew about him. 'I don't think they were having sex. It sounds as though Dean was pretty caught up with you. When did you get pregnant?'

'I think it was that party. The condom split. I didn't think too much about it until my period didn't start. They're really irregular so it took me a while to realise.'

'And did you tell Dean?'

Keira shook her head. 'I didn't know what to do. And now I can't tell him.' She put her hands to her face, shoulders shaking again.

'I know this is hard, Keira, but I need to ask you again about the night of your attack. The reason we believed Dean, or rather Zac, was responsible was because we found a condom in a bin in the Town Gardens. It had both yours and his DNA. What were you doing there?'

Keira wiped her face with a tissue. 'He texted me, saying he wanted to meet in the gardens. I knew what he wanted. I didn't tell you before because I was embarrassed. He has... or had, a thing for having sex outside. I think he liked the idea of being caught or being watched—' She stopped.

'What? Have you remembered something?'

'I thought someone was there. I could hear rustling but Dean said it was probably just an animal. I wondered if it was that creepy park guy. He's eyed me up before.'

'Park guy?'

'The one who looks after the gardens. Lives in the cottage. He sometimes walks around at night with his dog. We've been in there a few times and he nearly caught us once.'

Bernie looked at Kerry, who wrote something in her notebook.

'So you had sex in the gardens. What happened next?'

'Ugh. Dean got a call. Said it was urgent and he had to go. And that was the last time I saw him.'

Bernie saw that Keira was about to lose it again so she intervened quickly. 'So Zac left. Do you know which way he went? What did you do?'

Keira rubbed her head. 'That's what I'm not sure about. I remember giving Dean – Zac – a carrier bag to stick his condom in. My trainers had been wrapped up in it. We never left stuff lying about that kids might find. He went running off. He probably climbed over the fence by the top gate. There's a pathway that leads to a road. That's the way he'd normally come in and leave.'

Bernie nodded. That fitted with seeing the tag on the graffiti wall. 'Did he deal drugs in that road?'

Keira nodded. 'Yeah. Behind the houses. There's a lane there. I think he left me to go and do a deal. Anyway, I turned to pick up my bag and then, the next thing I knew, I was in hospital. I don't think Dean hit me. There must have been someone else there.'

Bernie thought about Jade Ambrose and her insistence that Zac would never attack a woman like that. The worrying thing was that if Zac wasn't the serial sex attacker, then the real culprit was still out there.

'Earlier you said to us you didn't know Rachel Bell. I guess you weren't telling the truth.'

'No. She was worried I might tell my parents about the parties. They don't know about them. But Rachel was great in ICU. She took good care of me. She said she'd contact Dean and let him know how I was doing. She knew it wouldn't be a good idea for him to come to the hospital. She passed on his messages.'

'So you had no idea that Zac, or Dean, was lying in a hospital bed only a few metres away from you?' Kerry asked. She'd been busy writing down everything Keira had said.

Alarm crept onto Keira's face. 'What? That can't be true. You haven't said how he died. Did someone kill him?'

'That's what we're trying to find out,' Bernie said. 'But I can tell you now that Rachel Bell knew Dean was in ICU so she was lying about the texts. Why would she do that?'

'I don't know. To protect me? She'd know I'd go hysterical if I knew.'

'Maybe. I think we're going to leave it there for the moment, Keira. It's important you rest.'

Keira gripped Bernie's hand. 'You'll find out what happened to Dean, won't you?'

'We'll do our very best, Keira. We'll be in touch.'

Bernie and Kerry left the ward quickly. Bernie looked at her sergeant. 'I think it's time to find Rachel Bell, don't you? I'm not convinced she was lying about the texts to protect Keira. And I'm not sure I want her seeing Keira again.'

62

There was no answer at the large white house in Lydiard Millicent. Bernie peered through a window.

'Very nice. Anthony Markham is clearly doing well for himself,' Kerry said. They walked back to the car.

'Hmm. I'm wondering now if Jade Ambrose had asked him to be her lawyer or if he had offered his services,' said Bernie. 'Rachel clearly knew who he was, even with a different name. God, I wish people would just use their real names. It's so bloody confusing.'

'Do you think they were worried Zac was going to spill the beans on their parties?'

Bernie looked at Kerry. 'Worried enough to kill him, you mean?'

Kerry nodded.

'It's a possibility. But we're going to need a lot more than just a hunch to get a warrant to search this place. I think our best bet is to have a little chat with Anthony Markham first. Just let him know we need to talk to Rachel in relation to Zac's death. Say we're now speaking formally to everyone to build up a picture of what happened that night.'

'So, back to Swindon?'

'For now. And then do you fancy driving over to Salisbury?'

'You're kidding. Back to the mortuary?'

Bernie opened the car door and got in. 'I think Dr White will respond better if we're actually there. Too easy to get out of a phone call.'

'OK. But we're grabbing some lunch before we go. Don't want you fainting in the morgue.'

Bernie looked at her watch. It was almost midday. 'Good thinking. Let's see what Anthony Markham has to say for himself, then we'll pop into a supermarket. I really fancy fish paste.'

'Fish paste? God, Bernie, I thought your Marmite craving was bad enough. You're seriously weird.'

'I'm afraid Mr Markham is in court today.' Joel smiled weakly. 'Can I take a message?'

Bernie paused. 'No. Actually, you might be able to help us. Mr Markham recently took on a new client, Jade Ambrose, on behalf of her son, Zac. Do you know when Mrs Ambrose first contacted you?' She smiled sweetly.

Joel shuffled uncomfortably in his chair and tugged at his pink shirt collar. 'I can't give out that information. You'll have to talk to Mr Markham yourself.'

Bernie nodded. 'That's fine. Oh, one other thing.' She lowered her voice. 'Have you ever been to any of the *special* parties at Anthony Markham's house?'

Joel said nothing but his face matched his pink shirt.

'Thank you, Joel. You've been a great help.' Bernie winked and walked out, Kerry following.

'How was he helpful?' Kerry asked as they got back in the car.

'Because Joel will go to Markham and tell him what I said. It'll wind him up. It'll be interesting to see what he does next.'

Kerry had her window wound down as they drove to Salisbury.

'It's a bit cold, Kerry.'

'It's also a bit stinky with that bloody fish paste. I'm never letting you in my car again with that muck.'

'I can't help it. The baby wants it.'

'I don't care if the Queen wants it. The window stays open until you finish it.'

Bernie laughed, brushing crumbs off her coat from the crusty roll she had chosen. The baker in the supermarket had been most surprised when she'd asked for a knife to spread the paste. There was obviously some particular nutrient she was craving. She couldn't quite believe what she was eating. Pops would have roared with laughter. It had been one of his favourite sandwich fillings.

She finished the roll and wiped her mouth with a tissue, before having a swig of water. 'All done. Now, please can you put the window up?'

Kerry pushed a button and the window rose, the sound of the whooshing wind decreasing.

'That's better. I promise I'll keep the fish paste for home. Although Dougie isn't very keen either.'

'You're on your own with that one then. I'm still a bit confused with this case. I rang the mortuary this morning and they said the post-mortem report wasn't ready. So why are we going?'

'Because the super hinted to me that Nick White has been asked to sit on the report. He'll wait for toxicology results.'

'But that's normal.'

'What did Olivia tell us earlier? Zac went into cardiac

arrest. So that's most likely what he died from. What caused the arrest is another matter. So why aren't we being told that?'

'Hmm. I think you're not telling me everything either.'

Bernie was quiet for a minute. 'Kerry, it's not that I don't want to…'

'I know. Your hands are tied. But I'm working in the dark here. I think I understand some of the things we've found out today. Zac Ambrose, aka Dean Foster, was known to Anthony and Rachel as a drug dealer. DCI Thornton may, or may not, have been at some of those parties. Maybe he saw Keira there. Isaac delivered a note to Zac that was possibly from Thornton. Adam Howard was in ICU on the evening Zac died. Keira's mystery man and father of her child is Zac. And it's now unlikely he attacked Keira. So in some ways we're back at square one with our unknown serial sex attacker.'

Bernie nodded. 'You're right. We are back at square one. With Keira anyway. Unless she was right about Malcolm Keats. As I already know, it's hard to alibi someone when you're asleep. I'm going to call Alice and ask her and Leigh to go back through the stuff you found at the park search. Maybe there'll be something in there. And then I'll get Matt and Mick to look at Keats more closely.'

She took out her phone and called MCIT. 'Hi, Alice. New task for you and Leigh. You're going to love this.'

Dr Nick White stepped out from the morgue, his scrubs splattered with blood and some other kind of fluid. Bernie decided not to ask what the yellow stain was.

'Detective Inspector Noel, what can I do for you?'

'Wanted to check in on the results for Zac Ambrose.'

There was a brief frown before White attempted a smile. 'I think my secretary spoke to your sergeant this morning. Nothing conclusive yet. We need to wait for tox.'

Bernie leaned her head to one side. 'So you have no idea at all? It's just that we spoke to an ICU nurse this morning who was there and she said Zac went into cardiac arrest.'

Nick White pursed his lips. 'Always one step ahead, aren't you, Detective Inspector?'

'I fully appreciate that you can't give a final report just yet but in your professional opinion, was cardiac arrest the cause of death? I don't need to know what caused the attack. Well, not for the moment.'

Nick shook his head. 'You'd make a good barrister. OK. He didn't die from his injuries from the accident. As far as I can tell, Zac Ambrose died from a cardiac arrest but I don't know what caused it. He was young and fit and his heart was in good condition. Even with all the other trauma he had suffered from the accident, his heart functioned well. I have no explanation – yet – as to why that changed. I think toxicology is going to be key in this. But don't quote me on that.'

Bernie smiled. 'I wouldn't dream of doing so.'

63

By the time they got back to headquarters, it was after three p.m.

'Certainly clocking up the miles on this case,' Kerry said as she pulled into the car park. 'I'll be glad to stretch my legs.'

'Thanks, Kerry. I'd have struggled doing all of that.'

'Oh, I don't mind. It was nice hanging out with you.'

Bernie undid her seat belt. 'You're finding Leigh difficult, aren't you?'

'That obvious, huh?'

'Yep.'

Kerry looked at Bernie. 'I just wish you'd told me earlier. I'll make more of an effort with her.'

'Thanks. I'm sure Leigh will appreciate that.'

Alice and Leigh were seated in front of Alice's computer.

'Afternoon,' Bernie said. 'Where are Mick and Matt?'

'Matt's watching the CCTV footage from the club,' answered Alice. 'And Mick's checking out this Keats guy.'

'OK. Have you two got anywhere yet with looking at Keira's case again?'

Leigh nodded. 'There are some pieces of evidence that weren't tested, probably because the condom was found. There was a small collection of cigarette butts that were found in a bush near to where the attack took place.'

Bernie joined them at the computer and looked at the evidence list on screen. 'Keira's told us that Zac Ambrose was her secret lover and the father of her child. They had sex there that night which explains the condom.'

'Why use a condom if she was already pregnant?' Alice said.

'Because she hadn't yet told him. And now she can't.' *But she can tell Jade.* 'Anyway, Zac had to leave suddenly. He got a call. We need to find out who rang him. Kerry, get on to Tom and ask him to check Zac's phone.'

'Sure,' Kerry said.

'Keira was about to leave when she was hit on the head,' Bernie continued. 'She thought there might have been someone else there. Said there was a rustling noise coming from a bush. Zac told her it was an animal but what if it wasn't? Perhaps it could be the owner of these cigarette butts. Let's get them tested asap for DNA. Ask for priority. Good work, Alice and Leigh.'

'Oh, it was all Leigh,' said Alice. 'She's the one who picked it up.'

Bernie resisted the urge to glance at Kerry. The search had been her domain. If she was annoyed about being upstaged by Leigh, Kerry wasn't displaying it.

'Afternoon, ma'am. I've got some good news for you.' Bernie turned to see Mick behind her.

'Oh yes. Something on Keats?'

'No, clean as a whistle. I spoke to his partner on the phone and she confirmed he was at home. Said she was woken up by the fox noise too. So, unless we find some evidence, he's not looking like a suspect at the moment. But, Adam Howard is downstairs waiting to see us. I managed to persuade him it was in his interest to come and see us sooner rather than later.'

'Excellent. I think I'd like to handle this myself. Do you want to join me, Mick?'

'Yes, ma'am. Shall I scribe?'

'That would be good. Thanks. Right, let's go and see what young Mr Howard has to say for himself.'

'Thank you for coming in, Adam. After our little chat in the hospital I have some questions that you might have the answers for.'

Adam had his hand raised to his mouth and was biting his fingernails. It was a habit Bernie hated and thought it particularly bad in a doctor, even a student one. After treating lots of patients you had no idea what would be trapped under those nails.

'Of course. Although Keira texted me earlier and said that her attacker had died. So I'm not sure what I can add really.'

Bernie leaned forward in her chair. 'Well, the interesting thing about the alleged attacker...'

Adam Howard frowned.

'...is that he was also in ICU at the same time as Keira. Obviously, not the exact same time – he came the next day. We didn't know he was possibly responsible until we got back some DNA results.'

'But he was still on the ward when you knew? How could you let Keira be anywhere near him?' Adam's face turned red with anger.

'Neither of them were well enough to be moved. Keira went to her current ward as quickly as possible. I can understand your frustration about that but our hands were tied. The reason I've asked you to come in is to talk about your last trip to ICU after Keira transferred.'

'I don't know what you mean.'

'We've been told you went there Saturday night.'

Adam looked puzzled. 'Did I? Oh, yes. I took chocolates for the staff to say thank you. I'm not sure what that has to do with anything.'

'Keira's alleged attacker died that night. We're investigating his death.'

Adam Howard stared at her. 'What? Are you suggesting what I think you are? I didn't even know this man was there.'

'Adam, we have to look at everyone who was there that evening, even the staff on duty. I'm not suggesting anything. We have to rule people out. Did you go into the ward at all?'

Adam shook his head. 'No. I gave the chocolates in and then spoke to Rachel.'

'We hadn't realised until recently that your family know Rachel.'

'Oh yes. Not particularly well but she was a great comfort to us all. We felt much happier knowing she was looking after Keira.'

'Hmm.' Bernie gave Mick a sideways glance. He was writing down what was being said. 'So you said Keira texted you earlier to let you know about the alleged attacker's death?'

'Yes. You keep saying "alleged". Are you sure or not?'

'Well, up until this morning we were fairly certain as we had found DNA evidence at the scene. However, since your sister texted you, we've had another chat with her. It turns out that she knew the *alleged* attacker. Rather than raping her, they had consensual sex in the gardens. And it wasn't their first sexual encounter. He's the father of her baby. She was attacked after he'd left.'

Adam started to breathe heavily. 'I don't understand what you're telling me. You just said Keira's attacker was in ICU with her and now you're saying she was having a relationship with him? And he's dead? The father of her child?' Adam stood up, his eyes darting round the room.

'Adam, is there anything you want to tell me?'

He shook his head violently. 'No. No. You're wrong.' He headed towards the door.

Bernie nodded to Mick who jumped up and grabbed Adam before he could leave.

'Adam Howard, I'm arresting you on suspicion of the murder of Zac Ambrose,' Bernie said. 'You do not have to say anything. But, it may harm your defence if you do not mention when questioned something you later rely on in court. Anything you do say may be given in evidence. Do you understand what I've just said to you?'

Adam nodded, his lips shut tight.

'Right, let's get you booked into custody.'

64

Bernie was buzzing. The ticking of the custody clock gave her more adrenalin than caffeine ever could. The rest of MCIT were itching to get going as well.

'Right. The clock has started. We have just under twenty-four hours to question Adam Howard and find any evidence that he's linked to the death of Zac Ambrose.'

'Shouldn't you have had that in place first?' said a voice by the door to the MCIT office.

Bernie looked over to the super standing there. 'Sir, it all happened very quickly. Adam Howard came in for us to ask him a few questions. His response to those questions and subsequent behaviour led me to believe he knows something about Zac's death. And in order to question him further, I needed to arrest him.'

DCS Wilson kept her gaze and then nodded. 'OK. But come to me first if you need an extension. Since you started talking to him earlier, I suggest you lead the interview.'

'Thank you, sir. Mick, perhaps you can join me for that. Matt, I'd like you to find out which hospital Adam Howard studies at. Get on to them and ask for an immediate audit of drugs. We're looking for something that would cause Zac heart problems.

'Kerry, ring Gable Cross and ask them to pick up Isaac Campbell. I think he's got more to tell us. And then get on to Forensics and say the cigarette butts are urgent. We now have DNA samples from Adam Howard so make sure they're sent.

'Alice and Leigh. Go and find Rachel Bell. She was there that evening and I want to know why. Oh, did Tom come back about Zac's phone and the call he received before Keira's attack?'

Kerry pulled a face. 'Zac's phone is missing. It was packaged up but it never made it to the lab.'

'Shit.' Bernie understood all too well what that could mean. Either Thornton had got hold of it, or it was with Thames Valley Police. 'OK. We'll go with what we've got for now.'

The phone on Kerry's desk began to ring. 'MCIT. Oh right, I'll let her know. Thanks.' She put the phone down. 'That was custody. Adam Howard's lawyer has turned up.'

'Great. But if it's anyone from Anthony bloody Markham's practice I'm kicking their backsides out of here. Let's go.'

Adam Howard was draped across the desk, sobbing.

'As you can tell, my client is in no fit state to be interviewed at present,' said an older man, his face as grey as his suit.

Bernie was relieved the lawyer was not Anthony Markham or any of his associates. Instead, he was the duty solicitor.

'I appreciate that but we're looking at a very serious charge here. Adam, I can see you're upset but it's important we question you.'

Adam raised his head. His face was blotchy and snot ran down his face like a toddler. Bernie passed him some tissues.

'Blow your nose and wipe your face. I want to explain why I arrested you. Earlier, we'd invited you in for a little chat as we need to speak to everyone who was in ICU on Saturday evening. Your reaction to my questions, as witnessed by DC Parris, was... a little suspicious. I think you know more about this than you're letting on.'

Adam blew his nose and then stuffed the tissues up his sweatshirt sleeve.

'Are you ready now?' Bernie asked.

'Yes.'

'OK. Let's start recording. The time is seventeen fifty hours. Present in the room is myself, Detective Inspector Bernadette Noel; Detective Constable Mick Parris; the suspect, Adam Howard; and his lawyer, Simon Taylor. The suspect has been arrested on suspicion of the murder of Zac Ambrose.

'So, Adam, let's start with why you were in ICU on Saturday evening.'

Adam wiped his sleeve across his face. 'Um, I was there to give some chocolates to the staff to say thank you for looking after Keira.'

The lawyer laid his hand on Adam's arm. 'Remember what I said. You don't have to answer their questions.'

Adam trembled. 'I'll answer what I can.'

'Thank you,' said Bernie. 'Did you speak to any of the nurses or doctors while you were there?'

'I said hello to some of the nurses I knew. In particular, I spoke to Rachel, who'd looked after Keira the most.'

'What did you talk about?'

'Nothing much. We know her a bit as Keira has a work placement at her husband's law firm.'

'Have you ever been to their house?'

Adam thought for a moment. 'I don't think so... no, wait, we went for a BBQ there last summer.'

'So you haven't been there for any other parties then?'

Adam shook his head.

'For the recording?' Bernie gestured to the machine.

'No. Just the BBQ.'

'OK. The chocolates you brought. Who did you give them to?'

Adam played with the cuff on his sweatshirt. 'I brought two boxes. I gave one to the nurse on reception and Rachel took the other. She said she was on shift the next day. Said if the box was left the night shift would eat them all.' He smiled weakly.

'So Rachel took the chocolates?'

'Yes.'

'Did you go into ICU at all to see any of the patients?'

'No, I didn't.'

'You're a medical student at Bristol?'

'Yes. Fourth year.'

'So I guess you've been let loose on the wards for quite a while then.'

Adam nodded. 'Poor patients.'

'When we spoke earlier, you were, firstly, very angry when we mentioned that Keira's alleged attacker was in ICU at the same time as Keira. I then explained to you that we discovered today that Zac Ambrose was in fact Keira's lover. You then became very upset and agitated. Is that fair to say?'

Adam stared at the table.

'Adam, is that right?'

There was a slight head movement.

'For the recording please, Adam.'

'Yes.'

'Why did your mood change so abruptly?'

Adam started to bite his fingernails. 'I guess I was upset that Keira's boyfriend had died. Is this going to take long? I really want to see Keira. She'll be upset.'

'That depends on how well you answer our questions. Did anyone else tell you, before today, that Zac Ambrose was responsible for Keira's attack?'

Adam kept his eyes down. 'No.'

'Are you sure about that?'

'Yes.'

Bernie glanced at Mick. She needed more evidence before she could continue. But equally it would give Adam time to consolidate a story. It was a risk she'd have to take.

'I think we'll take a break for a bit.'

65

'Do either of you have anything for me?'

Bernie looked at Matt and Kerry.

'I've spoken to the hospital,' said Matt. 'They weren't very happy with me, especially being near the end of the day. But they're doing an audit now. I explained it to them and they know what drugs to look at first. They're going to ring me later to give me an update. I did say we're against the clock.'

'OK. Kerry?'

'The lab are testing the cigarette butts as we speak. They should get Adam Howard's DNA in the next hour. But I don't think his DNA will match. I can't see Adam raping his own sister. And if he did, why kill Zac Ambrose?'

Bernie leaned against the desk. 'Assuming it was rape. Keira had definitely had consensual sex. Her internal injuries may have been caused by something else. An object put inside her.' She shuddered. She didn't want to think too much about that. 'And remember, Adam thought Keira might be pregnant before that night. Maybe he followed her. Couldn't cope with what he saw, and attacked her. And perhaps Zac had seen him.'

'But we're not asking him about that,' said Mick.

'Not yet. He's rattled though. Any news on Isaac Campbell or Rachel Bell?'

'Gable Cross can't find him – surprise, surprise. Mum didn't even know he'd been released. She thought he was still with us,' Kerry said. 'Alice and Leigh are stuck in traffic. They'll let us know when they get there.'

'Damn. I didn't think to check with Leigh about the working hours for this. I'm not sure if she's going to cope.'

'It's OK,' said Kerry. 'I checked with her. She was happy to stay on.'

Bernie raised her eyebrows.

'I was nice! In fact, I think she's quite excited about it all.'

'Yeah, I think she is,' said Matt. 'She was very keen to get out there.'

'OK then. I'd better go and see if my other half is still here and warn him I could be here late tonight. Let me know if anything useful comes in.'

Bernie made her way to the next floor to find Dougie. He was at his desk, surrounded by paperwork.

'That looks like fun.'

He groaned. 'They've put me on a case that's going to appeal. So I'm looking at all the paperwork. How are you doing?'

Bernie pulled a chair up to sit next to Dougie. 'I've arrested Keira Howard's brother, Adam, on suspicion of Zac Ambrose's murder.'

'What? Has it been confirmed as murder?'

'Not yet.'

'I suppose he has motive, given that Zac attacked his sister.'

'Except he didn't.'

Dougie frowned. 'What are you going on about?'

'Zac and Keira were in a relationship. They had sex that night in the gardens but he didn't attack her. You should have seen Adam's face when he realised Zac wasn't the attacker but the father of her baby.'

'Shit.'

'Exactly.'

'Had you told the Howard family about Zac Ambrose?'

'No. We were waiting for Keira to be moved and settled before we told them his name.'

'How did Adam find out?'

'I think from Rachel Bell, Anthony Markham's wife. She might have overheard me talking to Jack Thornton about it.'

'Maybe she thought she was doing the right thing in telling Adam.'

'Except the plot thickens.'

'Seriously?'

Bernie leaned into Anderson. 'An ICU nurse has confirmed that Anthony and Rachel do have raunchy, drug-fuelled sex parties – so not just a rumour – and Zac Ambrose was their dealer.'

Dougie pulled back and stared at her. 'You are kidding! I've been working on a boring old fraud case and you've found out all this stuff today. Fuck.' He shook his head. 'Rachel knew who Ambrose was then.'

'More than that. Keira has been to a couple of these parties and hooked up with Zac. Rachel knew they were together.'

'Now I'm confused. Why not tell the family? Unless she genuinely thought Zac had attacked Keira. You need to get her in.'

'I know. We're trying to locate her. And we're attempting to get Isaac back in as well except he's done a bunk.'

'I thought you'd cleared him.'

'I think I may have been hasty. Anyway, I came to say that I might not be home until late tonight.'

'Well, in that case, you need to eat something soon. I'm going to do this for about another ten minutes then I'm stopping. I'll go and get food for you all and keep you company for the evening. I can be your errand boy.'

Bernie kissed him. 'That's sweet of you. But what about my parents?'

'They're in Bath and are eating there. So let me know what you want and I'll go and buy it. Actually, it will be quite nice to be part of the old team again. I've missed it.'

Bernie was just taking a mouthful of pizza when her desk phone rang.

'Damn. Kerry, could you?'

DS Allen leaned across the desk and answered the phone. 'MCIT, DS Allen speaking... oh hi, wait a minute, I'll put you on speaker so we can all hear... OK, Alice, what have you got?'

'We're at Rachel Bell's house. She's not here but Anthony Markham is. He told us that Rachel had a family emergency and has gone to see her sister for a few days.'

Bernie swallowed her food. 'That's very handy.'

'Exactly. What do you want us to do now?'

'Hmm. We could do with speaking to Anthony Markham anyway. Are you still near the house?'

'Yes, we're just in the car outside. Do you want to speak to him now on the phone?'

'Yes please.'

'OK. Give me a minute.'

Bernie snuck another quick bite of her pizza as she could hear Alice's feet crunching on gravel and then a doorbell ringing.

'Oh, it's you again,' said a male voice.

'Sorry to disturb you again, Mr Markham, but DI Noel would like a word with you.'

Bernie imagined Alice handing over the phone.

'Yes, DI Noel, what can I do for you?' There was a weariness in his voice.

'Mr Markham, there are a few things I'd like to talk to you about in person.'

There was a sigh. 'I can see you tomorrow morning about ten.'

'I'm afraid it won't wait until the morning. My officers will bring you to headquarters now.'

'Is this really necessary? I've had a long day at court. I've not even eaten yet.'

There was something in his voice that caught Bernie's attention. He was tired. His usual precise, polished tone had slipped a little, along with a few consonants. His original accent was breaking through.

'We can feed you. It really is very urgent. We're investigating a murder, Mr Markham.'

'I know and I'm not deliberately being difficult. I really am very tired. So, unless you're going to arrest me, I'll see you at ten tomorrow morning. Do you need to speak to your officer again?'

Bernie sighed. Markham was right. She couldn't force him to come in. 'Yes please.'

There was a pause and then, 'Ma'am?'

'Leave Markham for now and come back to headquarters. If Leigh wants to go home she can.'

'OK. I'll check with her.'

'Thanks, Alice.'

Bernie hung up. 'Matt, did you get anywhere looking at the CCTV footage from the club?'

'No, not really.'

'Go and look again. And this time, check carefully for Anthony Markham.'

Kerry caught her eye. 'You think Markham could be the mysterious man that met Isaac in the club?'

'It's a possibility. When he was talking to me, I could hear a south London accent. Not very distinct but still there.'

Bernie had just picked up another slice of pizza when her phone rang again. 'Seriously?' She answered. 'DI Noel.'

'Ma'am, it's Alice again. We've just heard some chatter on the radio. Gloucestershire Police have fished a body out of one of the lakes in the Cotswold Water Park. One of the smaller ones that aren't used much by the public. Body's an IC3 male. They found a rather waterlogged photo ID card for Great Western Hospital.'

'Don't tell me – Dean Foster, right?'

'Yep. They're requesting support from Gable Cross. Do you want us to attend?'

'Yes please. Let me know if I need to come.'

'Of course. Bye, ma'am.'

'Bye, Alice.' Bernie put the phone down. 'Oh shit.'

'What?' Kerry asked.

'I think we might have found Isaac Campbell and it's not good.'

66

It was an hour before Alice rang back.

'Sorry, ma'am. It took a while to get here as we had to work out exactly which lake –there are so many. And then the road was closed and we had to walk down in the dark. I've seen the body – it is Isaac Campbell. Anyway, there are a few detectives from Gloucestershire here. We might have an issue over who's going to investigate. They want to run it. Classed as suspicious death at the moment.'

Bernie sat back in her chair. She wasn't surprised. 'It's their turf. Did you explain that we questioned Isaac only yesterday in relation to another possible murder?'

'Yes, and they're very happy to have our cooperation.'

'Shit.' Bernie rubbed her forehead. A stress headache was starting to build. Was it coincidence that Isaac's body had been found just over the county border or did someone know that that would mean another police force would investigate, pushing her away from the scene of the action? Was it the London gang after all? Or someone closer to home?

'Has his mother been informed?'

'No, not yet. They'd been looking up Dean Foster rather than Isaac Campbell.'

'Will they let us do that? It's the least we can do.'

'I'll ask.'

Bernie looked at the rest of her team. 'Not good news. Alice has confirmed it's Isaac.'

'Oh no,' said Kerry. 'Maybe we should have put surveillance on him.'

Anderson put his arm round Bernie. 'It's not your fault.'

'Isn't it? We questioned him about involvement in another possible murder and now he's dead. How can it not be related?'

'Ma'am?' It was Alice.

'Yes.'

'DI Brooks from Gloucestershire would like a word.'

'OK. Put him on.'

Bernie heard a distant 'sir' as Alice handed her phone over.

'Hi, DI Noel, this is DI Christopher Brooks. I understand from DC Hart that you have an interest in this case.' Brooks had the voice of a man born and bred in Gloucestershire.

'You could say that. We interviewed him yesterday in relation to a murder case but released him without charge last night. I wanted to talk to him again and asked Gable Cross to pick him up earlier this evening but he wasn't at home. His mother thought he was still being held.'

'So, he never made it home. Interesting. Hmm. Well, we'll definitely be needing your cooperation in all of this. Of course, until the post-mortem happens, we can't be sure what this is exactly – accident, suicide or something else. There's a head wound but we can't be sure if that happened to him before going into the water. Lakes round here were former quarry pits so there are plenty of rocks in them.'

'About the post-mortem. Am I right in thinking you're a different area from us?'

'Yes, and I know what you're going to ask. He's on our patch so the post-mortem is done our end. The pathologist is on standby.'

Bernie sighed. 'If Isaac's death is linked with our case, it would be better if our pathologist, Dr Nick White, could do it. He's done our murder victim. Plus we've had another victim with head injuries. If it's the same perpetrator then there's likely to be similarities.'

'All the better to have two experts in court when the time comes, then. Assuming it is murder. Until we know for certain, though, he stays with us.'

Bernie looked at her team and shook her head. DI Brooks was digging his heels in and, if she was honest with herself, she'd probably do the same if it was the other way round.

'Could we at least inform his mother for you?'

Brooks paused. Bernie could guess what he was thinking. No one willingly wanted to tell a family that a relative had died.

'That would be helpful, thank you. If you could tell her someone from my team will see her in the morning. Gable Cross has already passed the address on to us. Perhaps you could be kind enough to let me know how it goes. I'll give my number to DC Hart. Thank you for your cooperation, DI Noel. Goodbye.'

Shame I can't say the same. 'Bye, DI Brooks. Can you pass the phone back to Alice please?'

'Hi, ma'am. Do you want me to go to Ms Campbell?'

'No thanks, Alice. You and Leigh have done more than enough tonight. I'll go. See you tomorrow.'

Bernie put the phone down. Tiredness washed over her. The baby needed her to rest, not get in a car and drive over to Swindon.

'Right, so which one of us is going with you?' asked Kerry.

Bernie looked across at her DS. 'Not you. You've already driven the length of this county today.'

'I'll drive you,' said Anderson. 'I've been stuck here all day looking at paperwork.'

Bernie hesitated. 'Not sure if that's a good idea or not. If it is tied in with Zac's death—'

'I was close enough to hear what Brooks said. We don't know what this is yet. Consider me your driver. You can do all the talking.'

'Thanks, I think.'

Although she had offered to speak to Isaac's mother, it really was the job she hated the most.

67

It was just after nine p.m. when they got to Isaac's home in Swindon. The door was boarded over where the battering ram had been used to gain entry the day before.

Anderson rang the bell. 'Police,' he said loudly.

'I'm coming,' said a voice from inside. 'Don't break the bloody door down again.'

The door opened. Isaac's mother looked at Bernie. 'You again. Found him yet?'

Bernie took a deep breath. 'Yes. Perhaps we could talk inside.'

Ms Campbell's eyes widened as she held the door back to let them in. Bernie and Anderson followed her into the lounge.

'Ms Campbell, I didn't get the chance to introduce myself last time. I'm DI Bernie Noel and this is DI Dougie Anderson. I think it's best if we all sit down.'

Isaac's mother shook her head. 'I don't want to sit down. Because if I sit down, you're gonna tell me something bad about my boy and I don't want to hear it.'

'Ms Campbell—'

'Lauren. Please, don't say it. Please, don't say it.' Tears were spilling onto her face.

Bernie bit her lip. She hated this so much.

Anderson stepped forward, gently took Lauren Campbell by the arm and led her to the sofa. Bernie sat down next to her and took a deep breath.

'Lauren, I'm so sorry to have to tell you this but Isaac was found dead earlier this evening in one of the lakes at the Cotswold Water Park. We don't know the cause of death yet so we can't explain what happened. As soon as we have more information, we'll tell you.'

Lauren bent over and sobbed. Bernie gently placed her hand on her shoulder.

'Take your time, Lauren.'

After a few minutes, Lauren sat up and wiped her face with her hand. 'I don't understand. He was with you. You took him away. I wasn't here but my neighbour told me. How did he end up in a lake?'

Bernie glanced at Anderson.

'How about I make you some tea, Lauren?' he asked.

'I'd rather have something stronger, thanks. There's a bottle of vodka in the freezer.'

'Neat?'

Lauren nodded.

Bernie held up her finger and thumb to Anderson to indicate a small measure. She needed Lauren to stay coherent.

'We released Isaac without charge about six o'clock last night. He didn't come home?'

Lauren shook her head. 'Not while I was here but I didn't get back until after seven thirty.'

Anderson returned with a shot glass. Lauren swallowed it down in one and handed the glass back. 'Another please.'

'In a little while,' said Bernie. 'I need to ask you a few more questions first.'

Lauren sniffed. 'OK. Let's get this over with and then I can get pissed.'

Bernie glanced at Anderson. This wasn't going to be easy.

'How long has Isaac been working at the hospital for as a cleaner?'

'I'm not sure. A few weeks. He said he'd met a man who'd offered him the job and he needed the money. He's done nothing since getting kicked out of college.'

'Did he tell you anything about this man? Any particular details?'

'No. Isaac said it was an agency.'

'Did you ever see his work photo ID? It had a different name on it – Dean Foster.'

Lauren looked confused. 'That doesn't sound right. No, I don't think I ever saw it. Why would he have a different name?'

'That's what we asked him about yesterday. In fact...' Bernie paused, wondering how much she should tell Lauren and how best to phrase it. 'We were asking him about a suspicious death on ICU at Great Western Hospital. Isaac was working there that night. We've spoken to all the staff on duty. Isaac told us a few things about the man who organised the job for him. It wasn't as straightforward as joining an agency. I wanted to ask him more questions today.'

'That's why the police turned up earlier.'

'Yes.'

'You thought he knew more than he'd said. Did you think he was in danger when you released him?'

'No. I didn't get that sense from him and I wouldn't have released him if I'd thought that. Lauren, do you think Isaac would hurt himself?'

Lauren shook her head vehemently. 'Never. It's how his father died. Isaac was only thirteen at the time but he swore to me he'd never do that. You said he was found in a lake. Isaac can't swim. He's scared and doesn't go near water at all. If he was going to kill himself, he wouldn't do it like that. So it's not suicide and it's not an accident. Someone did this to Isaac. Someone killed my boy. And you'll find out who, won't you?'

Bernie clenched her hands together. 'The lake where Isaac was found is in Gloucestershire so it'll be that force leading the investigation. I spoke to a DI Brooks earlier and someone from his team will come and see you in the morning. So, go easy on the vodka tonight.'

'But, if Isaac's death is connected to this other one...'

'Until the post-mortem results are in, we don't know how Isaac died and whether it relates to our case. But we'll assist DI Brooks as much as we can. Is there anyone we can call who can come and be with you?'

Lauren shrugged. 'Not really. Maybe Irene next door. She's always liked Isaac. Bought him Christmas and birthday presents.'

'I'll go and knock now,' said Anderson. 'Which way?'

Lauren pointed right. 'That side.'

Bernie waited until Anderson had left the house before speaking again. 'I'm going to leave you my card, Lauren. Call me if there's anything you think of or want to ask.'

Lauren looked directly at her. Despite the shot of vodka, she appeared very sober. 'You think he was murdered, don't you?'

Bernie hesitated. She knew what her gut instinct was telling her and she didn't want to lie to Lauren Campbell. 'Yes. And I'm sure DI Brooks will do a good job. But the case I'm looking at is very complex. If Isaac's death is connected, DI Brooks won't even know where to start. I do. I'll find who's responsible. I promise.'

'What are you thinking then?' Anderson asked, as he handed Bernie a cup of herbal tea. They'd gone straight home after seeing Lauren Campbell and were now curled up on the sofa.

'I'm not thinking anything.'

'Yes, you are. You're doing that funny twitch thing you do when you're thinking.'

'I twitch?'

'Yep. Around your mouth. So spill.'

Bernie sighed. She clearly couldn't keep anything from Dougie. 'I was thinking about Isaac. I'm trying to remember if he had his photo ID on him when he was at Gable Cross with us. The ICU nurse we spoke to this morning said the cleaner hadn't turned up last night. I'm pretty sure it was meant to be Isaac.'

'So you're thinking he went home to get his pass and then headed on to work. But he didn't get there.'

'Exactly. If someone picked him up, it must have been before he reached the hospital. It might be worth looking at CCTV.'

'Well, you can pass that information on to DI Brooks for him to decide. Because it's not your case, is it?'

'But—'

'Is it?'

Bernie huffed. 'No, it's not my case. We'll assist. But you have to admit this is a really complex investigation. How do we even begin to explain it to Brooks? In fact, we might not even be allowed to because of DCI Thornton.'

'Talk to the super tomorrow. This is one for him and the chief constable to decide on. Not you. Now, it's after eleven. Time for bed.' Dougie stood and offered Bernie his hand.

'Haven't finished my tea.'

'You don't even like that stuff.'

'It's growing on me.'

Anderson raised his eyebrows. 'You're not getting your laptop out now and working. Bed. The baby needs you to rest, even if you don't think so. You can bring your tea with you.'

Bernie narrowed her eyes. 'You know me too well. Not sure if I like that.'

She took Anderson's hand and he pulled her up. He put his arm around her and kissed the top of her head.

'I also know that you've promised Lauren Campbell that you'll find her son's killer because that's the kind of officer you are. But you can't do that on no sleep. We'll get back to it in the morning.'

68

WEDNESDAY

Bernie arrived early in MCIT the next morning with a large white box from the bakery. They'd opened up especially for her. After the news about Isaac Campbell the previous night, she thought her team could do with a boost.

'Breakfast is here. Help yourself and we'll have a briefing in fifteen minutes.' She grabbed a large Danish pastry to go with her decaf coffee. She'd only taken one bite when her desk phone rang.

'How do people always know when I'm eating?' She answered. 'DI Noel.'

'It's Alan Turner, ma'am.'

Bernie smiled. She liked the custody sergeant. 'What can I do for you?'

'It's Adam Howard. He's in a dreadful state. I don't think he's slept at all. I'm not sure whether to get the nurse to check him over or whether he needs to talk to you. He's crying so much he's not making sense.'

'Has he eaten anything?'

'No. Refused dinner last night and nothing so far this morning.'

Bernie eyed the bakery box. 'Stick him in an interview room. I'll be there in ten minutes. Thanks, Alan.'

She turned to the rest of the team after putting the phone down. 'Change of plan. Mick, you're with me. I think Adam Howard is about to spill his guts.'

Bernie put the white box on the table and opened it. There wasn't much left but there was enough of a choice for Adam.

'Eat something, Adam. You'll feel much better for it.'

Adam eyed the box warily.

Bernie passed him a plate. 'Come on. I bet you're a maple pecan plait kind of guy. They're my favourite but I'm staying clear of nuts just to be on the safe side.'

Adam sniffed. 'That's a good idea. Better to be safe during pregnancy.' His hand hovered over the box before pulling out the maple pecan plait.

'I knew I was right.' Bernie moved the box onto the floor. 'Just let me know if you want another. Sergeant Turner told me you've had a bad night. I guess you've had some thinking to do.'

Adam nodded as he crammed the pastry into his mouth, barely chewing.

'Would you like us to get your solicitor?'

He shook his head, still eating his food. He swallowed and then had a mouthful of tea. There were a few nuts left on his plate and he picked them up with his fingers and stuffed them in his mouth.

Something about his eating habits made Bernie uneasy. Was he really just that hungry? She got up and opened the door. Alan Turner had had the foresight to put them in the interview room across from the custody desk. 'Alan?'

He looked up from the desk. 'Yes, ma'am?'

'Does Adam Howard have any allergies?'

'Let me just check.' Alan Turner tapped on his keyboard. 'Yes. Nuts.'

Bernie looked back at Adam. He started coughing, his hand going to his throat. 'Oh, you little...' She shook her head. 'We need an ambulance now, Alan. And check his belongings for an EpiPen.'

When Alan rushed back into the room a couple of minutes later, Bernie and Mick had already placed Adam in the recovery position and were trying to keep his airway clear.

'No EpiPen in his belongings,' said Alan. 'Is it in your car, Adam?'

Adam tried to speak but only a squeak came out. He nodded instead.

'In our car park?'

Another slight nod.

'OK, I'll send someone out to look for his car. We have the keys.'

Bernie stared at Adam, alarmed as to how quickly he was reacting. 'What about the paramedics? What's their ETA?'

'I left Sian calling them.' Alan raised his voice. 'Sian, ETA for paramedics?'

'Ten minutes, Sarge. I'll go and find the car. I have the registration.'

Adam's breathing became shallow.

'I think we might need to raise him,' said Bernie. 'He's struggling to breathe in this position.'

Mick and Alan propped Adam up against the table.

'Better?' Bernie asked.

Adam blinked at her, his pupils dilated, his breathing laboured.

'Hold on for me, Adam. Keira needs you.' Bernie squeezed his hand. She looked at the clock on the wall. They didn't have long.

It seemed ages before Sian arrived back but it had only been four minutes.

'Got it,' she said. 'Right, those jeans look a bit thick to me to go through. We'll need to wriggle them down and then I'll inject the EpiPen into his thigh. Don't worry, Adam, I've done this before.'

Bernie sat back as Alan and Mick pulled down Adam's jeans and Sian plunged the EpiPen into his thigh. The effect was almost immediate: Adam gasped and his pupils started to shrink.

'Oh, thank God,' said Bernie.

'Paramedics are here,' someone called from the custody desk.

Bernie moved away and let Sian and Alan explain what had happened to the two paramedics who rushed in. She steadied herself against a chair.

'Ma'am,' said Mick, 'let's leave them to it. There are too many of us in here anyway.'

Bernie caught Alan's eye. He nodded. She could trust Alan to take it from here.

'Well, that went well.' Bernie slammed the bakery box onto her desk.

'Why?' Kerry asked. 'What happened?'

'The little fucker ate a pastry with nuts in it,' said Mick. 'He's allergic to them.'

'Maybe he didn't know there were nuts in it,' said Alice.

'It was a maple pecan plait. It was bloody obvious. Now I'm going to get done for it, even though he didn't have his EpiPen with him. Thank God it was in his car.' Bernie rubbed her forehead. The headache was back.

'Would you like some good news then?' Matt asked.

'Yes please.'

'The guy at the Bristol hospital has come back to me. As well as checking the actual medicine, he's also been looking at who went into the room. There's a swipe system that logs who's gone in. Student doctors rarely do so. But Adam Howard went in the day before Zac's death. They're looking at the meds now.'

Bernie smiled. 'Finally we're getting somewhere. The clock has stopped on Adam's custody. If he thinks deliberately causing an allergic reaction gets him out of this then he's very much mistaken.'

69

Bernie sat waiting for news of Adam Howard. She'd told the super what had happened. He hadn't been impressed.

'But you arrested him and booked him in. Don't you remember him saying about allergies?'

'No, I really don't.'

She still couldn't recall it as she sat at her desk. Everyone was sitting around waiting for news from various places – the forensic lab, the Bristol hospital, DI Brooks. Isaac's post-mortem was due that morning. Before she'd even had the chance to ask, an email from the chief constable's office had told her the case would be staying with Gloucestershire. But Bernie was sure that whoever killed Zac was responsible for Isaac's death too.

The phone rang and Bernie pounced on it.

'DI Noel.'

'Ma'am, it's Alan Turner. I've checked with yesterday's custody sergeant. Adam Howard didn't declare his allergy until we offered him dinner. You're off the hook. On the other hand, I'm very much on the hook as I didn't tell you.'

'I'll back you, Alan, don't worry. Have you heard anything from the hospital?'

'No. But it'll be at least six hours before he's allowed back. And he'll need babysitting for twenty-four hours.'

Bernie checked her watch. Six hours meant Adam wouldn't be back until early afternoon.

'Well, depending on what happens, we might be able to bail and place him in the care of his parents. Oh, Alan, could you do me another favour please? Could you check with Gable Cross for the custody record for Isaac Campbell and see if he had his hospital work ID card on him when questioned on Monday?'

'Of course, no problem, ma'am.'

'Thanks, Alan. Bye.'

Bernie put the phone down and stood up. Looking across at Leigh, she realised she hadn't really had a chance to check on her properly since her meltdown. Leigh had her head bent over some files. Bernie wandered over to her.

'What are you looking at, Leigh?'

She lifted her head. 'The sex offences in Swindon, ma'am. If Keira's attack isn't connected then the assailant is still out there. I'll be straight back on to that once this case is over. Actually, I've been looking at Carl Smith, the barman from the Plaza. You were right. He has done time. Two counts of GBH. Both victims were male and the last one was from five years ago. So I don't think he's my man. But' – Leigh smiled – 'I'll keep an open mind.'

Bernie drew a chair up to sit next to her. 'Do you want to go back to Gable Cross? We have a HOLMES position coming up soon. You'd be an excellent candidate.'

Leigh smiled. 'Thank you, ma'am, but I like being an LCI. And as much as it's been good to meet new people, I miss the team back at Gable Cross.'

'The whole team or just one person in particular?'

Leigh blushed. 'One in particular. He came to see me Monday evening to make sure I was OK. We had a good chat. It's a start.'

'It is. Good on you, Leigh.'

Bernie's phone started to ring again.

'Excuse me.'

She darted back to her desk. 'MCIT. DI Noel speaking.'

'Good morning, DI Noel, this is Sally on reception. I have a rather irate man on the line for you. A Geoff Howard.'

'That's OK. Put him through.' Bernie waited for the click. 'Mr Howard, it's DI Noel. What can I do for you?'

'You can tell me why my son is in hospital after suffering an anaphylactic shock at your police station. What the bloody hell is going on?'

'Mr Howard, we gave Adam the choice to contact you yesterday but he declined. He didn't declare his allergy until after he'd been booked in so I didn't know about it, and he ate a pastry this morning knowing it had nuts in it. Thankfully, we picked up on it before he went into full shock. I'm waiting to hear from the hospital and once he's well enough he'll come back to custody.'

'But why was he with you in the first place?'

'We arrested Adam yesterday on suspicion of the murder of Zac Ambrose.'

'What? That's ridiculous. Who's Zac Ambrose anyway?'

'Did you see Keira yesterday?'

'Yes, of course. We see her every day.'

'Did she tell you that we'd been to see her?'

'No. Not a thing.'

'Mr Howard, I'm happy to tell you what's going on but I honestly think it would be better if you spoke to Keira first. Where are you?'

'At the hospital, trying to see my son. But a police officer has informed me that I can't.'

'That's right, I'm afraid. Adam is still in custody. Once he's well enough to leave hospital we have more questions for him. Please, go and see Keira now. I know it's not visiting time but I'll get one of my officers to notify the ward.' Bernie looked across at Kerry. She nodded and picked up her phone. 'And stay with Keira. She needs you. I'll be in contact about Adam. I'm sorry I can't tell you more for the moment, Mr Howard. I'll be in touch as soon as I can. Goodbye.'

She put the phone down. 'That felt brutal.'

'But necessary,' said Alice.

'Ma'am, I have an email through from Bristol,' said Matt.

'Oh yes, we have him.'

Bernie joined Matt at his desk to read the message. 'Brilliant. Now all we need is young Mr Howard back with us.'

'Ma'am.'

Bernie turned to see Alice behind her.

'Anthony Markham is here.'

'Oh great, barely get time to sit down.' Bernie sighed. 'Now I have to go and face Mr Hot-shot Lawyer.'

'Think I can help you with that too, ma'am,' said Matt, as he passed over a piece of paper with a picture on it.

Bernie looked at it and beamed. 'Oh, you beauty, Matt! Got him.'

70

Anthony Markham looked crumpled. Not just his clothes but his face too. Bernie was sure there were lines on his forehead that hadn't been there before. He obviously hadn't slept well. Something was weighing on him.

'So, DI Noel, what do you want to know?'

Bernie leaned back in her chair. 'The truth. Isn't that what we all want?'

Markham rubbed his face with his hand. 'I haven't come here to have a philosophical discussion. I don't have time to play games.'

'No, neither do I. Nor does Adam Howard. He's currently under arrest.'

'What?' Anthony sat up straight. 'Why? Do his parents know? Does he have representation?'

'He doesn't need you, that's for sure. He does need your wife though. But before we get to that, I have a question. Why did you pretend to not know Zac Ambrose?'

Anthony gave a wry smile. 'I didn't know Zac Ambrose.'

'OK, Dean Foster then.'

'Ah, Dean. Yes, well, it's a bit complicated.'

'Representing the family of your drug dealer – yes, I can imagine that would be complicated.' Bernie rubbed her head. Despite the food, a headache was brewing.

'My drug dealer? Do you have proof of that?'

'Tell me more about your parties.'

Another smile. 'Are you sure, DI Noel? I wouldn't want to upset your sensibilities, given your condition.'

Bernie resisted the temptation to roll her eyes. 'I'm pretty tough. And we see all sorts here.'

Anthony Markham pushed his sleeves up on his shirt. 'Rachel and I are swingers. We have a large house so we regularly hold parties for other swingers. Some are couples, some are single people. There's nothing illegal about it.'

'How did Dean fit in to all of this?'

'I met Dean last summer. A mutual friend introduced us. We invited him along.'

'You're telling me that Dean wanted to go to a swingers' party? Are you sure he wasn't there to provide you with drugs? I have a witness who saw lines of cocaine at one of your parties.'

'Really? I guess it would be the witness's word against mine.'

Bernie wanted to slap the arrogance out of him. 'Why did you invite Keira to a party?'

'Ah, Keira.' Anthony folded his arms. 'Well, I have to be honest and say that I was hopeful she might be interested in me. But it was not to be. She'd clearly met Dean before and I didn't stand a chance against him. Of course...' Anthony Markham stopped.

'Of course, what?'

He shook his head. 'It doesn't matter.'

Bernie looked at him. Anthony was hiding something, but he wasn't about to give it up easily. She pushed the piece of paper Matt had given her, a still from the CCTV at the club, across the table to him. 'This was taken last week at the Plaza. I believe it's you in the shot, talking to Isaac Campbell. Where are you from originally?'

Anthony gave her a quizzical look. 'South London. Why?'

'Because Isaac said he spoke to a man with a London accent. The man asked him to deliver a note to Zac Ambrose. Isaac was given the alias "Dean Foster" to use. Sloppy really, but I suspect there wasn't time to arrange anything else. What was in the note, Anthony?'

A vein in Anthony's neck pulsed as he swallowed. Then he relaxed. 'I'm sure you must know, *if* you have the note.'

Bernie thumped her fist down on the table between them. 'Time to stop playing games, Mr Markham.'

'Careful, Detective Inspector Noel, you seem a little aggressive there.' Anthony picked up the photo and examined it. 'Hmm, bit of a grainy shot but yes, that's me. Rachel had recognised Dean and told me his real name. And why he was there. Naturally, I couldn't give a note to Rachel to pass on. I knew about Isaac from Keira. I'd warned him off on behalf of the family last year. I knew how to get hold of him.'

'What was in the note?'

A smug smile appeared. 'You obviously don't have it otherwise we wouldn't be having this nice little chat. But I'll tell you. Rachel had told me that Dean, or Zac, was the main suspect for Keira's attack. I knew he wasn't responsible. I'd called him that night, asking to meet. I collected him from near Town Gardens.'

'Let me guess – the access road behind Goddard Avenue. We might have some footage of that. Why did you need to see him?'

'Um...' Markham's smile disappeared. 'Dean wanted to discuss something.'

'But you called him.'

'I was responding to a message he'd sent earlier.'

'How did he send that message?'

'By text.'

'Can I see it please?'

'I've deleted it.'

'That's OK. We can check your phone records. What did he want to discuss?'

Anthony Markham wiped his face with his hand. Bernie knew he was trying to think up something.

'He was worried he was about to be arrested.'

'What for?'

Markham hesitated. 'Drugs.'

'So he was a drug dealer then and provided you with cocaine for your parties.'

'No—'

'You see, this witness I was talking about, she's a nurse. A good, upstanding woman. I think her word would more than stand up against yours. So, I'm going to ask you again: why did you need to see Dean so urgently late on a Sunday night?'

Bernie kept eye contact with Markham until he broke away.

'I... needed a fix – cocaine.'

Bernie leaned her head on one hand. It hadn't been DCI Jack Thornton in the club. He hadn't sent the note to Zac.

'So,' Markham continued, 'I wrote a note saying I would be his alibi.'

'How do you know he didn't attack her before meeting you?'

'His demeanour was all wrong. He was happy, relaxed. He said he'd just been with Keira and she was on her way home. He told me how much he cared for her. There's no way he would have hurt her.'

'Then who did? And who killed him?'

Anthony Markham shook his head. 'I don't know.'

Bernie wasn't convinced. She remembered her earlier thought about an object being used to create Keira's injuries. You didn't have to be a man to do that. Things slotted into place. 'Where's your wife, Mr Markham? Where's Rachel?'

Anthony bit his lip.

'It won't take us long to find out where her sister lives, assuming she even has one. And I don't think it'll be long before Adam Howard admits his part in all of this. The hospital he works at has done an urgent audit on their drugs. They've found something. It would be stupid for Rachel to steal from her own hospital. You see' – Bernie leaned forward – 'I've been thinking long and hard about all of this. I thought it was about one thing in particular but I got it wrong. It's a very simplistic approach but generally most things come down to gold, glory or girls. Or in this case, boys. You said you liked Keira. You were going to say something else but stopped. I think Rachel liked Dean. Very much. Maybe she'd already had sex with him before he met Keira. How am I doing?'

Anthony dropped his eyes.

'As soon as we found the used condom, we thought Dean, or rather, Zac Ambrose, was responsible for Keira's rape so we didn't have to look any closer at the evidence. And Rachel was such a diligent nurse. To them both. She told Adam who was responsible for Keira's attack and persuaded him to get the drugs she needed to kill Zac, as she now knew him. Adam smuggled them in in a box of chocolates. Now at this point, I'm thinking there are two possibilities. Either Rachel administered the drug herself, or she made sure it was ready for the night shift nurse to give it. I suspect the latter. She's quite devious, isn't she?

'I think she also took your note when she found it in Zac's belongings. Rachel couldn't have you being an alibi for him. She needed you to be an alibi for her because she wasn't at work the Sunday night Keira was attacked. She was in Town Gardens, watching her former lover have sex with his new girlfriend. And after he left...'

'Stop.' Anthony Markham wiped sweat from his face. 'You can't prove it.'

'It's only a matter of time. Last night, Isaac Campbell's body was found. His post-mortem is happening as we speak. It'll be interesting to see what they come up with. If there are any similarities to Zac or Keira. She's killed twice and left another for dead. You may think you're buying her time but you're not. Time's running out. So, I'm going to ask you again, where's Rachel? Where's your wife? Is she really with her sister?'

Markham looked down. 'No.'

'Then where is she?'

He shrugged. 'I don't know.'

71

Bernie knocked on the super's door.

'Come in.'

She opened the door to see the chief constable sitting opposite DCS Wilson.

'What can I do for you, Bernie?' Wilson asked.

'Sorry to disturb you both but I thought you might like to know we've made some progress in the Ambrose case.'

Wilson pointed to the chair next to the chief constable. 'Tell us more.'

Bernie sat. 'I know we still don't have the full PM report but Nick White has suggested that the toxicology results might hold the answer to Zac's death. It's looking increasingly likely that Rachel Bell, an ICU nurse, was responsible. I also think she attacked Keira. Contrary to what we thought, Keira has told us that she and Zac were lovers – he didn't rape her. Except she knew him as Dean Foster. As did Rachel Bell. Turns out Zac, or Dean, was her drug dealer who supplied drugs for parties that she and Anthony Markham held – swingers' parties.'

'What?' said the chief constable. 'Anthony Markham, the lawyer? Sex parties? Drugs? Are you sure?'

'Yes, sir. We'd already heard about them from a colleague of Rachel's. Keira told us that she'd been to two parties and Anthony has just admitted it. Well, more or less.'

Wilson shook his head. 'Good God. Unless we catch them in the act, there's nothing we can do. Drugs, that is. Not the other.' He gave a nervous cough and blushed.

Bernie gave a small smile and looked from Wilson to the chief constable. 'There's more. It wasn't DCI Thornton who recruited Isaac Campbell to give a note to Zac. It was Anthony Markham offering his services as an alibi to Zac for Keira's attack. I suspect he didn't want to lose his drug dealer. Keira met Zac in Town Gardens for sex. Zac then got a call from Anthony who was in need of a fix. He left Keira to go to Anthony. It was someone else who attacked Keira.'

'And you think it was Rachel Bell. But why? What's her motive?' asked Wilson.

'Jealousy. I think Zac had probably slept with Rachel and she didn't like the fact that he'd moved on to Keira. And I know Gloucestershire is looking at Isaac Campbell but I think Rachel really did shoot the messenger – metaphorically speaking.'

'OK. What hard evidence do you have for this?'

Bernie swallowed. 'At the moment – none. But we have Keira Howard's brother in custody. Well, we did until he deliberately gave himself anaphylactic shock. I think Rachel persuaded him to steal some drugs from his hospital to kill Zac. We're still waiting on forensics. And the hospital where Adam is based has done an audit of their medication. We know he took some drugs out.'

'So where is Rachel Bell?' asked the chief constable.

'Good question. Anthony Markham claimed originally she'd gone to her sister but he's retracted that now. Says he doesn't know where she is.'

'Do you believe him?'

'No. I want to pull his phone records.'

The chief constable nodded. 'You have my full permission. I'll get my office to sort out the warrant. Keep me informed. But you're going to need hard evidence to proceed.'

Bernie stood up. 'Yes, sir. One more thing – do I need to report this to the IPCC or Thames Valley? From what we've got so far, it looks as though DCI Thornton is in the clear for Zac Ambrose's death.'

There was an uneasy glance between Wilson and the chief constable.

'Am I missing something?' Bernie asked.

'Not something – someone,' Wilson said. 'DCI Thornton has apparently vanished into thin air. That's on a need-to-know basis, Bernie.'

She understood Wilson completely. 'Of course, sir.' She remembered what Keira had said about seeing someone of Thornton's description at the parties. She couldn't decide whether to mention it or not but at the same time she didn't want to land herself in trouble. 'It may not be relevant but Keira mentioned that Zac met a man of DCI Thornton's description at the parties.'

'Thank you, Bernie. We'll let the IPCC know. Did you ask Anthony Markham about this?' asked Wilson.

'No.'

'Don't. Leave it to the IPCC. You concentrate on finding Rachel Bell.'

72

Bernie glanced at her watch – eleven a.m.

'Right, troops, sorry this briefing is so delayed. Lots going on this morning at my end and hopefully yours too. Who wants to go first?'

Kerry raised her hand. 'I've been talking to DI Brooks from Gloucestershire police. Isaac Campbell's post-mortem was done this morning – the pathologist started early. Initial COD is drowning. There's water in Isaac's lungs. However, the pathologist does think it likely that Isaac was incapacitated by a single blow to the head first and was unconscious when he went into the water.'

Bernie nodded. 'Good to hear we have a thorough pathologist on the case. When I spoke to Isaac's mother last night, she told me a couple of things. Firstly, his father took his own life when Isaac was thirteen. Lauren said that Isaac promised her he would never do that. Secondly, Isaac couldn't swim and was too scared to go near water. So even if he had broken his promise, he wouldn't drown himself.' Bernie paused for a moment. *Poor Isaac.* She couldn't help but feel responsible.

'As Isaac's body had his work pass, I think he went home to

pick it up,' she continued. 'I asked Alan Turner to check with Gable Cross and he didn't have his ID when we arrested him. So he must have gone home after leaving us but left for work before his mother got back. CCTV is going to be crucial for this. How did Isaac get to work? Bus? Walk some of the way perhaps? He lived the other side of town from the hospital.'

Matt groaned. 'No, you're going to make us trawl through hours of CCTV again. I hate that job.'

'Of course not, Matt. This isn't our case.' Bernie half-smiled. 'Having said that, maybe you could look at the different routes Isaac might have taken Monday evening and then, with Kerry, collate all the information DI Brooks is going to need. While he's looking for the evidence, we're going after the murderer – Rachel Bell.

'I had an interesting chat with Anthony Markham earlier. He's confessed that Rachel isn't with her sister but says he doesn't know where she is. I don't believe him. Tom, we have permission from the chief constable to look at Markham's phone records. His office is sorting out the warrant now and it will go in as urgent. Mick, if you can help Tom with that please. Alice, where are we up to with forensics and those cigarette butts?'

Alice checked her notes. 'Nothing's come in yet, ma'am. I'll chase them.'

'Great. After that, can you and Leigh start looking into the Markhams please? Not too sure what we're looking for but anything that might tell us where Rachel has gone. And it might be worth putting out an alert to all ports.'

Bernie looked round her team. 'I'll be honest with you. This is all theory at the moment. The chief constable has told me I need hard evidence to proceed. So, let's get the proof we need for an arrest warrant.'

. . .

Bernie had a map open on her computer. There were a ridiculous number of lakes on it.

'Alice, which lake was Isaac found in? I don't even know where to begin here.'

DC Hart pulled up a chair next to Bernie. 'It's lake number ninety-seven. This one here next to the A419. I'm so glad I had Leigh with me as it's not easy to reach and she showed me the way. I don't know much about it other than it's not one of the main lakes in the water park. If we go on to street view then I can show you a bit more.' Alice brought up a small road that ran alongside the lake. 'It was closed from this point and Leigh and I had to walk down here in the dark.'

'Oh God. Was Leigh OK? Did it affect her sensory-wise?'

'No, it was fine.' Alice lowered her voice. 'She did really well. Anyway, there's a gate here and then a short driveway to the lake.'

On the screen, Bernie could see the large metal farm gate was chained up. 'Was this locked when you got there?'

'No idea. Gloucestershire Police were already there by then.'

'Hmm. Isaac lived in Shrivenham Road. Where's that in relation to the lake?'

Alice typed the road name into search. 'It's here, near the football ground for Swindon FC. And if I zoom out...'

Bernie looked at the distance between the two. 'That's miles apart. Long way for Isaac to walk.'

'Yes. And not that easy to get to by car. You need to know the roads really well.'

'And if you know the roads, you probably know you're over the border. County lines gangs are organised but I'm not sure they know exactly where the boundaries are. Matt?'

DC Taylor turned round at his desk. 'Yes, ma'am.'

'If you haven't already checked, find out what car Rachel

Bell drives and put out an ANPR check for the A419 and surrounding roads.'

Matt grinned. 'Already ahead of you there, ma'am. Just waiting for results.'

'Glad you're on the ball.' Bernie looked at her watch. Almost one p.m. 'Think I need something to eat. Make sure you all get lunch. Because once we have everything we need to catch Rachel, it'll be all systems go.'

It was after two p.m. when Bernie got the phone call she'd been waiting for.

'Alan here, ma'am. Adam Howard's on his way back. ETA is thirty minutes. The doctor has cleared him for interview but has said to go easy on him. He'll probably be a bit twitchy as he's had adrenalin.'

'OK, thanks. See you in a bit, Alan.'

Bernie turned round in her chair. 'Mick, we've got about half an hour before Adam's back. Let's get our game plan sorted.'

73

'The time is fourteen forty-five hours. Detective Constable Parris is present along with myself, Detective Inspector Noel, continuing the interview of Adam Howard in relation to the murder of Zac Ambrose. Adam's lawyer, Simon Taylor, is also present. Before we get going, I just want to make sure you're feeling better, Adam.'

Adam looked slightly twitchy but nodded.

'For the recording please, Adam.'

'Yes.'

'While you were away at A&E, we had an interesting email about you. It shows us the time log when you entered the pharmacy at your hospital and which drug you took out – Propofol – an anaesthetic. We even have CCTV footage of you there. We've checked with your supervisors and you had no reason to take out that drug. What did you do with it, Adam?'

Adam buried his head in his hands. 'I know you think I ate the nuts to delay my interview but I didn't. I did it because I wanted to die. Ever since you told me about who Zac really was...' He shook his head. 'I spent all night thinking about it. I can't bear it. I hate myself for what I did.'

'What did you do, Adam?'

He looked up, his eyes red. 'I stole the medicine and gave it to Rachel Bell. She told me he deserved to die for what he did to Keira.'

'Whose idea was it?'

'Rachel's. She said she couldn't take the drug from her own pharmacy. I said I would.'

'What exactly did Rachel say to you?'

'She said she'd overheard the police say that Zac had attacked Keira. And she hated the fact they were both in ICU.'

'Why did you go along with it? You're a student doctor. You're meant to preserve life.'

'So is Rachel. I don't know. I was so angry about Keira. It felt awful to see her lying there, not knowing if she was going to live or not.'

'How did you get the medicine to Rachel?'

'I think you already know the answer to that, don't you? I hid the vial in the chocolates box. Rachel handled it from there.'

'Do you know what she did next?'

Adam shook his head. 'No. She said it would be given to him and it would look like he just took a turn for the worse and slipped away.'

Bernie looked at Mick taking notes. 'But of course, Zac wasn't Keira's attacker but her lover.'

'No, but Rachel wasn't to know that. She just told me what the police had said.'

Bernie bit her lip. It was hard to not feel sorry for the young man in front of her. What she was about to say would devastate him but it had to be said.

'Actually, Rachel did know. She knew Zac and Keira were lovers. They got together at a party at Rachel and Anthony's house last autumn.'

Adam paled visibly before them. 'No. No, that's not possible. Rachel wouldn't have lied to me like that.'

'I'm sorry, Adam, but she did.'
'But why? Why did she lie?'
'That's something we'd like to ask her ourselves.'
Bernie's mobile pinged. A text from Alice.

Lab results back on cigarette butts. DNA matches with Rachel Bell. She was there.

Bernie pushed the phone towards Mick.
'Shit,' he muttered under his breath.
'Adam, do you know where Rachel is?'
The young man shook his head.
'Adam, I'm worried for Keira. We've just had some results back from Forensics. We have evidence that puts Rachel Bell in Town Gardens, we believe, on the night of the attack. I think Rachel hurt Keira. And I'm worried she'll try again.'
'Why would she do that? None of this makes sense.'
'We think Rachel was having an affair with Zac Ambrose that started before he met Keira. He finished it to be with your sister. I think this all boils down to jealousy.'
Adam's face hardened. 'Jealousy? She made me do all this because she was jealous? Tell me what you want me to do.'

74

The team were gathered together around the table in the meeting room. Wilson was also there.

'OK, I think we have enough evidence to issue a warrant for Rachel Bell's arrest for her attack on Keira and for the murder of Zac Ambrose,' Bernie said. 'We have cigarette butts that place her at the scene for Keira, and Adam Howard has given a full disclosure statement, detailing his part in Zac's death and implicating Rachel. I suspect she's behind Isaac's death as well but obviously, that's not for us to decide. Out of interest, though, Matt, did you get anywhere with ANPR?'

Matt shook his head. 'No, not with her car. I've found some different routes that Isaac might have taken on Monday night on his way to the hospital and sent them over to DI Brooks. I also checked the CCTV at Gable Cross to make sure no one picked him up from there. Looks like he walked away by himself.'

'OK. Looking at the crime scene, there's no way Isaac walked all the way there, especially in the dark,' said Bernie.

Wilson raised his eyebrows at her. Bernie knew what that meant.

'Anyway, as I said, that's not for us to work on. Getting back to Rachel Bell – Tom and Mick, what have you come up with?'

Tom picked up a piece of paper and passed it to Bernie. 'These are Anthony Markham's calls and texts for the last few days. Rachel's number isn't there. But there is another one that's showed up a few times. It's pay-as-you-go but the texts have been at eight a.m. and eight p.m. for the last couple of days. It could be Rachel.'

'The timings are useful to know. We might be able to get a fix on her location and that would help with planning a raid. Can we speak to the mobile company?'

'Already done,' said Mick. 'Told them it's a murder inquiry so they're getting on to it straight away.'

'Good work, guys. Alice and Leigh, what have you found?'

'Leigh had the bright idea of looking at planning applications,' said Alice. 'The Markhams have extended into the loft and out to the side and rear. A planning application for a basement was turned down.'

Bernie rolled her eyes. 'I don't even want to think about what that was for. I'm guessing not a wine cellar.'

'There's something else,' said Leigh. 'They have another property in Cricklade.'

Bernie smiled. 'Bingo.'

'I bloody love Google,' Bernie said as they all gathered round Leigh and Alice. The street scene on the laptop showed a small, terraced house on the edge of the village. It looked a little rundown in the picture.

'I'm guessing they've bought this as an investment,' said Leigh. 'There are plans for a loft conversion and rear extension and they were passed a few weeks ago under permitted development. They may have started work.'

'Hmm. Leigh, ring Gable Cross and see if they can spare a

plain car to do a recce for us. We don't want to be running into a gutted house.'

'Ma'am,' said Mick. 'Phone company's come back. Think that number does belong to Rachel judging by the text Anthony Markham sent this morning.' He read from a sheet of paper: '"Trying to get everything organised. Do what you need to do and be ready to leave when I tell you." Looks like we don't have long, ma'am.'

Bernie rubbed her belly as the baby kicked her. 'No, we don't.'

Thirty minutes later they had eyes on the house. PC Tim Hills had gone. He was on the phone to Leigh. She put it on speakerphone.

'Tell me what you can see, Tim,' Bernie said.

'Well, there's no scaffolding outside so the planned work hasn't started yet. But they could be doing work inside, I suppose. Curtains are drawn but I saw a light go on in the bathroom a few minutes ago so someone is in.'

'Are you in uniform?'

'Yes. But I have my normal coat in the car. I can change quite easily. Do you want me to go and knock? I could say I've lost my cat.'

Bernie tapped her fingers on the desk. 'Tempting but no. I don't want to arouse any suspicion. Are you able to take some photos to send to us?'

'Yes. I'll do that now.'

There was a crackle and Bernie could hear Tim's radio in the background.

'I've taken some photos of the back. I'll do the front in a minute but then I think I'll have to go, ma'am. There's a bad RTA on the A419. They're asking for all units.'

'OK. No problem. Thanks for your help, Tim. Bye.'

Bernie tapped her fingers again. 'Damn. I was banking on getting Swindon to help with manpower for this. If they're caught up with an RTA they won't be able to spare anyone.'

'What about DI Anderson?' asked Kerry. 'Some of his team are in today.'

Bernie pulled a face. 'I'm not sure if he should, considering this is about Zac.'

'He doesn't have to deal with Rachel. He could lead the team at the house in Lydiard Millicent and sort out Anthony Markham. Then the rest of us can go to Cricklade and arrest Rachel, assuming she's there.'

There was a ping from Leigh's phone. 'Photos are here, ma'am. I think there's been a few changes since the street scene was done. There's an alleyway at the back of the property. It's overgrown on Google but is now cleared on Tim's photos.'

'Right, we'll definitely need a team at the back then.' Bernie looked at Kerry. 'Let's see what the super thinks.'

Wilson looked at them both. 'Well, a dual raid is a good idea. As for DI Anderson going... Hmm.'

'Sir, there's a good chance this overlaps with the original county lines case he was working on,' said Kerry. 'We really need the extra team and we don't have long.'

Wilson nodded slowly. 'OK. I'll set the warrants in place and include the Cricklade address too. When do you want to do this?'

'About nineteen thirty hours. Markham has been texting his wife at regular intervals of eight a.m. and eight p.m. I want to get in there before he texts her again,' Bernie said.

'Keep an eye on that. He might surprise you. Do you have anyone watching the properties?'

'We did have someone at Cricklade but he had to go. There's been an accident on the A419.'

'If you're joining forces then I suggest you send a couple of people from DI Anderson's team to keep watch. We don't want them sneaking off without our knowledge. You've only got a couple of hours to prepare.'

There was a frenzy of activity in MCIT as the two teams prepared the raid. Anderson had jumped at the chance of joining them and Bernie liked having him alongside her again as they planned their strategy. Two detectives had been dispatched to watch the houses and see if they could spot Anthony Markham and Rachel Bell. Bernie thought Markham probably had nothing to do with Keira's attack or Zac's or Isaac's deaths but he was certainly aiding and abetting his wife. The warrants came through and by eighteen fifteen hours they were ready to leave.

It was dusk as they pulled out of the car park. It wouldn't be long before the hour moved forward and the evenings were lighter. Bernie rubbed her belly. July would bring her baby girl and life would change for ever.

They drove in convoy until they reached West Swindon. Anderson's team peeled off to Lydiard Millicent while Bernie's continued to Cricklade. They'd planned to hit the targets at the same time. The village was quiet as they continued towards the house. A few people were heading to the pub and others were walking their dogs. Bernie was hoping for an easy, quiet takedown. The last thing she wanted was to draw an audience from the local residents.

They were in two cars and pulled up near the surveillance vehicle. Kerry jumped out to have a quick chat with the detective. Bernie looked at her watch. It was seven twenty-five. Five minutes to go. Kerry came back.

'There's little to report. Some lights have been switched on but he hasn't seen any movement because the curtains have been shut.'

'Hmm. I'm not very happy with where he's parked,' said Bernie. 'The house is on a corner and he's only had sight of the front. Let's hope she didn't go out the back. Right, can you get the rear team in place and then I'll go in the front with Mick and Leigh.'

'What do you mean, you're going in the front?'

Bernie was under strict instructions from Dougie to stay in the car during the raid and not to see Rachel until she'd been secured. She smiled. As if she ever did anything she was told to.

She rang Dougie. 'Ready your end?'

'Yes.'

'Then go.'

75

Mick banged on the door. 'Police. Open up please.'

There was silence. No sign of movement at all.

Bernie spoke quietly into her radio. 'Kerry, anything?'

'No, nothing, ma'am.'

Bernie nodded at Mick.

He banged again, louder this time. 'Police! Open up.'

Still nothing.

'OK, we'll have to use the battering ram.' She turned to Dougie's officer. 'Are you ready?'

'Yes, ma'am.'

'One more time, Mick, and give the warning.'

DC Mick Parris pounded on the door. 'Police. Open up or we'll break the door down.'

'She's not there, love.'

Bernie turned to her left, startled by the voice. A small old lady, bent over, was standing on her front step next door.

'Sorry, what did you say?'

'I said she's not there. She went out about fifteen minutes ago.'

'What?' Bernie pulled out her phone and found a picture of Rachel Bell that she'd got from the hospital. 'This woman?'

The old lady peered at the phone. 'Hang on a second.' She pushed her glasses up onto her head and beckoned for the phone. Bernie passed it over. 'Well, it looks like her but she's got different hair now.'

'What's it like?'

'Short and red.'

'And you definitely saw her leave?'

'Yes.'

Bernie glared at the surveillance detective – how had he missed her leaving the house?

'Although it was a bit funny, like.'

Bernie turned her attention back to the neighbour. 'Why's that?'

'Because I didn't hear her front door close. You have to pull it hard to make it shut. Always makes a bang. But I saw her walking down the road and get into her car. Blue, don't know what sort though. She came from that way.' The neighbour pointed behind her.

Bernie closed her eyes. Rachel had obviously used the back alley to get out. 'I don't suppose you saw which direction she was going when she drove off?'

'She turned left towards the A419. She was probably going to work.'

'Work?'

'Yes, dear. She's a nurse. She had her scrubs on. Although, that's a bit odd too. My granddaughter's a nurse and she gets changed at the hospital.'

Bernie left Mick, Alice and the other detective to enter the house. She, Kerry, Matt and Leigh jumped into Kerry's car.

'Dammit. When Anthony Markham texted "do what you

have to do", I wonder if he knew what Rachel had planned. And with her scrubs on, she can walk straight in.' Bernie tipped her head back against the seat rest.

'Do you want me to check that with DI Anderson, ma'am?' Leigh asked.

'Yes please. Matt, what car does Rachel Bell drive? The old lady said it was blue.'

'When I checked, she was the registered keeper of a white Toyota Yaris. Can't remember the registration off the top of my head. I can find out.'

'Don't worry. I think she's in a different car. That's probably why her number didn't come up on the ANPR. I'm going to find out if the A419 is cleared now. Just because she went that way, it doesn't mean she didn't change route.' Bernie picked up a radio. 'DI Noel to Control. Over.'

'Go ahead, DI Noel. Over.'

'Is the RTA on the A419 cleared now?'

'I'll check... yes, cleared and reopened to traffic about thirty minutes ago. Officers still at the scene.'

'OK. I need to get to the hospital urgently. We're joining at Cricklade. I could do with a patrol car to clear the way if possible please.'

'Give me a moment... patching you in to a patrol vehicle now. Go ahead, DI Noel.'

'Hi. This is DI Noel. We need an escort to the hospital. Whereabouts are you? Over.'

'Just south of Blunsdon. Over.'

Bernie recognised the voice. 'Hi, Tim. We're just coming up to there. Ah, I think I can see you moving.'

'Yes. You're in the black Fiesta?'

'Yep.'

'Great. Let's get going. My colleague is driving.'

'We'll probably need your help when we arrive. Target is Rachel Bell. I'll send you a photo but we have reason to believe she's cut her hair short and dyed it red. Last seen wearing hospital scrubs. She's wanted for murder so approach with caution. Over.'

Cars moved out of the way as the sirens blared down the road.

'Ma'am.'

Bernie turned to look at Leigh.

'Just spoken to DI Anderson. Markham claims he didn't know about Rachel leaving the house. She was supposed to sit tight until his text tonight. He was arranging false passports to get out of the country.'

'I think she's taken the opportunity to have one last crack at Keira. Ring the hospital and get Keira Howard moved to a secure room. And ask them to check their CCTV. Maybe we can find out where she is.'

Leaning back in the seat as the car's speed increased, Bernie felt a little woozy. She was glad Kerry was driving. She didn't need this now. She had to have a clear head to make sure the arrest went smoothly.

'Matt, can you get on to Gable Cross and find out if we can get any more officers to the hospital please?'

'Yes, ma'am.'

'Bernie.'

'Yes, Kerry.'

'Debs is working tonight. Give her a call and ask her to keep an eye out for Rachel.'

Bernie pulled out her phone and found Debs' number. It rang a few times.

'Bernie? Is everything OK?'

'Yes, fine. We're heading over to you now. If you see Rachel Bell, can you let me know please?'

'All right. Are you sure everything is OK? We've just had a call asking us to take Keira Howard back.'

Bernie looked at Leigh. She gave her a thumbs up. ICU was a very secure ward.

'Debs, Keira is coming for her own safety. Please don't let anyone into ICU unless you know them. We believe Rachel is dangerous and has probably changed her appearance. Sorry, I don't mean to alarm you. We're on our way now.'

There was a pause. 'Are you OK, Debs?'

'In what way changed?'

'We think she now has short, red hair.'

'Shit. I didn't see her come in. I've just been to the loo.'

'You mean she's already there?'

'Yes. And Keira's just arrived too.'

Bernie looked at Kerry. 'What's our ETA?'

'About five minutes.'

'Debs, can you hear me?'

'Yes.'

'We'll be with you in about five minutes. I want you to stay with Keira and not leave her, not even for one second. Leigh's on the phone to the hospital now. We'll send security to you.'

'OK. Be quick.' She hung up.

Bernie had heard the nervousness in Debs' voice. There was a pensive look on Kerry's face. 'You got the gist of that.'

'Yes,' Kerry said. She put her foot down. 'ETA is now three minutes.'

76

The lift seemed to take for ever to arrive. Kerry had given up and bounded up the stairs, despite the weight of her stab jacket. She needed to release the adrenalin somehow. She was outside ICU talking to a security guard when the rest of them arrived.

'Slow coaches.' The joke was another way of hiding her anxiety. She was bouncing on her feet.

Bernie reached out and touched her arm. 'You need to calm down before we go in. At the moment you're not safe.'

'Debs is in there. You asked her to stay with Keira.'

'I know. But I can't have you rushing in there. If you don't calm down, you'll have to stay out here.'

Kerry stared at Bernie. Despite her agitation, her eyes were hard. Bernie had no doubt that Kerry could hurt Rachel very badly given the opportunity. Kerry swallowed, then nodded. 'I'll stay at the back and wait for your order. If I need to disarm Rachel, I will. But only on your say-so.'

Bernie turned to the security guard. 'Has anyone else gone in there?'

'Not since I arrived. I turned away a couple of visitors. As far as I'm aware, there should be six patients in there, including

Keira Howard, two doctors and five nurses. Plus Rachel Bell. But there was a big car accident earlier so some of the staff may be in A&E.'

'Have you heard any noise?'

'No, it's all very quiet. But that's normal, to be honest with you.'

'OK, thanks.' Bernie turned back to her team – Kerry, Leigh, Matt, PC Tim Hills and another uniformed officer. 'I have no idea if Rachel is armed or what her intentions are. So' – Bernie looked at the two PCs – 'I want you to stay out here. We'll have open comms on the radio. If you hear me say that Rachel has a gun, one of you needs to contact Control on another channel to get the tactical team in. They're on standby. We all have stab vests on. But I think she's more likely to have a bloody great big needle ready.' Bernie rubbed her head. She still didn't feel quite right and the weight of the jacket didn't help. 'Our best bet is to try and talk to her. Get her to come quietly.'

'And if she doesn't?' said Matt.

'Then Kerry can use her ninja skills.'

Bernie turned to the security guard. 'Can you let us in please?'

The man tapped in a code and the door catch released.

It was quiet, just as the security guard said. There were faint beeping sounds of heart rates being monitored. No voices. There was no one on reception, which bothered Bernie. She almost reached automatically for the hand gel then stopped. She didn't think anyone would mind today.

They walked through into the ward. The curtains were pulled around all the beds except one at the end. Bernie saw Keira, her eyes wide with fear. Debs was sitting on a chair near to her with her mouth taped and hands behind her back. Bernie assumed they were tied. The temptation was to move quickly but Bernie waited for Rachel to show herself. Sweat trickled down her back. It was warm in ICU.

Kerry nudged Bernie and pointed to the curtained area next to Keira's bed. There were feet.

'Rachel, it's DI Bernie Noel. Back again, like a bad penny. We need to talk.'

The feet moved slightly.

'Rachel, I know you're here. Let's have a chat.'

Bernie took a few steps forward towards Keira's bed when the curtain was suddenly pulled back. In an instant, Rachel was beside Keira with a syringe in her hand.

'Don't come any closer.'

Bernie stopped. 'OK. I like your hair. It suits you.'

Rachel screwed up her face. 'What the fuck are you talking about? I'm standing here waiting to finish off this slag and you're talking about my hair?'

'We can talk about something else if you like. How about Dean Foster?'

Keira whimpered.

'Oh, shut up, you snivelling child! He was mine long before he was yours,' Rachel snarled.

'How long had you known him?' Bernie asked.

'Since last summer. He was gorgeous – and so good in bed.' Rachel laughed.

Bernie clenched her fists.

'I told him I wanted to leave Anthony. Go away with him somewhere. But he wasn't so keen. Didn't want to give up the drug dealing. Or so he said. And then she appeared.' Rachel spat the words out at Keira. 'Little Miss Goody-Two-Shoes.' She shook her head. 'If only she'd done what she was supposed to do and opened her legs for my husband, then I might have got Dean to go with me. But no, she refused and Dean made a move. I watched them. And then she came again to the New Year's Eve party. We didn't invite her – Dean did. And they were at it in the alleyway. They probably didn't notice the camera above the security light, filming them. You don't know how many times I've watched that.'

'When did you decide to hurt Keira? Was it when you treated the woman who overdosed after being sexually assaulted by the Swindon attacker?'

'Patients – families too – tell you all sorts of things when you're a nurse. You become their confidante. She told me everything about the attack. I helped her by listening and in return, she helped me. Gave me all the details I needed to make it look authentic. I just stepped it up a gear. That's what attackers do, don't they? They escalate. I didn't hit her hard enough though. She wasn't supposed to survive, and with her parents there all the time in ICU, I couldn't do anything about it.'

Rachel's eyes glazed over slightly. Bernie risked a step and then another.

'No closer.' Rachel held up the syringe. She moved slowly round the bed until she was between Debs and Keira. She bit her lip. 'Eeny meeny miny moe...'

Kerry began breathing heavily. Bernie could almost feel the tension radiating off her DS.

'We've been speaking to Adam Howard, Rachel. He explained everything to us. It was a clever idea to get the drugs from another hospital.'

'It was, wasn't it? Obviously I thought of that. God, he was so easy to manipulate. I didn't even have to sleep with him. Thought he was doing right by his sister.' Rachel looked at Keira. 'Did you know that? Did you know your lovely brother stole the drug that killed your precious Dean?' She laughed.

Bernie edged forward again. She wondered if Rachel had taken something. She was definitely unstable. 'Except he wasn't really Dean, was he?' Bernie said. 'He was Zac Ambrose. And if you thought you loved him, it was nothing compared to his mother. You ought to be grateful she's not here. She'd take you out in a flash.'

Rachel shook her head. 'Nah, not that one. She's all talk.'

'What's in the syringe, Rachel? Is it what you gave Zac?'

'Oh, I didn't give it to Zac or Dean. The nurse on duty did that. I merely left the medication ready. My fingerprints weren't on it. This isn't the same though. As much as I hated Dean at that point, I also still loved him. But he was awake and talking and he'd have realised that I had hurt Keira. I couldn't risk him dropping me in it. I did the kindest thing and put him to sleep. My Sleeping Beauty for ever.' She looked at the syringe. 'This one is my own concoction. No antidote. But just who to give it to?' Rachel swung the syringe between the two women.

Bernie's back was now completely damp. Beads of sweat glistened on her forehead. The room was so hot and her temples ached. 'Rachel, you don't have to do this. Dean's gone now. Hurting Keira won't bring him back. And she's carrying his child. You don't want to hurt the baby.'

Rachel sagged slightly and sighed. 'You're right. I don't want to hurt Dean's baby.' She looked up and stared at Bernie, her eyes as dark as coal. 'But yours on the other hand...'

Rachel lunged. Bernie realised that although she had moved closer to Rachel, her team hadn't and were a few steps behind. Rivulets of sweat ran down her face. Rachel appeared to be flying towards her, arms outstretched, the syringe in her hand. Kerry pushed past her into Rachel's path. Bernie stepped back, tripping over her own feet. Then she felt Matt's arms around her, pulling her back up.

Rachel crashed to the floor. Kerry kicked the syringe away and was immediately on top of Rachel, cuffing her. Kerry looked up. 'Do you want the honours, ma'am?'

'Yes, thank you. Rachel Bell, I'm arresting you on suspicion of the attempted murder of Keira Howard, the murder of Zac Ambrose and the murder of Isaac Campbell. You do not have to say anything. But, it may harm your defence if you do not mention, when questioned, something which you later rely on in court. Do you understand?'

'Who the fuck's Isaac Campbell?'

'Do you understand, Rachel?'

'Yes, I understand. Now, get me off the fucking floor.'

'Matt, can you get PC Hills and the other officer in, please, to take Rachel Bell to headquarters?'

'Yes, ma'am.'

Bernie went over to Keira. She was sobbing. She took the young woman's hands. 'It's OK, Keira. It's over now. Rachel can't hurt you any more.'

Keira wiped her face. 'I can't believe she killed Dean and Isaac. And that she tried to kill me too.'

Leigh passed Keira a tissue from her pocket. 'It's clean. Ma'am, I asked PC Hills for his bodycam just before we came in. I got all of Rachel's confession.'

'That's brilliant. Good thinking.'

'Leigh,' said Kerry, 'can you come round here and film Debs and how she's been tied up? We need to document this.' Kerry scratched gently at one top corner of the plaster covering Debs' mouth. 'One, two, three.' She pulled the plaster off in one go. Debs bent forward in pain. 'I'm sorry, darling, it was better that way. Let's sort out your hands.'

'Oh, Debs, I'm so sorry,' said Bernie. 'I put you in danger. I still don't understand how Rachel fell like that. It looked like she was flying.'

Debs smiled and then winced. 'Still stings. I tripped her. She was about to tie my legs up when you arrived. You need to look for my colleagues. I'm sure she's done something to them. And please check the other patients.'

Leigh and Matt went off to find them. Bernie turned back to Keira, who was still crying.

'Oh, Keira. We'll get your parents here as fast as we can.'

'Was it true what Rachel said? Did Adam get the drug that killed Dean?'

Bernie nodded. 'I'm afraid so. But Rachel told him that Dean, or Zac, had attacked you. He did it because he thought he was protecting you.'

Keira sniffed. 'Such a horrible woman. I can't believe Dean slept with her. You know, I always thought Dean didn't suit him as a name. Zac's much better. If the baby's a boy, I think I'll call him Zac.'

Bernie smiled. 'I think Zac's mum would like that.'

'I'd like to meet her, if she's still around.'

Bernie thought of Jade, broken since her son's death. She could do with some good news. 'I think that can be arranged.'

77

The gel was cold on Bernie's abdomen, but this time she welcomed it; it was refreshing. Stripped of her stab jacket, she was beginning to cool down.

'We're just going to make sure baby is all right,' said the sonographer. Bernie was having déjà vu as it was the same woman she had seen before. 'And this time it's lovely that Dad's here too.' She beamed at Dougie. Bernie didn't have the energy to correct her.

He took Bernie's hand and kissed it. 'Yes. Although I would have preferred it under different circumstances.'

A picture appeared on the screen. 'Well, everything is looking OK so far. Heartbeat is good. Baby doesn't seem to have suffered any ill-effects from you falling over, Bernie. Having said that, I'm going to book you an appointment with your consultant. From what you've described to me, I think you were close to fainting again.'

'I just hadn't eaten enough and it was very hot in there. I was under a lot of stress...'

'Even so, maybe best to let your team handle the action stuff.'

Dougie stroked her hair. It was damp. 'She's supposed to do that anyway as a DI.'

'Huh. You can talk.'

The sonographer grabbed some paper towels and started wiping the gel off. 'My recommendation now is to go home and get straight into bed.'

Bernie shook her head. 'I can't. I have to go back to work. We have a suspect in custody who needs questioning.'

Dougie took her hand again. 'It can wait until tomorrow and Kerry can handle it.'

'She probably can but I just want to see the super. And after that, I'll promise we'll go home.'

They were almost at the main entrance when Bernie spotted a woman she recognised.

'Jade.'

The woman turned, concern etched on her face. 'Thank God, you're OK. Your boss rang to tell me what happened. I was coming to see you.' She lowered her eyes. 'Thank you for catching her.'

Bernie never thought she'd hear Jade Ambrose thank her for anything. 'Was just doing my job.'

Jade looked up. 'Maybe. I know you didn't do it for my sake but I like to think you did it for Joshua.'

Bernie nodded. 'He's a very special boy. Tell him I say hi.'

'I will.' Jade pointed towards Bernie's bump. 'Take care of yourself and little one. Enjoy the time while he or she's small. It's hard going but nothing compared to the pain they can cause you when they're older.'

Bernie looked at Jade. Her hard-face mask had dropped and to her surprise, Bernie saw vulnerability. She thought about Keira's request.

'Zac had a girlfriend called Keira Howard. She's in the

hospital. You can't visit tonight but it might be worth seeing her before you go back home. She'd like to see you.'

Jade's eyes lit up slightly. 'Thank you. It would be good to meet her.'

'I've kept my end of the bargain, Jade. Your turn to give me some information.'

'Oh, Bernie. I don't have to tell you that. You've known all along. Isn't it always the people we trust the most that betray us?'

Jade gave a weak smile. 'Nice to meet you, DI Anderson. Take care of her and the baby. See you around.' She turned and left the lobby through the automatic doors.

'That's her gone then,' said Dougie.

'For now.' Bernie was quite sure she and Jade would cross paths again. She'd said see you around, not goodbye.

Bernie knocked lightly on Wilson's door.

'Come in... Oh, Bernie, thank God you're all right.'

The super got up from his desk and came round to her. For a moment she thought he was going to hug her but he stopped short of that. He patted her arm instead.

'Such a relief. You all did a good job tonight. Although, really, I should be cross with you, putting yourself in jeopardy like that. I trust baby is OK.'

Bernie smiled. 'Yes, she's fine.'

'A girl? That's wonderful. I mean, a boy would be wonderful too. Oh, you know what I mean.'

Bernie laughed. 'Yes, I do. Sir, I just wanted to ask about DCI Thornton. Is there any news?'

Wilson bowed his head slightly. 'Yes. Come and sit down for a minute.'

Bernie sat while Wilson perched on the edge of his desk.

'Welsh Police picked him up this evening. Obviously he's in

the clear for Zac Ambrose's death but there are other things he needs to be questioned about. Bernie, you need to be prepared for the worst. There may be a trial and it's very likely that all of his past cases will be looked at. There may be appeals. And you may be called to appear in court.'

Bernie nodded. She knew exactly what Wilson was getting at. 'Danny Ambrose. That's why Jade's been here. Not just for Zac. She'd do anything to get Danny out of prison.'

'Yes. I'm afraid so. But we don't know anything for sure yet. In the meantime, you can come in for the interviews tomorrow, but after that, I'm ordering you to go home and not come back in until Monday. Same with DI Anderson. And on Monday, we'll talk about your role until you go on maternity leave. No more heroics from you.'

Bernie smiled. As much as she didn't want to be sitting behind a desk, she wasn't going to risk losing her baby. 'Yes, sir.'

Bernie sank into the car seat. She was glad Dougie was driving home.

'How was the raid on Markham's house?' she asked.

'Very successful. Found far more than we bargained for. Lucy was still processing the garage when I left. There's a baseball bat with blood stains on it that's on its way to Therese. We're guessing it might be Keira's or Isaac's blood, or maybe even both, from their head injuries. You already knew he had a personal drug habit but we found about twenty grand's worth of cocaine. It was hidden in his fishing gear. God, what a stupid man.'

Something triggered in Bernie's brain. 'Fishing gear?'

'Yes, what about it?'

'Isaac was found in a lake not used much by the public. What if it's used for private fishing? When I arrested Rachel, I included Isaac but she said she didn't know who he was.'

'Well, no. He'd been using a different name.'

'But it was the same name Zac had used. She would have picked up on that if she'd met Isaac as Dean. And she was only in for a short time the night Zac died so she probably wouldn't have seen Isaac. And he wouldn't have seen her. Which means, the only person who actually knew him is Anthony Markham. I think he killed Isaac. We need to go back so I can check the ANPR for Markham's car and contact DI Brooks—'

'No, you don't. You can do that in the morning. Anthony Markham won't be going anywhere for a while.' Dougie took Bernie's hand. 'We're going home.'

78

THURSDAY

Anthony Markham looked even worse than the day before. But a night in the cells normally had that effect on people.

Bernie glanced across at DI Christopher Brooks, who was ready to take notes. They'd agreed that Bernie would lead. The rest of the team were crammed into the viewing room. Not the most professional way of handling it but they all wanted to see Bernie take down Markham.

'I trust you've had breakfast, Mr Markham,' said Bernie.

He looked at her witheringly. 'If you can call insipid tea and lukewarm toast with less jam than a war ration "breakfast", then yes, I've eaten.'

'Ah, the custody special. Let's begin.'

Bernie pressed the buttons on the recorder.

'Time is ten fifteen and present in the room is DI Bernadette Noel, DI Christopher Brooks, Anthony Markham – the suspect – and his lawyer, Richard Dunne.

'Mr Markham, you were arrested last night for possession of drugs with intent to supply. We'll start there. A large quantity of cocaine was found in your garage, with a street value of around twenty thousand pounds. Does it belong to you?'

Markham leaned back in his chair. 'No comment.'

Bernie had expected him to do this. 'Does it belong to your wife, Rachel?'

'No comment.'

'If it doesn't belong to either of you, who is the owner of the drugs?'

'No comment.'

'You told me that you met Zac Ambrose, aka Dean Foster, a week ago on Sunday to score some cocaine from him. If you had twenty thousand pounds' worth of cocaine in your house, why did you need to get more?'

'No comment.'

'Did you really buy a small amount from Dean that night, or did you drive him to his house to collect the cocaine we found at your property yesterday? Were you storing it for him so it wouldn't be found when the police raided where he was living?'

'No comment.'

'Were you supposed to hold on to the cocaine until DCI Jack Thornton picked it up from you? We have reports that he was at your house when Zac was too. Did he give you the false papers for Isaac Campbell?'

'No comment.'

Bernie looked down at her notes, which included some forensic reports just in from Therese. Time for a change of subject.

'Where were you Monday evening from six p.m. onwards?'

'No comment.'

'Oh. Does that mean you don't have an alibi?'

'No comment.'

Bernie opened a folder and took out a photograph. 'Handily for you, we know where you were. This is a shot from an ANPR camera on the A419, showing you driving towards Cirencester at twenty-three fifteen hours. We know from the next camera along that you turned off before then.'

'No comment.'

Bernie pulled out another photograph. 'Of course, I asked where you were from around six p.m. That's because CCTV in Shrivenham Road in Swindon shows your car was there.' She placed the photo in front of him. 'Isaac Campbell lived in Shrivenham Road. And we know that after speaking to us on Monday, he went home to pick up his hospital work pass but he never showed up for his shift. Did you see Isaac Campbell? Did you speak to him? You admitted to me yesterday that you knew him. That you knew where to find him. Did you kill him, Mr Markham? Did you murder Isaac? Were you tying up loose ends, worried that Isaac had read your note?'

Richard Dunne coughed. 'If you wish to ask my client about the death of Isaac Campbell, you'll have to rearrest him. Assuming you have evidence.'

Markham smirked.

Bernie looked at Dunne and then Markham. 'Of course, you're right. Anthony Markham, I'm arresting you—'

Markham laughed.

'What's so funny? Murder is a very serious crime, as you well know.'

Anthony Markham looked directly at her. 'You can't arrest me.'

'Why not? Lack of evidence? We have the photos of your car, which is currently being thoroughly searched. And there's a fine spatter of blood in your garage that you missed when cleaning up, after hitting Isaac in the head with a baseball bat. Forensics are scrutinising that bat as we speak. I suspect it might have Keira's DNA on it too – both ends, considering what your wife did to her. I had a quick chat with Keira's father, Geoff Howard, this morning who told me that you and he sometimes go fishing at lake number ninety-seven in the Cotswold Water Park, which is where Isaac was found, and that you have a key for the padlock. But, look at me, giving away the evidence.'

Bernie leaned back. 'Of course, that's not why you think I can't arrest you. It's because Isaac's body was found in Gloucestershire. You knew that when you put his body there. That it wouldn't be my case. Didn't stop me finding you, though, did it? I think you've forgotten that the law does allow me to arrest you but for the sake of argument...' Bernie looked at Brooks.

DI Brooks pulled out his warrant card, showing Gloucestershire Police. 'Anthony Markham, I'm arresting you on suspicion of the murder of Isaac Campbell. You do not have to say anything. But, it may harm your defence if you do not mention when questioned something which you later rely on in court. Anything you do say may be given in evidence. Do you understand?'

Markham's face drained of colour. He nodded.

'For the recording please, Mr Markham,' Bernie said.

'Yes, I understand.'

The team in MCIT cheered as Bernie and DI Brooks came into the office.

'Well done, ma'am,' said Mick. 'That was perfect. His face when DI Brooks took his warrant out. Classic.'

Bernie sat down at her desk. 'It was rather satisfying. Thanks for your help, Christopher.'

'Pleasure to run a joint operation with you, Bernie.'

She smiled. DI Brooks was nicer in person than on the phone. 'Right, I think a cuppa is in order before I tackle Rachel Bell. Who wants to join me for interview?'

'No one has to.'

Bernie turned round to see the super at the door.

'Rachel Bell's given a full confession, though she's citing mental health issues. So, good job all round. And, I'm sure your team will back me up, time for you to go home and rest, Bernie, as we agreed last night.'

Bernie opened her mouth to speak but Kerry got there first.

'Absolutely right, sir. We can hold the fort until next week. Go home. Rest. Hang out with your parents before they go back to London.' Kerry hugged her.

'What about my cuppa?'

'Ma'am, I'm very happy to make you one but wouldn't you rather go and find a decent hot chocolate somewhere?' said Alice.

Bernie grinned. 'Yes, you're right.' She stood up and collected her bag and coat. 'If you're all sure, I'll see you Monday. I'm expecting a lot of progress.'

Bernie was almost by the lift when she heard a voice behind her.

'Ma'am?' It was Leigh.

Bernie turned and smiled. 'Yes?'

Leigh looked down. 'I won't be here on Monday. I'm going back to Gable Cross. The super's said that Alice can come and help me with the sex attacker case. We might have a new lead. The CCTV images have been shown to all the bus drivers in Swindon. One of them thinks he was on his bus yesterday. There's a clearer picture of his face. I'm determined to find him.'

'And you will, Leigh. I have faith in you. You're a good officer. Who else would have thought about doing a planning permission search on the Markhams?' Bernie smiled again. 'We've really benefitted having you on the team. You've certainly made me think a lot about how best to look after my officers. Thank you. Take care of yourself, Leigh.'

'You too, ma'am.'

SUNDAY

The church bell tolled for the morning service. Bernie moaned. Paul Bentley had nearly raised enough money to buy more. She couldn't decide if a peal of bells would be any better than a single one. Dougie pushed the duvet back and got out of bed.

'Why are you getting up?' she murmured.

Dougie was pulling on his clothes. 'I promised your parents I'd take them to church.'

Bernie rubbed her eyes and blinked. 'Seriously, you're taking my parents to church? An Anglican church?'

'Yes. They asked me a couple of days ago.'

'Why do they want to go?'

'Said they wanted to experience village life here. But I feel bad leaving you. I'm sure they won't mind if I cancel.'

'No, it's fine. I'll make myself some breakfast and then potter around this morning. Have a long bath. I promise I'll relax.'

'OK.' Dougie bent over and kissed her. 'I'll have my phone so just text me if you feel unwell. Your mum's already booked us into the pub for lunch so you don't have to worry about that.

We'll be back around twelve. Maybe earlier if Paul gives a short sermon.'

'What's the time now?'

'Just after ten. I'll see you soon.'

Bernie was on her third slice of Marmite toast when the doorbell rang. She was lying on the sofa watching TV. She didn't really want to get up. The bell rang again, followed by a knock. She glanced at the clock. It was 11.45 a.m. She'd been watching TV longer than she'd realised. *Maybe it's Mum and Gary, come to get me for lunch but I'm sure we gave them a key.* She pushed herself off the sofa and padded out to the hallway. She opened the door.

'I thought we gave you a key— Oh.'

A blonde-haired woman, slim and petite, stood on the doorstep. She smiled. Her make-up was immaculate. Her clothes seemed expensive. Bernie didn't even want to think how she looked this morning in her dressing gown and hair sticking out everywhere.

'I was looking for Dougie Anderson. I understand he lives here.'

Bernie recognised the voice instantly. She'd heard it on the phone the year before.

'You must be Louise Anderson.'

'Yes, well, I was. I've gone back to my maiden name now. You must be Bernie. I spoke to you last year.' She looked up and down, taking in everything.

'What do you want, Louise?'

She held out a plastic bag. 'The last few things of Dougie's. I found them a couple of weeks ago. I was in Bristol for a work conference this week so I thought I'd drop them by in person. Say hello. I got the address from Dougie's sister. Funnily enough, she didn't mention you.' Louise tipped her head to one side. 'And she certainly didn't mention that.' She gestured to Bernie's bump and then shook her head.

'I'm pregnant. So what?'

'Well, I mean, does he know?'

'Know what?'

'Oh God, he doesn't.' Louise laughed. She put her hand to her mouth. 'I'm sorry. But don't you think you should tell him?'

Bernie gripped the door. Her blood pressure was starting to go up. 'Tell him what?'

'That it's not his baby. It can't be. It's not possible. Dougie can't have kids. He's firing blanks. We tried for a year before we found out. Then moved on to IVF and it didn't work.' She laughed again. 'Mind you, Dougie always did believe in miracles.'

Bernie was tempted to wipe the smirk off Louise's face. Louise had lied to her before. She was sure Dougie's ex-wife was lying again. Wasn't she?

'I don't believe you.'

'Really? Then tell me why his family don't know about you and the baby. You haven't met them, have you?' Louise took a step closer. 'You really ought to tell him now that it's not his. He's got one hell of a temper.'

'Shut up, Louise,' said a familiar voice.

Bernie looked past the woman in front of her and saw Dougie. His face was red with anger. He reached out, grabbed Louise by the arm and pulled her away from the door.

'Dougie, let go. You're hurting me. You need to listen to me. That woman's been lying to you. You're not the father of her baby.'

'Where's your car, Louise?'

'In the pub car park. But Dougie...'

Bernie froze as Dougie dragged Louise away from the

house. Louise had lied to her before but the look on Dougie's face... Doubts started to creep into her mind. Was Louise right? Did Dougie already know he wasn't her baby's father? Was that why she hadn't met his family? But then why was he so insistent on the paternity test being done? Nothing made sense.

A hand was on her arm. Her mother. She was pushing her back into the house. Leading her to the sofa. Sitting her down gently. Her parents sat either side.

'I don't understand. Has he been lying to me all this time? I can't stay with him if he's lied to me. You know how much I hate that. And Alex's new girlfriend is pregnant so he's not going to help me. What am I going to do? I can't do this alone.'

'You don't have to decide anything right now. And you're not alone. We're here.' Denise gently squeezed her hand.

The front door slammed shut. Dougie came into the lounge, his face still red with anger.

'Bernie, I know you probably don't want to hear what I have to say—'

'Damned right about that.'

'Please. You know what Louise is like. You can't believe everything she says.'

'Can't I?' Bernie stood up. 'She has a point though. You haven't told your family about me or the baby.'

'That's why I want to do the paternity test. To be sure.' Dougie looked at Bernie's parents. 'Gary and Denise, would you mind giving us some space please? There are some personal things I want to tell Bernie.'

Denise tightened her grip on her daughter's hand.

'It's OK, Mum. You and Gary can go over to the pub. I'll join you soon.'

Bernie waited until they had left before speaking again. 'You have five minutes.'

Dougie nodded. 'Louise and I did have fertility problems

and it was more me than her. I'm not completely infertile though. I have a low sperm count and low mobility. But it's not impossible. The IVF just didn't work for us. So when you said you were pregnant, I think that was the happiest moment of my life. Then you mentioned Alex and my heart sank. For a while it wasn't too bad. I could pretend that the baby was definitely mine and that Alex wouldn't take her away from me. Or take you. Then the doubts started growing in my mind. I wanted to tell you but I couldn't. So that's why I asked about the paternity test. To know for sure. And that way I wouldn't have to tell you about my... problem. God, Bernie, I'm so sorry. I don't want to lose you. And it doesn't matter if I'm not the real father. I'll still be the best dad I can possibly be. Because I want to do this with you.' He took a step closer to her. 'Please.'

Bernie looked at Dougie. There were tears in his eyes. Her heart was telling her he was sincere but her head wasn't quite there. Yet, they both shared the same fear – of losing one another if Alex was the father. 'Will you tell your family about me and the baby?'

'Yes. But I'll only say what you want me to say.'

Bernie put her hand to her abdomen. Little Bun was squirming. 'Then I'd better do the paternity test before you speak to them.'

Ten days later, the email arrived.

'Ready?' Bernie asked. They were sat together on the sofa, her laptop balanced on her thighs.

'Yes. No. Wait.' Dougie turned to look at her. 'No matter what that says, I want to stay with you and the baby – if you'll have me.'

Bernie nodded. The previous ten days had been tense. Her heart raced as she opened the email. Just a year before she'd opened a similar one that had told her Gary was her father. She read the paternity result, the enormity of it hitting her hard.

'So,' she said.

Dougie bit his lip.

Bernie took his hand. 'Miracles really do happen.'

A LETTER FROM JOY

Dear reader,

I want to say a huge thank you for choosing to read *Left for Dead*. If you did enjoy it, and want to keep up to date with all my latest releases, just sign up at the following link. Your email address will never be shared and you can unsubscribe at any time.

www.bookouture.com/joy-kluver

I hope you loved *Left for Dead* and if you did I would be very grateful if you could write a review. I'd love to hear what you think, and it makes such a difference helping new readers to discover one of my books for the first time.

There were two main crimes I wanted to address in the book – violence against women and county lines drugs cases. Thankfully, Wiltshire Police are being proactive in their policing in both these areas. They've introduced Project Vigilant to target perpetrators of violence against women, to ensure they can have a safe night out. Likewise, another team, Operation Fortitude, deals with county lines and aims to shut down the gangs using young people to carry and sell drugs.

I also wanted to look at autism. Unlike the armed forces, autistic people are allowed to serve in the police force which is fantastic. Leigh struggles when her working routines are changed but she brings a different mindset to the case and thinks of ideas that no one else has. If you want to know more about autism then The National Autistic Society is a good place to start.

I love hearing from my readers – you can get in touch on my Facebook page, through Twitter, Goodreads or my website.

Thanks,

Joy

kluver.co.uk

facebook.com/joykluverauthor
twitter.com/JoyKluver

ACKNOWLEDGEMENTS

I'm going to start with my Bookouture editor, Therese Keating. I couldn't have asked for a better editor to start my career with and I'm going to miss you hugely. All the best as you move on. To Noelle Holten, my publicist, I apologise now for all the Twitter notifications. Thank you to the rest of the Bookouture family for all your support. To Anne Williams, my agent, thank you for always being there with calm reassurance.

Once more, I've used a bit of artistic licence with the police procedural side of things but thank you to Graham Bartlett, Rebecca Bradley, Lisa Cutts and Karen Bates for making sure I didn't go completely overboard. There's nothing like discovering that your crime scene is in a different county.

I've wanted to write a medical crime for a while and include a hospital in the setting. Thank you to my anonymous doctor friend who gave some guidance on drugs and procedures. I have to confess now that I haven't actually been to the Great Western Hospital in Swindon, so apologies for any errors. When I initially wrote this, I hadn't been on an ICU ward either. However, when I started editing, the worst happened – a family member was taken into ICU and this book is dedicated to him. It might appear a bit cynical to some but the only way I could process the experience was to write about it. So Pops's reflections on Bernie being in ICU are actually my own.

I won't name them but I want to thank all the wonderful autistic people I know. I'm still learning and still getting it wrong – sometimes on a daily basis. I hope Leigh is a good reflection of a neurodivergent person.

The first draft of *Left for Dead* was written while I was still at the Malden Centre Writing Class, under the watchful eye of Elizabeth Kay. Huge thanks to her and the rest of the class for all your support – John, Viviane, Jean, Mike, Sue, Aleks, Marilyn, Caroline, Clare and Loraine.

To Vicki Goldman and Alex Caan – thank you for keeping me sane.

I might not have gone to the hospital in Swindon but I did go to Town Gardens! It's a really lovely place to visit. Thank you to John and Esther Dusting for hosting us again and looking after the children. Research trips are much easier without them. And thanks to Kirk Dusting for giving me the lowdown on Swindon nightclubs.

Huge thanks to my family. I think my mother, Rosalie, may have to go on commission for the amount of books she's sold – thank you for all your support. To my husband, Phil – I promise the next book will be for you. And to my children, James, Beth and Hayden, thank you for coping with me working over the summer holidays for the first time ever.

Finally (and this may seem a bit strange), thank you to DI Bernadette Noel. In the very first novel I wrote, Bernie was a minor character but by the time I finished, it was clear she needed to be the protagonist. I love writing a strong (but not flawless), female, biracial police officer, and I long to see this reflected in TV dramas. It's certainly time for a female person of colour to be the star of a police show.

Printed in Great Britain
by Amazon